HELM GREYCASTLE

created by

HENRY BARAJAS & **BRYAN VALENZA**

Published by **TOP COW PRODUCTIONS, INC.**
LOS ANGELES

IMAGE COMICS, INC. • Todd McFarlane: President • Jim Valentino: Vice President • Marc Silvestri: Chief Executive Officer • Erik Larsen: Chief Financial Officer • Robert Kirkman: Chief Operating Officer • Eric Stephenson: Publisher / Chief Creative Officer • Nicole Lapalme: Controller • Leanna Caunter: Accounting Analyst • Sue Korpela: Accounting & HR Manager • Marla Eizik: Talent Liaison • Jeff Boison: Director of Sales & Publishing Planning • Dirk Wood: Director of International Sales & Licensing • Alex Cox: Director of Direct Market Sales • Chloe Ramos: Book Market & Library Sales Manager • Emilio Bautista: Digital Sales Coordinator • Jon Schlaffman: Specialty Sales Coordinator • Kat Salazar: Director of PR & Marketing • Drew Fitzgerald: Marketing Content Associate • Heather Doornink: Production Director • Drew Gill: Art Director • Hilary DiLoreto: Print Manager • Tricia Ramos: Traffic Manager • Melissa Gifford: Content Manager • Erika Schnatz: Senior Production Artist • Ryan Brewer: Production Artist • Deanna Phelps: Production Artist • IMAGECOMICS.COM

For Top Cow Productions, Inc.
Marc Silvestri - CEO
Matt Hawkins - President & COO
Elena Salcedo - Vice President of Operations
Vincent Valentine - Production Manager

ASTLE ™

story by **HENRY BARAJAS**

color artist **BRYAN VALENZA**

penciler **RAHMAT M. HANDOKO**

letter artists **GABRIELA DOWNIE** et **DAVID LANPHEAR**

script assist & editor **CLAIRE NAPIER**

senior editor **ELENA SALCEDO**

designer **SASHA E. HEAD** et **VINCENT VALENTINE**

proofreader **KATE NEWTON**

cover art by **RAHMAT M. HANDOKO** et **BRYAN VALENZA**

dedicated to **FRANCINE** & **DEBORAH**
special thanks to **CHEYENNE, KAITI, WENDO, PATRICK, MAMA DM,
AZTEC EMPIRE**, and **PAUL GUINAN'S PATREON PAGE**

Introduction

As a kid growing up in Mexico, all of my favorite movies and cartoons were American. In my teen years, I watched a lot of anime. I don't remember when I realized that none of the stuff I was watching took place in my home country, but when I did, it was glaring. Whenever Mexico would show up in a high-budget film, it was through a foreign lens-- usually dusty, dirty, and dangerous. Even then I knew there was much more to Mexico than Hollywood portrayed.

And I knew that behind every mystical Aztec artifact uncovered by the American protagonist in an action film, there was deep, complex Mesoamerican lore. The mythology of the Americas is every bit as interesting as the Greek, Norse, Arthurian legends we are all familiar with, and yet, all I could ever seem to find were exaggerated depictions of savagery or conspiracy theories about ancient aliens.

I waited for Disney's first Mayan princess throughout my youth, and she never came. I waited for an epic fantasy-adventure set in precolonial Mexico made with all the love of something like *Lord of the Rings*, and it never came. So when I had the opportunity to create *Onyx Equinox*, I wanted to create the thing I wanted to badly in my youth-- a loving depiction of Mexico, respectful of the individual cultures that make up our populace while still being able to play in the rich magic and fantasy that Mesoamerican myth lends itself to so well.

Henry Barajas illustrates that same appreciation in *HELM GREYCASTLE*. The beauty of this comic is a seamless introduction of the Mexica cultures as part of its fantasy. This isn't an ancient, ruined civilization lost and forgotten to time. This ancient Mexico is in its full splendor, thriving and vibrant as it was at the peak of pre-hispanic civilization. Henry's passion for inclusion of Mesoamerica in pop culture is palpable in the pages of this book. From the beautiful art, the lovingly researched setting, and the fun and very human characters. The twist of including the Mexica as part of the main plot, with interesting and multifaceted characters, was a breath of fresh air.

As you begin reading, you're introduced to a world we've become all-too-familiar with thanks to tabletop games like Dungeons and Dragons, which may help readers unfamiliar with our culture, feel a little more included. Much like Helm Greycastle and his comrades, the reader is an outsider to these foreign lands, and will be guided alongside the heroes as they learn about the world and its people. There's plenty of exposition of the world but not in a way that feels like a history course. These are historical facts and prominent figures that blend perfectly with the story as part of the introduction to set the big plot and the heroes' journey. It's all even more facilitated thanks to the very charismatic group of characters we join.

I feel incredibly honored to be invited to introduce you to this exciting adventure. A big thank you to Henry for allowing me to be a small part of this journey with you. I hope you enjoy exploring the world through the lens of noble warriors of all races, and you too, feel the inkling to delve into and explore more into Mesoamerica and the beautiful, vibrant culture that it still is today.

– Sofia E. Alexander
Creator of *Onyx Equinox*

PRELUDE

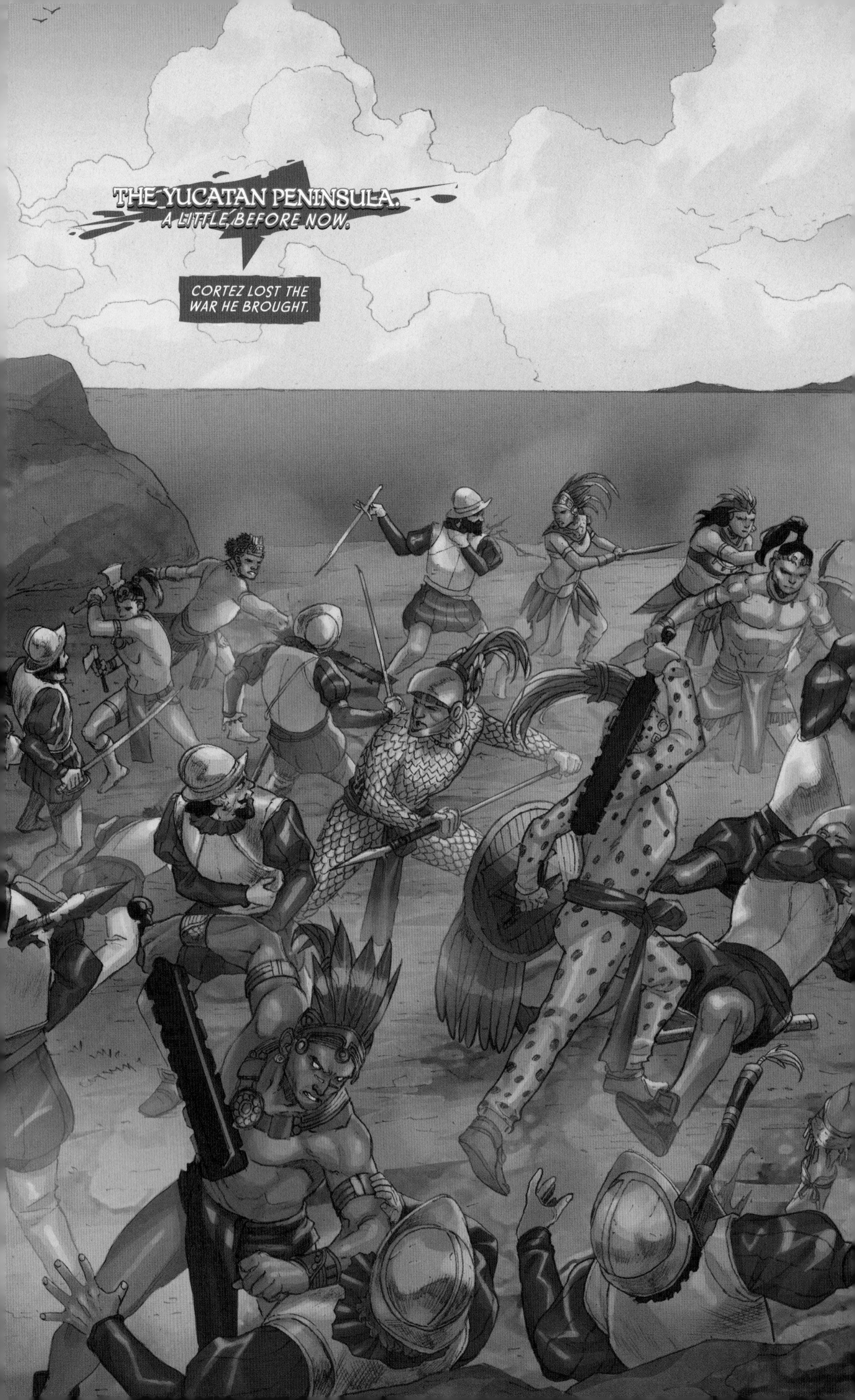
THE YUCATAN PENINSULA.
A LITTLE BEFORE NOW.
CORTEZ LOST THE WAR HE BROUGHT.

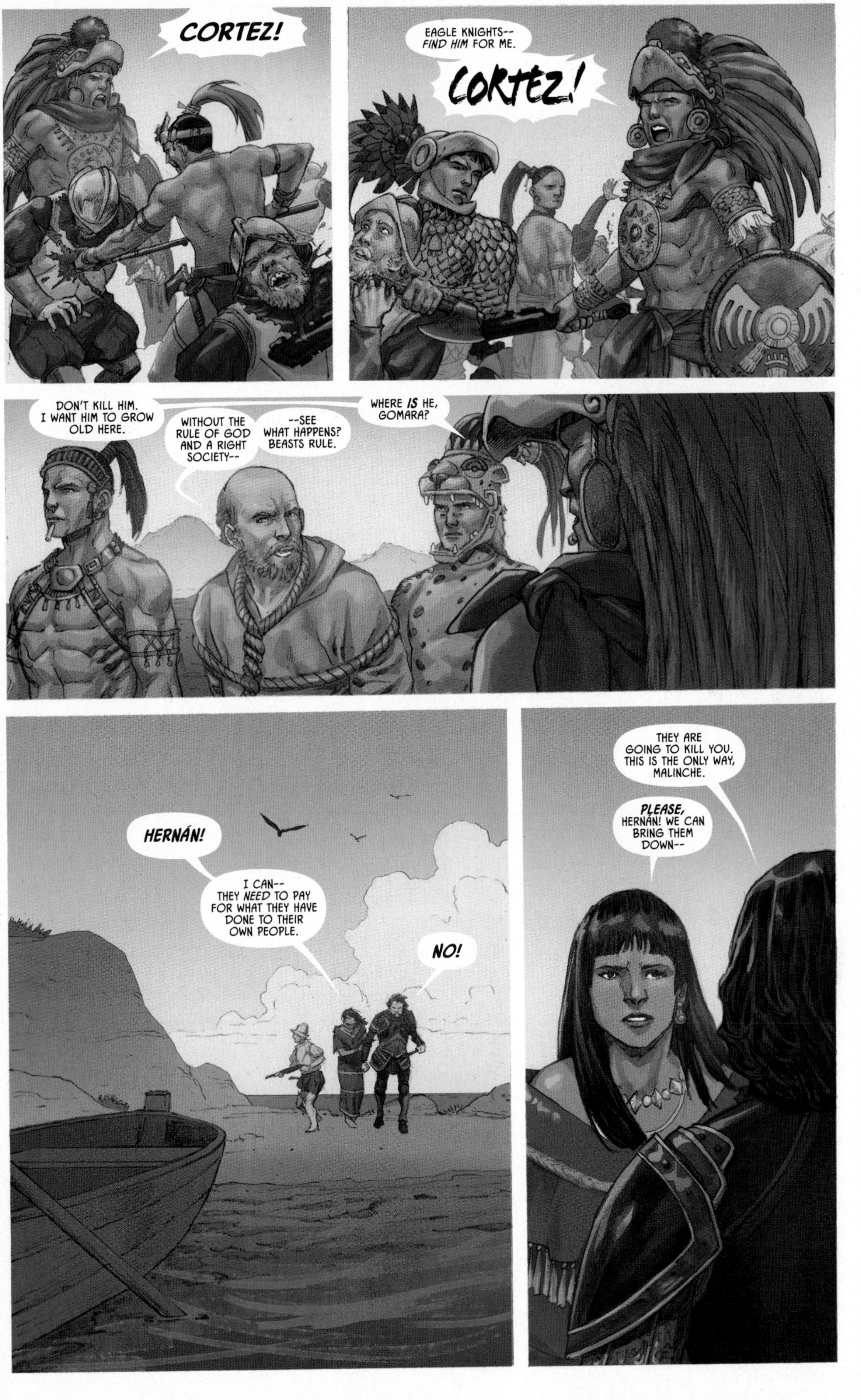
CORTEZ!
EAGLE KNIGHTS--
FIND HIM FOR ME.
CORTEZ!
DON'T KILL HIM. I WANT HIM TO GROW OLD HERE.
WITHOUT THE RULE OF GOD AND A RIGHT SOCIETY--
--SEE WHAT HAPPENS? BEASTS RULE.
WHERE IS HE, GOMARA?
HERNÁN!
I CAN-- THEY NEED TO PAY FOR WHAT THEY HAVE DONE TO THEIR OWN PEOPLE.
NO!
THEY ARE GOING TO KILL YOU. THIS IS THE ONLY WAY, MALINCHE.
PLEASE, HERNÁN! WE CAN BRING THEM DOWN--

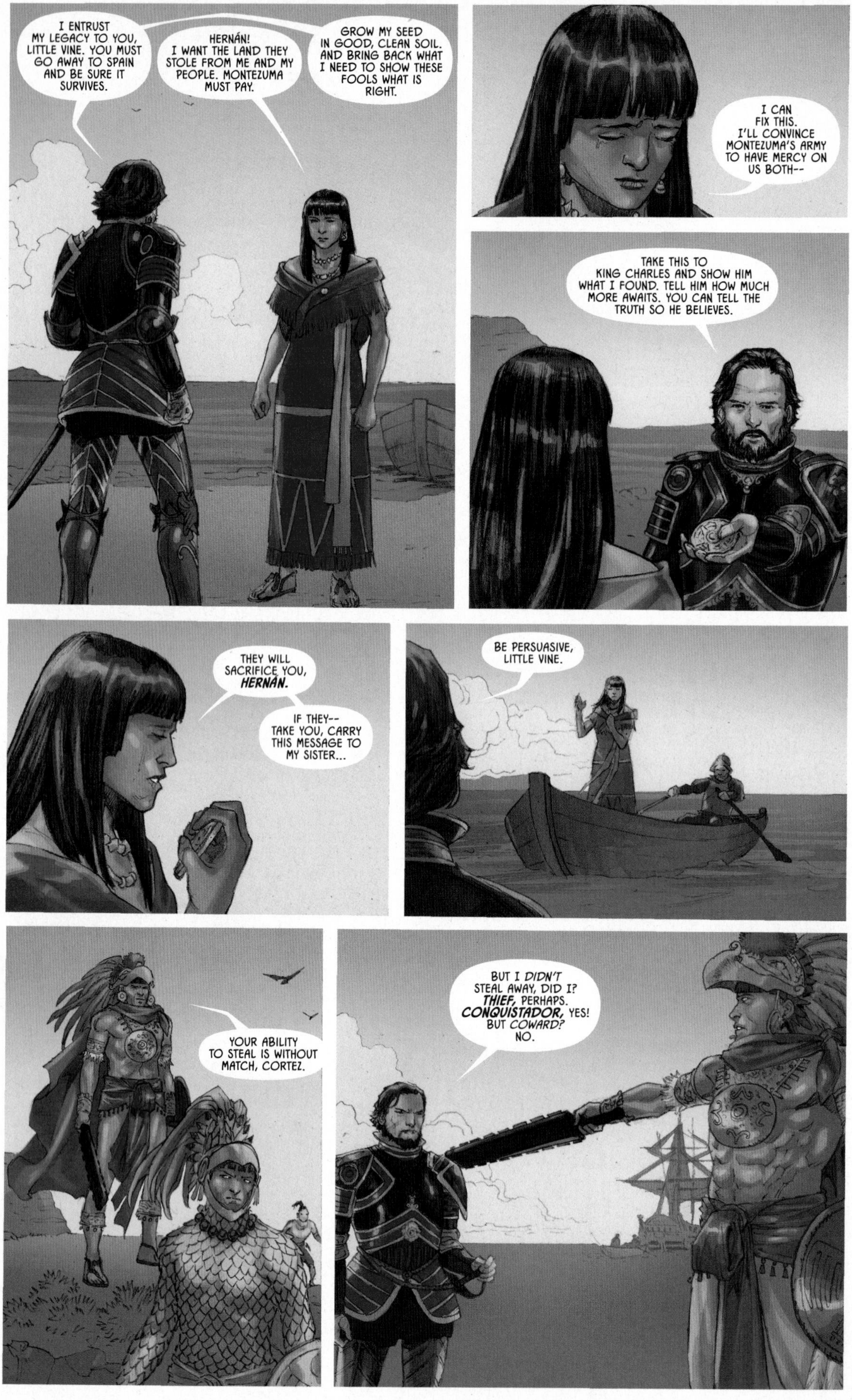
I ENTRUST MY LEGACY TO YOU, LITTLE VINE. YOU MUST GO AWAY TO SPAIN AND BE SURE IT SURVIVES.
HERNÁN! I WANT THE LAND THEY STOLE FROM ME AND MY PEOPLE. MONTEZUMA MUST PAY.
GROW MY SEED IN GOOD, CLEAN SOIL. AND BRING BACK WHAT I NEED TO SHOW THESE FOOLS WHAT IS RIGHT.
I CAN FIX THIS. I'LL CONVINCE MONTEZUMA'S ARMY TO HAVE MERCY ON US BOTH--
TAKE THIS TO KING CHARLES AND SHOW HIM WHAT I FOUND. TELL HIM HOW MUCH MORE AWAITS. YOU CAN TELL THE TRUTH SO HE BELIEVES.
THEY WILL SACRIFICE YOU, ***HERNÁN.***
IF THEY-- TAKE YOU, CARRY THIS MESSAGE TO MY SISTER...
BE PERSUASIVE, LITTLE VINE.
YOUR ABILITY TO STEAL IS WITHOUT MATCH, CORTEZ.
BUT I *DIDN'T* STEAL AWAY, DID I? ***THIEF,*** PERHAPS. ***CONQUISTADOR,*** YES! BUT *COWARD?* NO.

DEVOTION & DESIRE

01

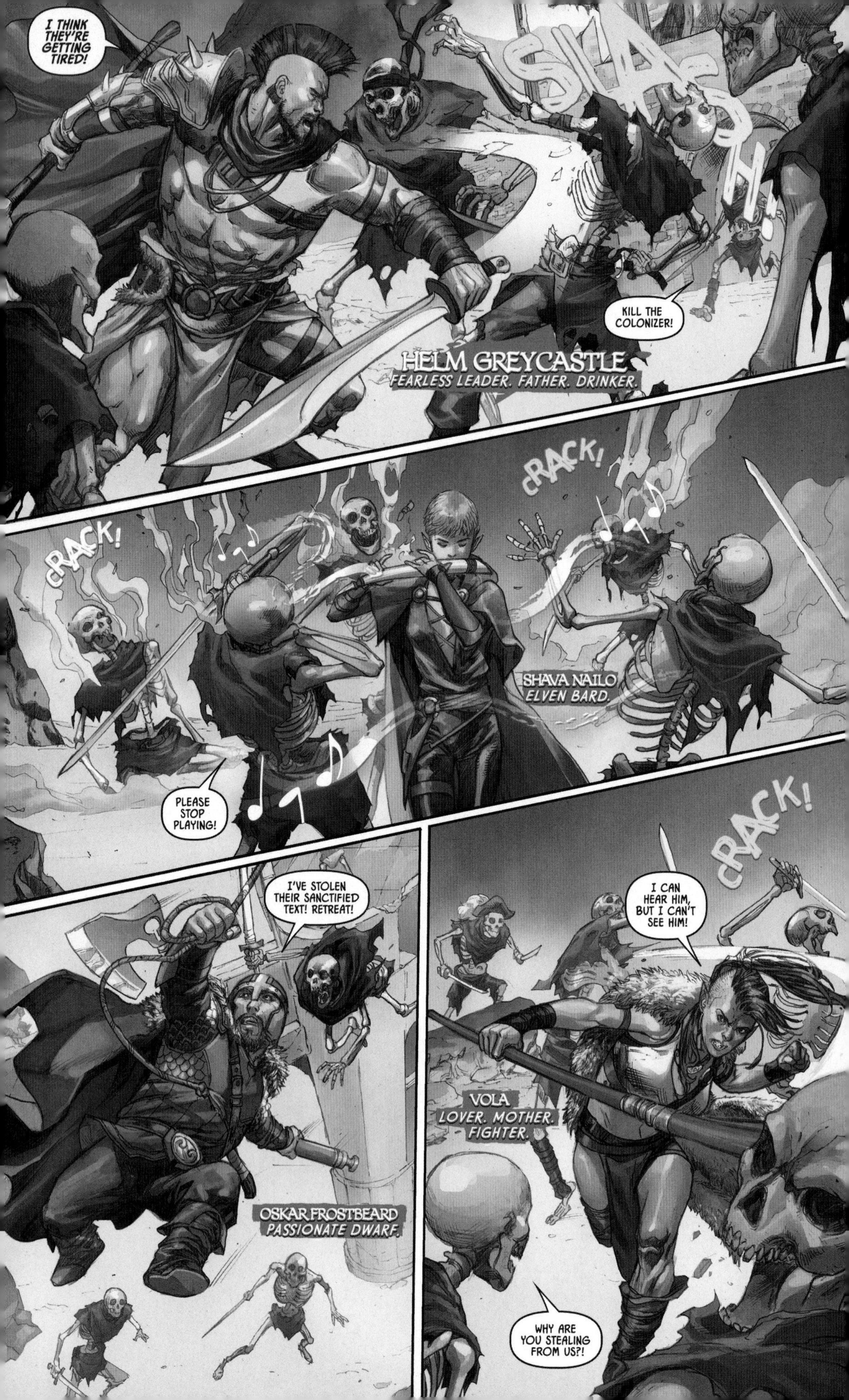
I THINK THEY'RE GETTING TIRED!
SHAAAH!
KILL THE COLONIZER!
HELM GREYCASTLE
FEARLESS LEADER. FATHER. DRINKER.
CRACK!
CRACK!
SHAVA NAILO
ELVEN BARD.
PLEASE STOP PLAYING!
I'VE STOLEN THEIR SANCTIFIED TEXT! RETREAT!
OSKAR FROSTBEARD
PASSIONATE DWARF.
CRACK!
I CAN HEAR HIM, BUT I CAN'T SEE HIM!
VOLA
LOVER. MOTHER. FIGHTER.
WHY ARE YOU STEALING FROM US?!

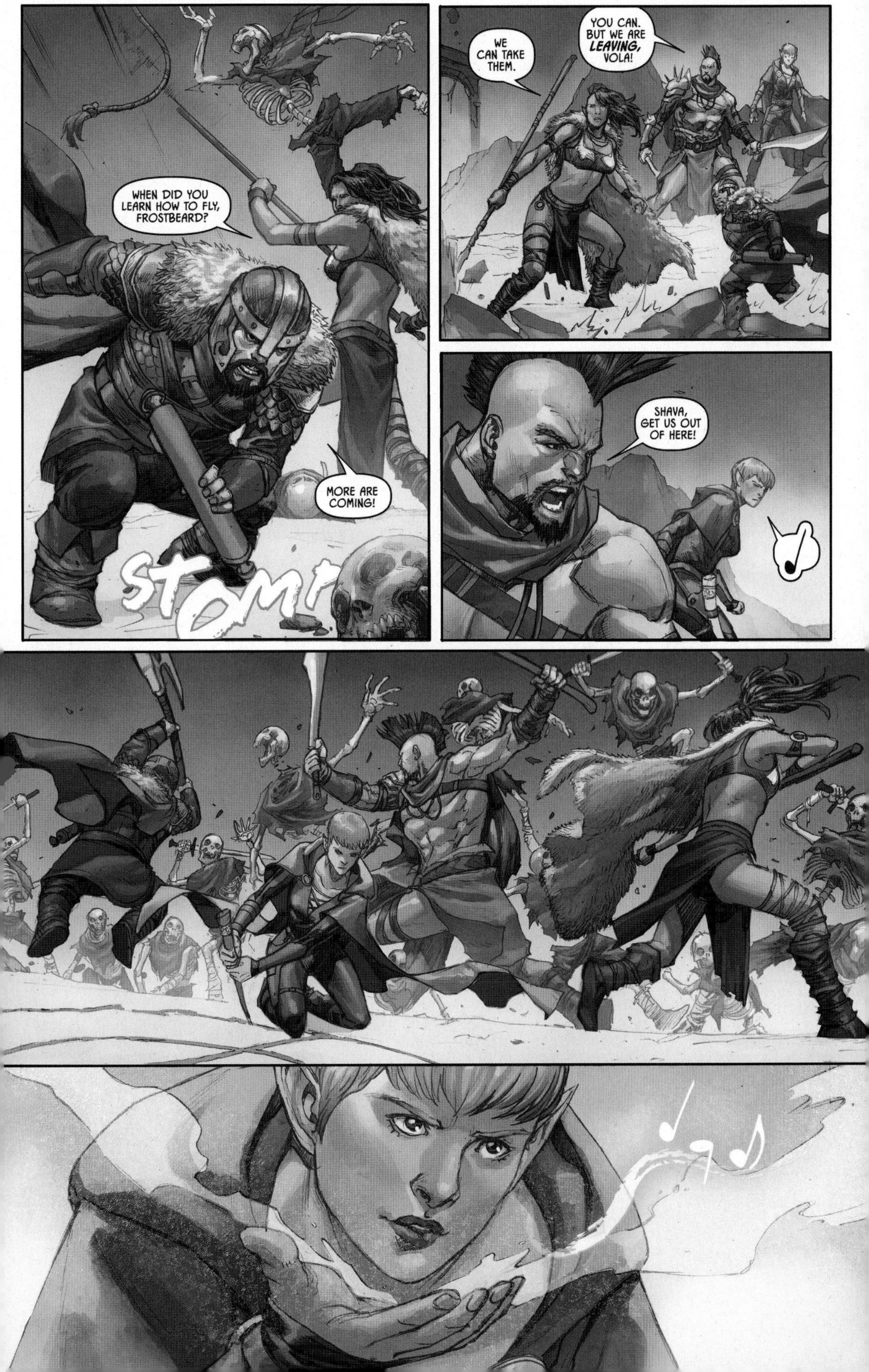
WHEN DID YOU LEARN HOW TO FLY, FROSTBEARD?
MORE ARE COMING!
STOMP
WE CAN TAKE THEM.
YOU CAN. BUT WE ARE *LEAVING,* VOLA!
SHAVA, GET US OUT OF HERE!

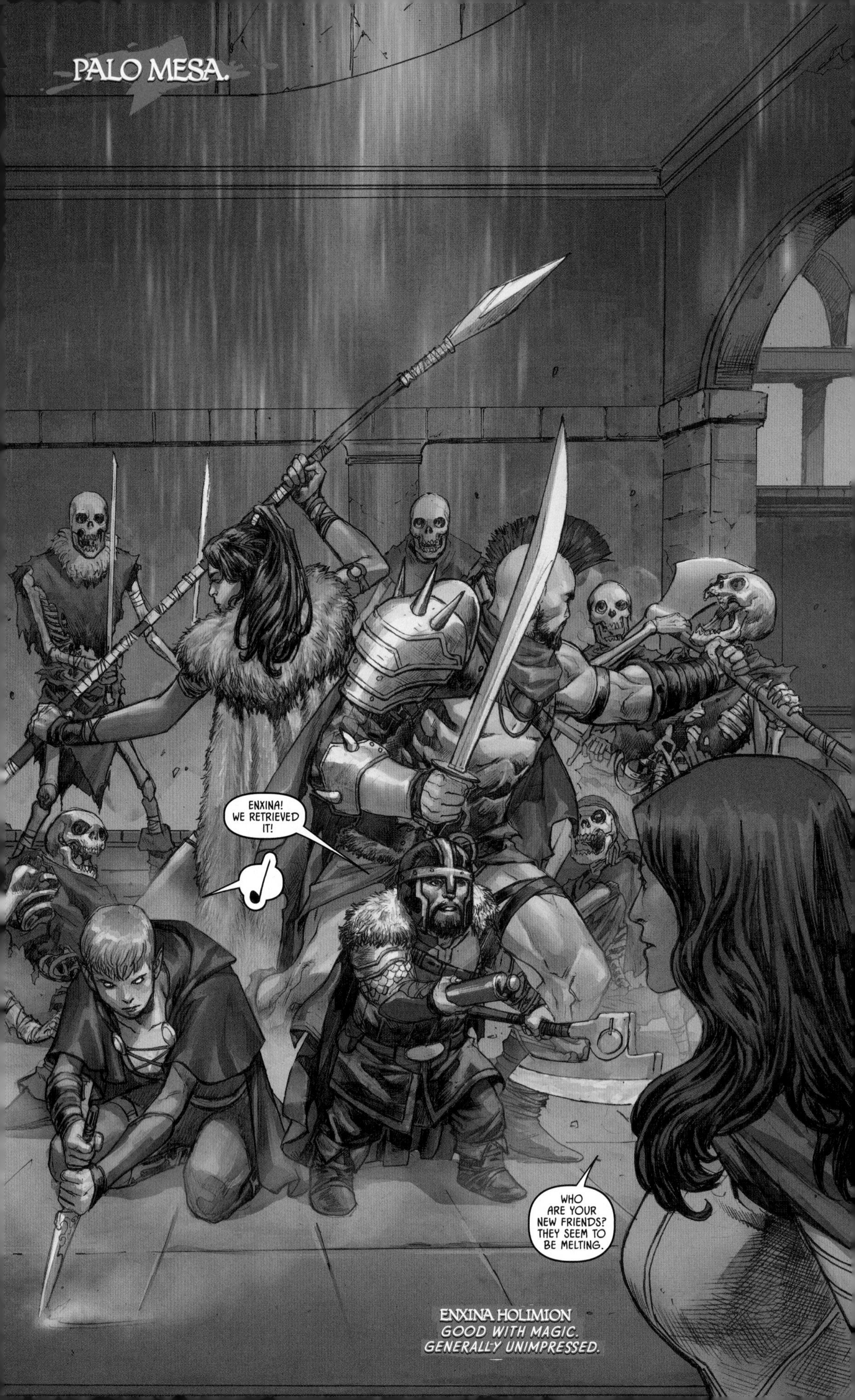

PALO MESA.
ENXINA! WE RETRIEVED IT!
WHO ARE YOUR NEW FRIENDS? THEY SEEM TO BE MELTING.
ENXINA HOLIMION
GOOD WITH MAGIC. GENERALLY UNIMPRESSED.

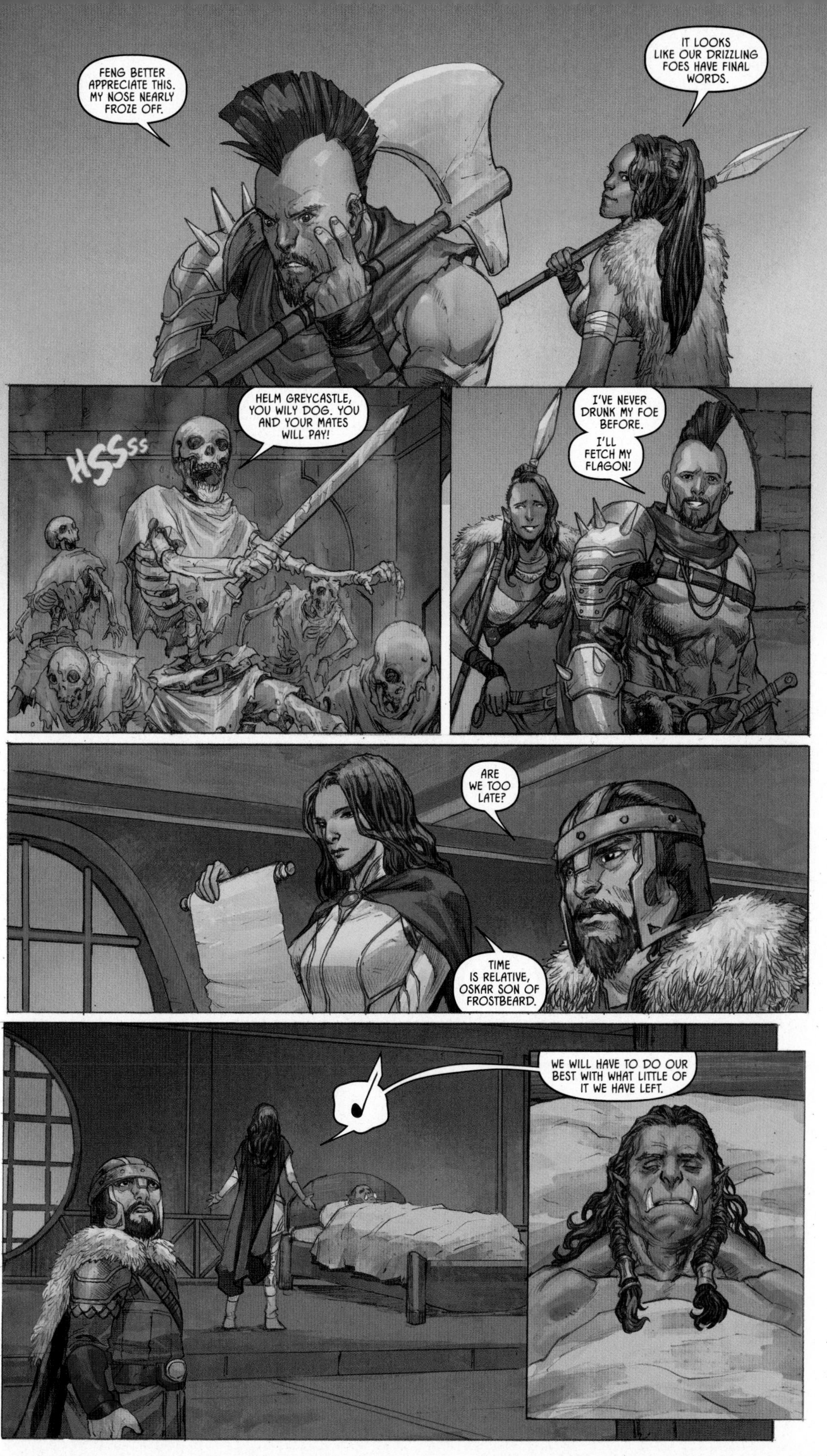
FENG BETTER APPRECIATE THIS. MY NOSE NEARLY FROZE OFF.
IT LOOKS LIKE OUR DRIZZLING FOES HAVE FINAL WORDS.
HSSss
HELM GREYCASTLE, YOU WILY DOG. YOU AND YOUR MATES WILL PAY!
I'VE NEVER DRUNK MY FOE BEFORE.
I'LL FETCH MY FLAGON!
ARE WE TOO LATE?
TIME IS RELATIVE, OSKAR SON OF FROSTBEARD.
WE WILL HAVE TO DO OUR BEST WITH WHAT LITTLE OF IT WE HAVE LEFT.

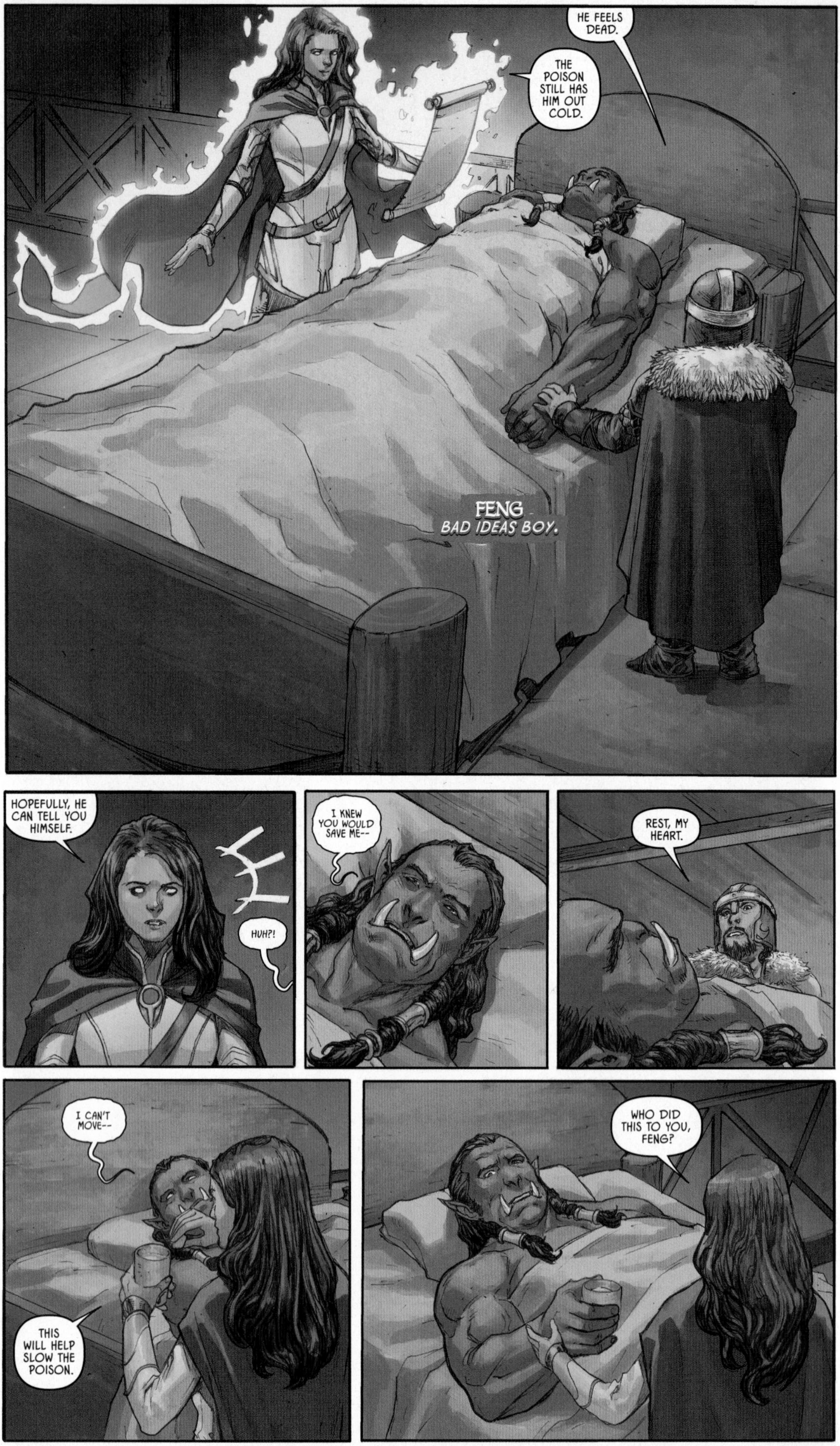
HE FEELS DEAD.
THE POISON STILL HAS HIM OUT COLD.
FENG
BAD IDEAS BOY.
HOPEFULLY, HE CAN TELL YOU HIMSELF.
HUH?!
I KNEW YOU WOULD SAVE ME--
REST, MY HEART.
I CAN'T MOVE--
THIS WILL HELP SLOW THE POISON.
WHO DID THIS TO YOU, FENG?

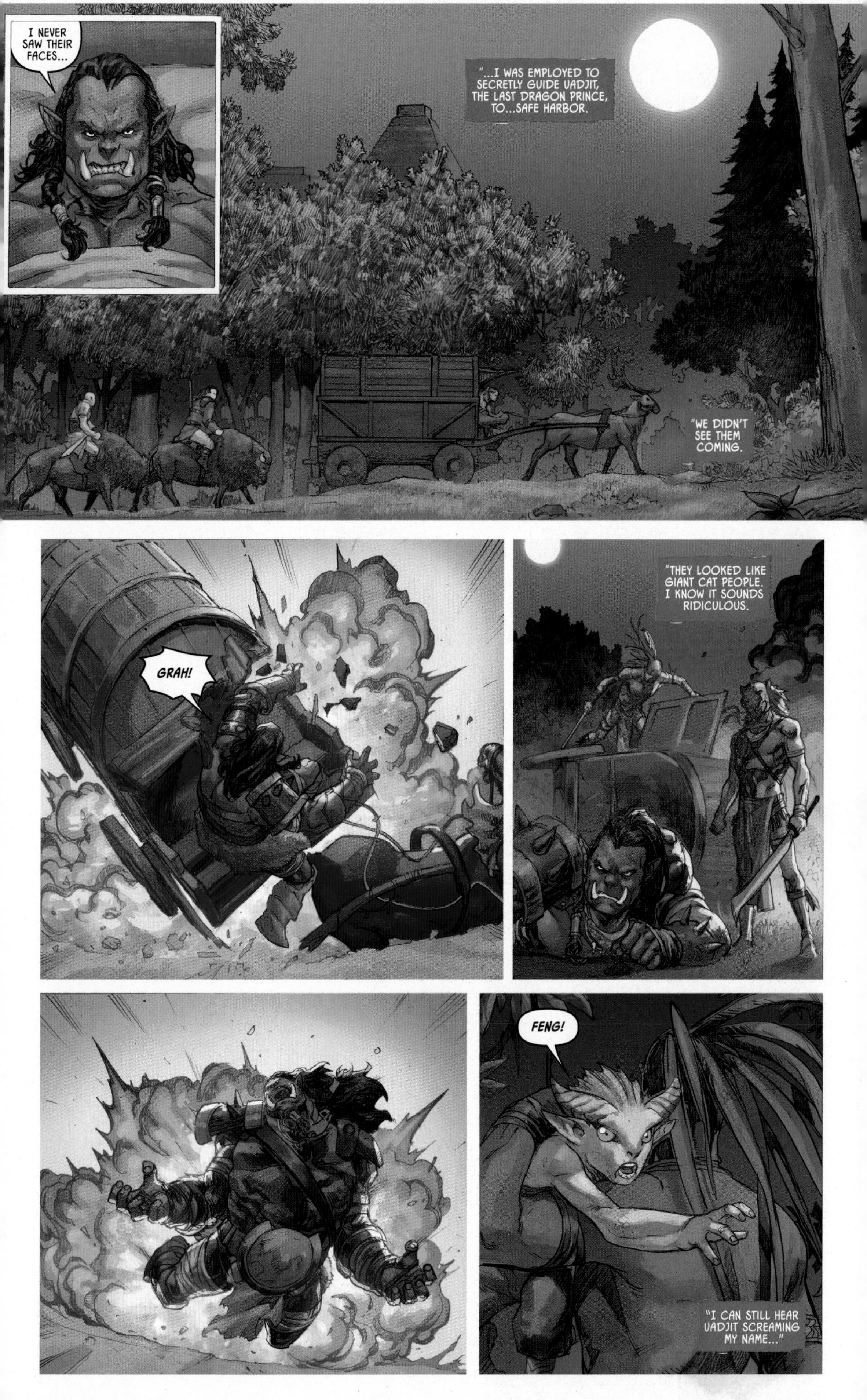

I NEVER SAW THEIR FACES...
"...I WAS EMPLOYED TO SECRETLY GUIDE UADJIT, THE LAST DRAGON PRINCE, TO...SAFE HARBOR.
"WE DIDN'T SEE THEM COMING.
GRAH!
"THEY LOOKED LIKE GIANT CAT PEOPLE. I KNOW IT SOUNDS RIDICULOUS.
FENG!
"I CAN STILL HEAR UADJIT SCREAMING MY NAME..."

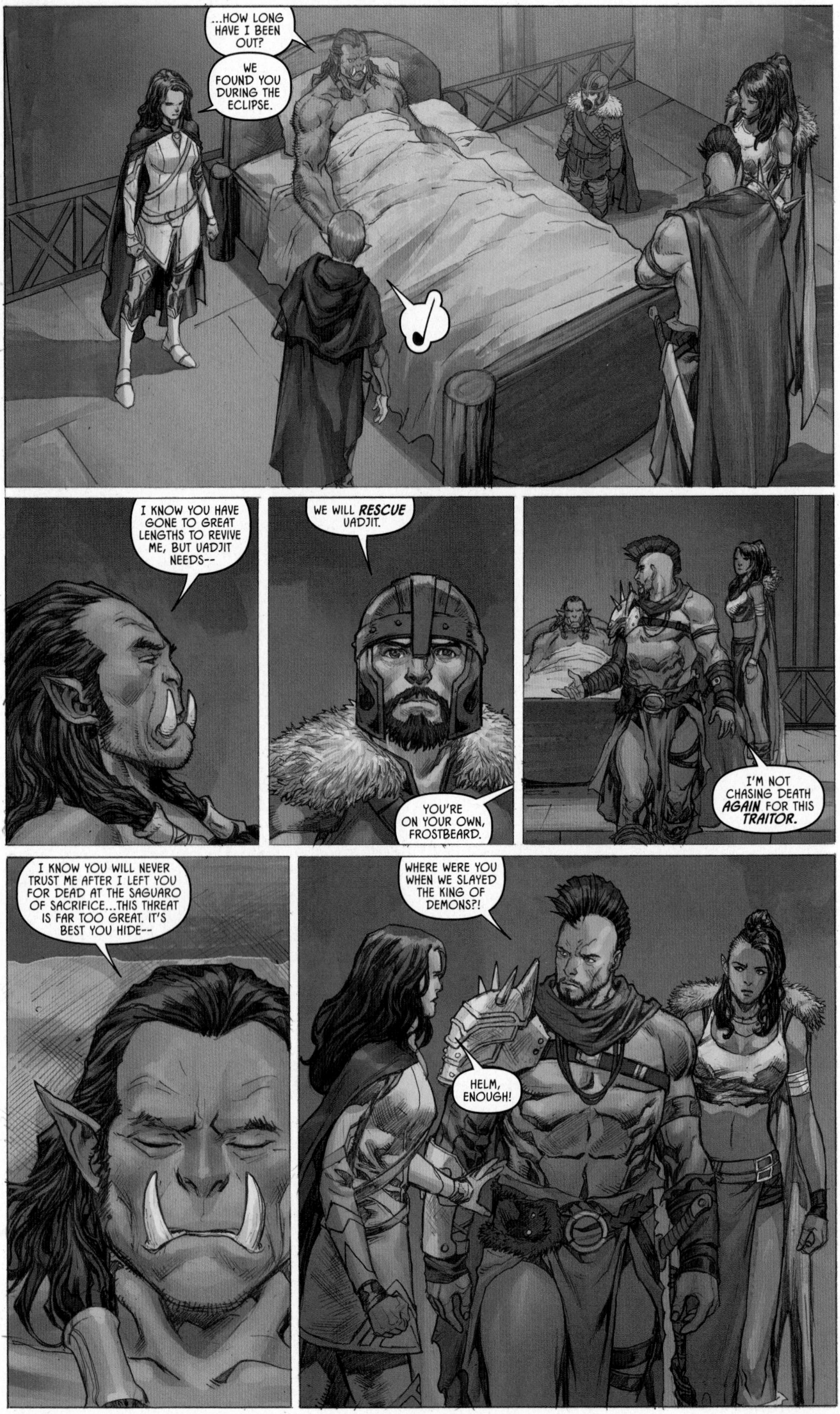
...HOW LONG HAVE I BEEN OUT?
WE FOUND YOU DURING THE ECLIPSE.
I KNOW YOU HAVE GONE TO GREAT LENGTHS TO REVIVE ME, BUT VADJIT NEEDS--
WE WILL RESCUE VADJIT.
YOU'RE ON YOUR OWN, FROSTBEARD.
I'M NOT CHASING DEATH AGAIN FOR THIS TRAITOR.
I KNOW YOU WILL NEVER TRUST ME AFTER I LEFT YOU FOR DEAD AT THE SAGUARO OF SACRIFICE...THIS THREAT IS FAR TOO GREAT. IT'S BEST YOU HIDE--
WHERE WERE YOU WHEN WE SLAYED THE KING OF DEMONS?!
HELM, ENOUGH!

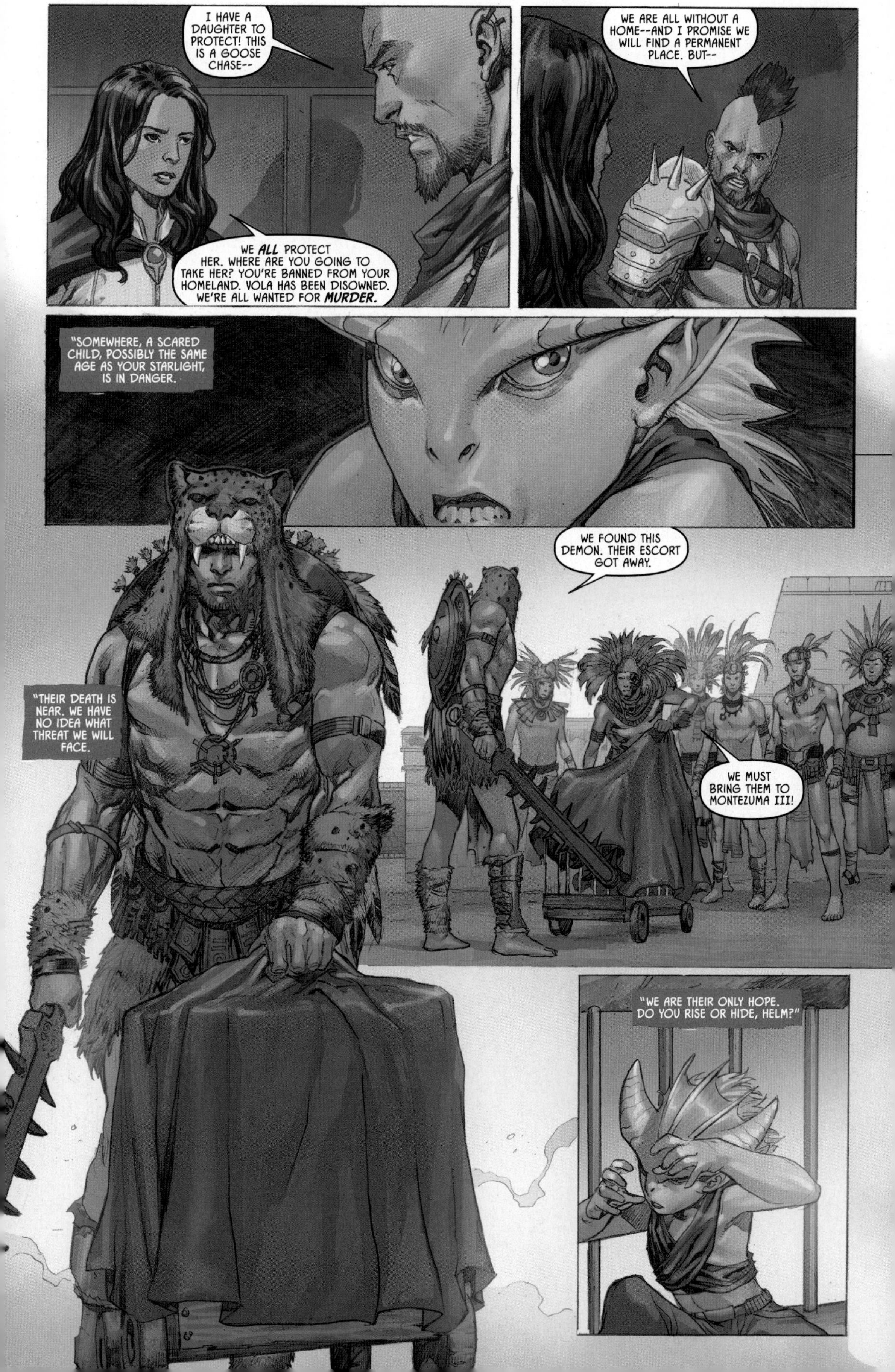

I HAVE A DAUGHTER TO PROTECT! THIS IS A GOOSE CHASE--
WE ALL PROTECT HER. WHERE ARE YOU GOING TO TAKE HER? YOU'RE BANNED FROM YOUR HOMELAND. VOLA HAS BEEN DISOWNED. WE'RE ALL WANTED FOR MURDER.
WE ARE ALL WITHOUT A HOME--AND I PROMISE WE WILL FIND A PERMANENT PLACE. BUT--
"SOMEWHERE, A SCARED CHILD, POSSIBLY THE SAME AGE AS YOUR STARLIGHT, IS IN DANGER.
WE FOUND THIS DEMON. THEIR ESCORT GOT AWAY.
"THEIR DEATH IS NEAR. WE HAVE NO IDEA WHAT THREAT WE WILL FACE.
WE MUST BRING THEM TO MONTEZUMA III!
"WE ARE THEIR ONLY HOPE. DO YOU RISE OR HIDE, HELM?"

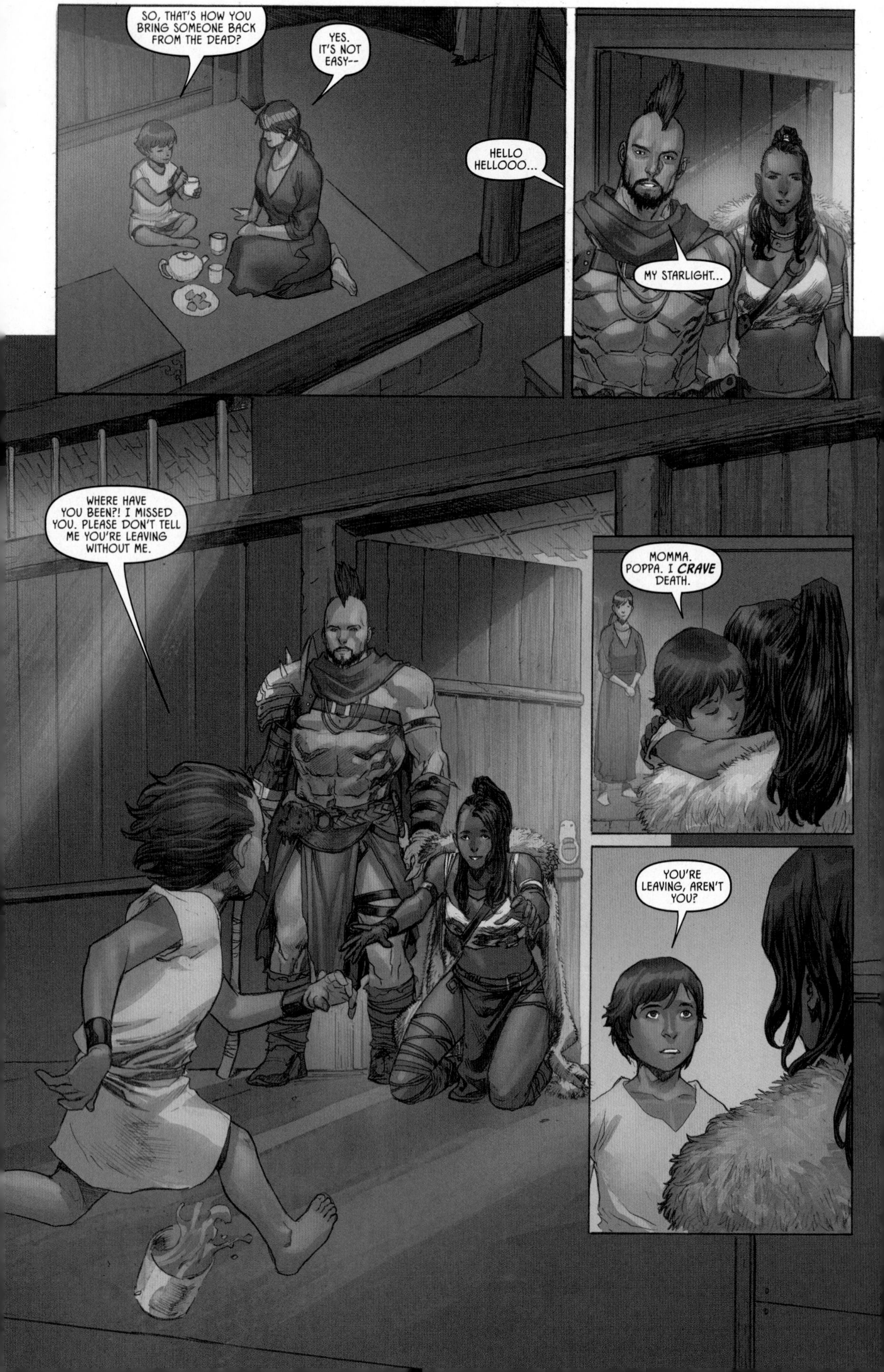
SO, THAT'S HOW YOU BRING SOMEONE BACK FROM THE DEAD?
YES. IT'S NOT EASY--
HELLO HELLOOO...
MY STARLIGHT...
WHERE HAVE YOU BEEN?! I MISSED YOU. PLEASE DON'T TELL ME YOU'RE LEAVING WITHOUT ME.
MOMMA. POPPA. I *CRAVE* DEATH.
YOU'RE LEAVING, AREN'T YOU?

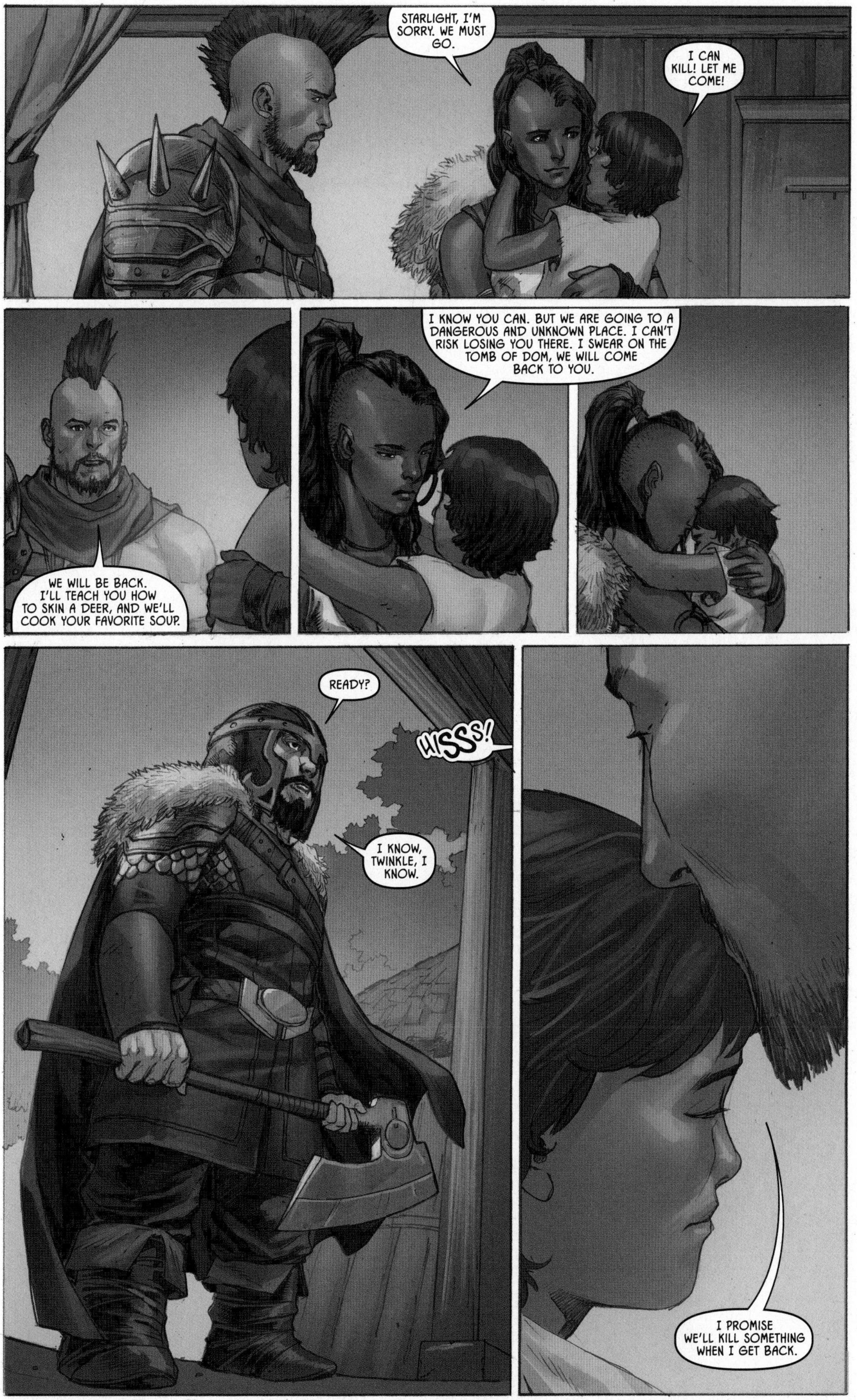
STARLIGHT, I'M SORRY. WE MUST GO.
I CAN KILL! LET ME COME!
WE WILL BE BACK. I'LL TEACH YOU HOW TO SKIN A DEER, AND WE'LL COOK YOUR FAVORITE SOUP.
I KNOW YOU CAN. BUT WE ARE GOING TO A DANGEROUS AND UNKNOWN PLACE. I CAN'T RISK LOSING YOU THERE. I SWEAR ON THE TOMB OF DOM, WE WILL COME BACK TO YOU.
READY?
HISSS!
I KNOW, TWINKLE, I KNOW.
I PROMISE WE'LL KILL SOMETHING WHEN I GET BACK.

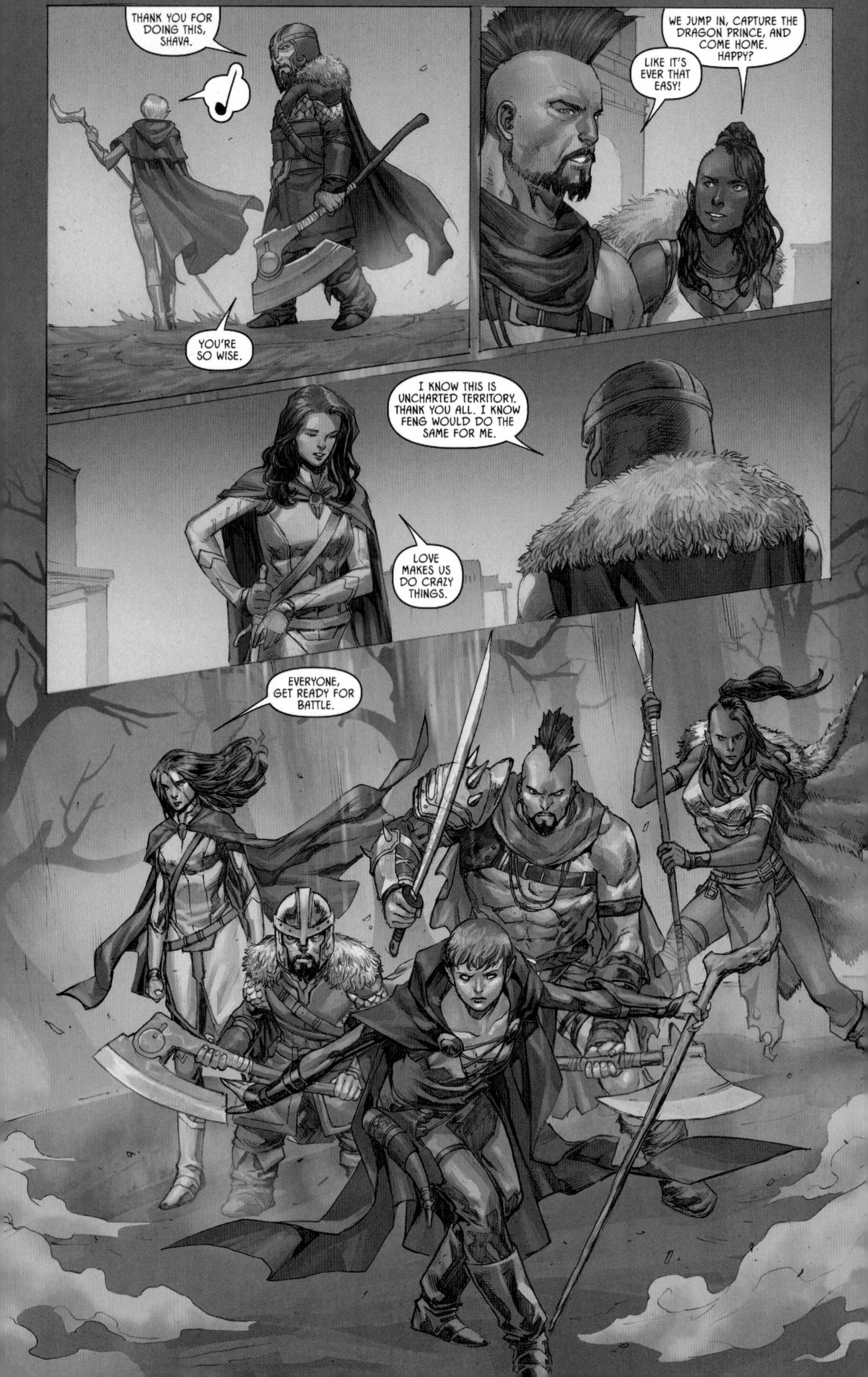
THANK YOU FOR DOING THIS, SHAVA.
YOU'RE SO WISE.
WE JUMP IN, CAPTURE THE DRAGON PRINCE, AND COME HOME. HAPPY?
LIKE IT'S EVER THAT EASY!
I KNOW THIS IS UNCHARTED TERRITORY. THANK YOU ALL. I KNOW FENG WOULD DO THE SAME FOR ME.
LOVE MAKES US DO CRAZY THINGS.
EVERYONE, GET READY FOR BATTLE.

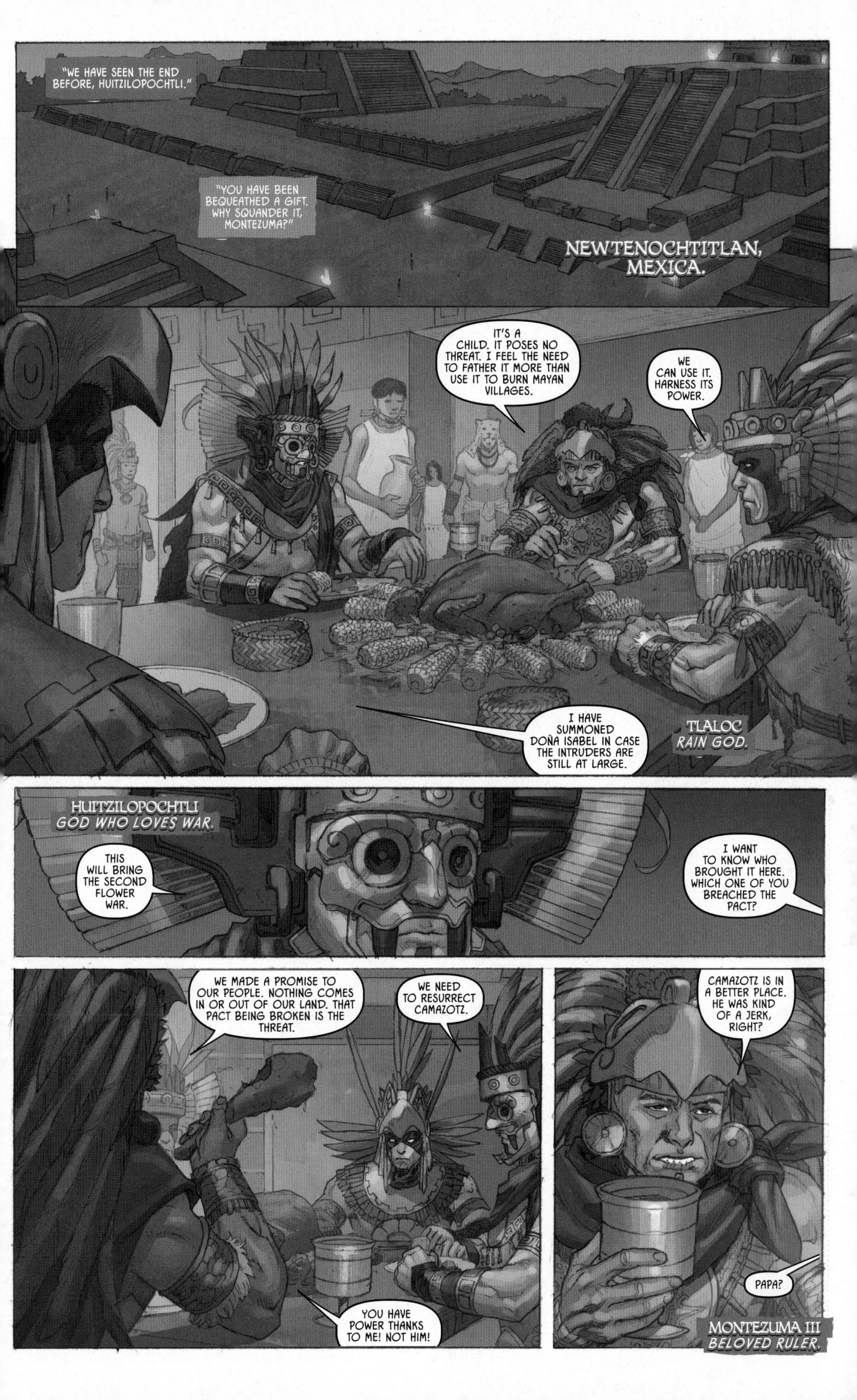
"WE HAVE SEEN THE END BEFORE, HUITZILOPOCHTLI."
"YOU HAVE BEEN BEQUEATHED A GIFT. WHY SQUANDER IT, MONTEZUMA?"
NEWTENOCHTITLAN, MEXICA.
IT'S A CHILD. IT POSES NO THREAT. I FEEL THE NEED TO FATHER IT MORE THAN USE IT TO BURN MAYAN VILLAGES.
WE CAN USE IT. HARNESS ITS POWER.
I HAVE SUMMONED DOÑA ISABEL IN CASE THE INTRUDERS ARE STILL AT LARGE.
TLALOC
RAIN GOD.
HUITZILOPOCHTLI
GOD WHO LOVES WAR.
THIS WILL BRING THE SECOND FLOWER WAR.
I WANT TO KNOW WHO BROUGHT IT HERE. WHICH ONE OF YOU BREACHED THE PACT?
WE MADE A PROMISE TO OUR PEOPLE. NOTHING COMES IN OR OUT OF OUR LAND. THAT PACT BEING BROKEN IS THE THREAT.
WE NEED TO RESURRECT CAMAZOTZ.
YOU HAVE POWER THANKS TO ME! NOT HIM!
CAMAZOTZ IS IN A BETTER PLACE. HE WAS KIND OF A JERK, RIGHT?
PAPA?
MONTEZUMA III
BELOVED RULER.

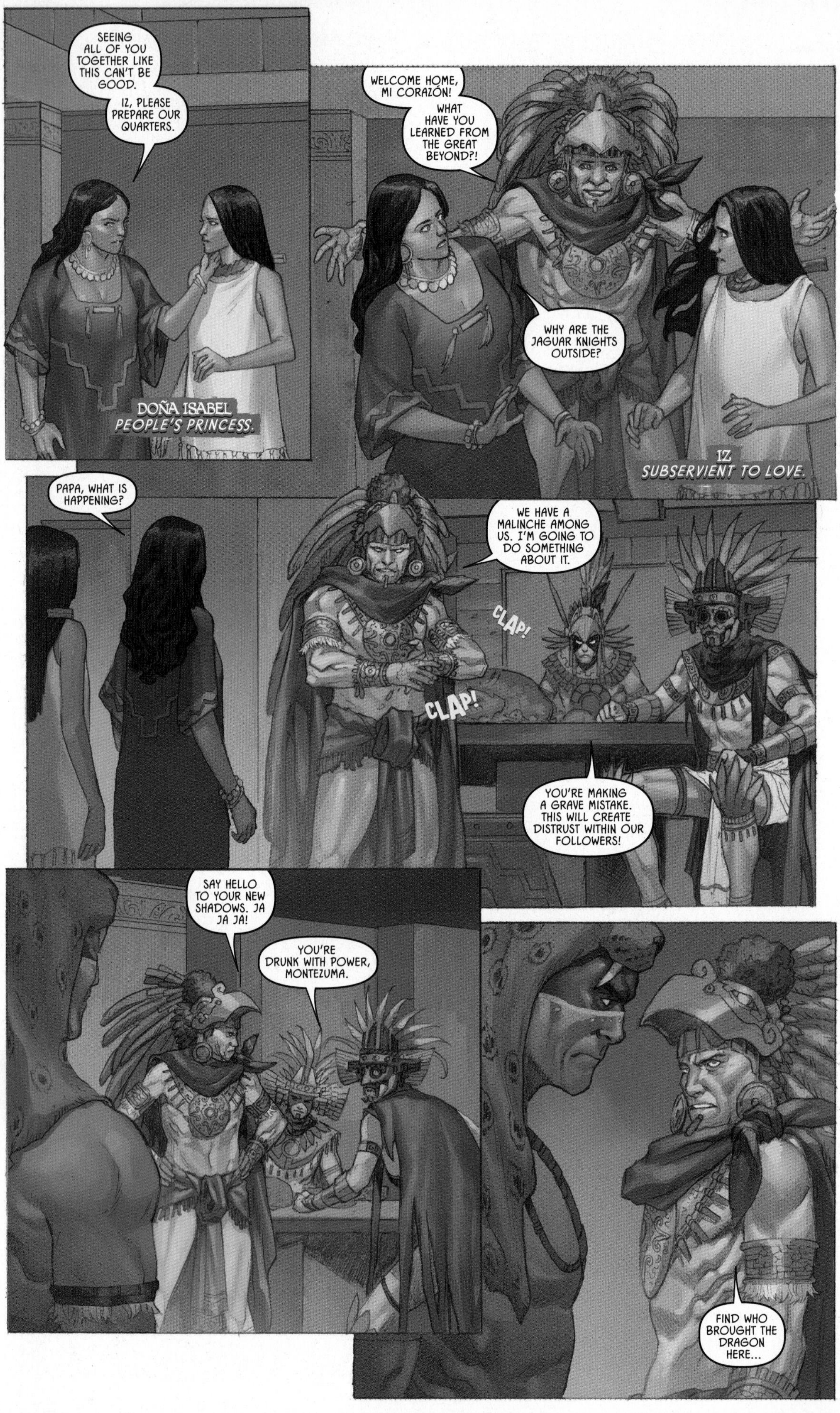
SEEING ALL OF YOU TOGETHER LIKE THIS CAN'T BE GOOD.
IZ, PLEASE PREPARE OUR QUARTERS.
DOÑA ISABEL
PEOPLE'S PRINCESS.
WELCOME HOME, MI CORAZÓN!
WHAT HAVE YOU LEARNED FROM THE GREAT BEYOND?!
WHY ARE THE JAGUAR KNIGHTS OUTSIDE?
IZ
SUBSERVIENT TO LOVE.
PAPA, WHAT IS HAPPENING?
WE HAVE A MALINCHE AMONG US. I'M GOING TO DO SOMETHING ABOUT IT.
CLAP!
CLAP!
YOU'RE MAKING A GRAVE MISTAKE. THIS WILL CREATE DISTRUST WITHIN OUR FOLLOWERS!
SAY HELLO TO YOUR NEW SHADOWS. JA JA JA!
YOU'RE DRUNK WITH POWER, MONTEZUMA.
FIND WHO BROUGHT THE DRAGON HERE...

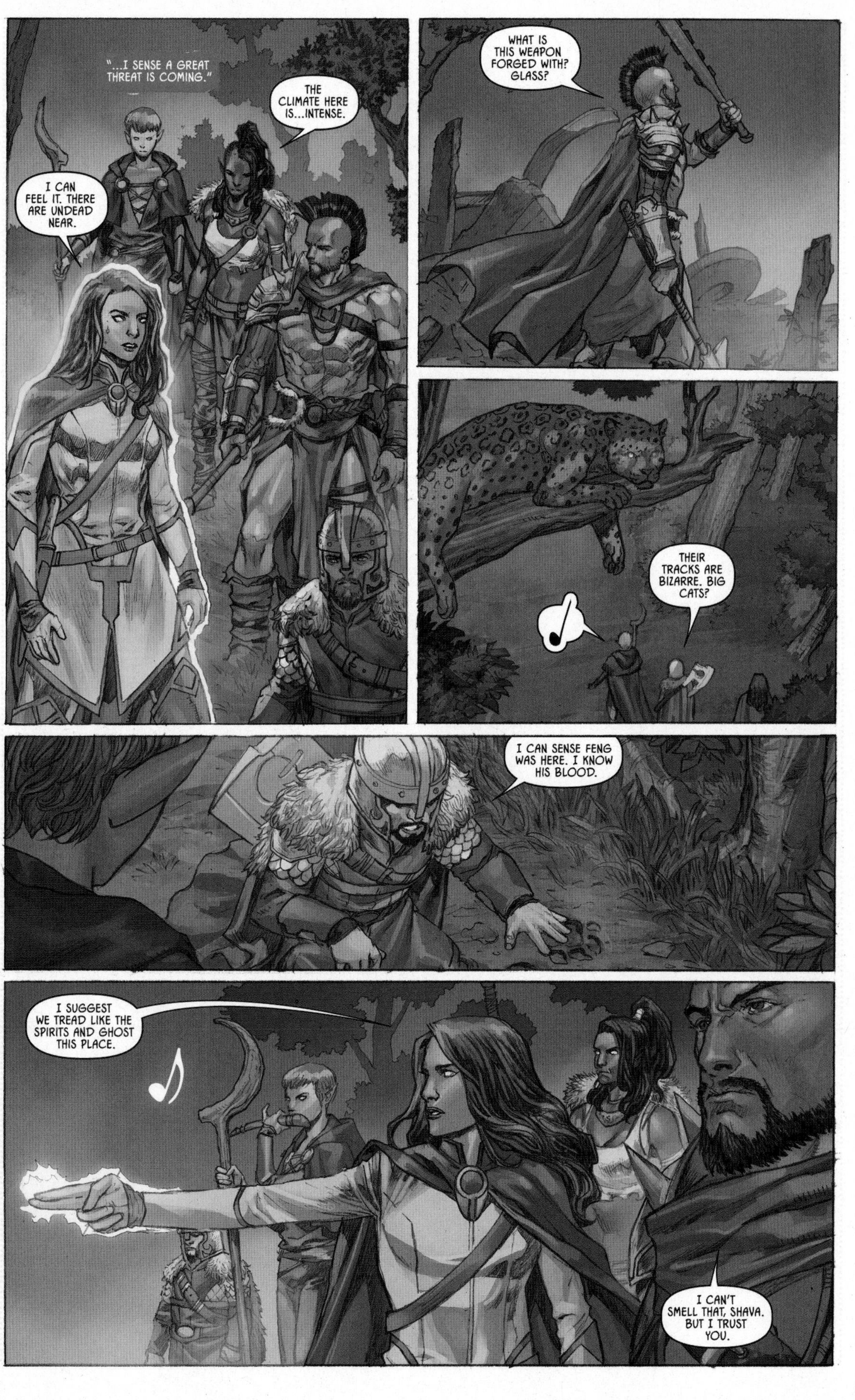
"...I SENSE A GREAT THREAT IS COMING."
THE CLIMATE HERE IS...INTENSE.
I CAN FEEL IT. THERE ARE UNDEAD NEAR.
WHAT IS THIS WEAPON FORGED WITH? GLASS?
THEIR TRACKS ARE BIZARRE. BIG CATS?
I CAN SENSE FENG WAS HERE. I KNOW HIS BLOOD.
I SUGGEST WE TREAD LIKE THE SPIRITS AND GHOST THIS PLACE.
I CAN'T SMELL THAT, SHAVA. BUT I TRUST YOU.

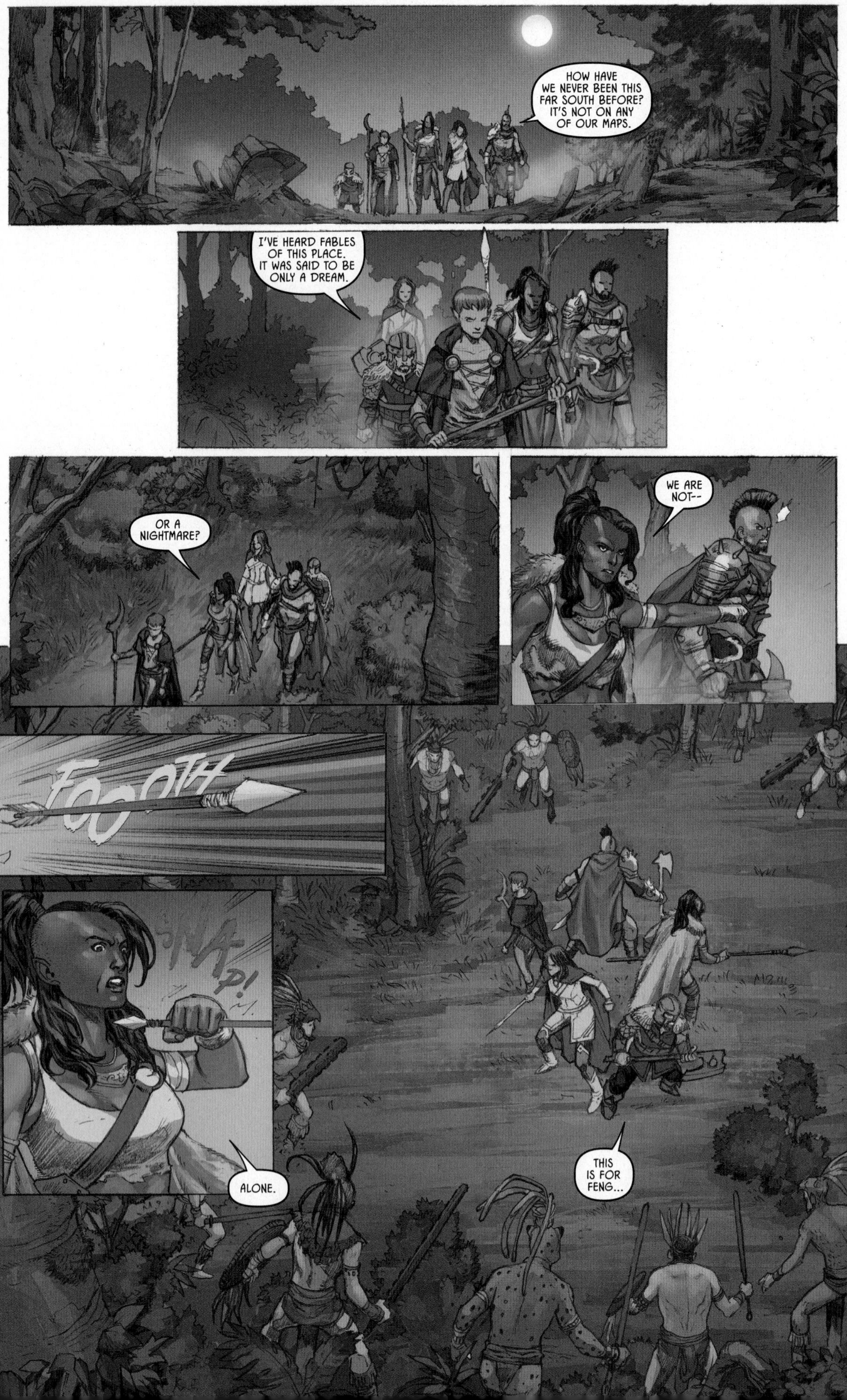
HOW HAVE WE NEVER BEEN THIS FAR SOUTH BEFORE? IT'S NOT ON ANY OF OUR MAPS.
I'VE HEARD FABLES OF THIS PLACE. IT WAS SAID TO BE ONLY A DREAM.
OR A NIGHTMARE?
WE ARE NOT--
FOOOTH
ALONE.
THIS IS FOR FENG...

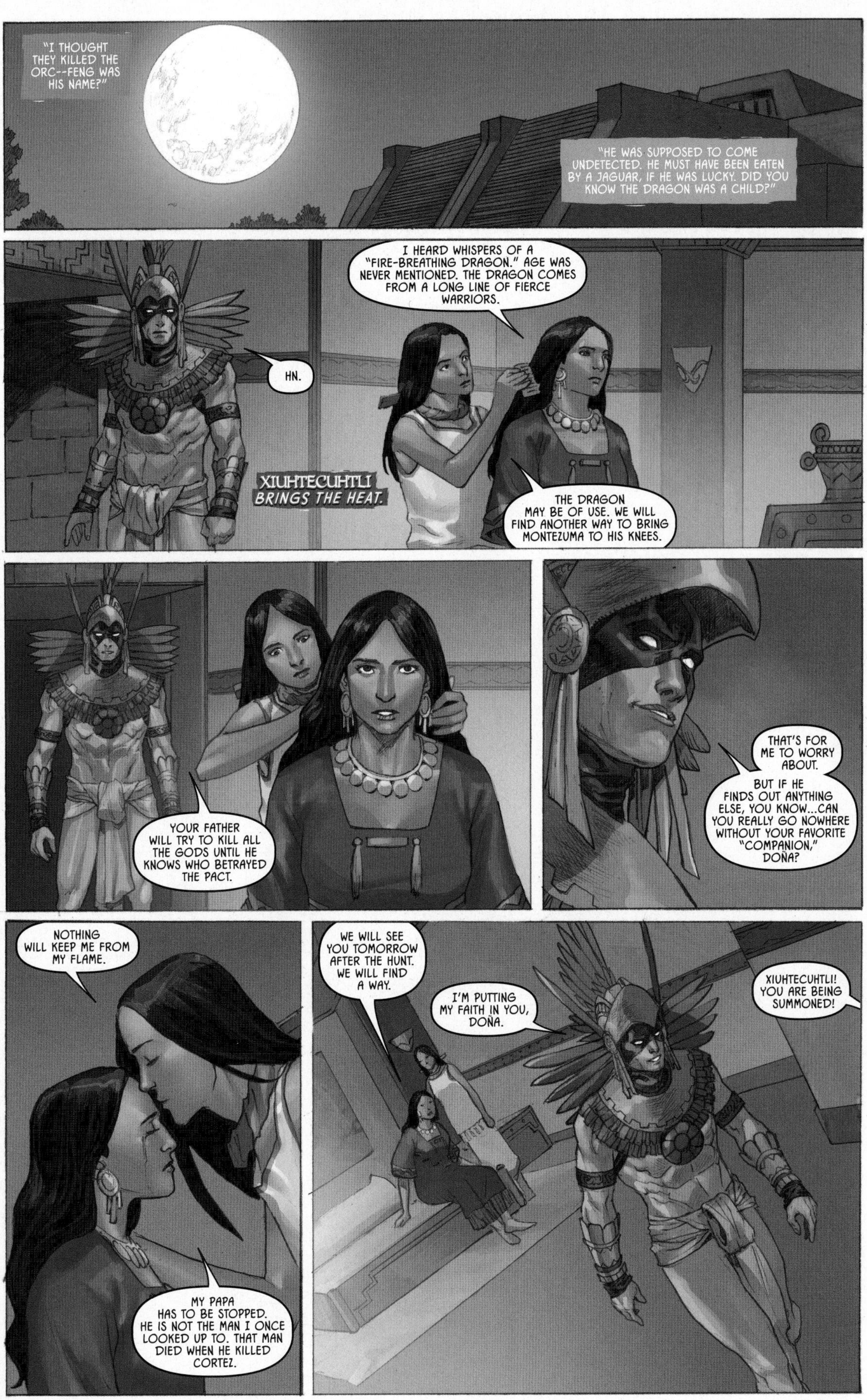
"I THOUGHT THEY KILLED THE ORC--FENG WAS HIS NAME?"
"HE WAS SUPPOSED TO COME UNDETECTED. HE MUST HAVE BEEN EATEN BY A JAGUAR, IF HE WAS LUCKY. DID YOU KNOW THE DRAGON WAS A CHILD?"
I HEARD WHISPERS OF A "FIRE-BREATHING DRAGON." AGE WAS NEVER MENTIONED. THE DRAGON COMES FROM A LONG LINE OF FIERCE WARRIORS.
HN.
XIUHTECUHTLI BRINGS THE HEAT.
THE DRAGON MAY BE OF USE. WE WILL FIND ANOTHER WAY TO BRING MONTEZUMA TO HIS KNEES.
YOUR FATHER WILL TRY TO KILL ALL THE GODS UNTIL HE KNOWS WHO BETRAYED THE PACT.
THAT'S FOR ME TO WORRY ABOUT.
BUT IF HE FINDS OUT ANYTHING ELSE, YOU KNOW...CAN YOU REALLY GO NOWHERE WITHOUT YOUR FAVORITE "COMPANION," DOÑA?
NOTHING WILL KEEP ME FROM MY FLAME.
MY PAPA HAS TO BE STOPPED. HE IS NOT THE MAN I ONCE LOOKED UP TO. THAT MAN DIED WHEN HE KILLED CORTEZ.
WE WILL SEE YOU TOMORROW AFTER THE HUNT. WE WILL FIND A WAY.
I'M PUTTING MY FAITH IN YOU, DOÑA.
XIUHTECUHTLI! YOU ARE BEING SUMMONED!

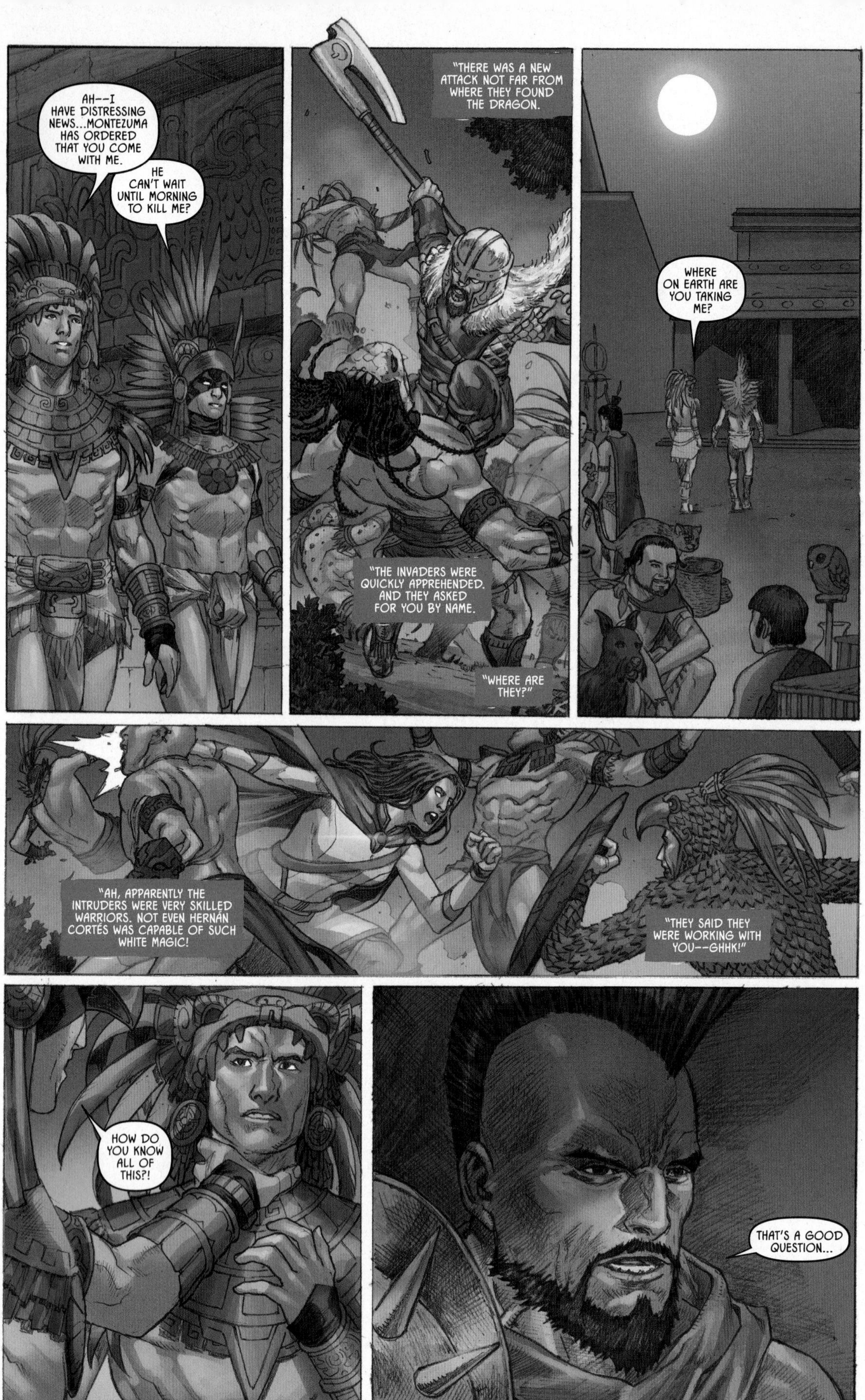
AH--I HAVE DISTRESSING NEWS...MONTEZUMA HAS ORDERED THAT YOU COME WITH ME.
HE CAN'T WAIT UNTIL MORNING TO KILL ME?
"THERE WAS A NEW ATTACK NOT FAR FROM WHERE THEY FOUND THE DRAGON.
"THE INVADERS WERE QUICKLY APPREHENDED. AND THEY ASKED FOR YOU BY NAME.
"WHERE ARE THEY?"
WHERE ON EARTH ARE YOU TAKING ME?
"AH, APPARENTLY THE INTRUDERS WERE VERY SKILLED WARRIORS. NOT EVEN HERNÁN CORTÉS WAS CAPABLE OF SUCH WHITE MAGIC!
"THEY SAID THEY WERE WORKING WITH YOU--GHHK!"
HOW DO YOU KNOW ALL OF THIS?!
THAT'S A GOOD QUESTION...

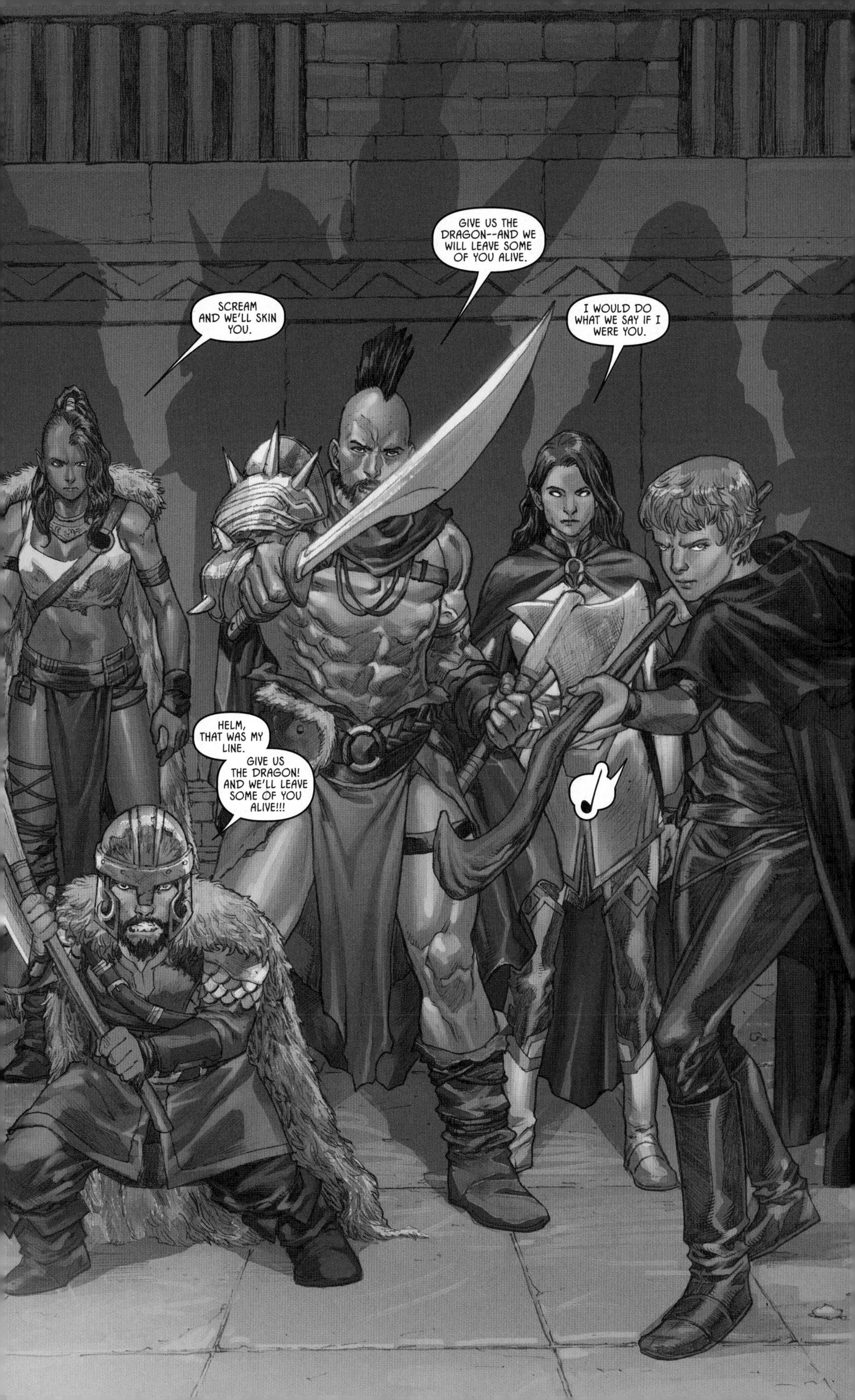
GIVE US THE DRAGON--AND WE WILL LEAVE SOME OF YOU ALIVE.
SCREAM AND WE'LL SKIN YOU.
I WOULD DO WHAT WE SAY IF I WERE YOU.
HELM, THAT WAS MY LINE.
GIVE US THE DRAGON! AND WE'LL LEAVE SOME OF YOU ALIVE!!!

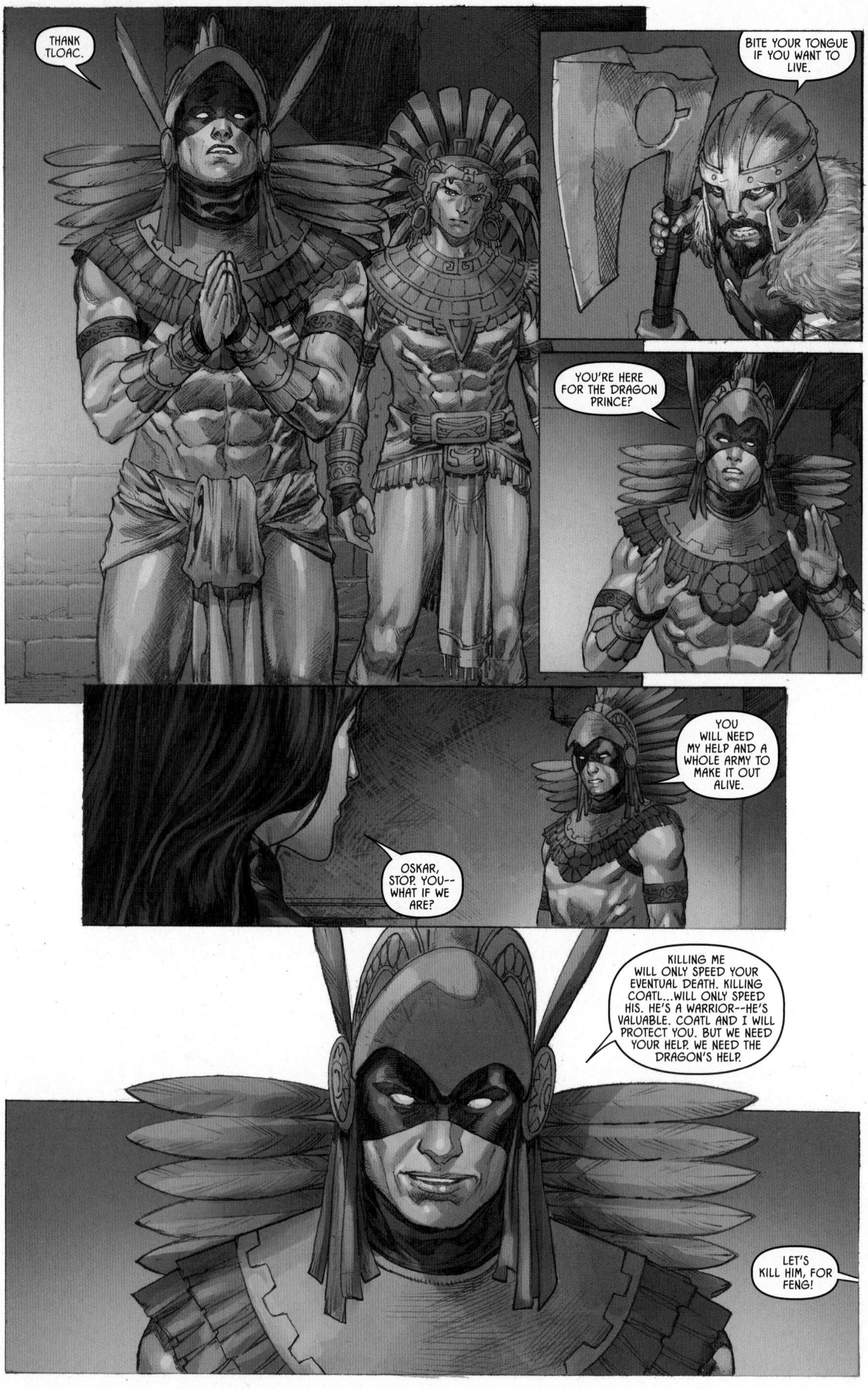
THANK TLOAC.
BITE YOUR TONGUE IF YOU WANT TO LIVE.
YOU'RE HERE FOR THE DRAGON PRINCE?
YOU WILL NEED MY HELP AND A WHOLE ARMY TO MAKE IT OUT ALIVE.
OSKAR, STOP. YOU-- WHAT IF WE ARE?
KILLING ME WILL ONLY SPEED YOUR EVENTUAL DEATH. KILLING COATL...WILL ONLY SPEED HIS. HE'S A WARRIOR--HE'S VALUABLE. COATL AND I WILL PROTECT YOU. BUT WE NEED YOUR HELP. WE NEED THE DRAGON'S HELP.
LET'S KILL HIM, FOR FENG!

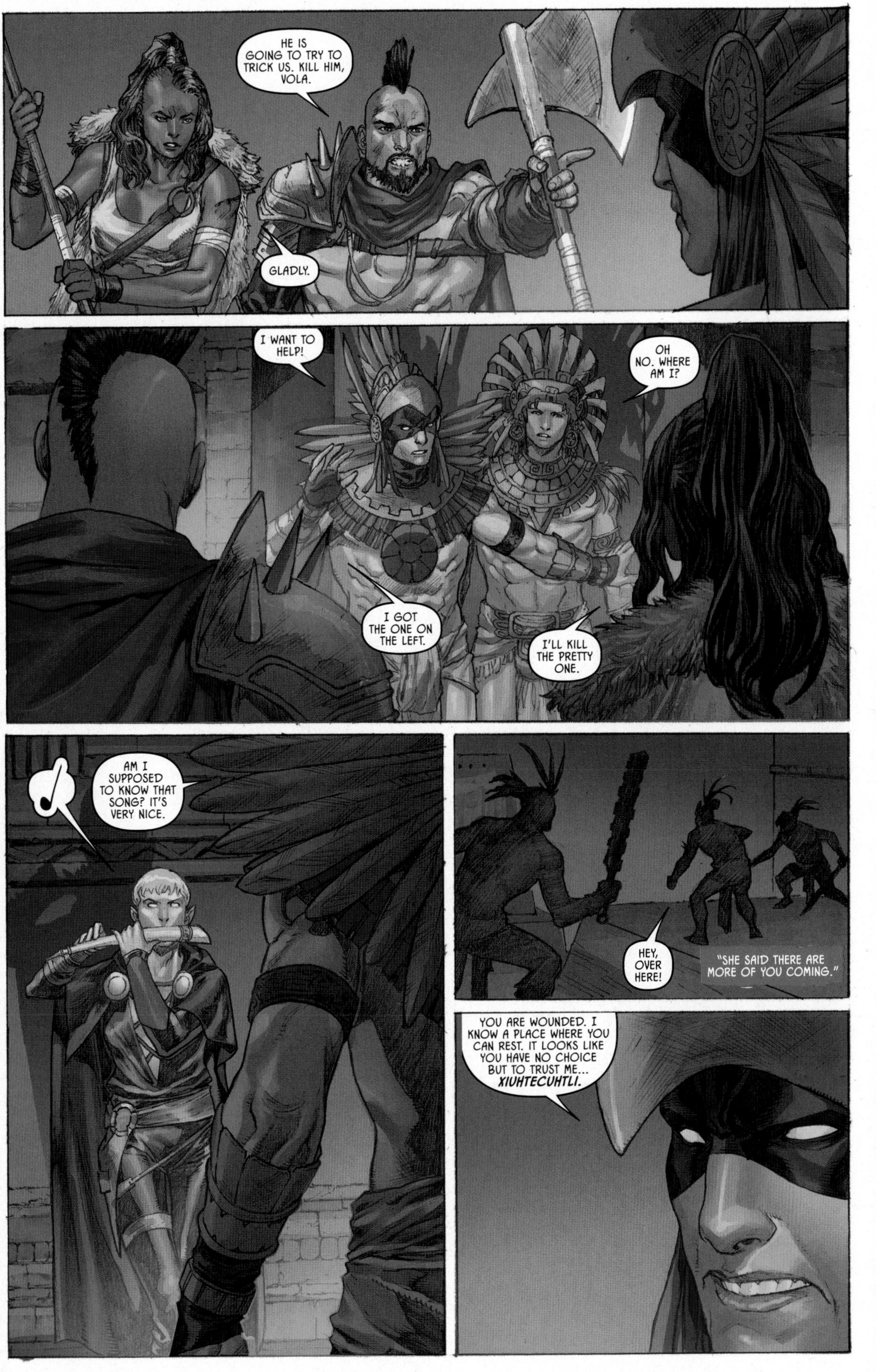
HE IS GOING TO TRY TO TRICK US. KILL HIM, VOLA.
GLADLY.
I WANT TO HELP!
OH NO. WHERE AM I?
I GOT THE ONE ON THE LEFT.
I'LL KILL THE PRETTY ONE.
AM I SUPPOSED TO KNOW THAT SONG? IT'S VERY NICE.
HEY, OVER HERE!
"SHE SAID THERE ARE MORE OF YOU COMING."
YOU ARE WOUNDED. I KNOW A PLACE WHERE YOU CAN REST. IT LOOKS LIKE YOU HAVE NO CHOICE BUT TO TRUST ME... XIUHTECUHTLI.

MEET ME IN MICTLĀN

02

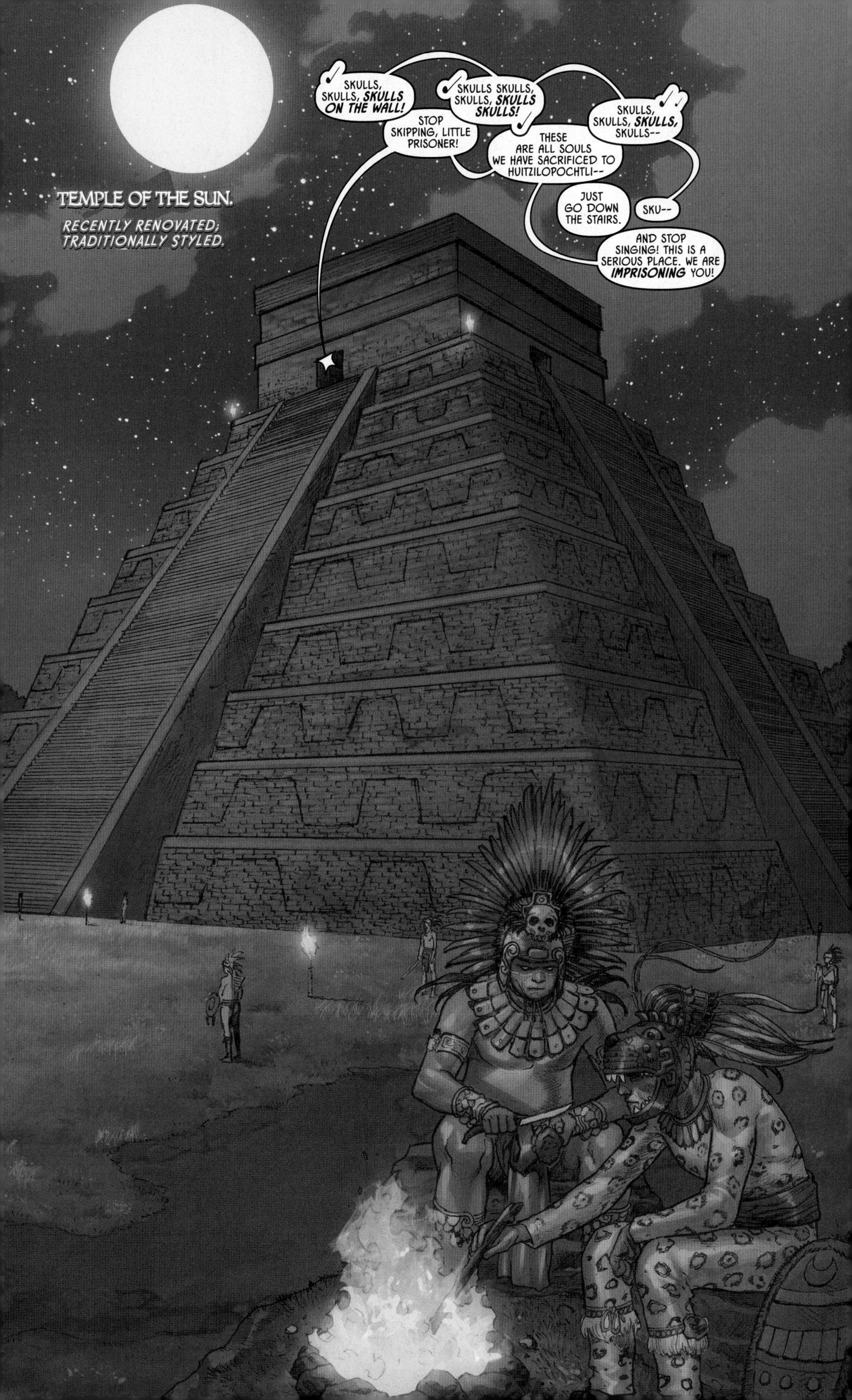
TEMPLE OF THE SUN.
RECENTLY RENOVATED; TRADITIONALLY STYLED.
SKULLS, SKULLS, SKULLS ON THE WALL!
STOP SKIPPING, LITTLE PRISONER!
SKULLS SKULLS, SKULLS, SKULLS SKULLS!
THESE ARE ALL SOULS WE HAVE SACRIFICED TO HUITZILOPOCHTLI--
SKULLS, SKULLS, SKULLS, SKULLS--
JUST GO DOWN THE STAIRS.
SKU--
AND STOP SINGING! THIS IS A SERIOUS PLACE. WE ARE IMPRISONING YOU!

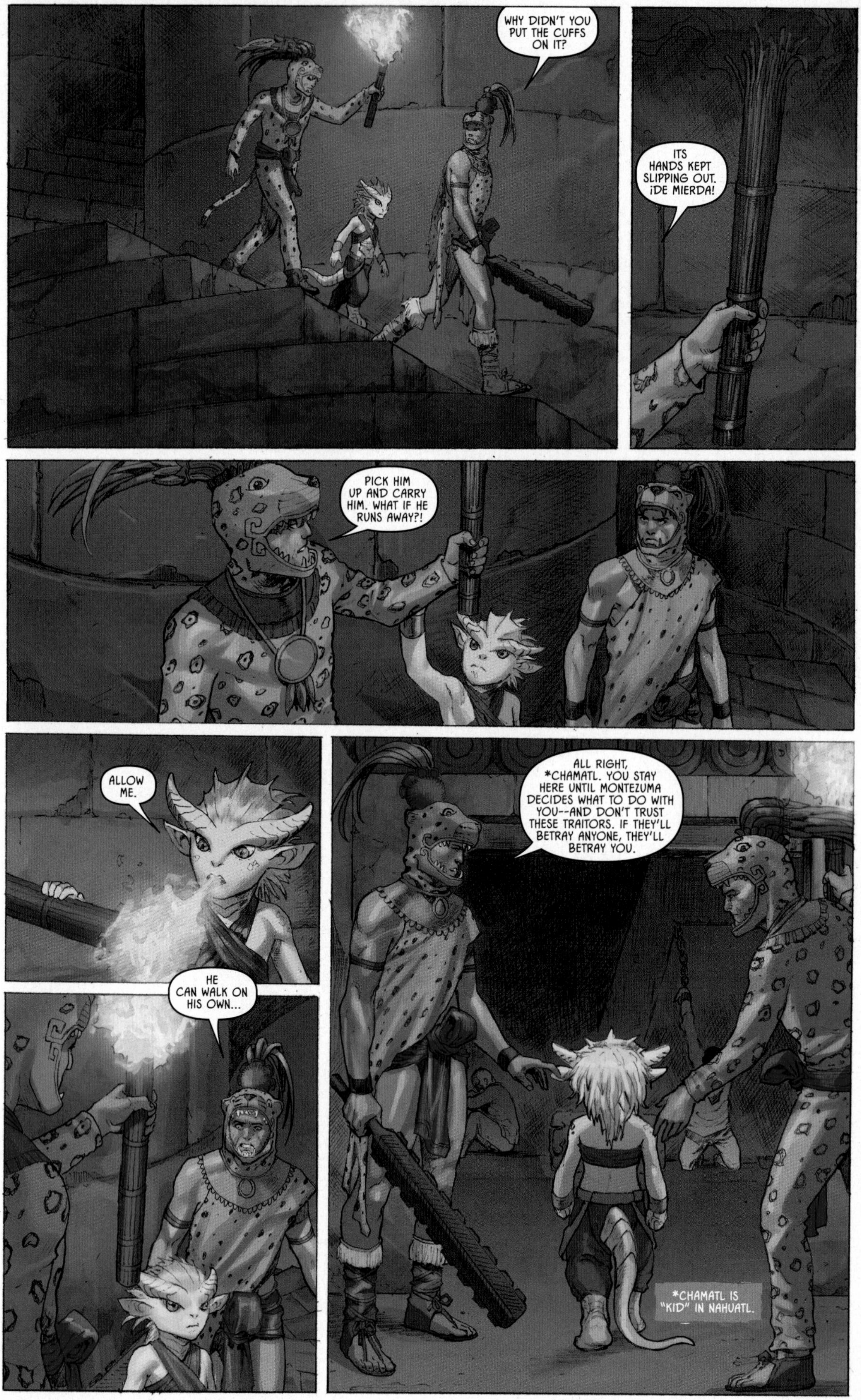
WHY DIDN'T YOU PUT THE CUFFS ON IT?
ITS HANDS KEPT SLIPPING OUT. ¡DE MIERDA!
PICK HIM UP AND CARRY HIM. WHAT IF HE RUNS AWAY?!
ALLOW ME.
HE CAN WALK ON HIS OWN...
ALL RIGHT, *CHAMATL. YOU STAY HERE UNTIL MONTEZUMA DECIDES WHAT TO DO WITH YOU--AND DON'T TRUST THESE TRAITORS. IF THEY'LL BETRAY ANYONE, THEY'LL BETRAY YOU.
*CHAMATL IS "KID" IN NAHUATL.

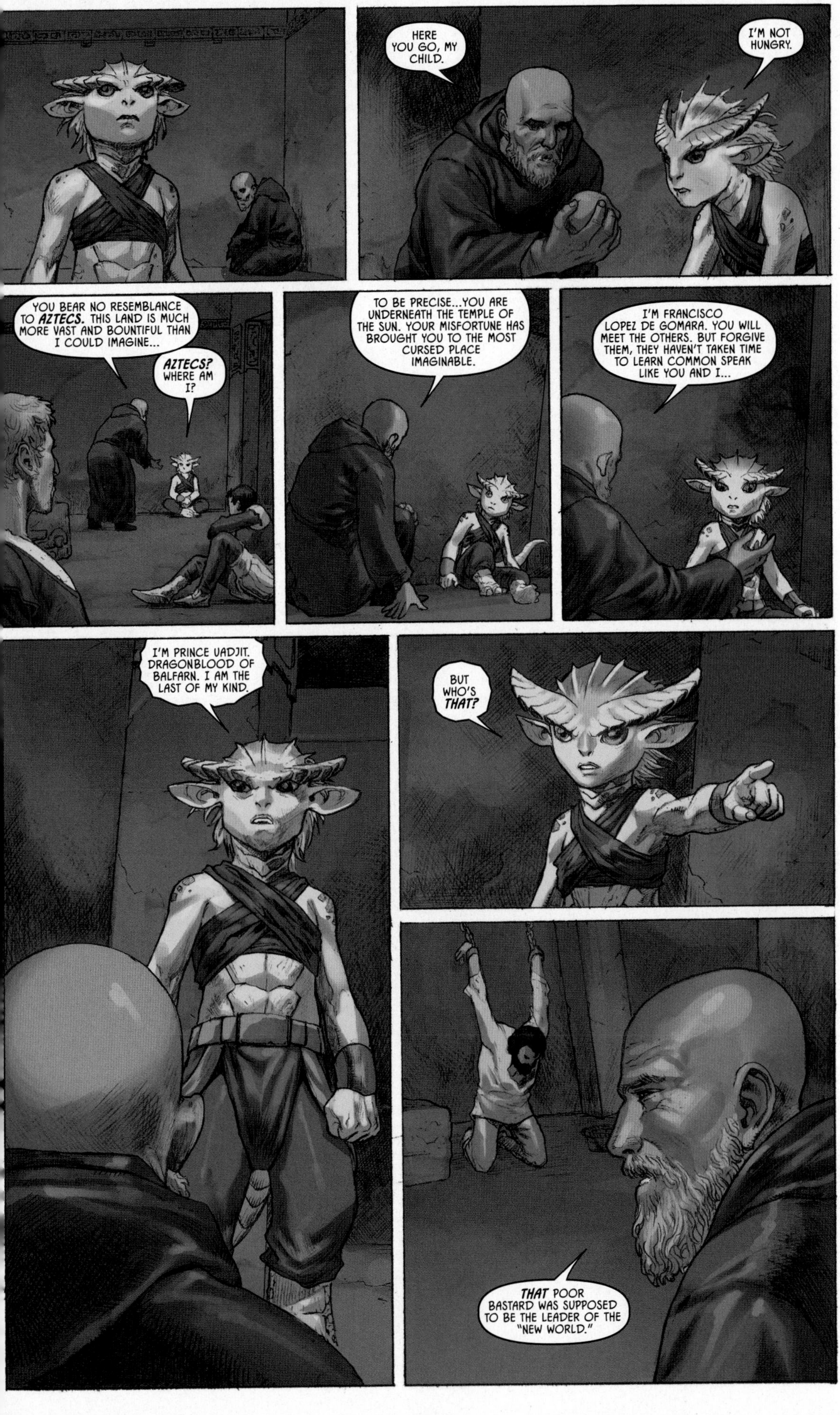
HERE YOU GO, MY CHILD.
I'M NOT HUNGRY.
YOU BEAR NO RESEMBLANCE TO AZTECS. THIS LAND IS MUCH MORE VAST AND BOUNTIFUL THAN I COULD IMAGINE...
AZTECS? WHERE AM I?
TO BE PRECISE...YOU ARE UNDERNEATH THE TEMPLE OF THE SUN. YOUR MISFORTUNE HAS BROUGHT YOU TO THE MOST CURSED PLACE IMAGINABLE.
I'M FRANCISCO LOPEZ DE GOMARA. YOU WILL MEET THE OTHERS. BUT FORGIVE THEM, THEY HAVEN'T TAKEN TIME TO LEARN COMMON SPEAK LIKE YOU AND I...
I'M PRINCE UADJIT. DRAGONBLOOD OF BALFARN. I AM THE LAST OF MY KIND.
BUT WHO'S THAT?
THAT POOR BASTARD WAS SUPPOSED TO BE THE LEADER OF THE "NEW WORLD."

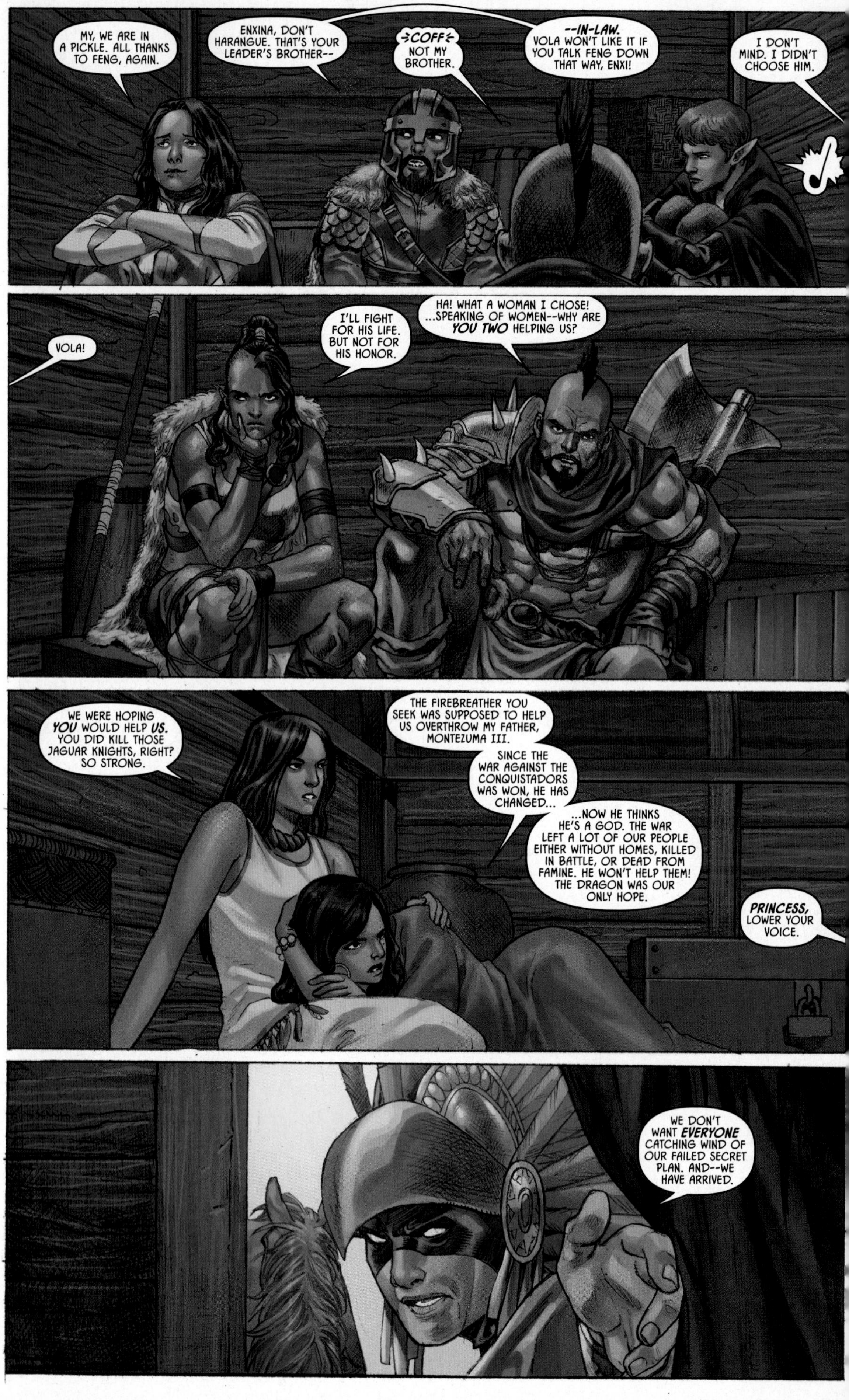

MY, WE ARE IN A PICKLE. ALL THANKS TO FENG, AGAIN.
ENXINA, DON'T HARANGUE. THAT'S YOUR LEADER'S BROTHER--
COFF NOT MY BROTHER.
--IN-LAW. VOLA WON'T LIKE IT IF YOU TALK FENG DOWN THAT WAY, ENXI!
I DON'T MIND. I DIDN'T CHOOSE HIM.
VOLA!
I'LL FIGHT FOR HIS LIFE. BUT NOT FOR HIS HONOR.
HA! WHAT A WOMAN I CHOSE! ...SPEAKING OF WOMEN--WHY ARE YOU TWO HELPING US?
WE WERE HOPING YOU WOULD HELP US. YOU DID KILL THOSE JAGUAR KNIGHTS, RIGHT? SO STRONG.
THE FIREBREATHER YOU SEEK WAS SUPPOSED TO HELP US OVERTHROW MY FATHER, MONTEZUMA III.
SINCE THE WAR AGAINST THE CONQUISTADORS WAS WON, HE HAS CHANGED...
...NOW HE THINKS HE'S A GOD. THE WAR LEFT A LOT OF OUR PEOPLE EITHER WITHOUT HOMES, KILLED IN BATTLE, OR DEAD FROM FAMINE. HE WON'T HELP THEM! THE DRAGON WAS OUR ONLY HOPE.
PRINCESS, LOWER YOUR VOICE.
WE DON'T WANT EVERYONE CATCHING WIND OF OUR FAILED SECRET PLAN. AND--WE HAVE ARRIVED.

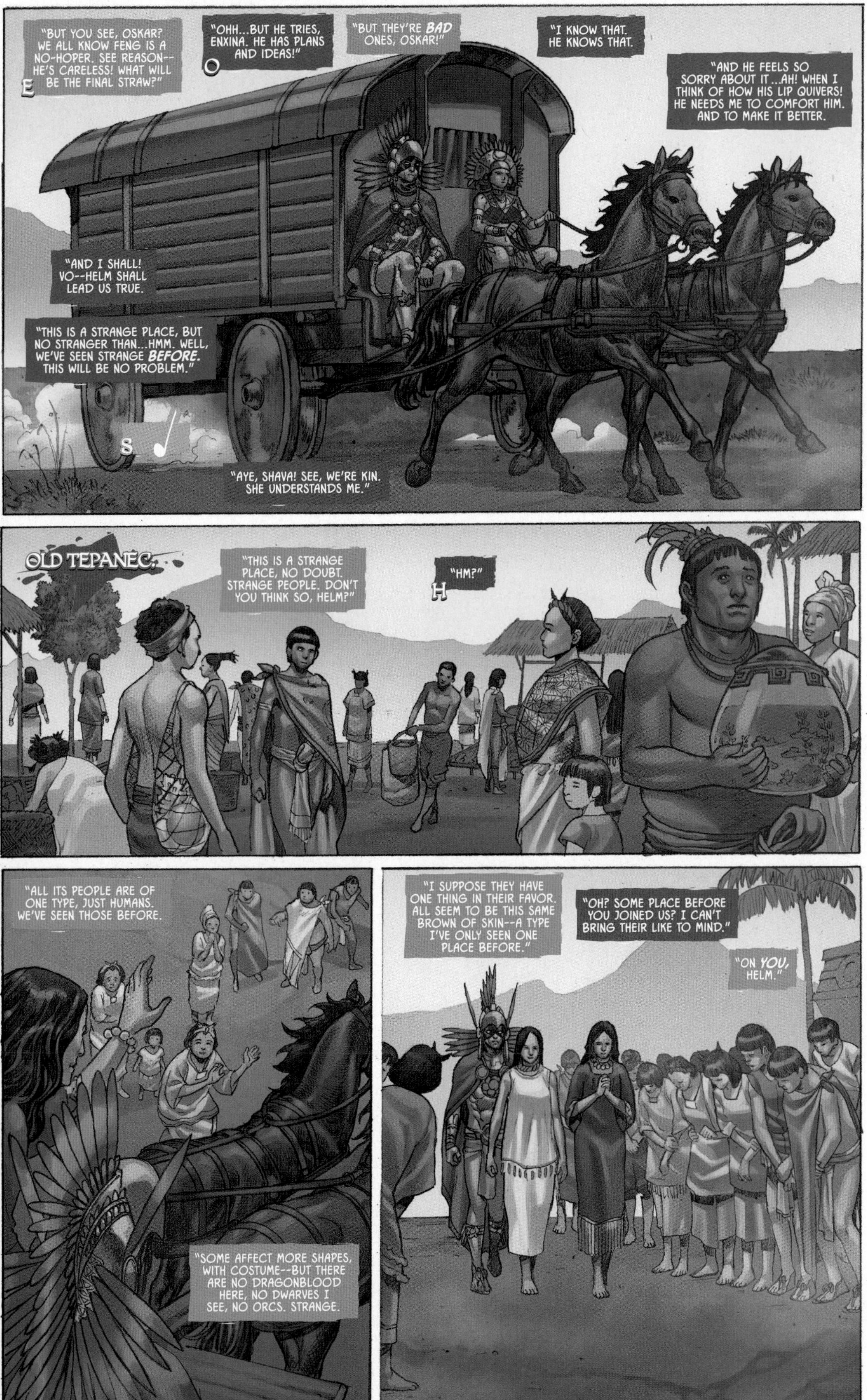

"BUT YOU SEE, OSKAR? WE ALL KNOW FENG IS A NO-HOPER. SEE REASON-- HE'S CARELESS! WHAT WILL BE THE FINAL STRAW?"
"OHH...BUT HE TRIES, ENXINA. HE HAS PLANS AND IDEAS!"
"BUT THEY'RE *BAD* ONES, OSKAR!"
"I KNOW THAT. HE KNOWS THAT.
"AND HE FEELS SO SORRY ABOUT IT...AH! WHEN I THINK OF HOW HIS LIP QUIVERS! HE NEEDS ME TO COMFORT HIM. AND TO MAKE IT BETTER.
"AND I SHALL! VO--HELM SHALL LEAD US TRUE.
"THIS IS A STRANGE PLACE, BUT NO STRANGER THAN...HMM. WELL, WE'VE SEEN STRANGE ***BEFORE***. THIS WILL BE NO PROBLEM."
"AYE, SHAVA! SEE, WE'RE KIN. SHE UNDERSTANDS ME."
OLD TEPANEC.
"THIS IS A STRANGE PLACE, NO DOUBT. STRANGE PEOPLE. DON'T YOU THINK SO, HELM?"
"HM?"
"ALL ITS PEOPLE ARE OF ONE TYPE, JUST HUMANS. WE'VE SEEN THOSE BEFORE.
"SOME AFFECT MORE SHAPES, WITH COSTUME--BUT THERE ARE NO DRAGONBLOOD HERE, NO DWARVES I SEE, NO ORCS. STRANGE.
"I SUPPOSE THEY HAVE ONE THING IN THEIR FAVOR. ALL SEEM TO BE THIS SAME BROWN OF SKIN--A TYPE I'VE ONLY SEEN ONE PLACE BEFORE."
"OH? SOME PLACE BEFORE YOU JOINED US? I CAN'T BRING THEIR LIKE TO MIND."
"ON *YOU*, HELM."

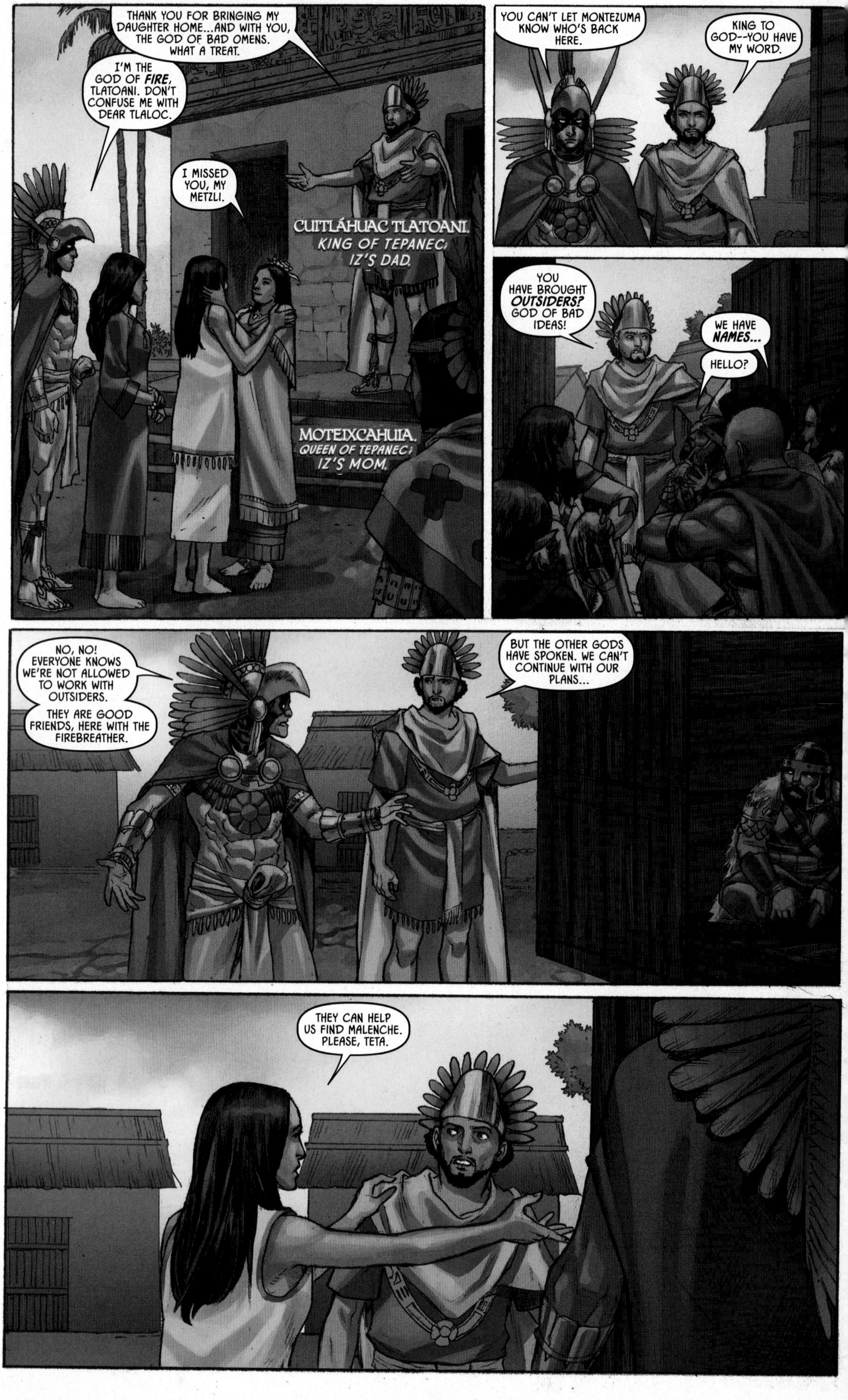
THANK YOU FOR BRINGING MY DAUGHTER HOME...AND WITH YOU, THE GOD OF BAD OMENS. WHAT A TREAT.
I'M THE GOD OF FIRE, TLATOANI. DON'T CONFUSE ME WITH DEAR TLALOC.
I MISSED YOU, MY METZLI.
CUITLÁHUAC TLATOANI. KING OF TEPANEC; IZ'S DAD.
MOTEIXCAHUIA. QUEEN OF TEPANEC; IZ'S MOM.
YOU CAN'T LET MONTEZUMA KNOW WHO'S BACK HERE.
KING TO GOD--YOU HAVE MY WORD.
YOU HAVE BROUGHT OUTSIDERS? GOD OF BAD IDEAS!
WE HAVE NAMES...
HELLO?
NO, NO! EVERYONE KNOWS WE'RE NOT ALLOWED TO WORK WITH OUTSIDERS.
THEY ARE GOOD FRIENDS, HERE WITH THE FIREBREATHER.
BUT THE OTHER GODS HAVE SPOKEN. WE CAN'T CONTINUE WITH OUR PLANS...
THEY CAN HELP US FIND MALENCHE. PLEASE, TETA.

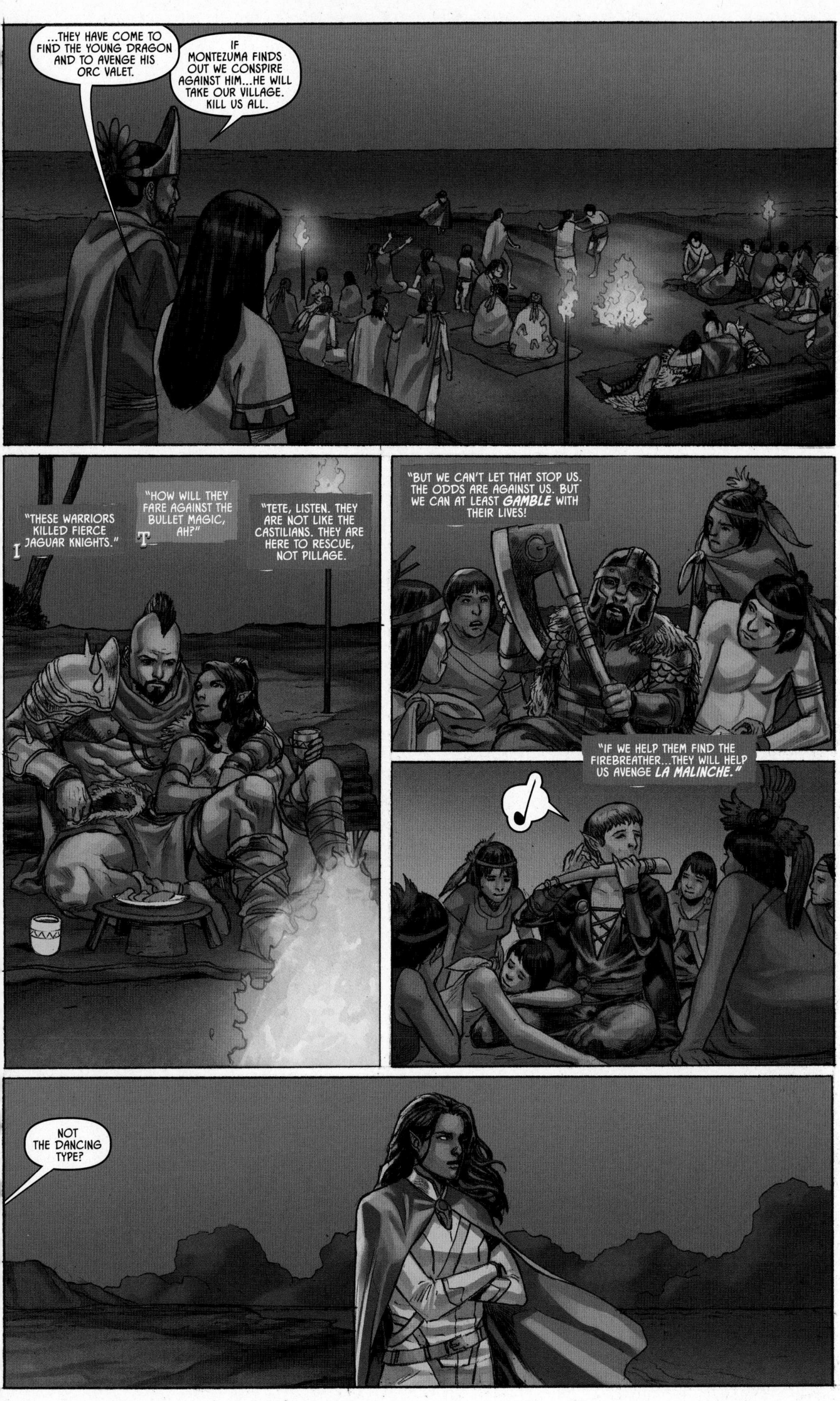
...THEY HAVE COME TO FIND THE YOUNG DRAGON AND TO AVENGE HIS ORC VALET.
IF MONTEZUMA FINDS OUT WE CONSPIRE AGAINST HIM...HE WILL TAKE OUR VILLAGE. KILL US ALL.
"THESE WARRIORS KILLED FIERCE JAGUAR KNIGHTS."
"HOW WILL THEY FARE AGAINST THE BULLET MAGIC, AH?"
"TETE, LISTEN. THEY ARE NOT LIKE THE CASTILIANS. THEY ARE HERE TO RESCUE, NOT PILLAGE.
"BUT WE CAN'T LET THAT STOP US. THE ODDS ARE AGAINST US. BUT WE CAN AT LEAST GAMBLE WITH THEIR LIVES!
"IF WE HELP THEM FIND THE FIREBREATHER...THEY WILL HELP US AVENGE LA MALINCHE."
NOT THE DANCING TYPE?

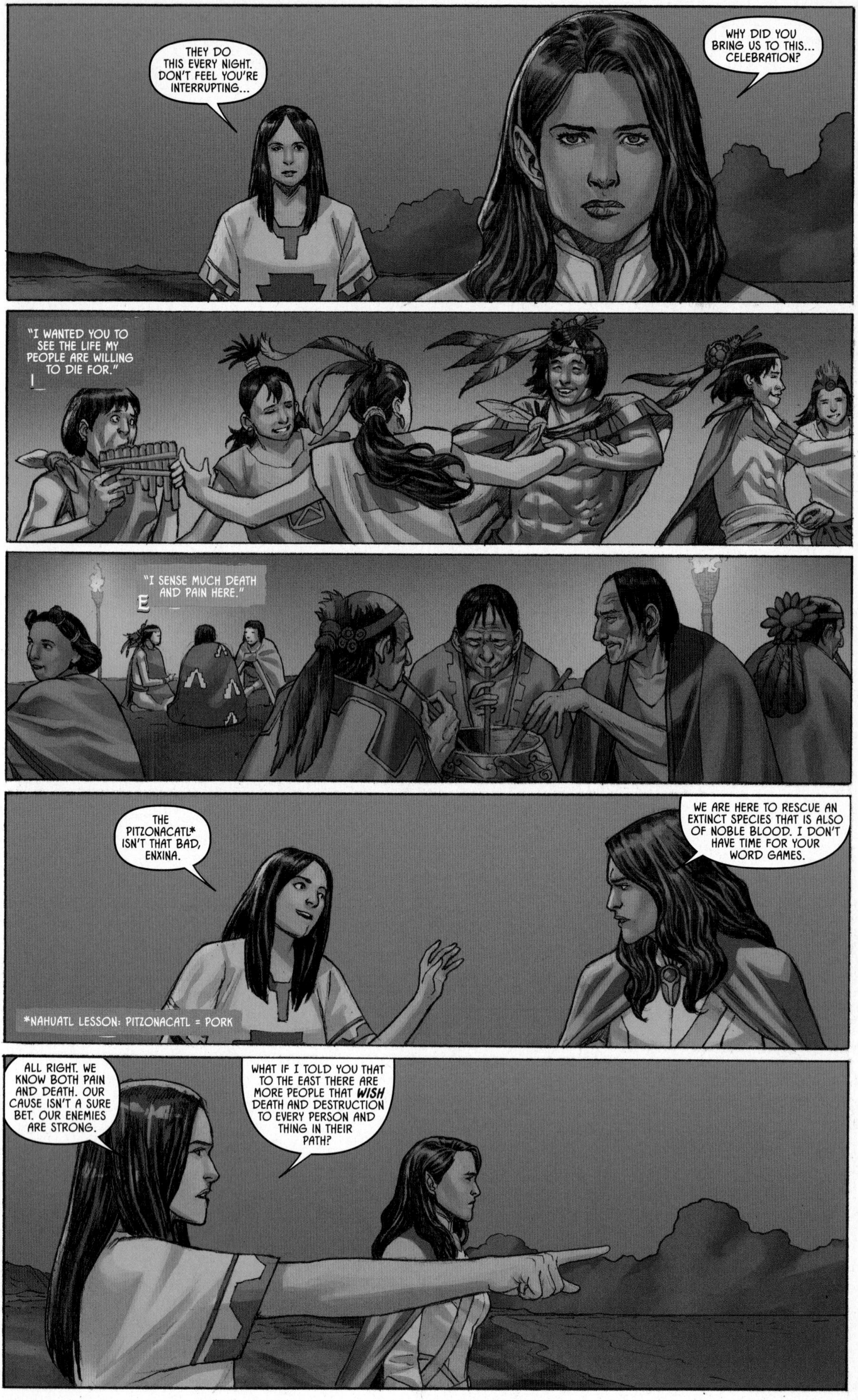
THEY DO THIS EVERY NIGHT. DON'T FEEL YOU'RE INTERRUPTING...
WHY DID YOU BRING US TO THIS... CELEBRATION?
"I WANTED YOU TO SEE THE LIFE MY PEOPLE ARE WILLING TO DIE FOR."
"I SENSE MUCH DEATH AND PAIN HERE."
THE PITZONACATL* ISN'T THAT BAD, ENXINA.
WE ARE HERE TO RESCUE AN EXTINCT SPECIES THAT IS ALSO OF NOBLE BLOOD. I DON'T HAVE TIME FOR YOUR WORD GAMES.
*NAHUATL LESSON: PITZONACATL = PORK
ALL RIGHT. WE KNOW BOTH PAIN AND DEATH. OUR CAUSE ISN'T A SURE BET. OUR ENEMIES ARE STRONG.
WHAT IF I TOLD YOU THAT TO THE EAST THERE ARE MORE PEOPLE THAT ***WISH*** DEATH AND DESTRUCTION TO EVERY PERSON AND THING IN THEIR PATH?

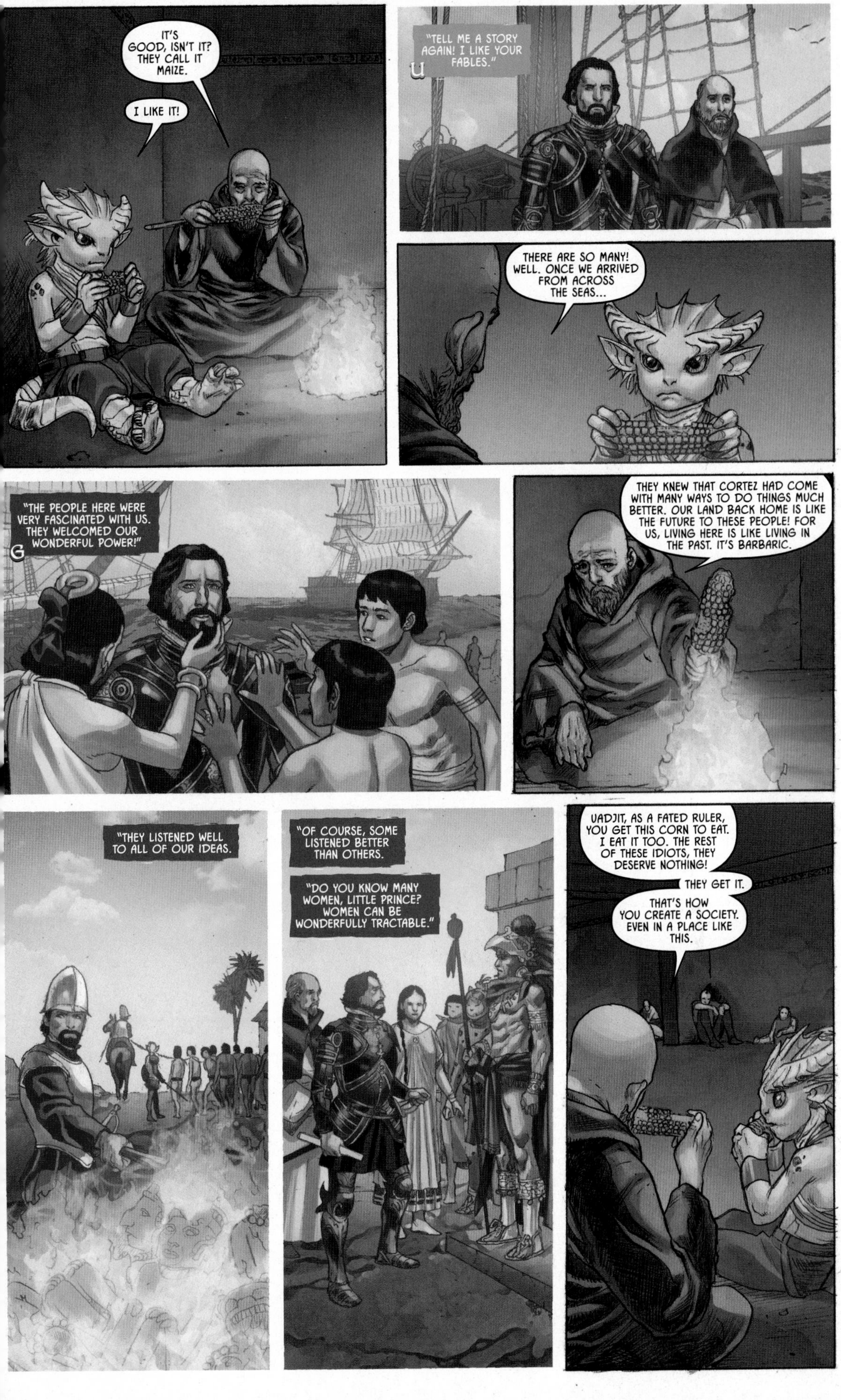
IT'S GOOD, ISN'T IT? THEY CALL IT MAIZE.
I LIKE IT!
"TELL ME A STORY AGAIN! I LIKE YOUR FABLES."
THERE ARE SO MANY! WELL. ONCE WE ARRIVED FROM ACROSS THE SEAS...
"THE PEOPLE HERE WERE VERY FASCINATED WITH US. THEY WELCOMED OUR WONDERFUL POWER!"
THEY KNEW THAT CORTEZ HAD COME WITH MANY WAYS TO DO THINGS MUCH BETTER. OUR LAND BACK HOME IS LIKE THE FUTURE TO THESE PEOPLE! FOR US, LIVING HERE IS LIKE LIVING IN THE PAST. IT'S BARBARIC.
"THEY LISTENED WELL TO ALL OF OUR IDEAS.
"OF COURSE, SOME LISTENED BETTER THAN OTHERS.
"DO YOU KNOW MANY WOMEN, LITTLE PRINCE? WOMEN CAN BE WONDERFULLY TRACTABLE."
UADJIT, AS A FATED RULER, YOU GET THIS CORN TO EAT. I EAT IT TOO. THE REST OF THESE IDIOTS, THEY DESERVE NOTHING!
THEY GET IT.
THAT'S HOW YOU CREATE A SOCIETY. EVEN IN A PLACE LIKE THIS.

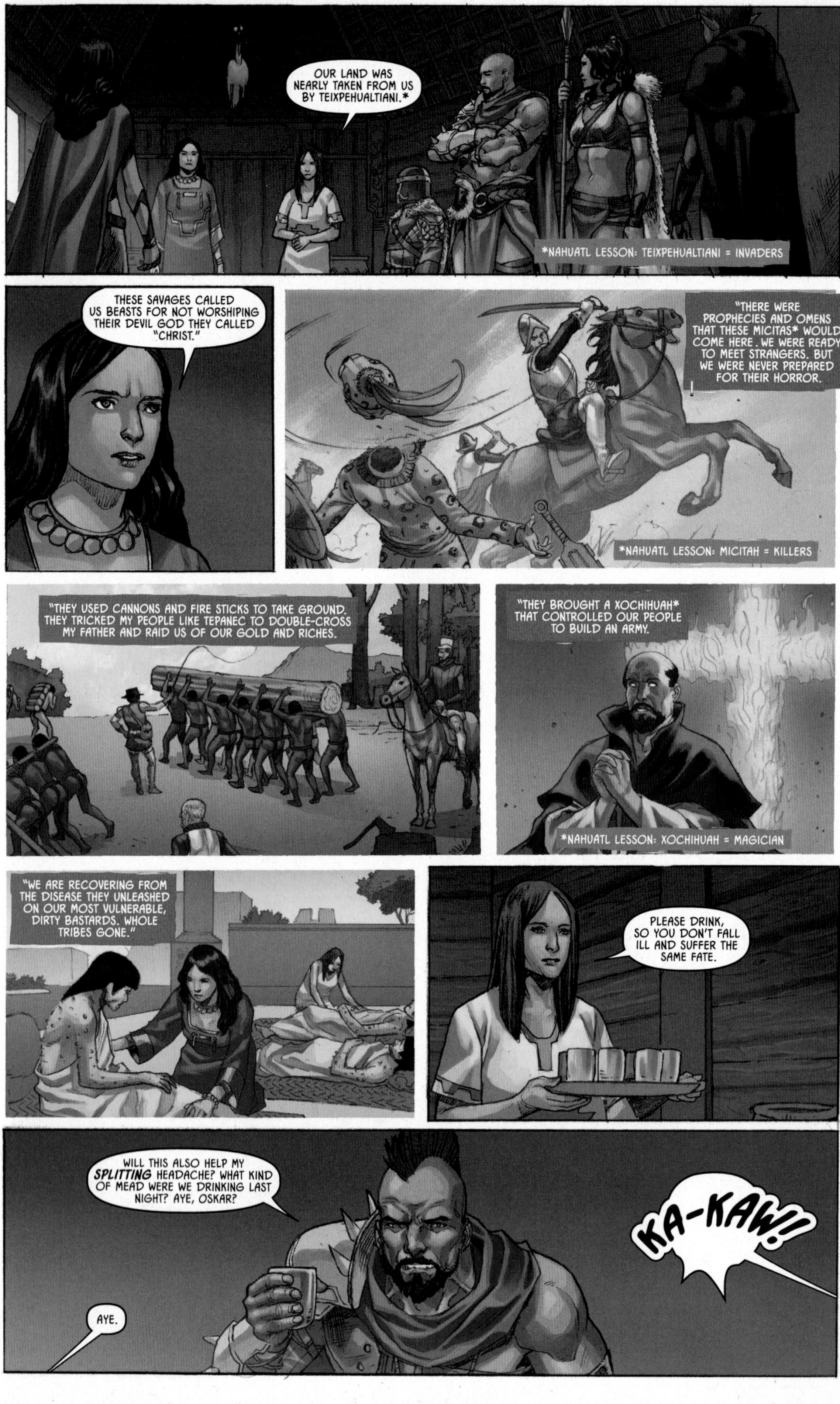
OUR LAND WAS NEARLY TAKEN FROM US BY TEIXPEHUALTIANI.*
*NAHUATL LESSON: TEIXPEHUALTIANI = INVADERS
THESE SAVAGES CALLED US BEASTS FOR NOT WORSHIPING THEIR DEVIL GOD THEY CALLED "CHRIST."
"THERE WERE PROPHECIES AND OMENS THAT THESE MICITAS* WOULD COME HERE. WE WERE READY TO MEET STRANGERS. BUT WE WERE NEVER PREPARED FOR THEIR HORROR.
*NAHUATL LESSON: MICITAH = KILLERS
"THEY USED CANNONS AND FIRE STICKS TO TAKE GROUND. THEY TRICKED MY PEOPLE LIKE TEPANEC TO DOUBLE-CROSS MY FATHER AND RAID US OF OUR GOLD AND RICHES.
"THEY BROUGHT A XOCHIHUAH* THAT CONTROLLED OUR PEOPLE TO BUILD AN ARMY.
*NAHUATL LESSON: XOCHIHUAH = MAGICIAN
"WE ARE RECOVERING FROM THE DISEASE THEY UNLEASHED ON OUR MOST VULNERABLE, DIRTY BASTARDS. WHOLE TRIBES GONE."
PLEASE DRINK, SO YOU DON'T FALL ILL AND SUFFER THE SAME FATE.
WILL THIS ALSO HELP MY SPLITTING HEADACHE? WHAT KIND OF MEAD WERE WE DRINKING LAST NIGHT? AYE, OSKAR?
KA-KAW!!
AYE.

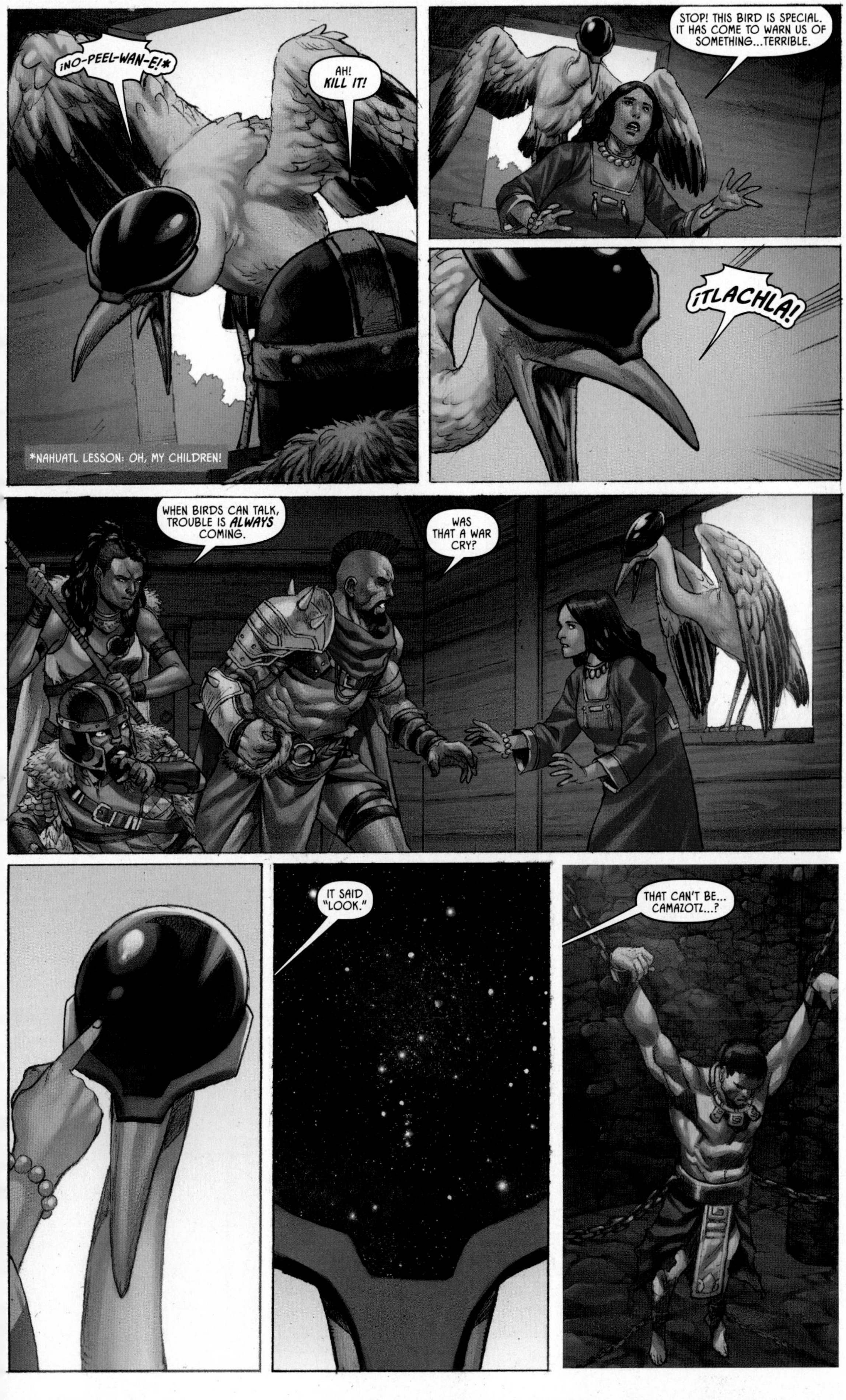

¡NO-PEEL-WAN-E!*
AH! KILL IT!
*NAHUATL LESSON: OH, MY CHILDREN!
STOP! THIS BIRD IS SPECIAL. IT HAS COME TO WARN US OF SOMETHING...TERRIBLE.
¡TLACHLA!
WHEN BIRDS CAN TALK, TROUBLE IS ALWAYS COMING.
WAS THAT A WAR CRY?
IT SAID "LOOK."
THAT CAN'T BE... CAMAZOTZ...?

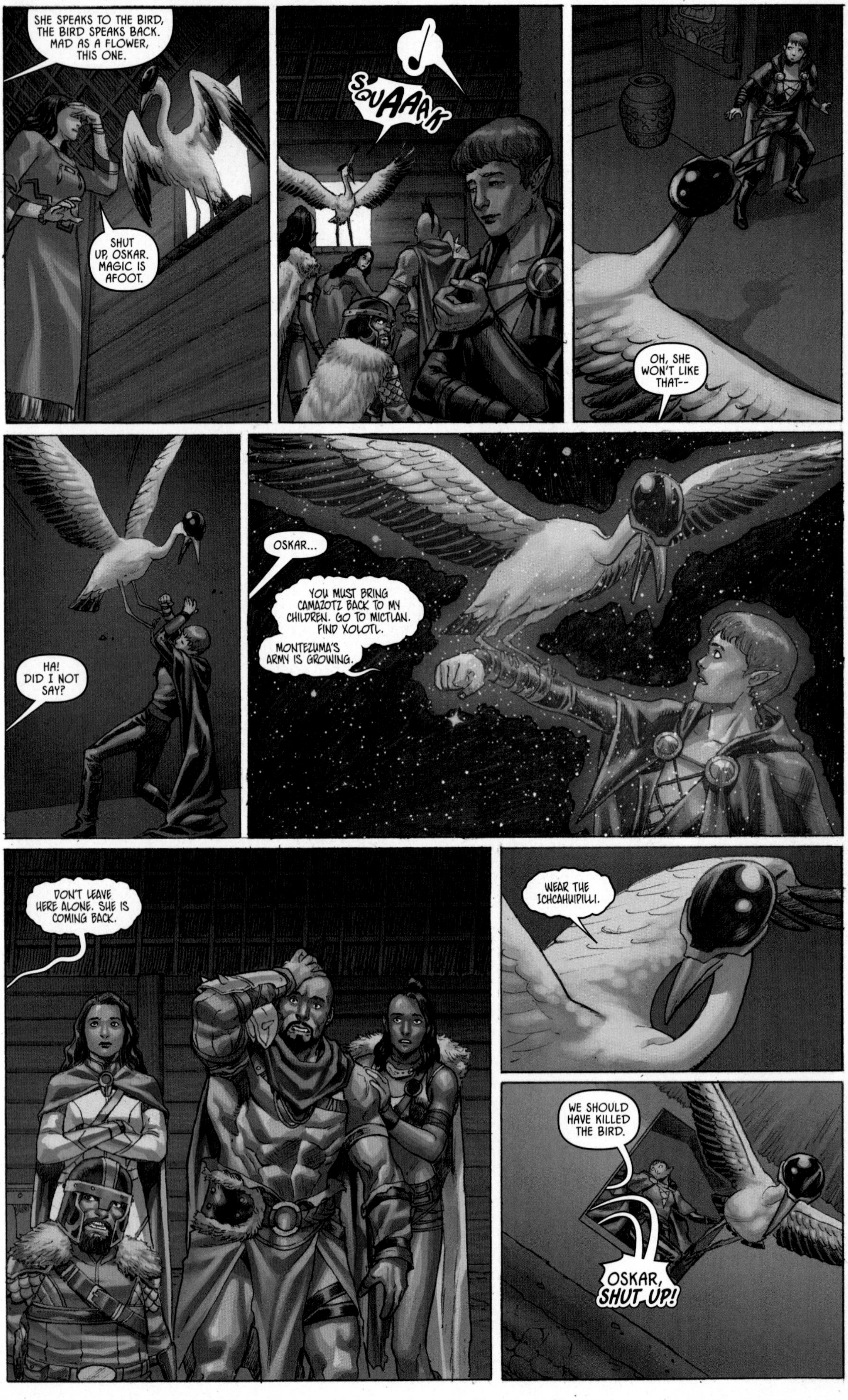
SHE SPEAKS TO THE BIRD, THE BIRD SPEAKS BACK. MAD AS A FLOWER, THIS ONE.
SHUT UP, OSKAR. MAGIC IS AFOOT.
SQUAAAK
OH, SHE WON'T LIKE THAT--
HA! DID I NOT SAY?
OSKAR...
YOU MUST BRING CAMAZOTZ BACK TO MY CHILDREN. GO TO MICTLAN. FIND XOLOTL.
MONTEZUMA'S ARMY IS GROWING.
DON'T LEAVE HERE ALONE. SHE IS COMING BACK.
WEAR THE ICHCAHUIPILLI.
WE SHOULD HAVE KILLED THE BIRD.
OSKAR, SHUT UP!

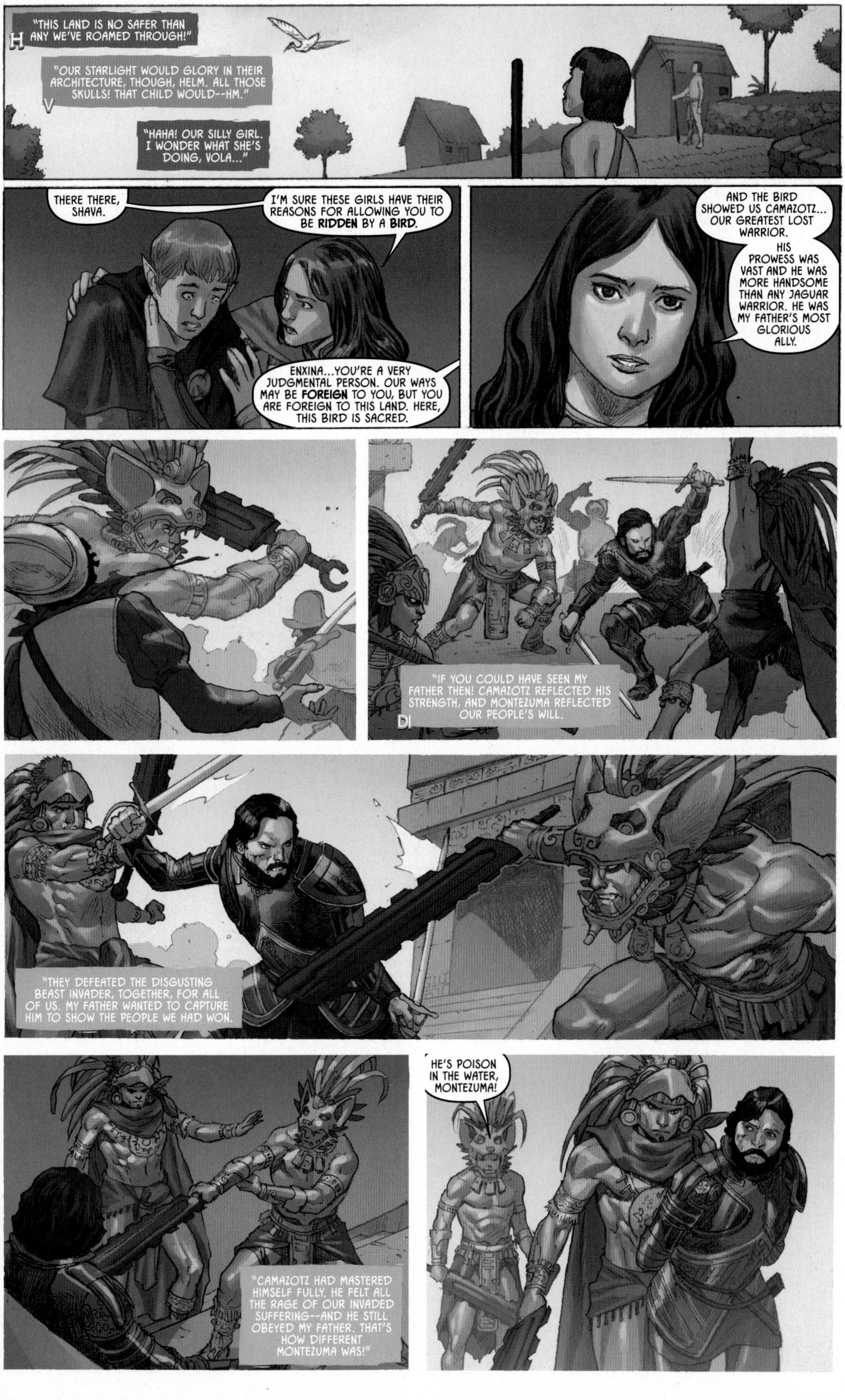
"THIS LAND IS NO SAFER THAN ANY WE'VE ROAMED THROUGH!"
H
"OUR STARLIGHT WOULD GLORY IN THEIR ARCHITECTURE, THOUGH, HELM. ALL THOSE SKULLS! THAT CHILD WOULD--HM."
V
"HAHA! OUR SILLY GIRL. I WONDER WHAT SHE'S DOING, VOLA..."
THERE THERE, SHAVA.
I'M SURE THESE GIRLS HAVE THEIR REASONS FOR ALLOWING YOU TO BE RIDDEN BY A BIRD.
ENXINA...YOU'RE A VERY JUDGMENTAL PERSON. OUR WAYS MAY BE FOREIGN TO YOU, BUT YOU ARE FOREIGN TO THIS LAND. HERE, THIS BIRD IS SACRED.
AND THE BIRD SHOWED US CAMAZOTZ... OUR GREATEST LOST WARRIOR.
HIS PROWESS WAS VAST AND HE WAS MORE HANDSOME THAN ANY JAGUAR WARRIOR. HE WAS MY FATHER'S MOST GLORIOUS ALLY.
"IF YOU COULD HAVE SEEN MY FATHER THEN! CAMAZOTZ REFLECTED HIS STRENGTH, AND MONTEZUMA REFLECTED OUR PEOPLE'S WILL.
DI
"THEY DEFEATED THE DISGUSTING BEAST INVADER, TOGETHER, FOR ALL OF US. MY FATHER WANTED TO CAPTURE HIM TO SHOW THE PEOPLE WE HAD WON.
"CAMAZOTZ HAD MASTERED HIMSELF FULLY. HE FELT ALL THE RAGE OF OUR INVADED SUFFERING--AND HE STILL OBEYED MY FATHER. THAT'S HOW DIFFERENT MONTEZUMA WAS!"
HE'S POISON IN THE WATER, MONTEZUMA!

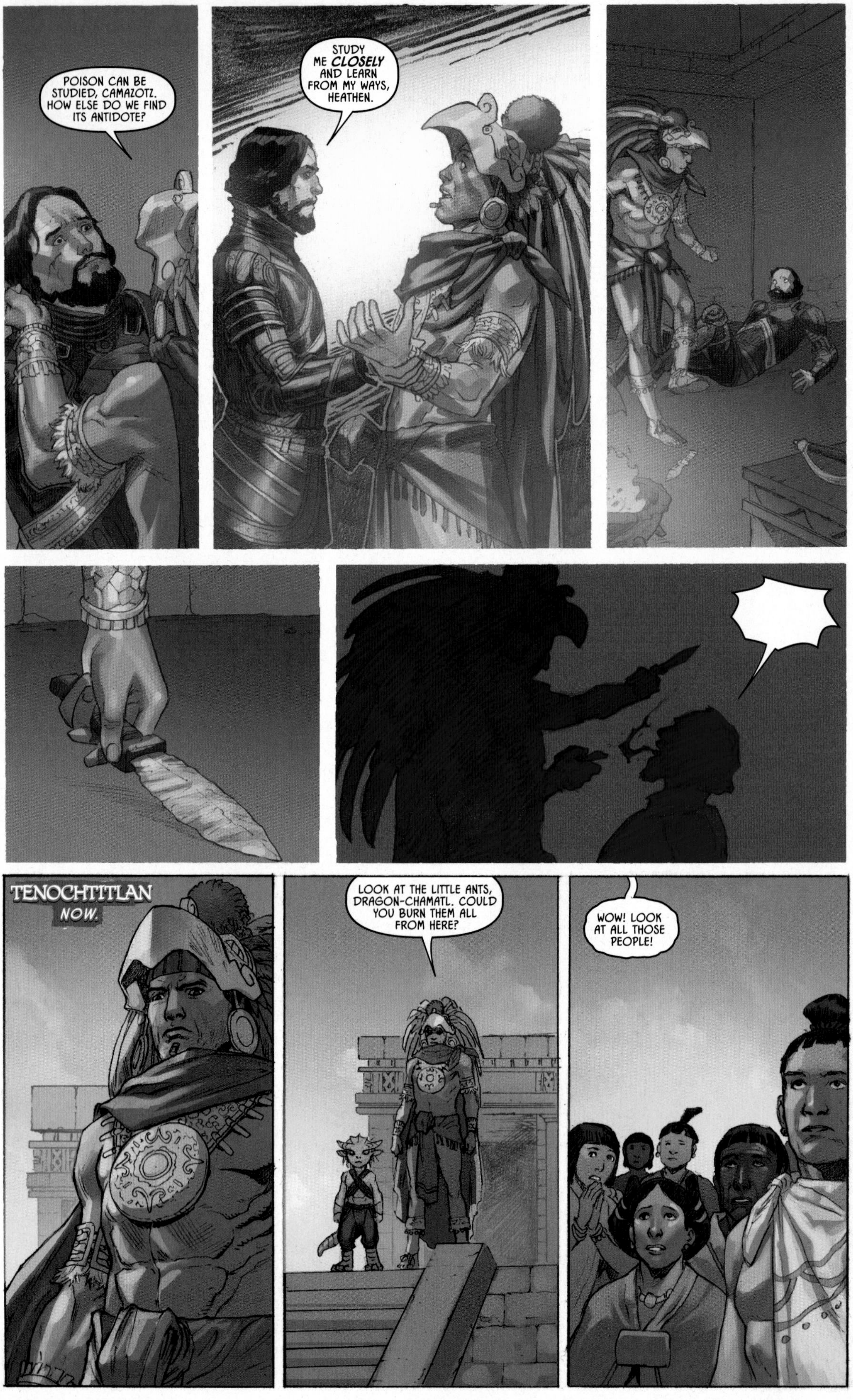
POISON CAN BE STUDIED, CAMAZOTZ. HOW ELSE DO WE FIND ITS ANTIDOTE?
STUDY ME CLOSELY AND LEARN FROM MY WAYS, HEATHEN.
TENOCHTITLAN NOW.
LOOK AT THE LITTLE ANTS, DRAGON-CHAMATL. COULD YOU BURN THEM ALL FROM HERE?
WOW! LOOK AT ALL THOSE PEOPLE!

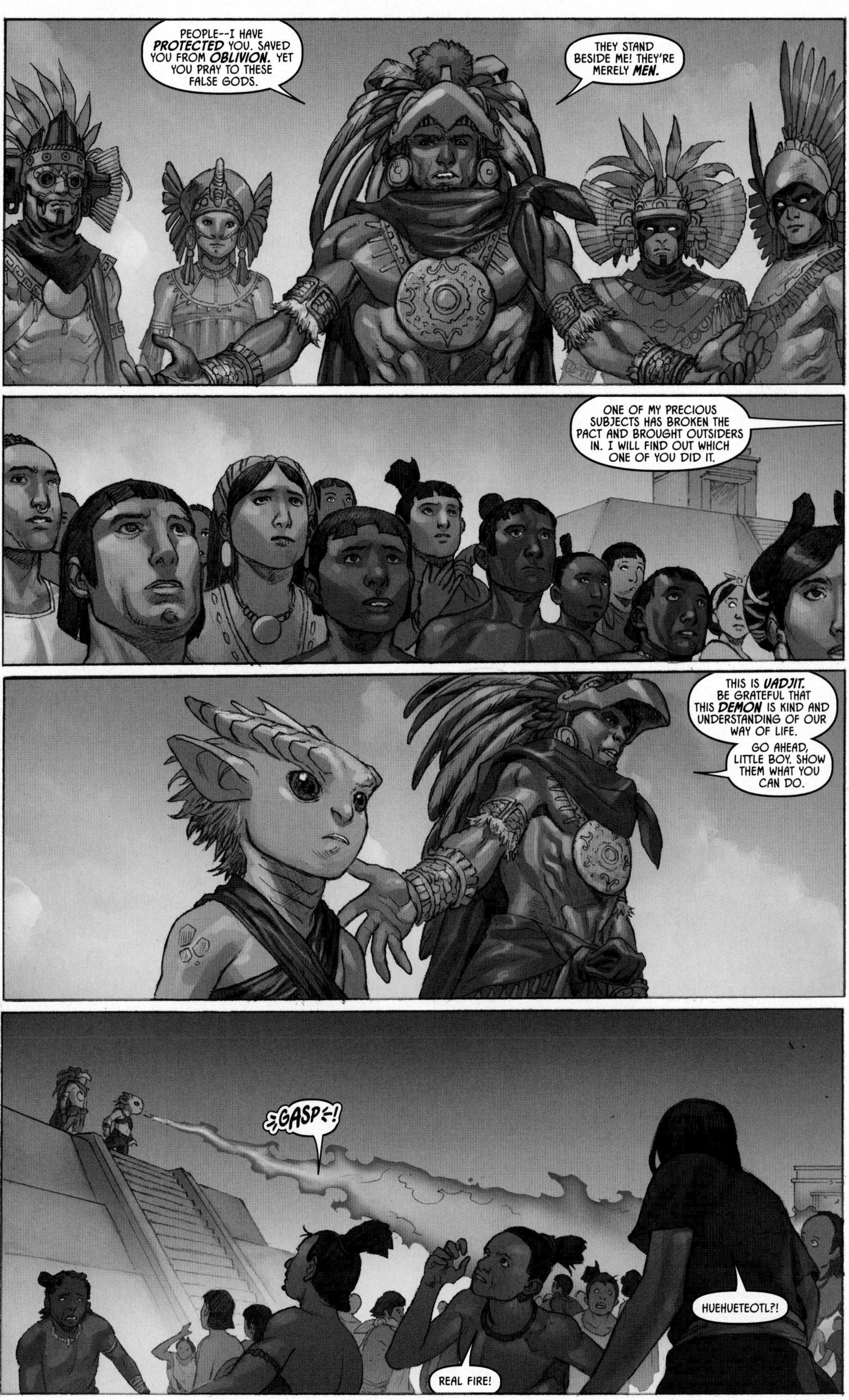
PEOPLE--I HAVE PROTECTED YOU. SAVED YOU FROM OBLIVION. YET YOU PRAY TO THESE FALSE GODS.
THEY STAND BESIDE ME! THEY'RE MERELY MEN.
ONE OF MY PRECIOUS SUBJECTS HAS BROKEN THE PACT AND BROUGHT OUTSIDERS IN. I WILL FIND OUT WHICH ONE OF YOU DID IT.
THIS IS UADJIT. BE GRATEFUL THAT THIS DEMON IS KIND AND UNDERSTANDING OF OUR WAY OF LIFE.
GO AHEAD, LITTLE BOY. SHOW THEM WHAT YOU CAN DO.
GASP!
HUEHUETEOTL?!
REAL FIRE!

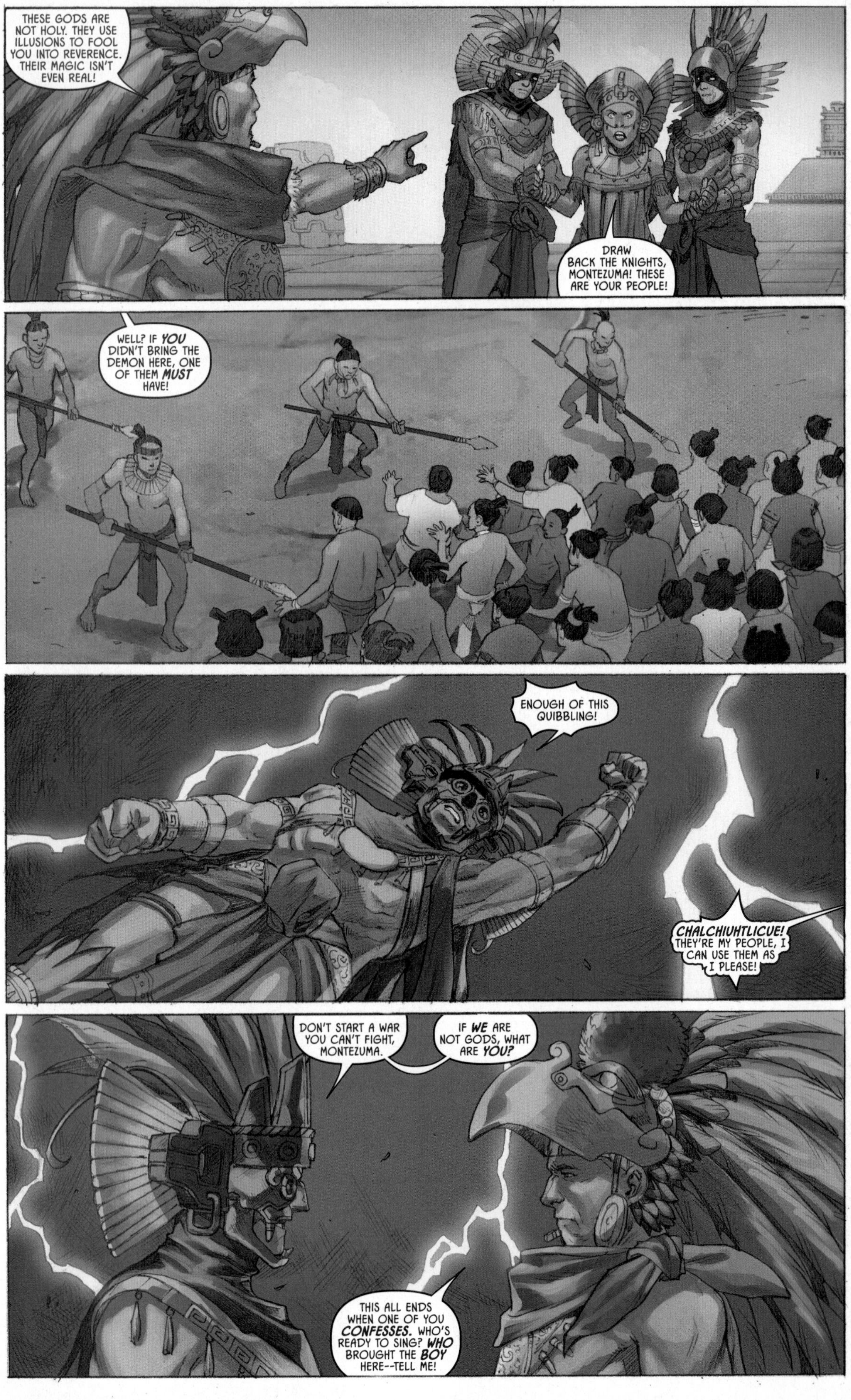
THESE GODS ARE NOT HOLY. THEY USE ILLUSIONS TO FOOL YOU INTO REVERENCE. THEIR MAGIC ISN'T EVEN REAL!
DRAW BACK THE KNIGHTS, MONTEZUMA! THESE ARE YOUR PEOPLE!
WELL? IF YOU DIDN'T BRING THE DEMON HERE, ONE OF THEM MUST HAVE!
ENOUGH OF THIS QUIBBLING!
CHALCHIUHTLICUE! THEY'RE MY PEOPLE, I CAN USE THEM AS I PLEASE!
DON'T START A WAR YOU CAN'T FIGHT, MONTEZUMA.
IF WE ARE NOT GODS, WHAT ARE YOU?
THIS ALL ENDS WHEN ONE OF YOU CONFESSES. WHO'S READY TO SING? WHO BROUGHT THE BOY HERE--TELL ME!

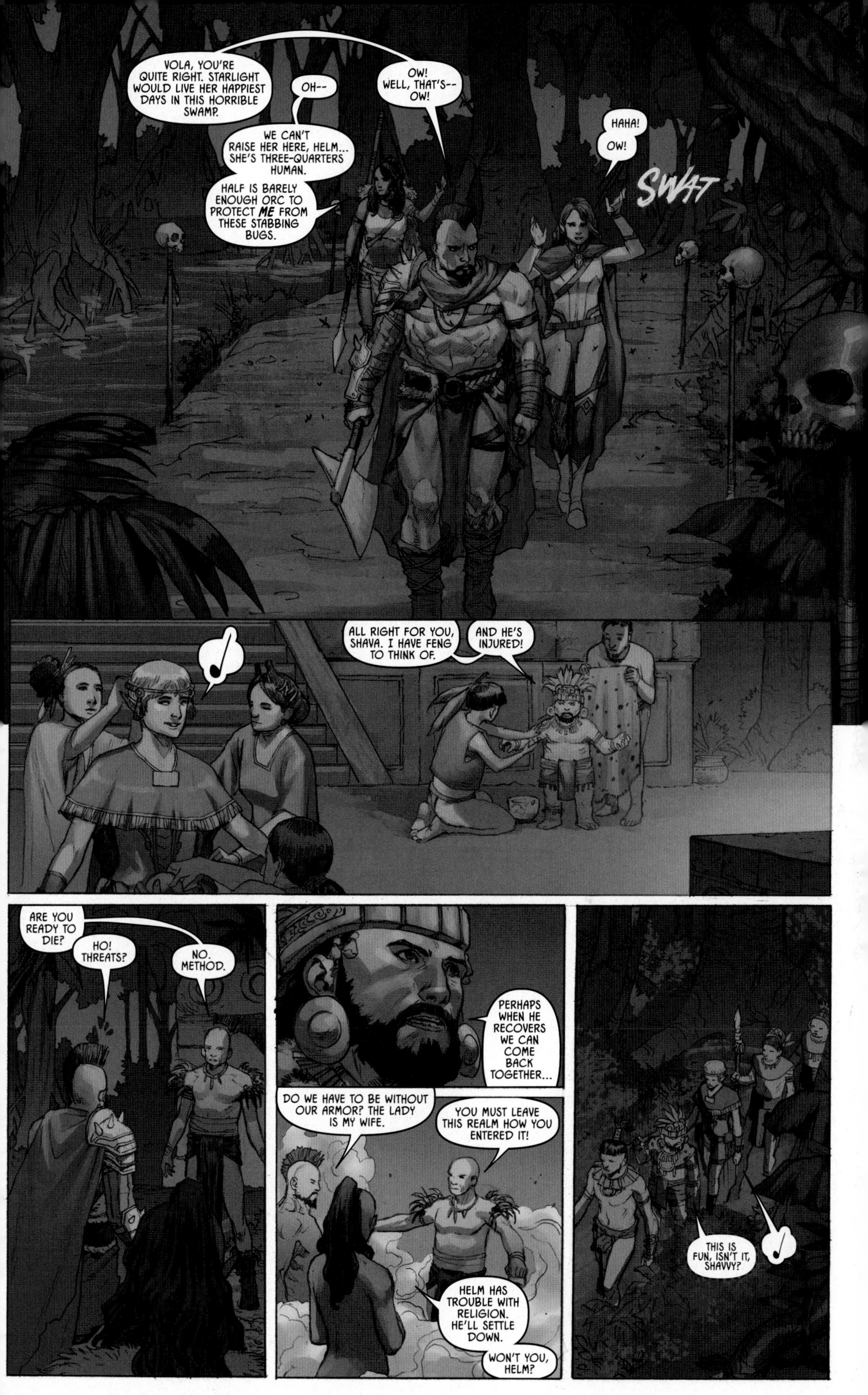
VOLA, YOU'RE QUITE RIGHT. STARLIGHT WOULD LIVE HER HAPPIEST DAYS IN THIS HORRIBLE SWAMP.
OH--
OW! WELL, THAT'S-- OW!
WE CAN'T RAISE HER HERE, HELM... SHE'S THREE-QUARTERS HUMAN.
HALF IS BARELY ENOUGH ORC TO PROTECT ME FROM THESE STABBING BUGS.
HAHA!
OW!
SWAT
ALL RIGHT FOR YOU, SHAVA. I HAVE FENG TO THINK OF.
AND HE'S INJURED!
ARE YOU READY TO DIE?
HO! THREATS?
NO. METHOD.
PERHAPS WHEN HE RECOVERS WE CAN COME BACK TOGETHER...
DO WE HAVE TO BE WITHOUT OUR ARMOR? THE LADY IS MY WIFE.
YOU MUST LEAVE THIS REALM HOW YOU ENTERED IT!
HELM HAS TROUBLE WITH RELIGION. HE'LL SETTLE DOWN.
WON'T YOU, HELM?
THIS IS FUN, ISN'T IT, SHAVVY?

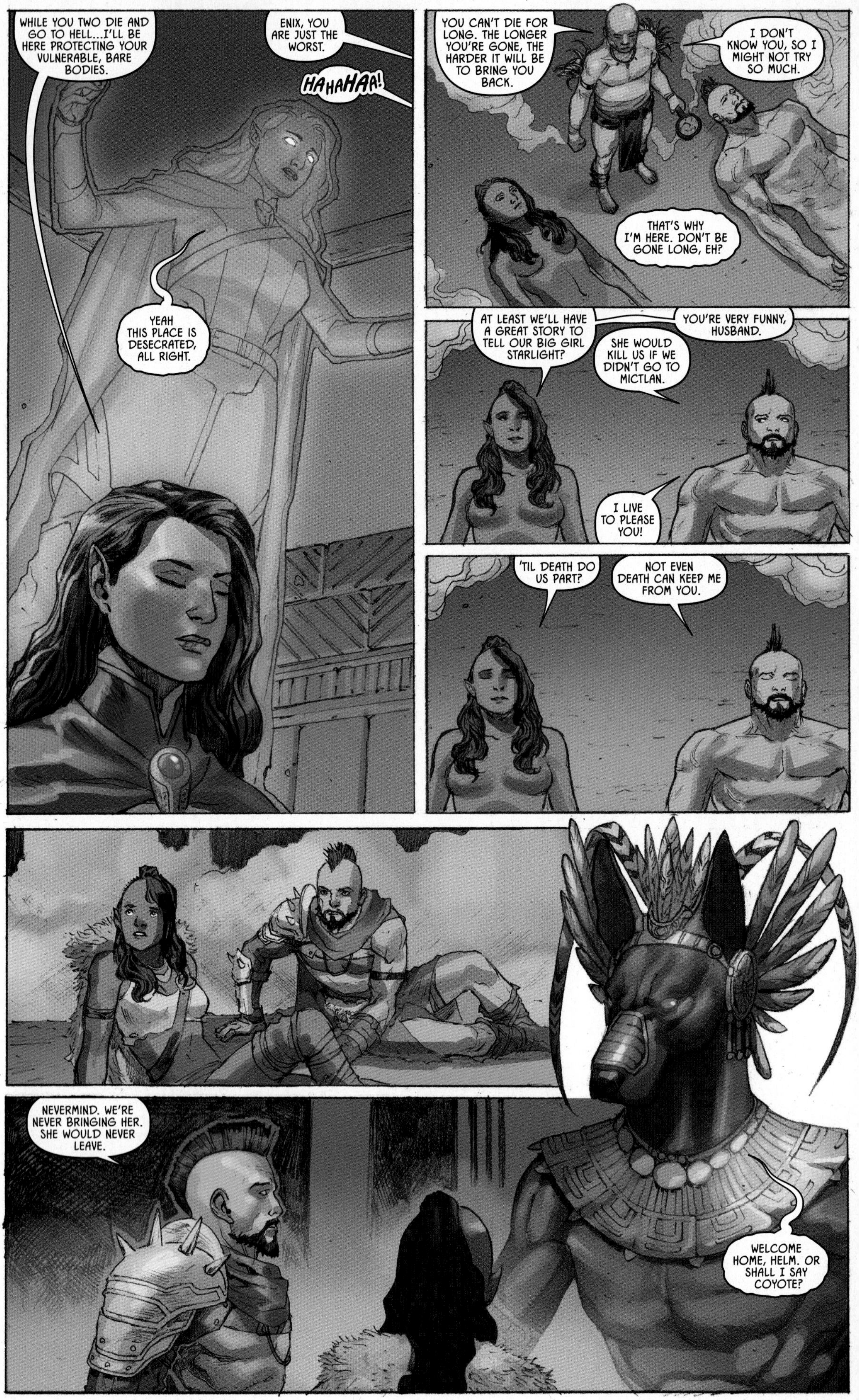

WHILE YOU TWO DIE AND GO TO HELL...I'LL BE HERE PROTECTING YOUR VULNERABLE, BARE BODIES.
ENIX, YOU ARE JUST THE WORST.
HAHAHAHA!
YEAH THIS PLACE IS DESECRATED, ALL RIGHT.
YOU CAN'T DIE FOR LONG. THE LONGER YOU'RE GONE, THE HARDER IT WILL BE TO BRING YOU BACK.
I DON'T KNOW YOU, SO I MIGHT NOT TRY SO MUCH.
THAT'S WHY I'M HERE. DON'T BE GONE LONG, EH?
AT LEAST WE'LL HAVE A GREAT STORY TO TELL OUR BIG GIRL STARLIGHT?
YOU'RE VERY FUNNY, HUSBAND.
SHE WOULD KILL US IF WE DIDN'T GO TO MICTLAN.
I LIVE TO PLEASE YOU!
'TIL DEATH DO US PART?
NOT EVEN DEATH CAN KEEP ME FROM YOU.
NEVERMIND. WE'RE NEVER BRINGING HER. SHE WOULD NEVER LEAVE.
WELCOME HOME, HELM. OR SHALL I SAY COYOTE?

DEAR YOUR HOLINESS

03

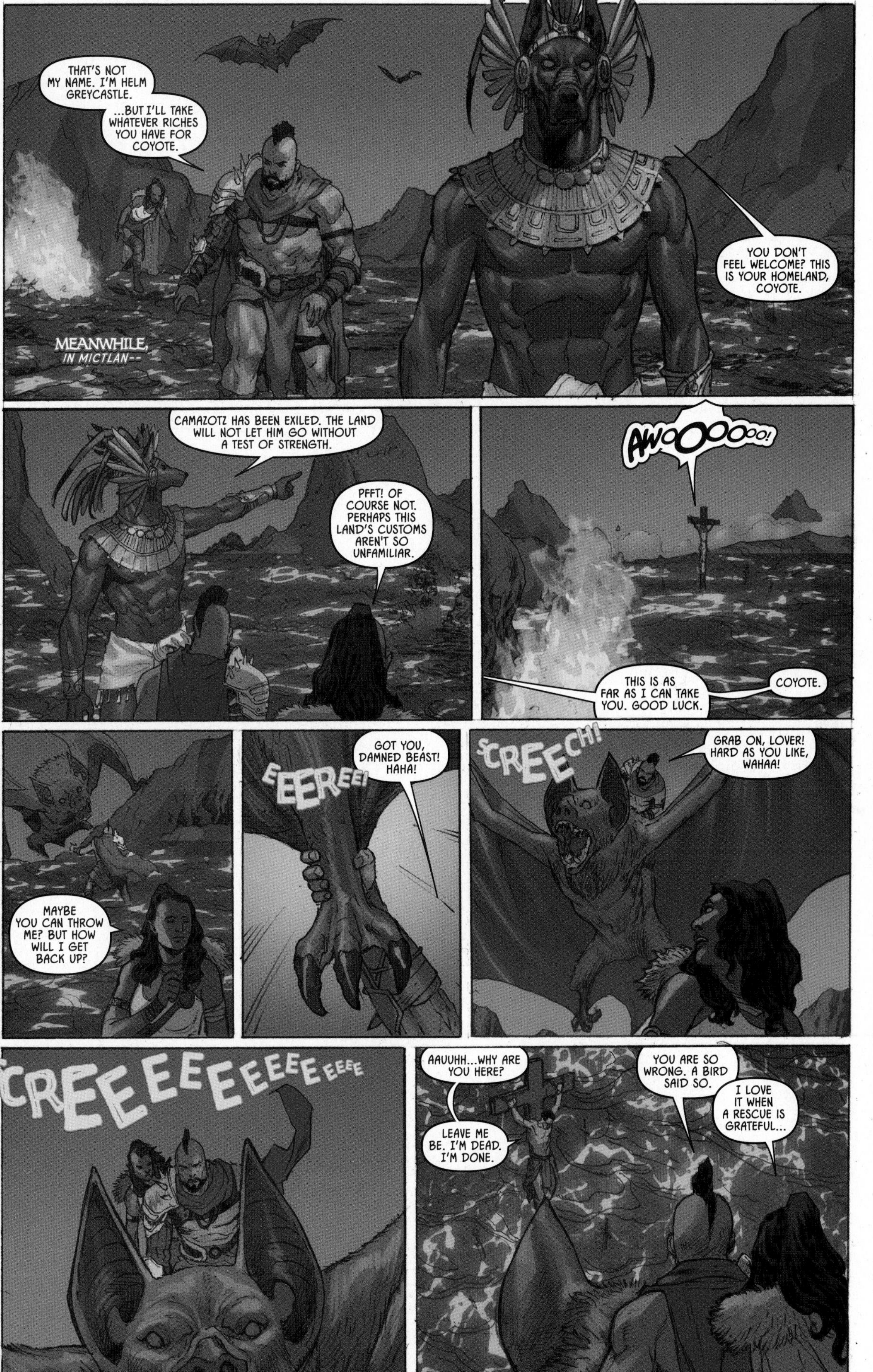
THAT'S NOT MY NAME. I'M HELM GREYCASTLE.
...BUT I'LL TAKE WHATEVER RICHES YOU HAVE FOR COYOTE.
YOU DON'T FEEL WELCOME? THIS IS YOUR HOMELAND, COYOTE.
MEANWHILE, IN MICTLAN--
CAMAZOTZ HAS BEEN EXILED. THE LAND WILL NOT LET HIM GO WITHOUT A TEST OF STRENGTH.
PFFT! OF COURSE NOT. PERHAPS THIS LAND'S CUSTOMS AREN'T SO UNFAMILIAR.
AWOOOOOOO!
THIS IS AS FAR AS I CAN TAKE YOU. GOOD LUCK.
COYOTE.
MAYBE YOU CAN THROW ME? BUT HOW WILL I GET BACK UP?
EEEREE!
GOT YOU, DAMNED BEAST! HAHA!
SCREECH!
GRAB ON, LOVER! HARD AS YOU LIKE, WAHAA!
SCREEEEEEEEEE
AAUUHH...WHY ARE YOU HERE?
LEAVE ME BE. I'M DEAD. I'M DONE.
YOU ARE SO WRONG. A BIRD SAID SO.
I LOVE IT WHEN A RESCUE IS GRATEFUL...

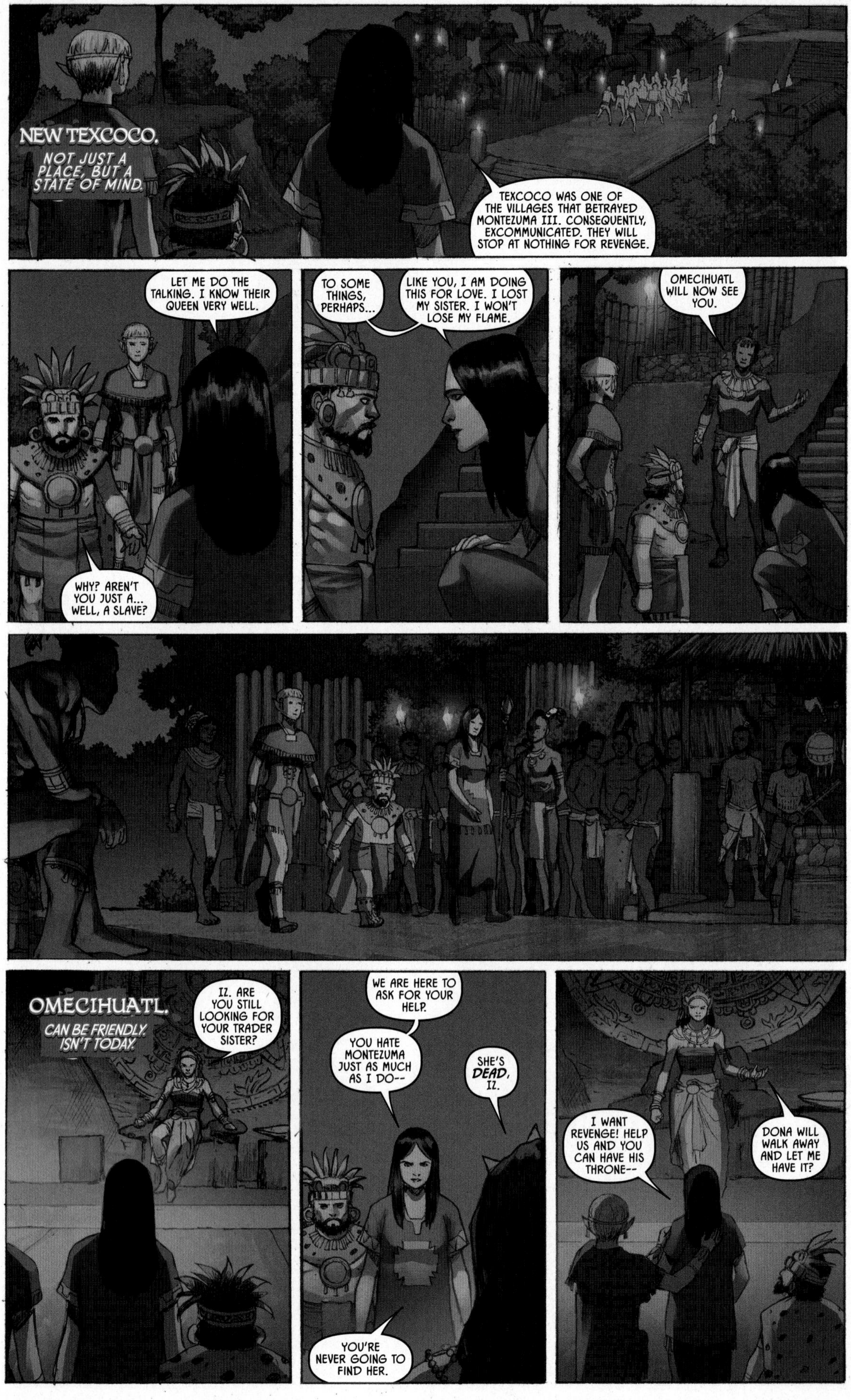
NEW TEXCOCO.
NOT JUST A PLACE, BUT A STATE OF MIND.
TEXCOCO WAS ONE OF THE VILLAGES THAT BETRAYED MONTEZUMA III. CONSEQUENTLY, EXCOMMUNICATED. THEY WILL STOP AT NOTHING FOR REVENGE.
LET ME DO THE TALKING. I KNOW THEIR QUEEN VERY WELL.
WHY? AREN'T YOU JUST A... WELL, A SLAVE?
TO SOME THINGS, PERHAPS...
LIKE YOU, I AM DOING THIS FOR LOVE. I LOST MY SISTER. I WON'T LOSE MY FLAME.
OMECIHUATL WILL NOW SEE YOU.
OMECIHUATL.
CAN BE FRIENDLY. ISN'T TODAY.
IZ. ARE YOU STILL LOOKING FOR YOUR TRADER SISTER?
WE ARE HERE TO ASK FOR YOUR HELP.
YOU HATE MONTEZUMA JUST AS MUCH AS I DO--
SHE'S DEAD, IZ.
YOU'RE NEVER GOING TO FIND HER.
I WANT REVENGE! HELP US AND YOU CAN HAVE HIS THRONE--
DONA WILL WALK AWAY AND LET ME HAVE IT?

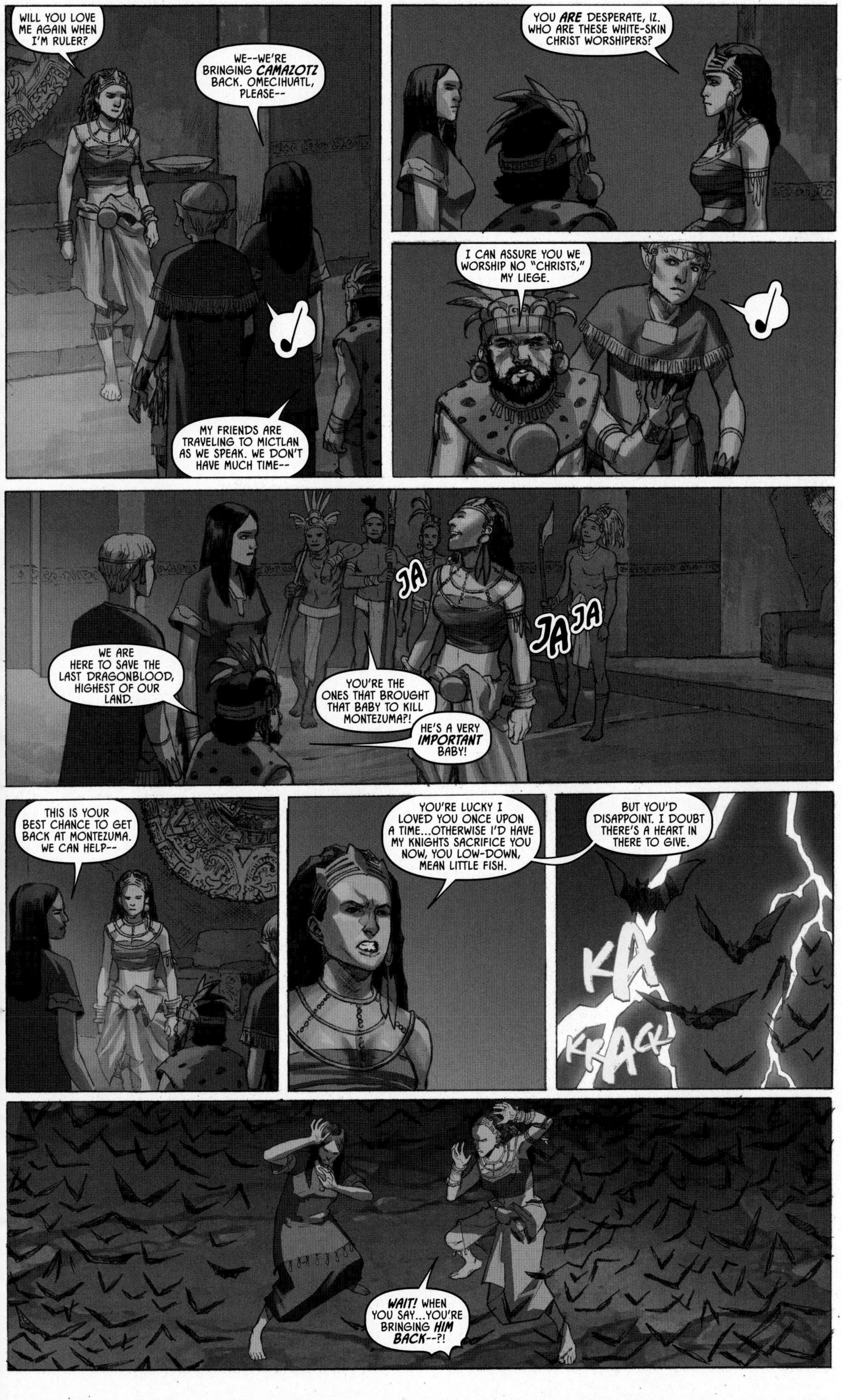
WILL YOU LOVE ME AGAIN WHEN I'M RULER?
WE--WE'RE BRINGING CAMAZOTZ BACK. OMECIHUATL, PLEASE--
MY FRIENDS ARE TRAVELING TO MICTLAN AS WE SPEAK. WE DON'T HAVE MUCH TIME--
YOU ARE DESPERATE, IZ. WHO ARE THESE WHITE-SKIN CHRIST WORSHIPERS?
I CAN ASSURE YOU WE WORSHIP NO "CHRISTS," MY LIEGE.
JA
JA JA
WE ARE HERE TO SAVE THE LAST DRAGONBLOOD, HIGHEST OF OUR LAND.
YOU'RE THE ONES THAT BROUGHT THAT BABY TO KILL MONTEZUMA?!
HE'S A VERY IMPORTANT BABY!
THIS IS YOUR BEST CHANCE TO GET BACK AT MONTEZUMA. WE CAN HELP--
YOU'RE LUCKY I LOVED YOU ONCE UPON A TIME...OTHERWISE I'D HAVE MY KNIGHTS SACRIFICE YOU NOW, YOU LOW-DOWN, MEAN LITTLE FISH.
BUT YOU'D DISAPPOINT. I DOUBT THERE'S A HEART IN THERE TO GIVE.
KA
KRACK
WAIT! WHEN YOU SAY...YOU'RE BRINGING HIM BACK--?!

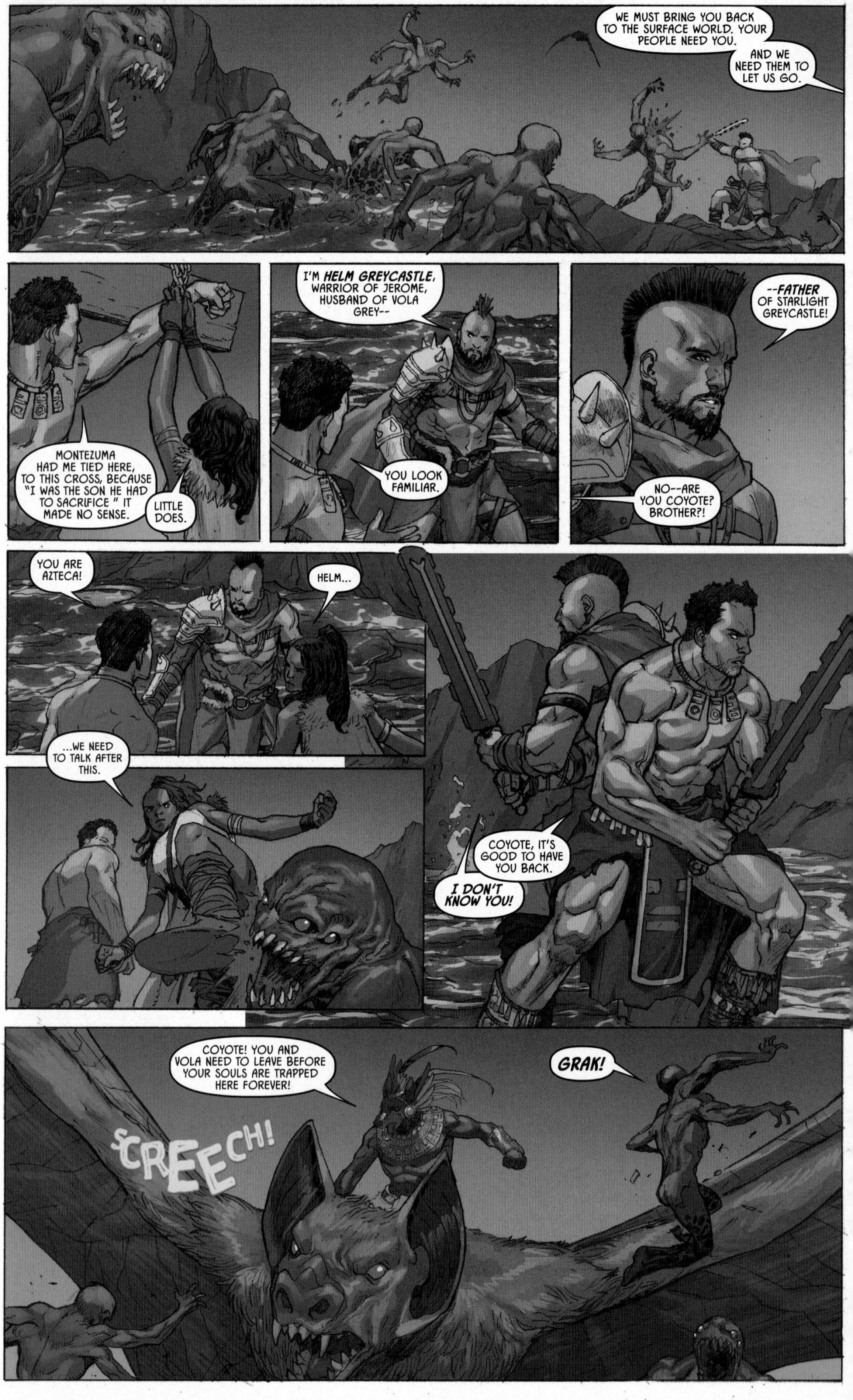

WE MUST BRING YOU BACK TO THE SURFACE WORLD. YOUR PEOPLE NEED YOU.
AND WE NEED THEM TO LET US GO.
MONTEZUMA HAD ME TIED HERE, TO THIS CROSS, BECAUSE "I WAS THE SON HE HAD TO SACRIFICE." IT MADE NO SENSE.
LITTLE DOES.
I'M HELM GREYCASTLE, WARRIOR OF JEROME, HUSBAND OF VOLA GREY--
YOU LOOK FAMILIAR.
--FATHER OF STARLIGHT GREYCASTLE!
NO--ARE YOU COYOTE? BROTHER?!
YOU ARE AZTECA!
HELM...
...WE NEED TO TALK AFTER THIS.
COYOTE, IT'S GOOD TO HAVE YOU BACK.
I DON'T KNOW YOU!
COYOTE! YOU AND VOLA NEED TO LEAVE BEFORE YOUR SOULS ARE TRAPPED HERE FOREVER!
GRAK!
SCREECH!

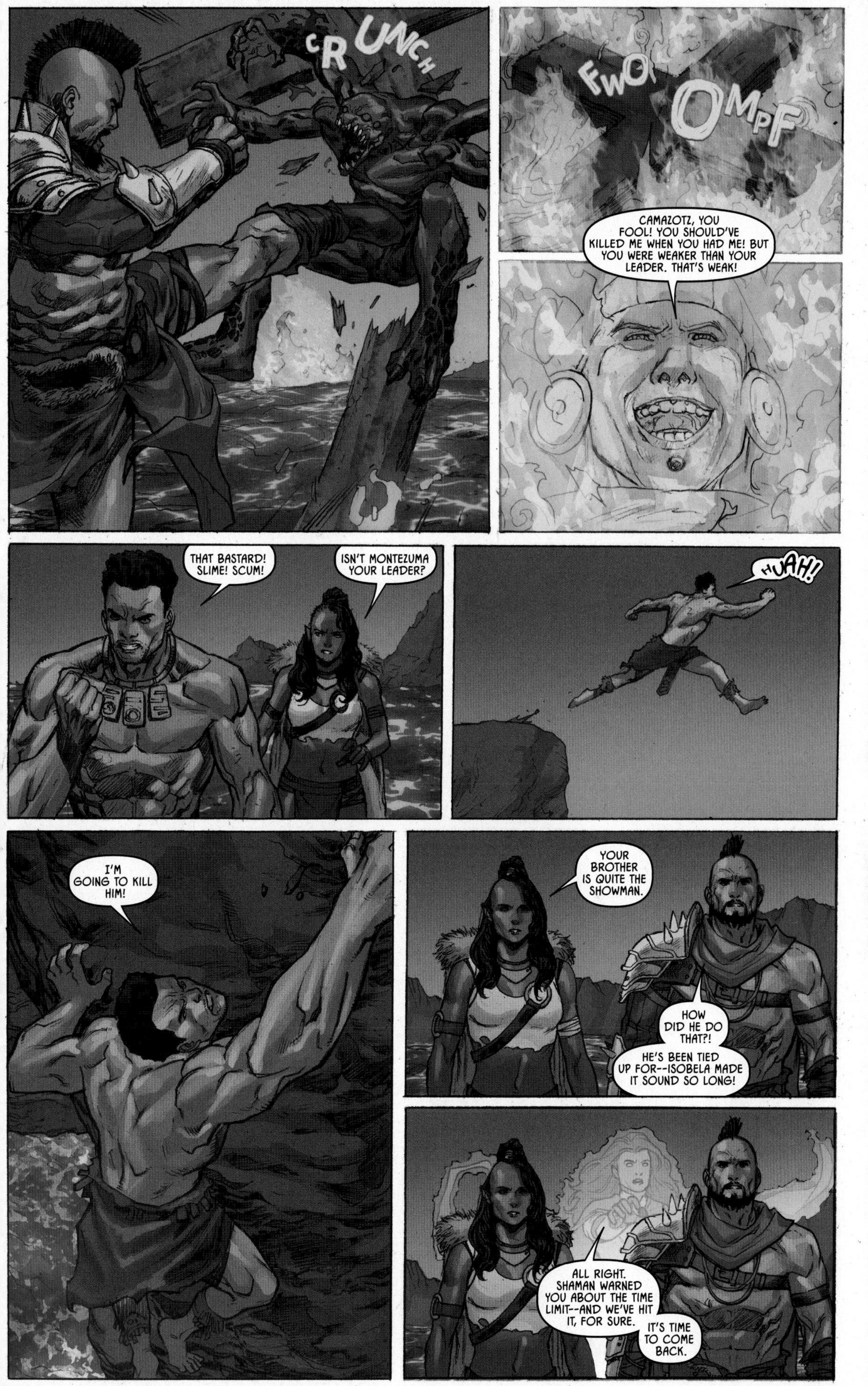
CRUNCH
FWOOMPF
CAMAZOTZ, YOU FOOL! YOU SHOULD'VE KILLED ME WHEN YOU HAD ME! BUT YOU WERE WEAKER THAN YOUR LEADER. THAT'S WEAK!
THAT BASTARD! SLIME! SCUM!
ISN'T MONTEZUMA YOUR LEADER?
HUAH!
I'M GOING TO KILL HIM!
YOUR BROTHER IS QUITE THE SHOWMAN.
HOW DID HE DO THAT?!
HE'S BEEN TIED UP FOR--ISOBELA MADE IT SOUND SO LONG!
ALL RIGHT. SHAMAN WARNED YOU ABOUT THE TIME LIMIT--AND WE'VE HIT IT, FOR SURE.
IT'S TIME TO COME BACK.

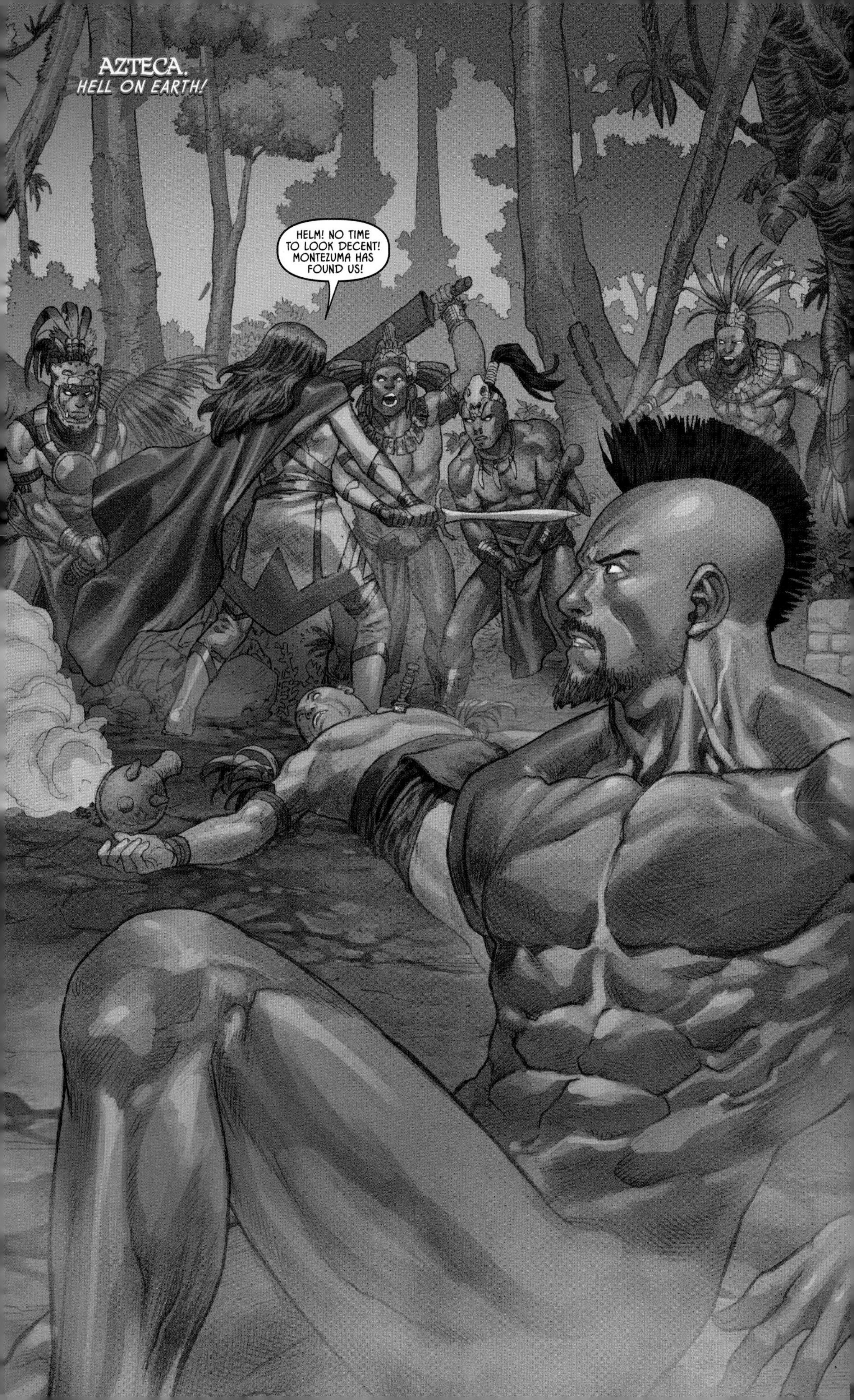
AZTECA.
HELL ON EARTH!
HELM! NO TIME TO LOOK DECENT! MONTEZUMA HAS FOUND US!

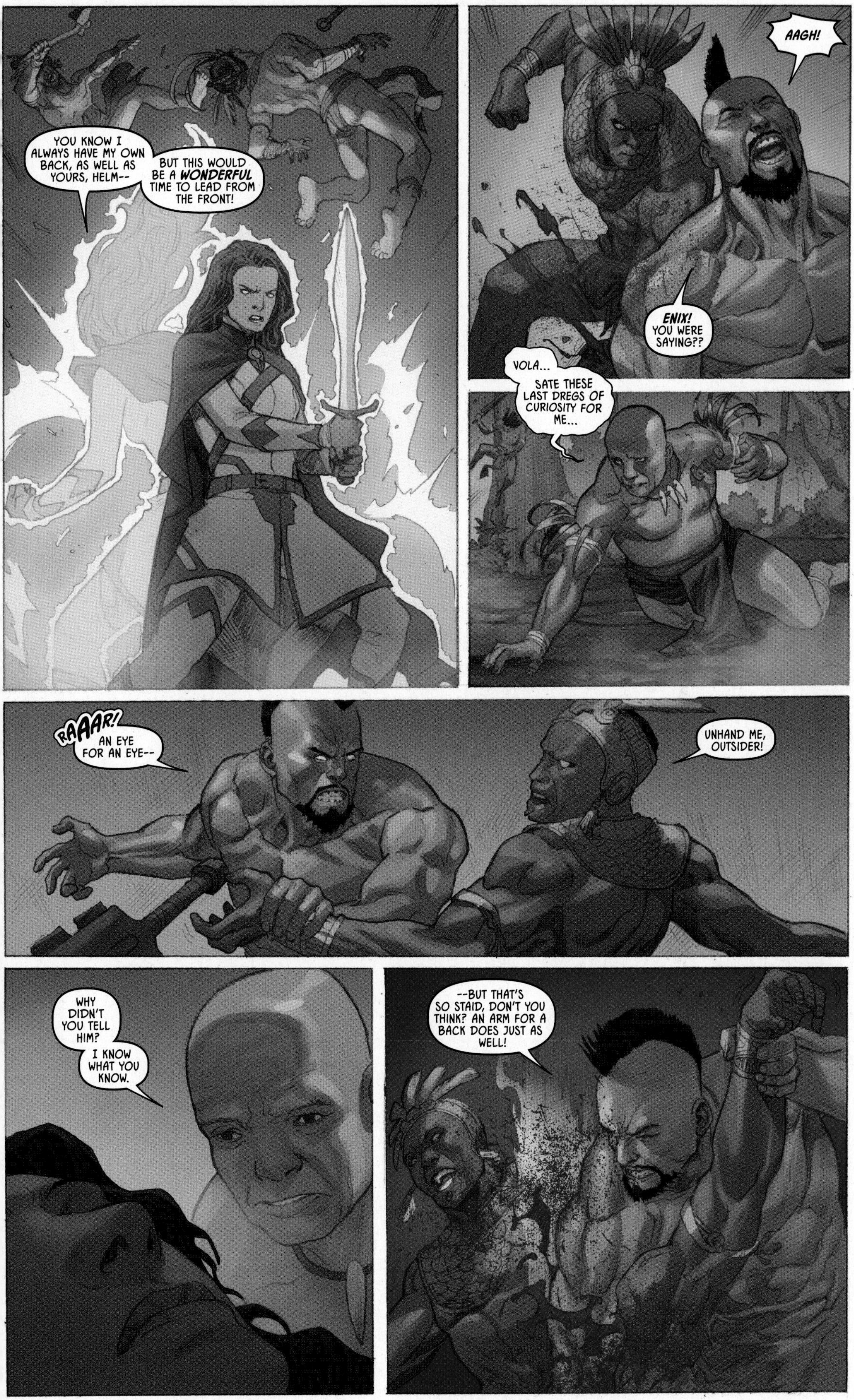
YOU KNOW I ALWAYS HAVE MY OWN BACK, AS WELL AS YOURS, HELM--
BUT THIS WOULD BE A **WONDERFUL** TIME TO LEAD FROM THE FRONT!
AAGH!
ENIX! YOU WERE SAYING??
VOLA... SATE THESE LAST DREGS OF CURIOSITY FOR ME...
RAAAR!
AN EYE FOR AN EYE--
UNHAND ME, OUTSIDER!
WHY DIDN'T YOU TELL HIM?
I KNOW WHAT YOU KNOW.
--BUT THAT'S SO STAID, DON'T YOU THINK? AN ARM FOR A BACK DOES JUST AS WELL!

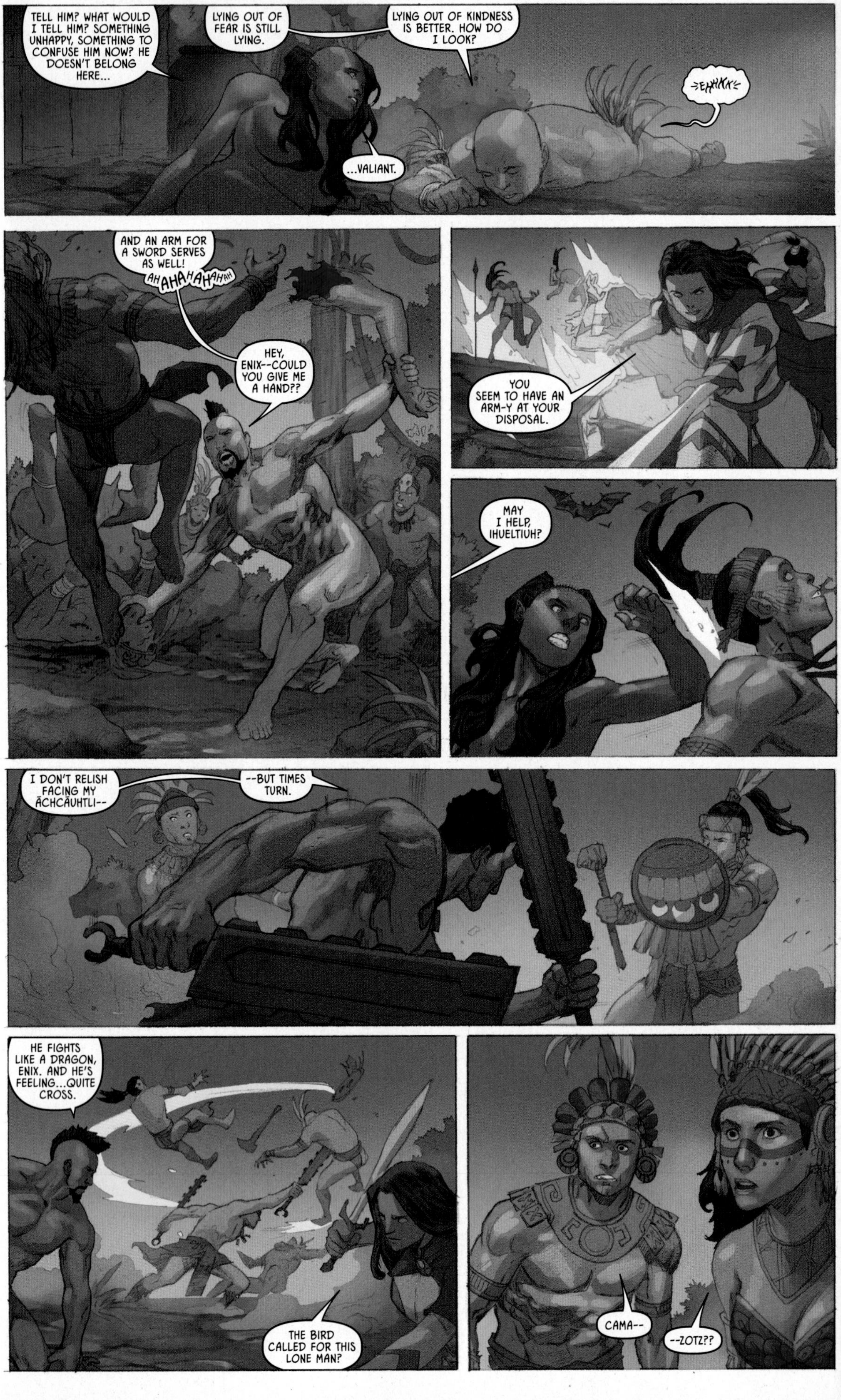
TELL HIM? WHAT WOULD I TELL HIM? SOMETHING UNHAPPY, SOMETHING TO CONFUSE HIM NOW? HE DOESN'T BELONG HERE...
LYING OUT OF FEAR IS STILL LYING.
LYING OUT OF KINDNESS IS BETTER. HOW DO I LOOK?
...VALIANT.
EHHKK
AND AN ARM FOR A SWORD SERVES AS WELL!
AHAHAHAHAHAH
HEY, ENIX--COULD YOU GIVE ME A HAND??
YOU SEEM TO HAVE AN ARM-Y AT YOUR DISPOSAL.
MAY I HELP, IHUELTIUH?
I DON'T RELISH FACING MY ĀCHCĀUHTLI--
--BUT TIMES TURN.
HE FIGHTS LIKE A DRAGON, ENIX. AND HE'S FEELING...QUITE CROSS.
THE BIRD CALLED FOR THIS LONE MAN?
CAMA--
--ZOTZ??

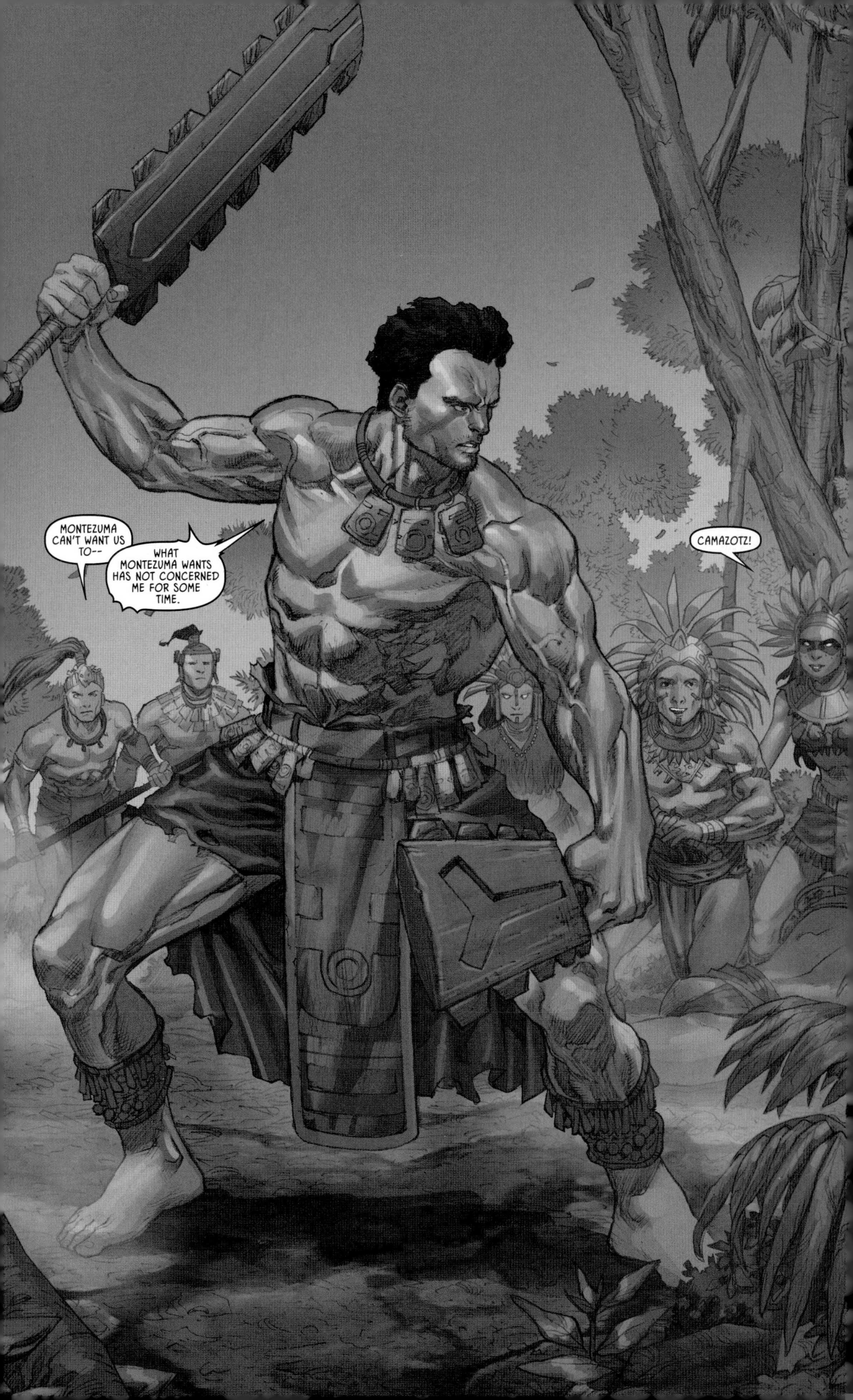
MONTEZUMA CAN'T WANT US TO--
WHAT MONTEZUMA WANTS HAS NOT CONCERNED ME FOR SOME TIME.
CAMAZOTZ!

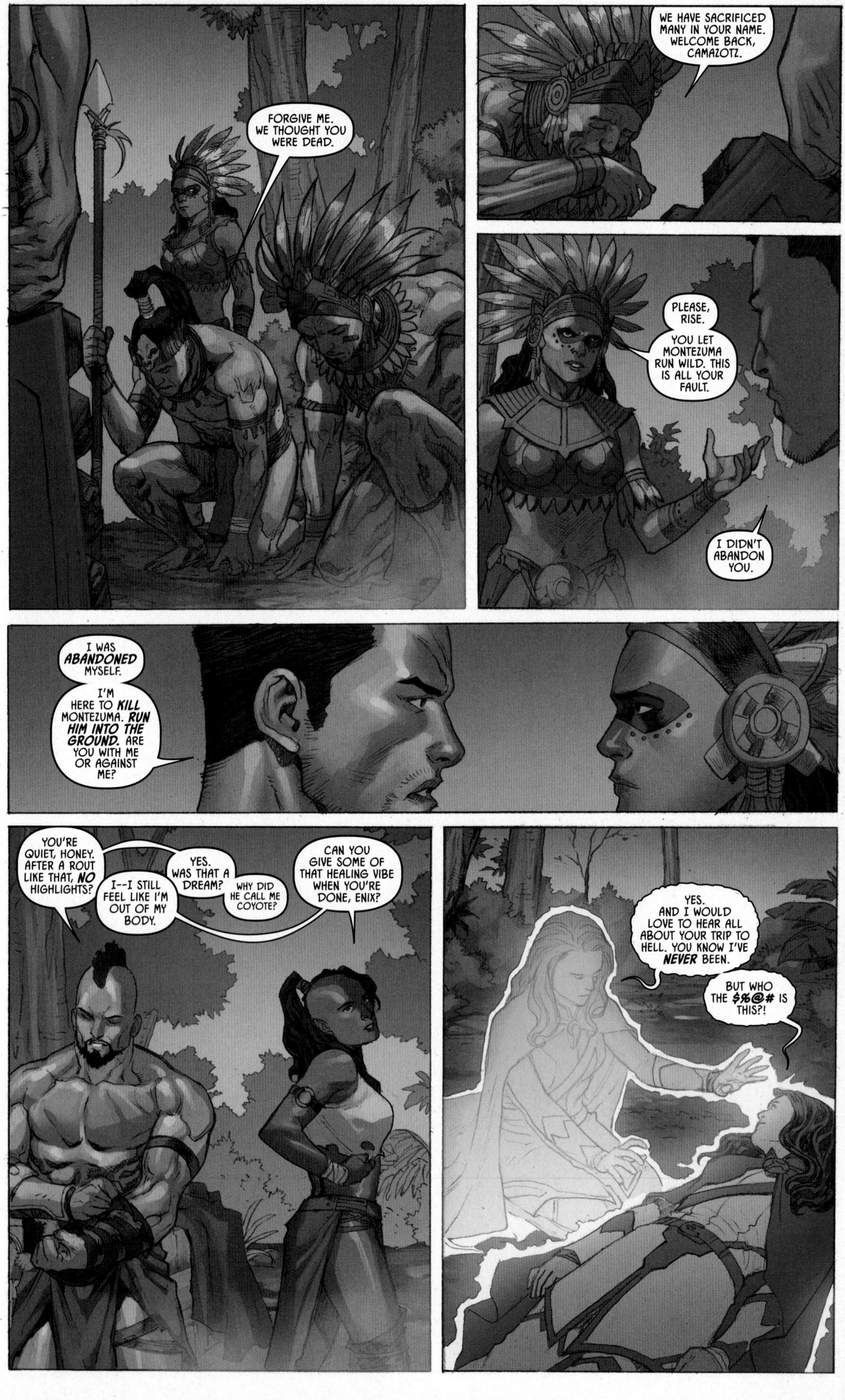
FORGIVE ME. WE THOUGHT YOU WERE DEAD.
WE HAVE SACRIFICED MANY IN YOUR NAME. WELCOME BACK, CAMAZOTZ.
PLEASE, RISE.
YOU LET MONTEZUMA RUN WILD. THIS IS ALL YOUR FAULT.
I DIDN'T ABANDON YOU.
I WAS ABANDONED MYSELF.
I'M HERE TO KILL MONTEZUMA. RUN HIM INTO THE GROUND. ARE YOU WITH ME OR AGAINST ME?
YOU'RE QUIET, HONEY. AFTER A ROUT LIKE THAT, NO HIGHLIGHTS?
YES. WAS THAT A DREAM?
WHY DID HE CALL ME COYOTE?
I--I STILL FEEL LIKE I'M OUT OF MY BODY.
CAN YOU GIVE SOME OF THAT HEALING VIBE WHEN YOU'RE DONE, ENIX?
YES. AND I WOULD LOVE TO HEAR ALL ABOUT YOUR TRIP TO HELL. YOU KNOW I'VE NEVER BEEN.
BUT WHO THE $%@# IS THIS?!

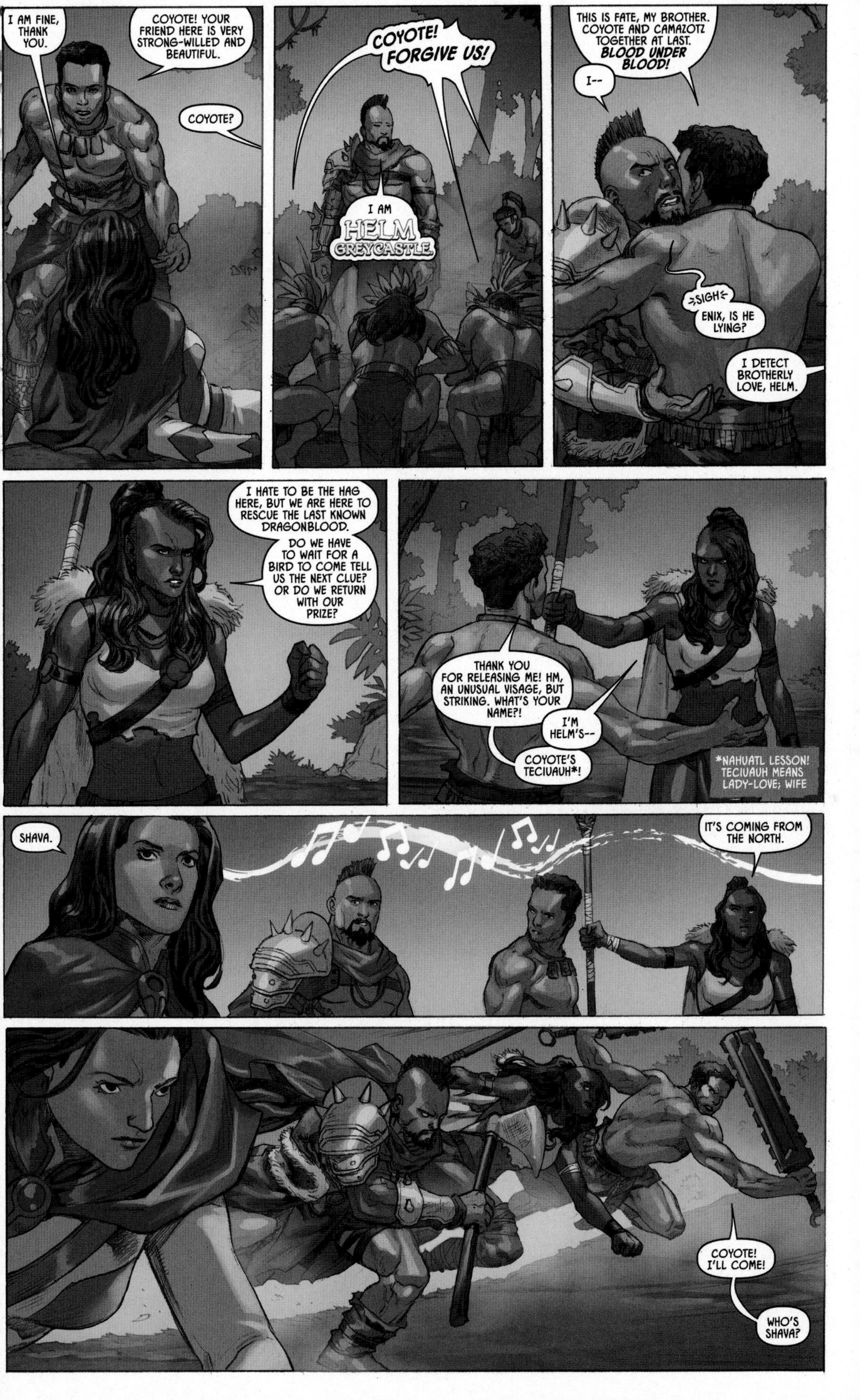
I AM FINE, THANK YOU.
COYOTE! YOUR FRIEND HERE IS VERY STRONG-WILLED AND BEAUTIFUL.
COYOTE?
COYOTE! FORGIVE US!
I AM HELM GREYCASTLE.
THIS IS FATE, MY BROTHER. COYOTE AND CAMAZOTZ TOGETHER AT LAST. BLOOD UNDER BLOOD!
I--
SIGH
ENIX, IS HE LYING?
I DETECT BROTHERLY LOVE, HELM.
I HATE TO BE THE HAG HERE, BUT WE ARE HERE TO RESCUE THE LAST KNOWN DRAGONBLOOD.
DO WE HAVE TO WAIT FOR A BIRD TO COME TELL US THE NEXT CLUE? OR DO WE RETURN WITH OUR PRIZE?
THANK YOU FOR RELEASING ME! HM, AN UNUSUAL VISAGE, BUT STRIKING. WHAT'S YOUR NAME?!
I'M HELM'S--
COYOTE'S TECIUAUH*!
*NAHUATL LESSON! TECIUAUH MEANS LADY-LOVE; WIFE
SHAVA.
IT'S COMING FROM THE NORTH.
COYOTE! I'LL COME!
WHO'S SHAVA?

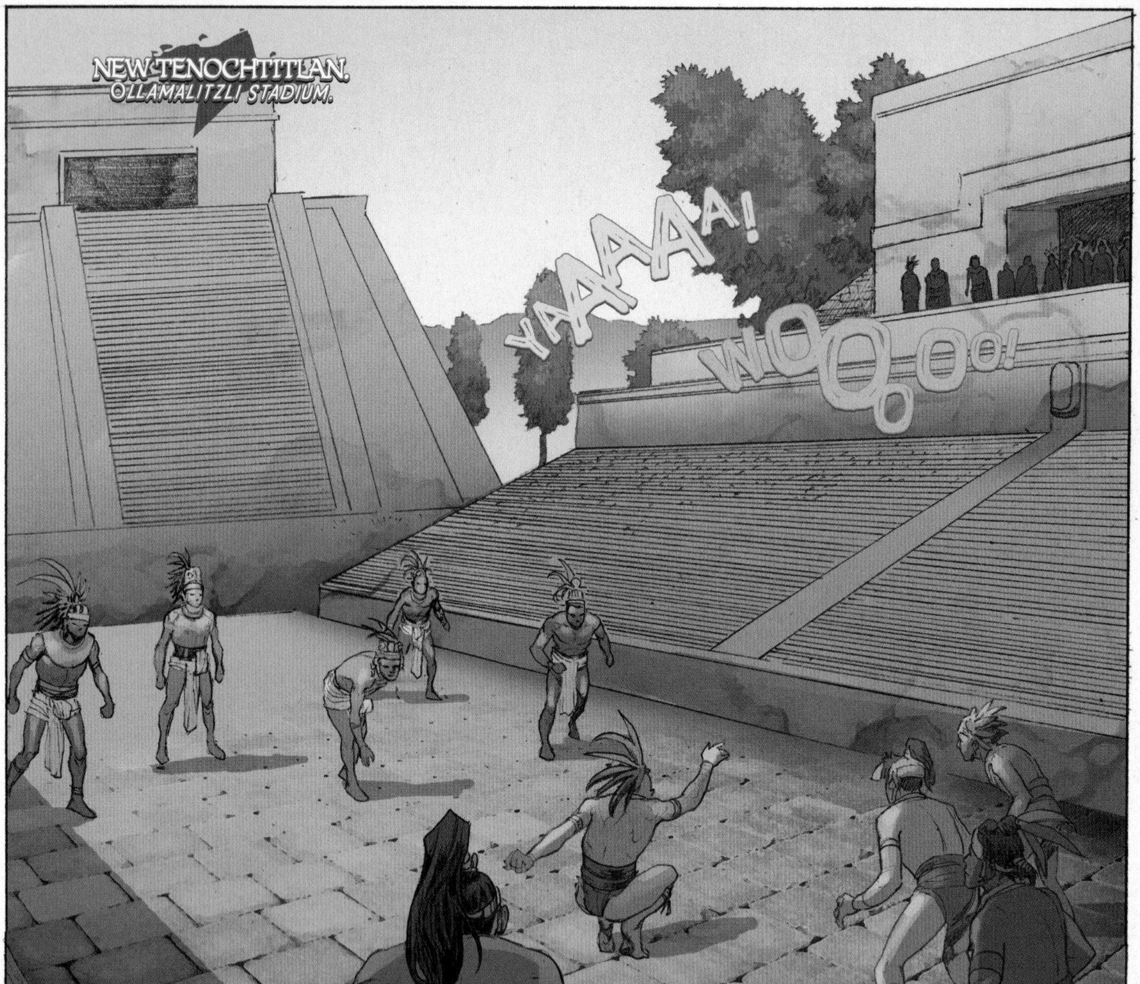
NEW TENOCHTITLAN.
OLLAMALITZLI STADIUM.
YAAAAAA!
WOOOOOO!

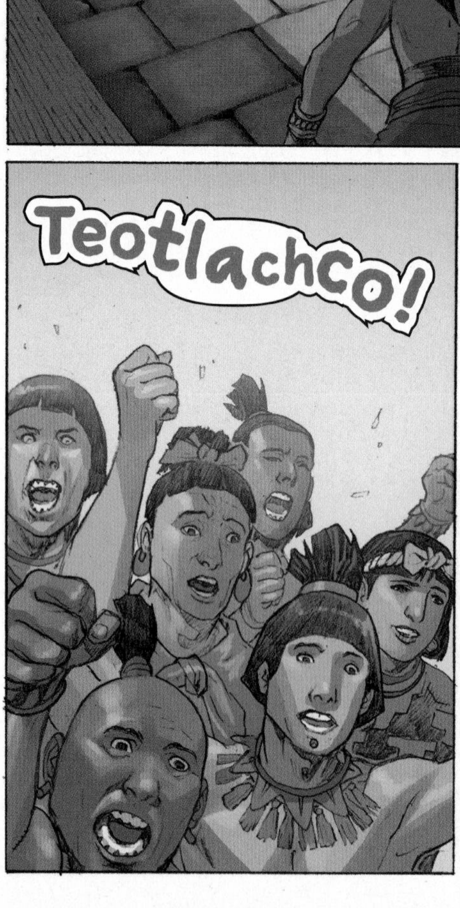
Teotlachco!

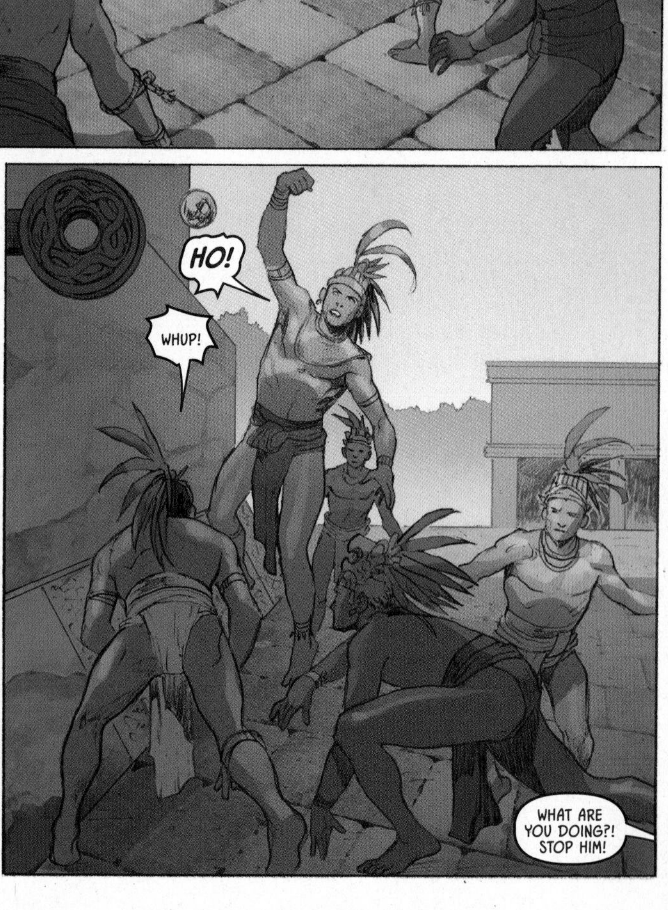
HO!
WHUP!
WHAT ARE YOU DOING?! STOP HIM!

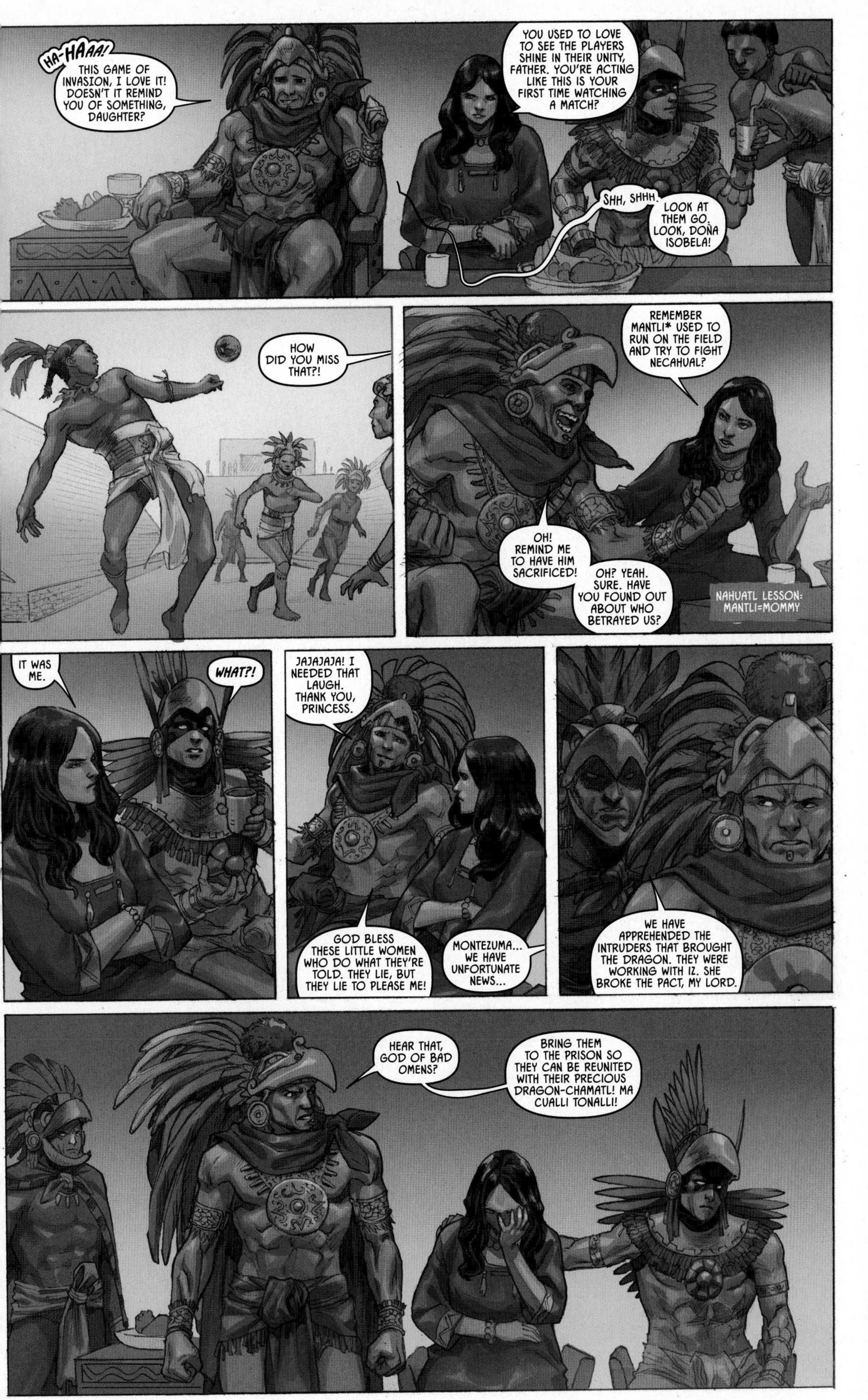
HA-HAAA!
THIS GAME OF INVASION, I LOVE IT! DOESN'T IT REMIND YOU OF SOMETHING, DAUGHTER?
YOU USED TO LOVE TO SEE THE PLAYERS SHINE IN THEIR UNITY, FATHER. YOU'RE ACTING LIKE THIS IS YOUR FIRST TIME WATCHING A MATCH?
SHH, SHHH.
LOOK AT THEM GO. LOOK, DOÑA ISOBELA!
HOW DID YOU MISS THAT?!
REMEMBER MANTLI* USED TO RUN ON THE FIELD AND TRY TO FIGHT NECAHUAL?
OH! REMIND ME TO HAVE HIM SACRIFICED!
OH? YEAH. SURE. HAVE YOU FOUND OUT ABOUT WHO BETRAYED US?
NAHUATL LESSON: MANTLI=MOMMY
IT WAS ME.
WHAT?!
JAJAJAJA! I NEEDED THAT LAUGH. THANK YOU, PRINCESS.
GOD BLESS THESE LITTLE WOMEN WHO DO WHAT THEY'RE TOLD. THEY LIE, BUT THEY LIE TO PLEASE ME!
MONTEZUMA... WE HAVE UNFORTUNATE NEWS...
WE HAVE APPREHENDED THE INTRUDERS THAT BROUGHT THE DRAGON. THEY WERE WORKING WITH IZ. SHE BROKE THE PACT, MY LORD.
HEAR THAT, GOD OF BAD OMENS?
BRING THEM TO THE PRISON SO THEY CAN BE REUNITED WITH THEIR PRECIOUS DRAGON-CHAMATL! MA CUALLI TONALLI!

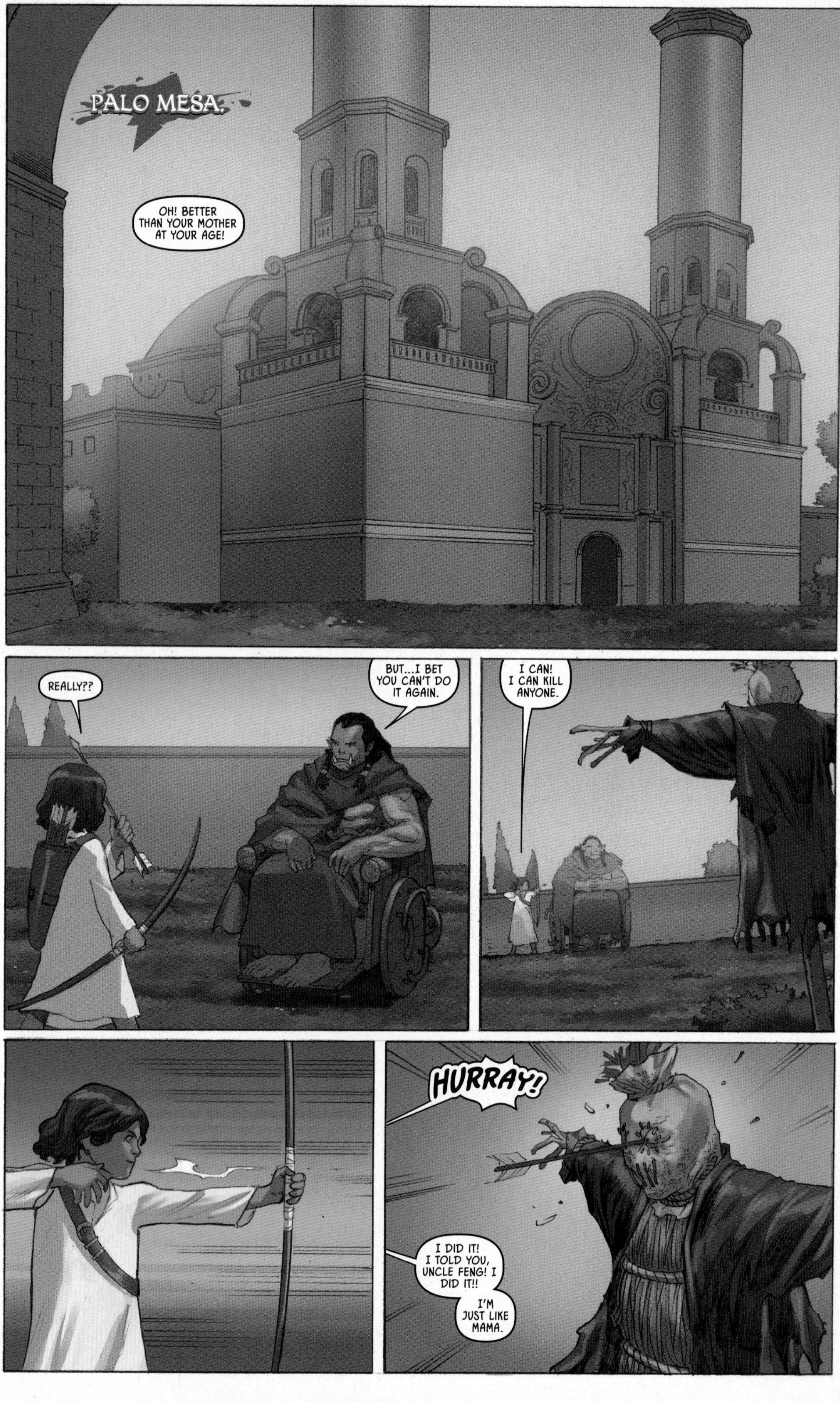
PALO MESA.
OH! BETTER THAN YOUR MOTHER AT YOUR AGE!
REALLY??
BUT...I BET YOU CAN'T DO IT AGAIN.
I CAN! I CAN KILL ANYONE.
HURRAY!
I DID IT! I TOLD YOU, UNCLE FENG! I DID IT!!
I'M JUST LIKE MAMA.

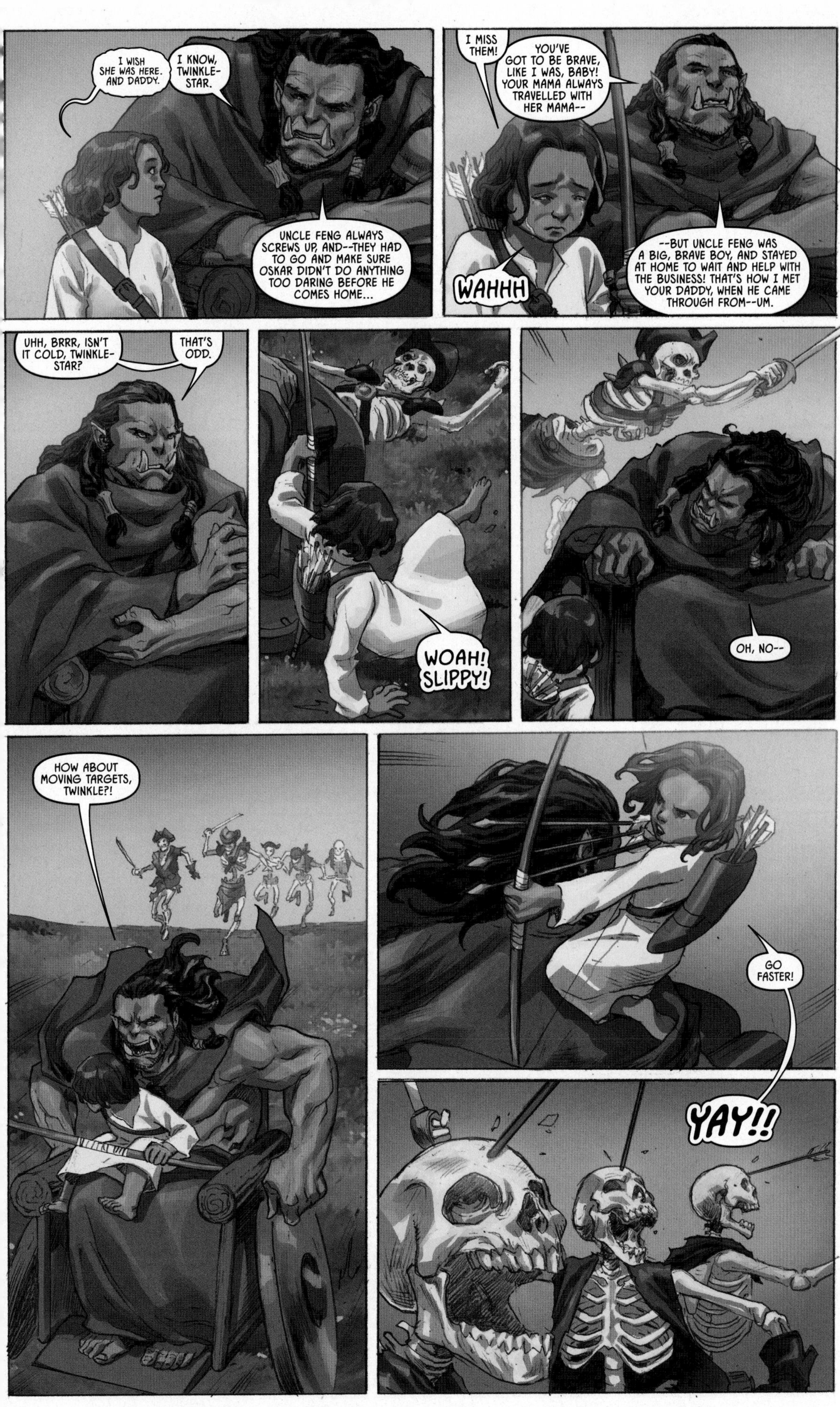
I WISH SHE WAS HERE. AND DADDY.
I KNOW, TWINKLE-STAR.
UNCLE FENG ALWAYS SCREWS UP, AND--THEY HAD TO GO AND MAKE SURE OSKAR DIDN'T DO ANYTHING TOO DARING BEFORE HE COMES HOME...
I MISS THEM!
YOU'VE GOT TO BE BRAVE, LIKE I WAS, BABY! YOUR MAMA ALWAYS TRAVELLED WITH HER MAMA--
WAHHH
--BUT UNCLE FENG WAS A BIG, BRAVE BOY, AND STAYED AT HOME TO WAIT AND HELP WITH THE BUSINESS! THAT'S HOW I MET YOUR DADDY, WHEN HE CAME THROUGH FROM--UM.
UHH, BRRR, ISN'T IT COLD, TWINKLE-STAR?
THAT'S ODD.
WOAH! SLIPPY!
OH, NO--
HOW ABOUT MOVING TARGETS, TWINKLE?!
GO FASTER!
YAY!!

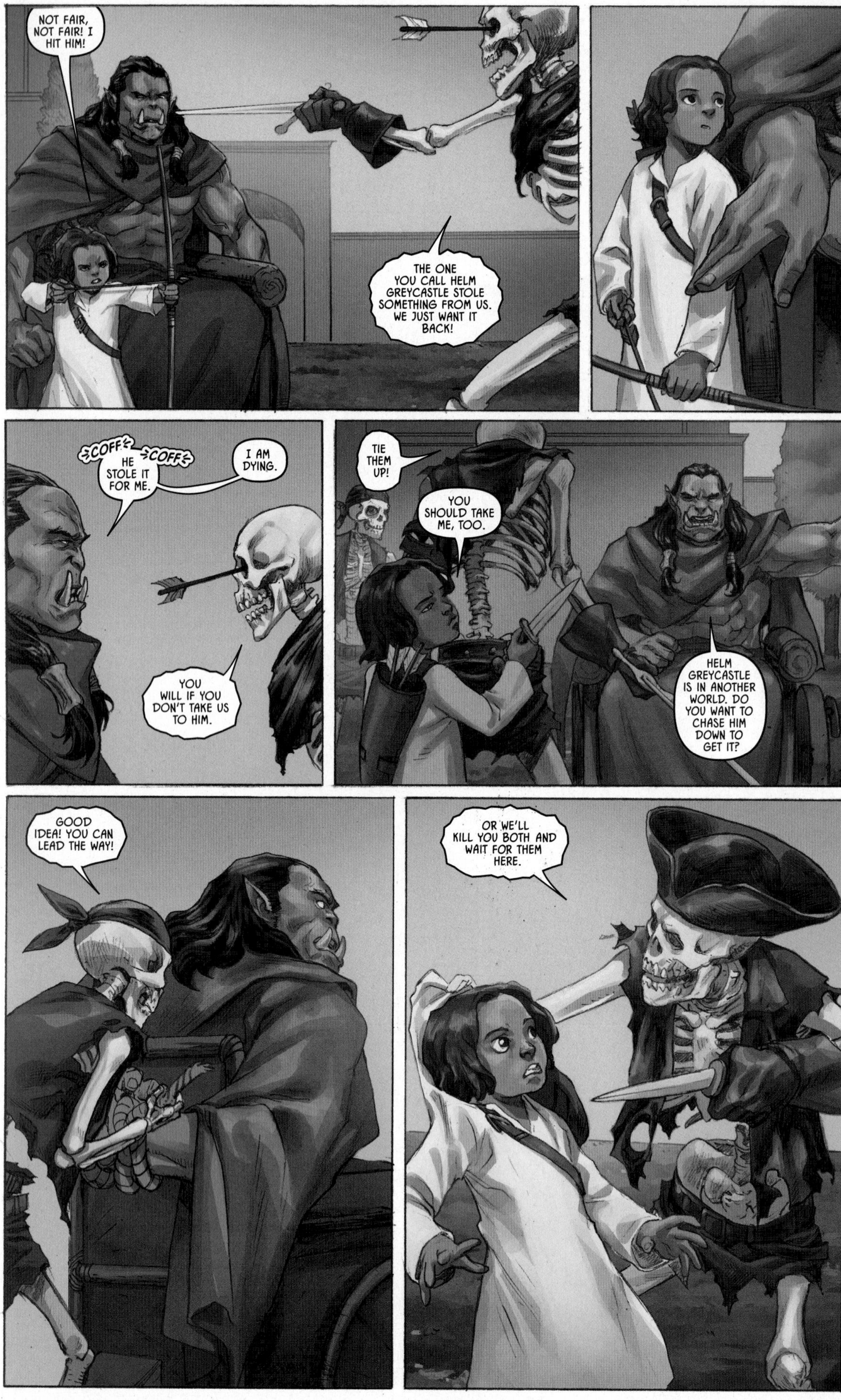
NOT FAIR, NOT FAIR! I HIT HIM!
THE ONE YOU CALL HELM GREYCASTLE STOLE SOMETHING FROM US. WE JUST WANT IT BACK!
COFF COFF
HE STOLE IT FOR ME.
I AM DYING.
YOU WILL IF YOU DON'T TAKE US TO HIM.
TIE THEM UP!
YOU SHOULD TAKE ME, TOO.
HELM GREYCASTLE IS IN ANOTHER WORLD. DO YOU WANT TO CHASE HIM DOWN TO GET IT?
GOOD IDEA! YOU CAN LEAD THE WAY!
OR WE'LL KILL YOU BOTH AND WAIT FOR THEM HERE.

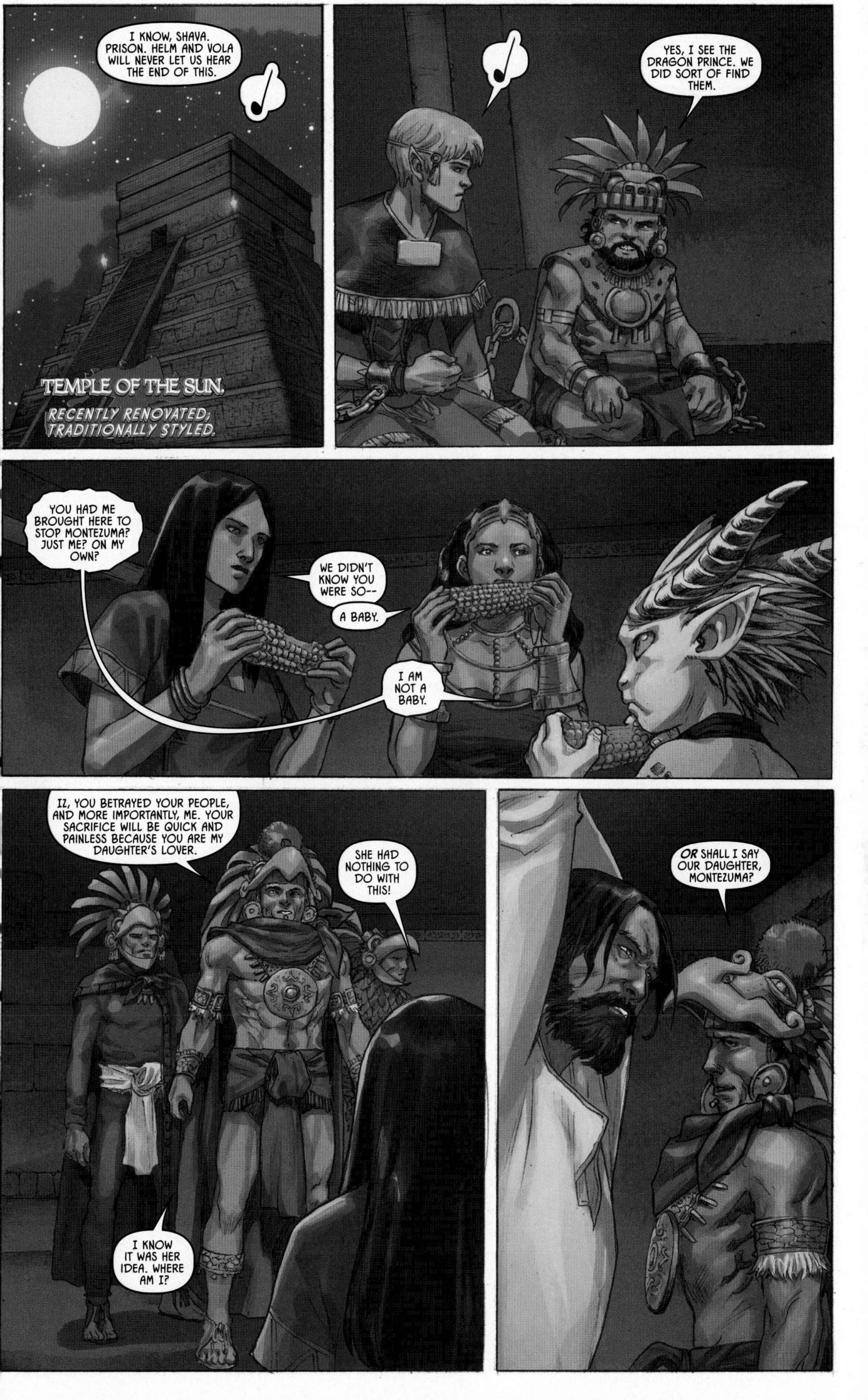
I KNOW, SHAVA. PRISON. HELM AND VOLA WILL NEVER LET US HEAR THE END OF THIS.
TEMPLE OF THE SUN.
RECENTLY RENOVATED; TRADITIONALLY STYLED.
YES, I SEE THE DRAGON PRINCE. WE DID SORT OF FIND THEM.
YOU HAD ME BROUGHT HERE TO STOP MONTEZUMA? JUST ME? ON MY OWN?
WE DIDN'T KNOW YOU WERE SO--
A BABY.
I AM NOT A BABY.
IZ, YOU BETRAYED YOUR PEOPLE, AND MORE IMPORTANTLY, ME. YOUR SACRIFICE WILL BE QUICK AND PAINLESS BECAUSE YOU ARE MY DAUGHTER'S LOVER.
SHE HAD NOTHING TO DO WITH THIS!
I KNOW IT WAS HER IDEA. WHERE AM I?
OR SHALL I SAY OUR DAUGHTER, MONTEZUMA?

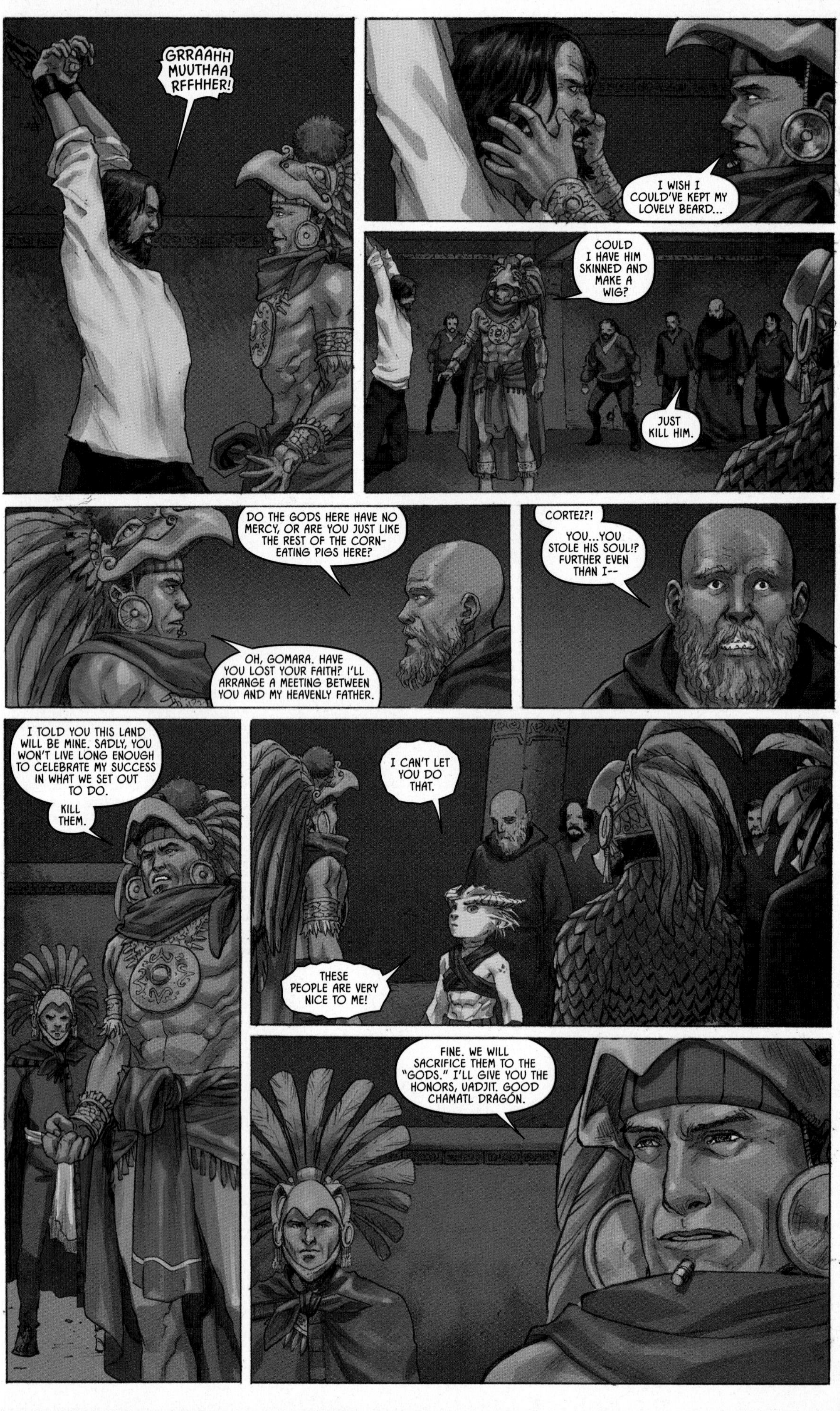
GRRAAHH MUUTHAA RFFHHER!
I WISH I COULD'VE KEPT MY LOVELY BEARD...
COULD I HAVE HIM SKINNED AND MAKE A WIG?
JUST KILL HIM.
DO THE GODS HERE HAVE NO MERCY, OR ARE YOU JUST LIKE THE REST OF THE CORN-EATING PIGS HERE?
OH, GOMARA. HAVE YOU LOST YOUR FAITH? I'LL ARRANGE A MEETING BETWEEN YOU AND MY HEAVENLY FATHER.
CORTEZ?!
YOU...YOU STOLE HIS SOUL!? FURTHER EVEN THAN I--
I TOLD YOU THIS LAND WILL BE MINE. SADLY, YOU WON'T LIVE LONG ENOUGH TO CELEBRATE MY SUCCESS IN WHAT WE SET OUT TO DO.
KILL THEM.
I CAN'T LET YOU DO THAT.
THESE PEOPLE ARE VERY NICE TO ME!
FINE. WE WILL SACRIFICE THEM TO THE "GODS." I'LL GIVE YOU THE HONORS, UADJIT. GOOD CHAMATL DRAGÓN.

BLAME IT ON BAD LUCK

04

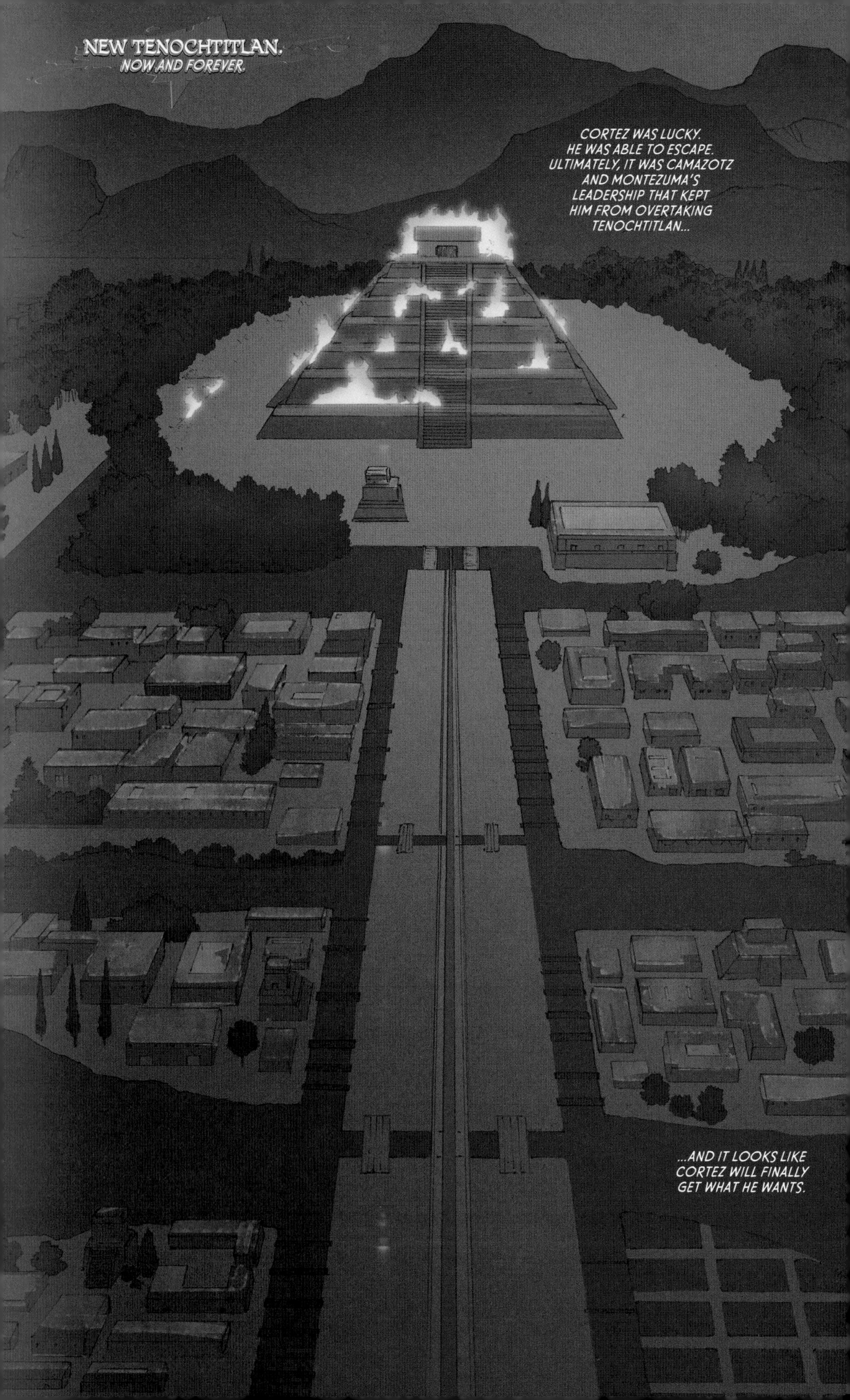
NEW TENOCHTITLAN.
NOW AND FOREVER.
CORTEZ WAS LUCKY. HE WAS ABLE TO ESCAPE. ULTIMATELY, IT WAS CAMAZOTZ AND MONTEZUMA'S LEADERSHIP THAT KEPT HIM FROM OVERTAKING TENOCHTITLAN...
...AND IT LOOKS LIKE CORTEZ WILL FINALLY GET WHAT HE WANTS.

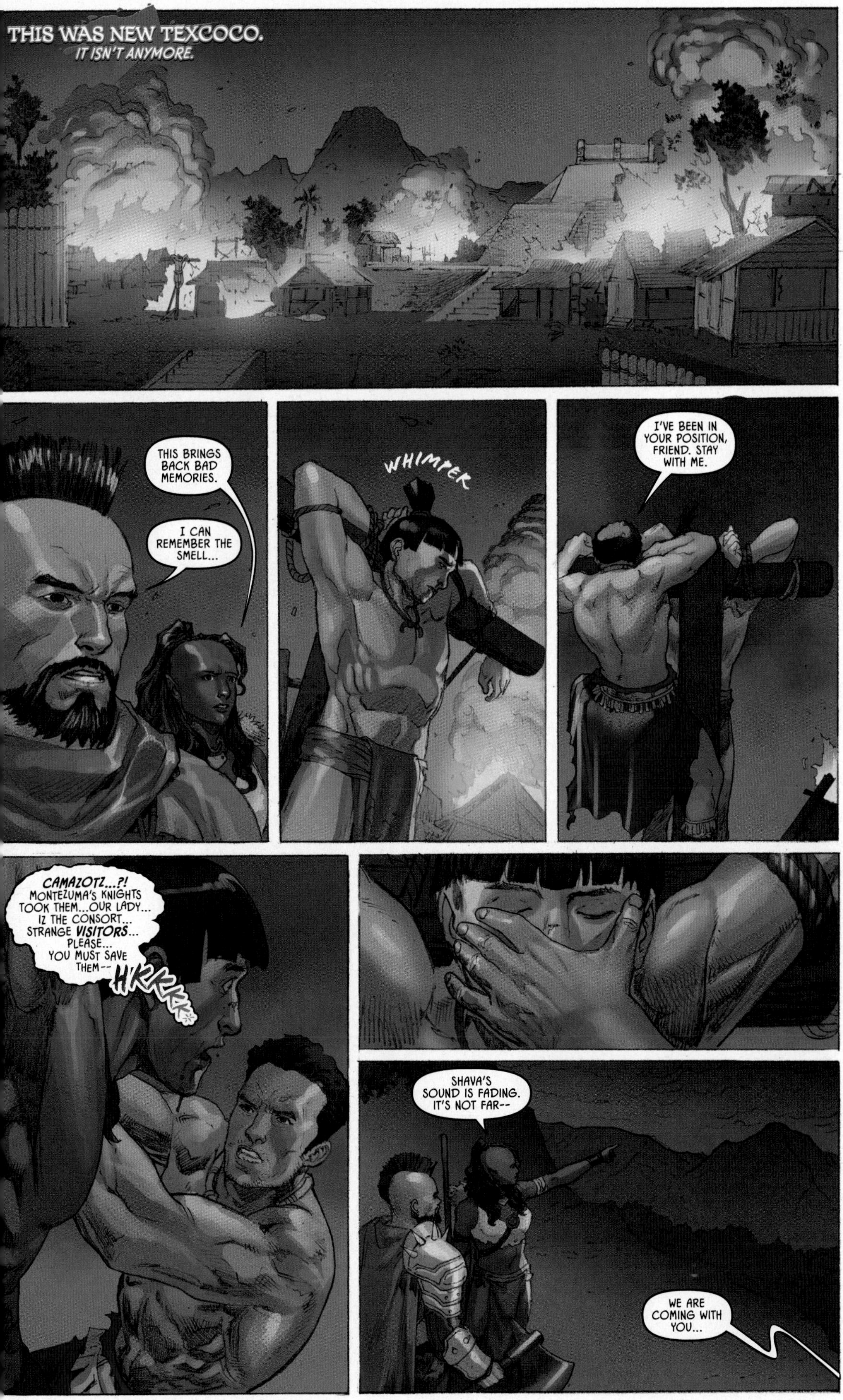
THIS WAS NEW TEXCOCO.
IT ISN'T ANYMORE.
THIS BRINGS BACK BAD MEMORIES.
I CAN REMEMBER THE SMELL...
WHIMPER
I'VE BEEN IN YOUR POSITION, FRIEND. STAY WITH ME.
CAMAZOTZ...?! MONTEZUMA'S KNIGHTS TOOK THEM...OUR LADY... IZ THE CONSORT... STRANGE VISITORS... PLEASE... YOU MUST SAVE THEM--
HKKKK
SHAVA'S SOUND IS FADING. IT'S NOT FAR--
WE ARE COMING WITH YOU...

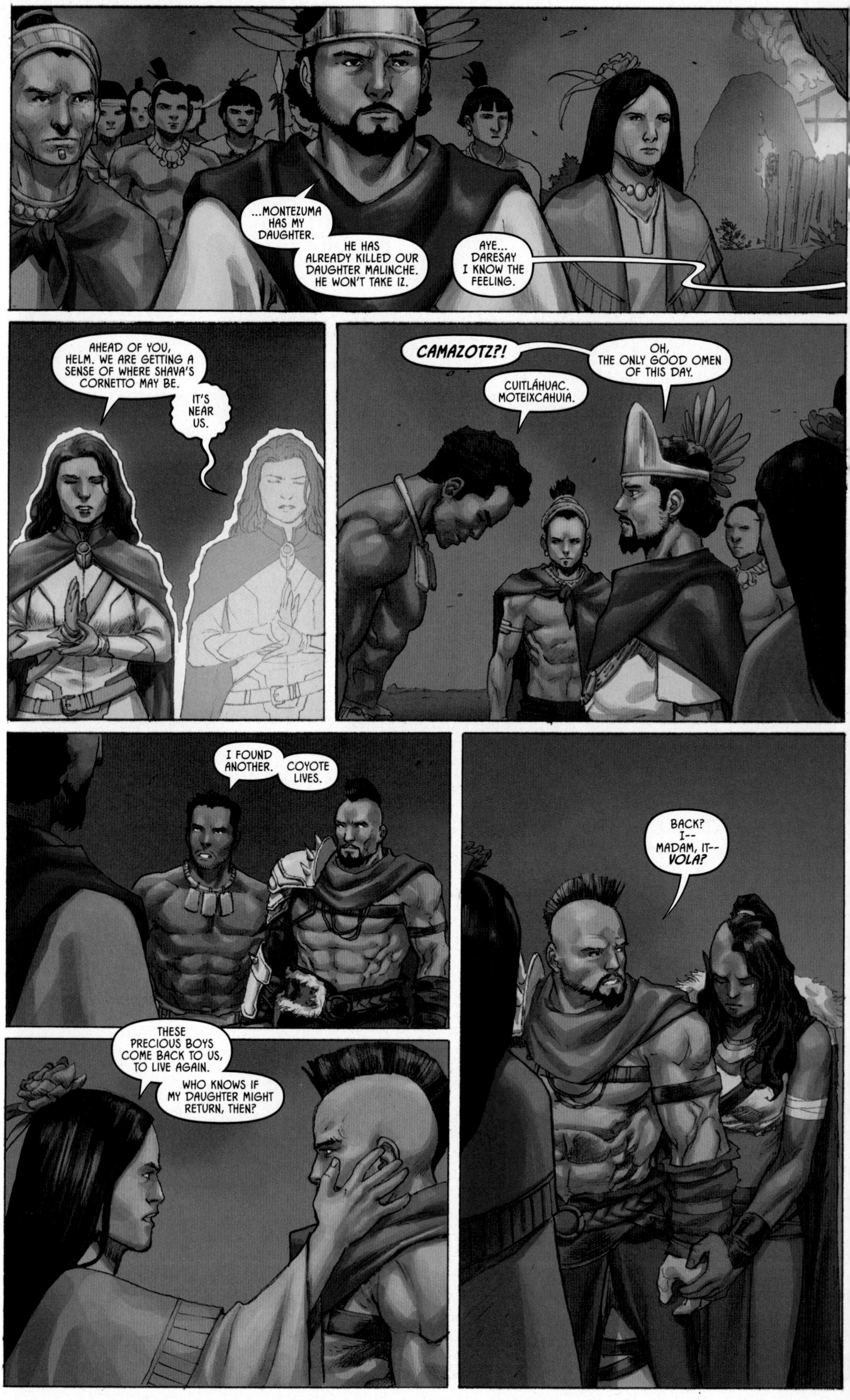
...MONTEZUMA HAS MY DAUGHTER.
HE HAS ALREADY KILLED OUR DAUGHTER MALINCHE. HE WON'T TAKE IZ.
AYE... DARESAY I KNOW THE FEELING.
AHEAD OF YOU, HELM. WE ARE GETTING A SENSE OF WHERE SHAVA'S CORNETTO MAY BE.
IT'S NEAR US.
CAMAZOTZ?!
OH, THE ONLY GOOD OMEN OF THIS DAY.
CUITLÁHUAC. MOTEIXCAHUIA.
I FOUND ANOTHER.
COYOTE LIVES.
THESE PRECIOUS BOYS COME BACK TO US, TO LIVE AGAIN.
WHO KNOWS IF MY DAUGHTER MIGHT RETURN, THEN?
BACK? I-- MADAM, IT-- VOLA?

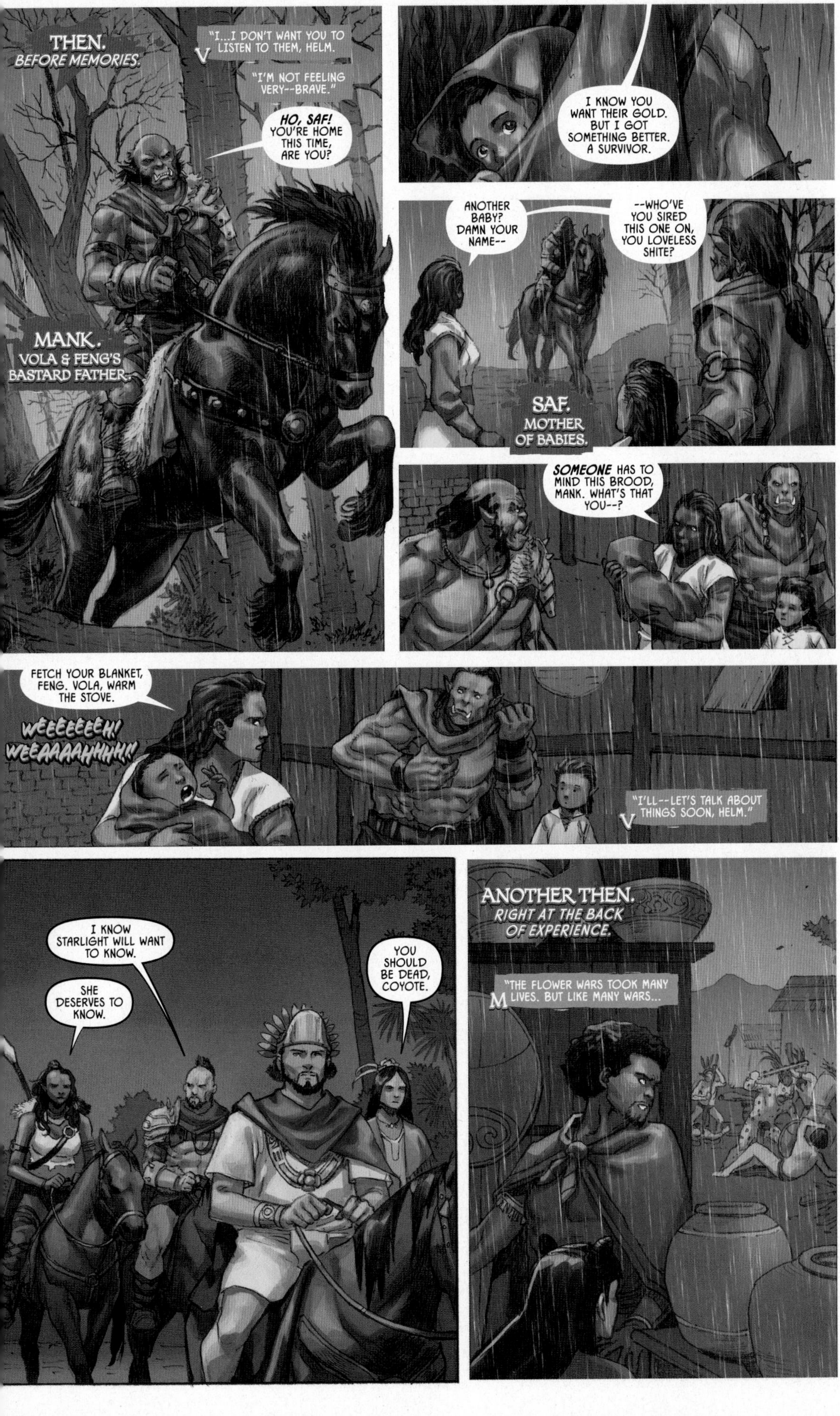
THEN.
BEFORE MEMORIES.
"I...I DON'T WANT YOU TO LISTEN TO THEM, HELM.
"I'M NOT FEELING VERY--BRAVE."
V
HO, SAF! YOU'RE HOME THIS TIME, ARE YOU?
MANK.
VOLA & FENG'S BASTARD FATHER.
I KNOW YOU WANT THEIR GOLD. BUT I GOT SOMETHING BETTER. A SURVIVOR.
ANOTHER BABY? DAMN YOUR NAME--
--WHO'VE YOU SIRED THIS ONE ON, YOU LOVELESS SHITE?
SAF.
MOTHER OF BABIES.
SOMEONE HAS TO MIND THIS BROOD, MANK. WHAT'S THAT YOU--?
FETCH YOUR BLANKET, FENG. VOLA, WARM THE STOVE.
WEEEEEEEH! WEEAAAAHHHH!!
"I'LL--LET'S TALK ABOUT THINGS SOON, HELM."
V
I KNOW STARLIGHT WILL WANT TO KNOW.
SHE DESERVES TO KNOW.
YOU SHOULD BE DEAD, COYOTE.
ANOTHER THEN.
RIGHT AT THE BACK OF EXPERIENCE.
"THE FLOWER WARS TOOK MANY LIVES. BUT LIKE MANY WARS...
M

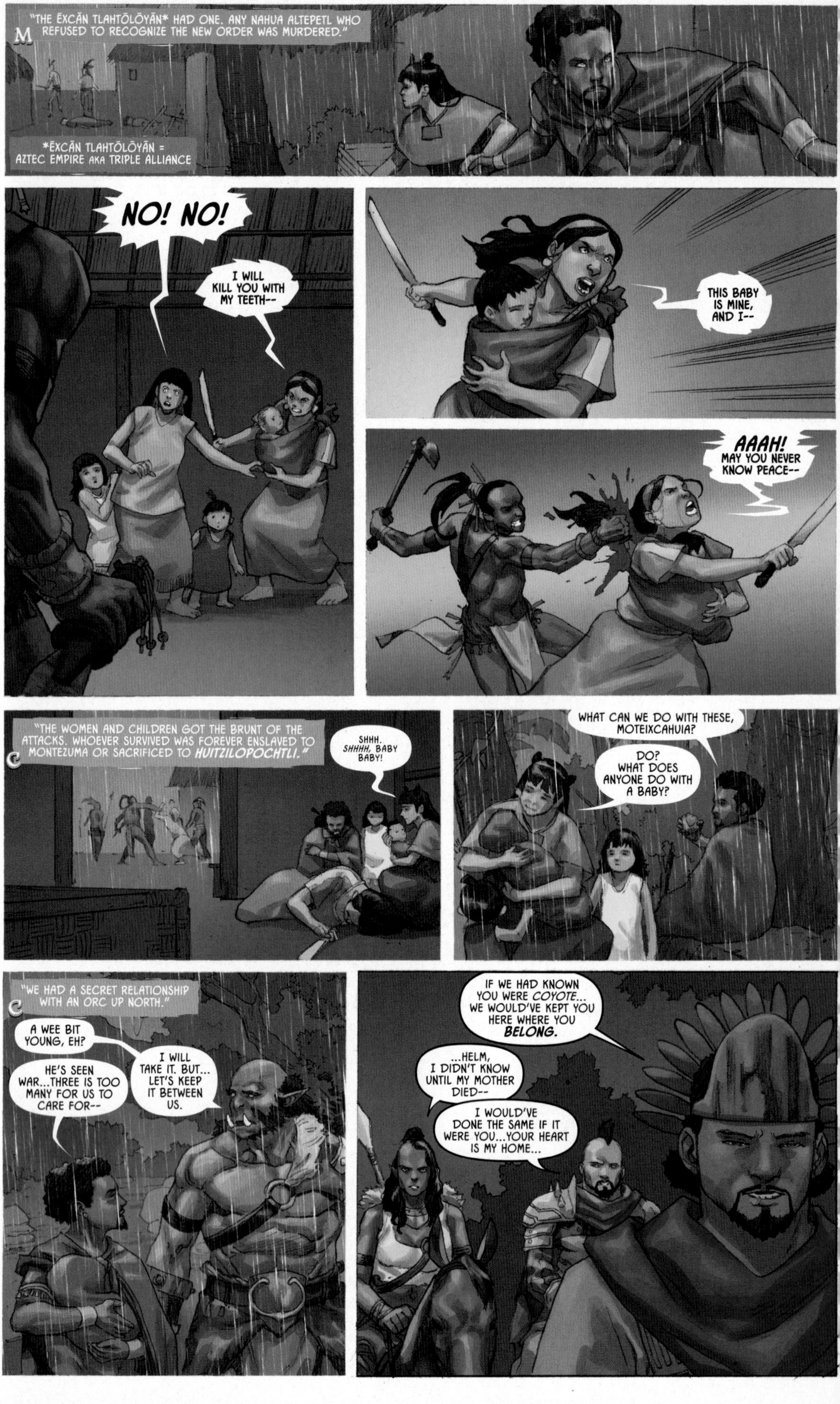
"THE ĒXCĀN TLAHTŌLŌYĀN* HAD ONE. ANY NAHUA ALTEPETL WHO REFUSED TO RECOGNIZE THE NEW ORDER WAS MURDERED."
*ĒXCĀN TLAHTŌLŌYĀN = AZTEC EMPIRE AKA TRIPLE ALLIANCE
NO! NO!
I WILL KILL YOU WITH MY TEETH--
THIS BABY IS MINE, AND I--
AAAH! MAY YOU NEVER KNOW PEACE--
"THE WOMEN AND CHILDREN GOT THE BRUNT OF THE ATTACKS. WHOEVER SURVIVED WAS FOREVER ENSLAVED TO MONTEZUMA OR SACRIFICED TO HUITZILOPOCHTLI."
SHHH. SHHHH, BABY BABY!
WHAT CAN WE DO WITH THESE, MOTEIXCAHUIA?
DO? WHAT DOES ANYONE DO WITH A BABY?
"WE HAD A SECRET RELATIONSHIP WITH AN ORC UP NORTH."
A WEE BIT YOUNG, EH?
HE'S SEEN WAR...THREE IS TOO MANY FOR US TO CARE FOR--
I WILL TAKE IT. BUT... LET'S KEEP IT BETWEEN US.
IF WE HAD KNOWN YOU WERE COYOTE... WE WOULD'VE KEPT YOU HERE WHERE YOU BELONG.
...HELM, I DIDN'T KNOW UNTIL MY MOTHER DIED--
I WOULD'VE DONE THE SAME IF IT WERE YOU...YOUR HEART IS MY HOME...

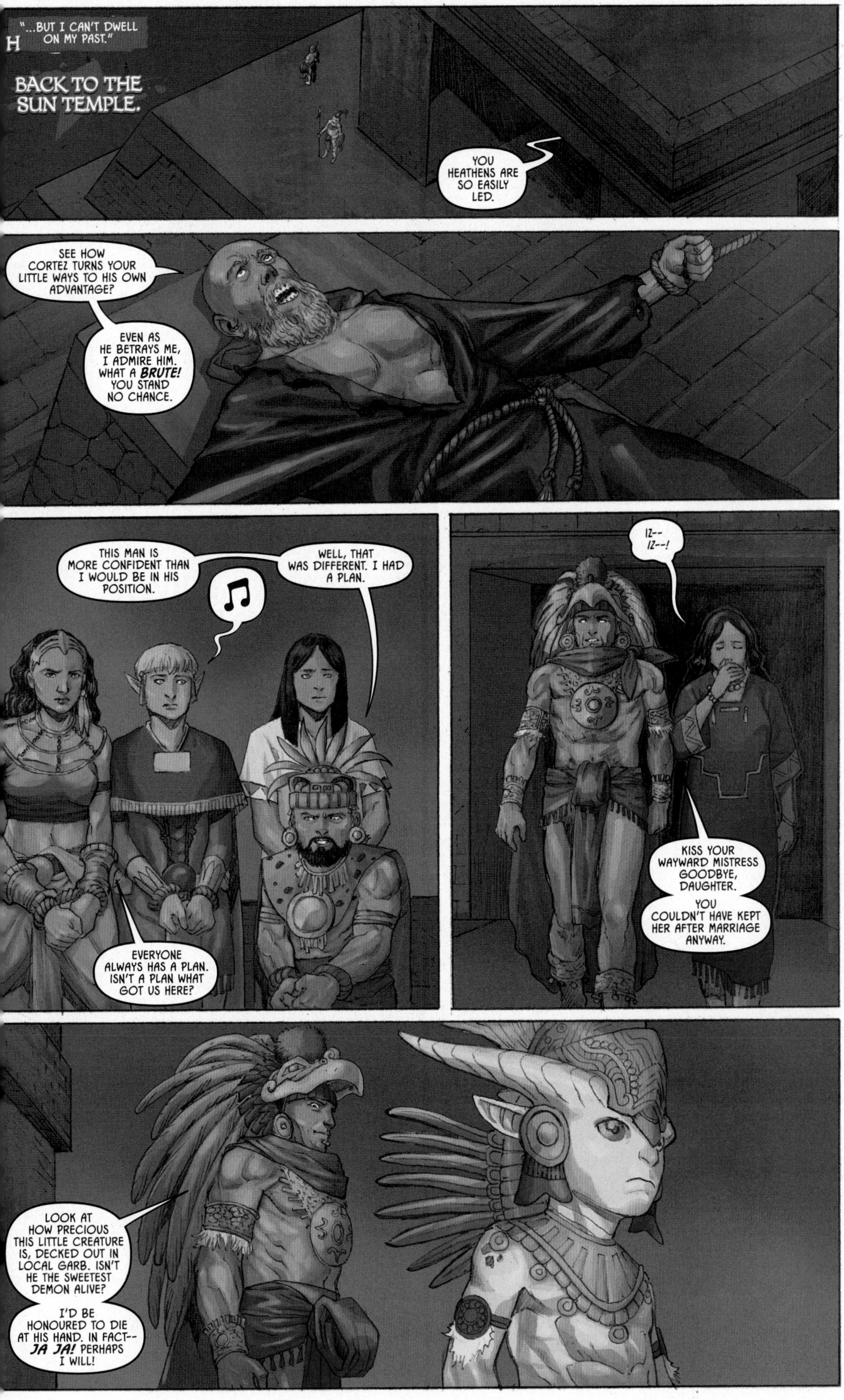
"...BUT I CAN'T DWELL ON MY PAST."
BACK TO THE SUN TEMPLE.
YOU HEATHENS ARE SO EASILY LED.
SEE HOW CORTEZ TURNS YOUR LITTLE WAYS TO HIS OWN ADVANTAGE?
EVEN AS HE BETRAYS ME, I ADMIRE HIM. WHAT A BRUTE! YOU STAND NO CHANCE.
THIS MAN IS MORE CONFIDENT THAN I WOULD BE IN HIS POSITION.
♫
WELL, THAT WAS DIFFERENT. I HAD A PLAN.
EVERYONE ALWAYS HAS A PLAN. ISN'T A PLAN WHAT GOT US HERE?
IZ-- IZ--!
KISS YOUR WAYWARD MISTRESS GOODBYE, DAUGHTER.
YOU COULDN'T HAVE KEPT HER AFTER MARRIAGE ANYWAY.
LOOK AT HOW PRECIOUS THIS LITTLE CREATURE IS, DECKED OUT IN LOCAL GARB. ISN'T HE THE SWEETEST DEMON ALIVE?
I'D BE HONOURED TO DIE AT HIS HAND. IN FACT-- JA JA! PERHAPS I WILL!

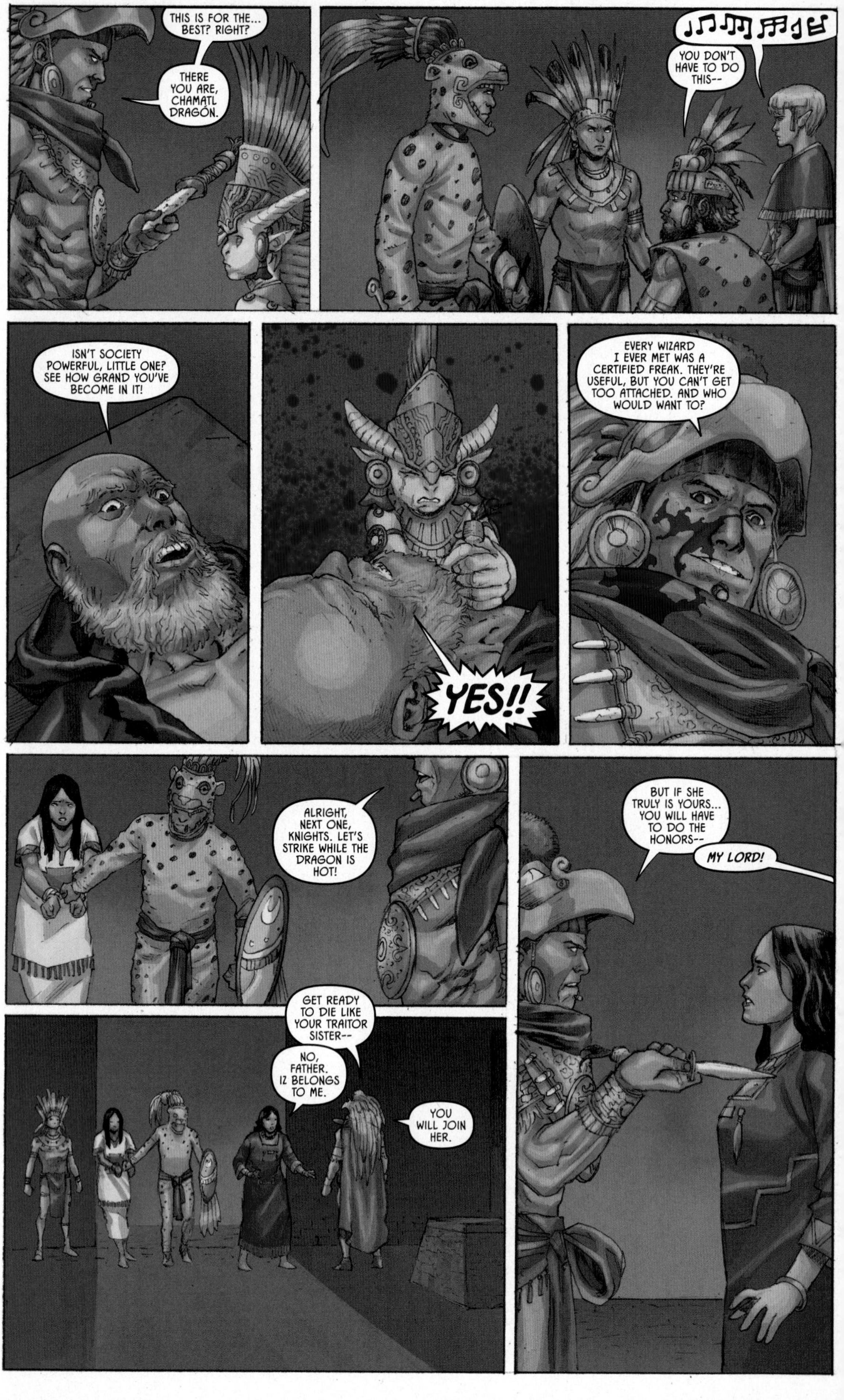
THIS IS FOR THE... BEST? RIGHT?
THERE YOU ARE, CHAMATL DRAGÓN.
YOU DON'T HAVE TO DO THIS--
ISN'T SOCIETY POWERFUL, LITTLE ONE? SEE HOW GRAND YOU'VE BECOME IN IT!
YES!!
EVERY WIZARD I EVER MET WAS A CERTIFIED FREAK. THEY'RE USEFUL, BUT YOU CAN'T GET TOO ATTACHED. AND WHO WOULD WANT TO?
ALRIGHT, NEXT ONE, KNIGHTS. LET'S STRIKE WHILE THE DRAGON IS HOT!
GET READY TO DIE LIKE YOUR TRAITOR SISTER--
NO, FATHER. IZ BELONGS TO ME.
YOU WILL JOIN HER.
BUT IF SHE TRULY IS YOURS... YOU WILL HAVE TO DO THE HONORS--
MY LORD!

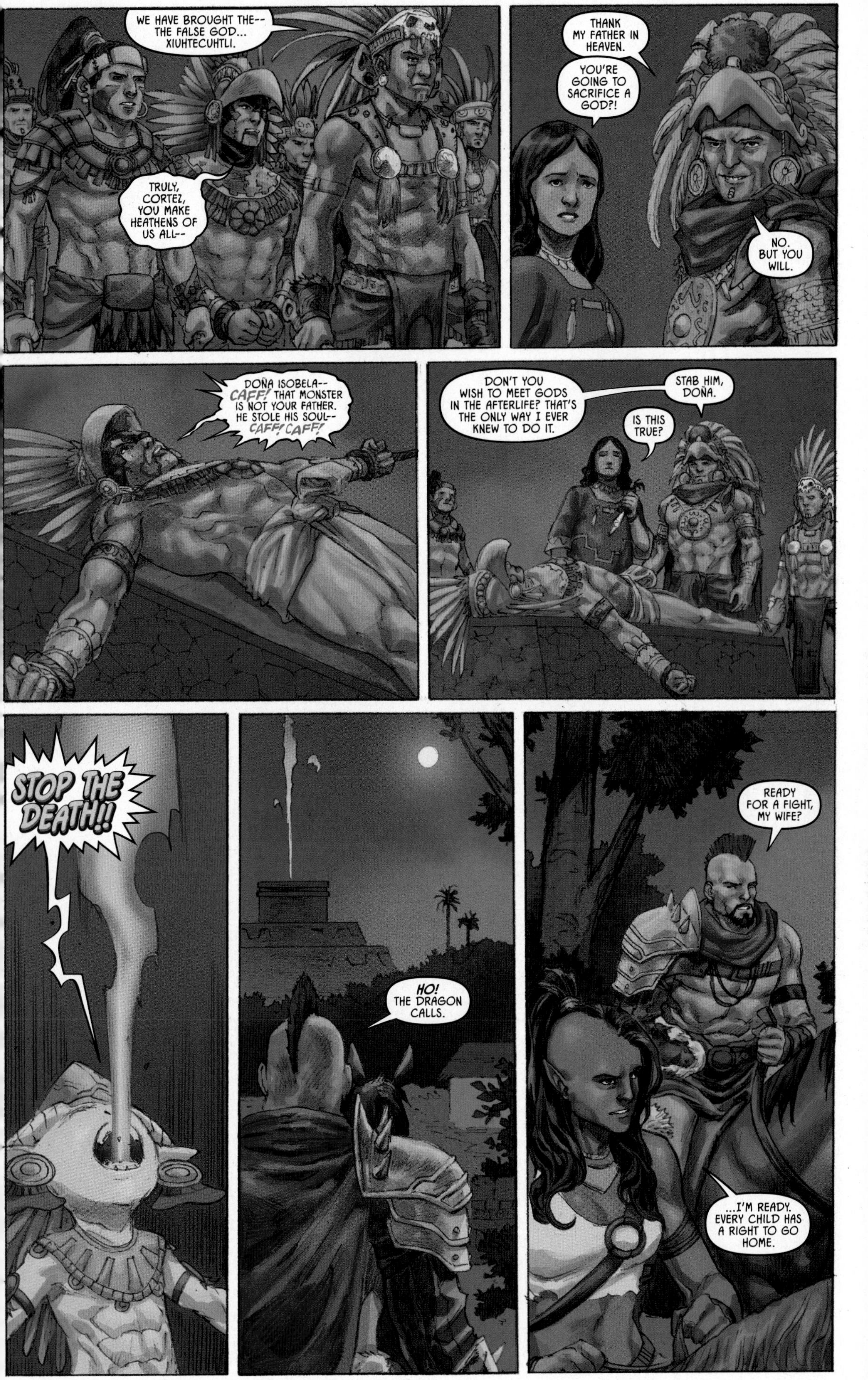
WE HAVE BROUGHT THE-- THE FALSE GOD... XIUHTECUHTLI.
TRULY, CORTEZ, YOU MAKE HEATHENS OF US ALL--
THANK MY FATHER IN HEAVEN.
YOU'RE GOING TO SACRIFICE A GOD?!
NO. BUT YOU WILL.
DOÑA ISOBELA-- CAFF! THAT MONSTER IS NOT YOUR FATHER. HE STOLE HIS SOUL-- CAFF! CAFF!
DON'T YOU WISH TO MEET GODS IN THE AFTERLIFE? THAT'S THE ONLY WAY I EVER KNEW TO DO IT.
STAB HIM, DOÑA.
IS THIS TRUE?
STOP THE DEATH!!
HO! THE DRAGON CALLS.
READY FOR A FIGHT, MY WIFE?
...I'M READY. EVERY CHILD HAS A RIGHT TO GO HOME.

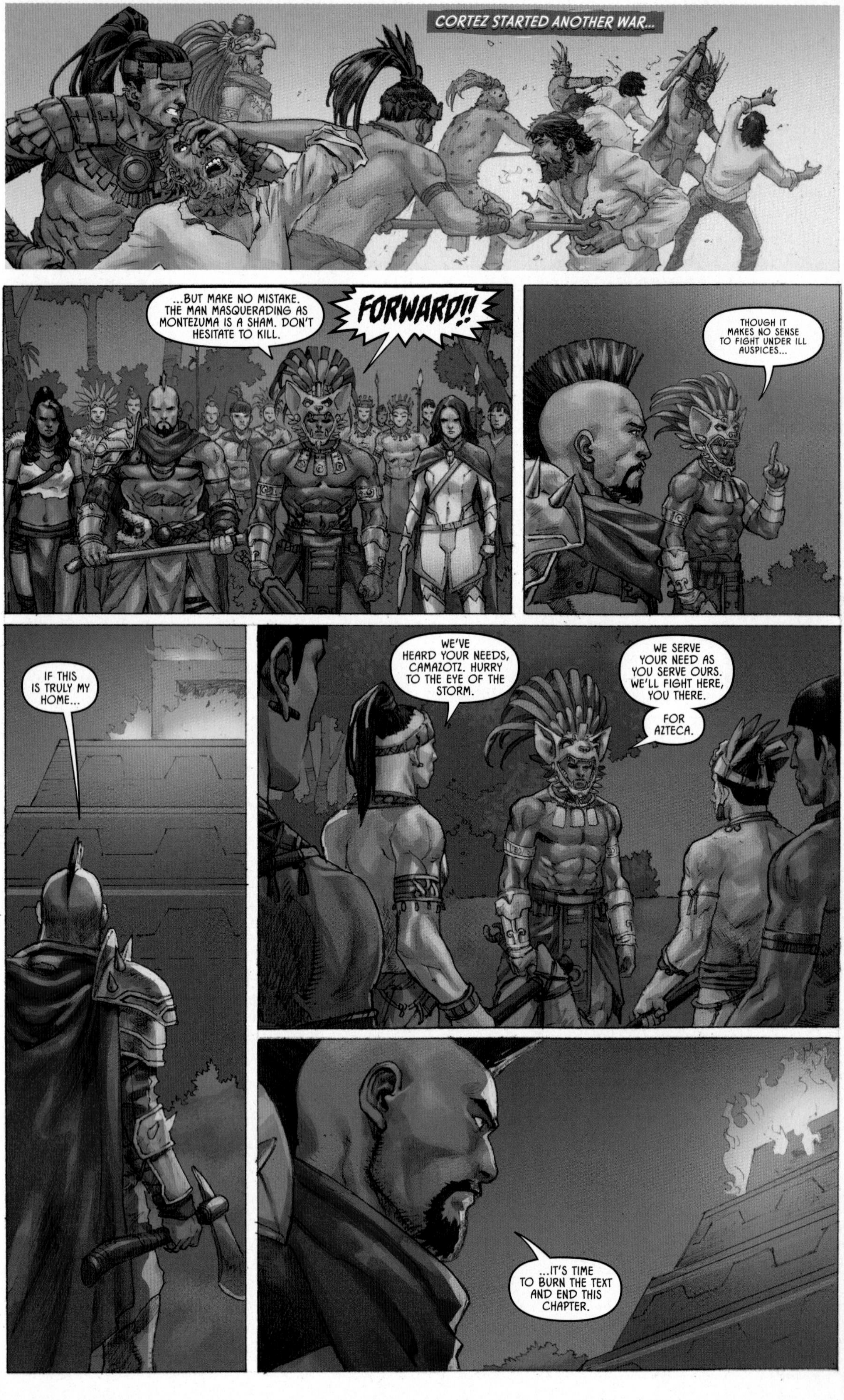
CORTEZ STARTED ANOTHER WAR...
...BUT MAKE NO MISTAKE. THE MAN MASQUERADING AS MONTEZUMA IS A SHAM. DON'T HESITATE TO KILL.
FORWARD!!
THOUGH IT MAKES NO SENSE TO FIGHT UNDER ILL AUSPICES...
IF THIS IS TRULY MY HOME...
WE'VE HEARD YOUR NEEDS, CAMAZOTZ. HURRY TO THE EYE OF THE STORM.
WE SERVE YOUR NEED AS YOU SERVE OURS. WE'LL FIGHT HERE, YOU THERE.
FOR AZTECA.
...IT'S TIME TO BURN THE TEXT AND END THIS CHAPTER.

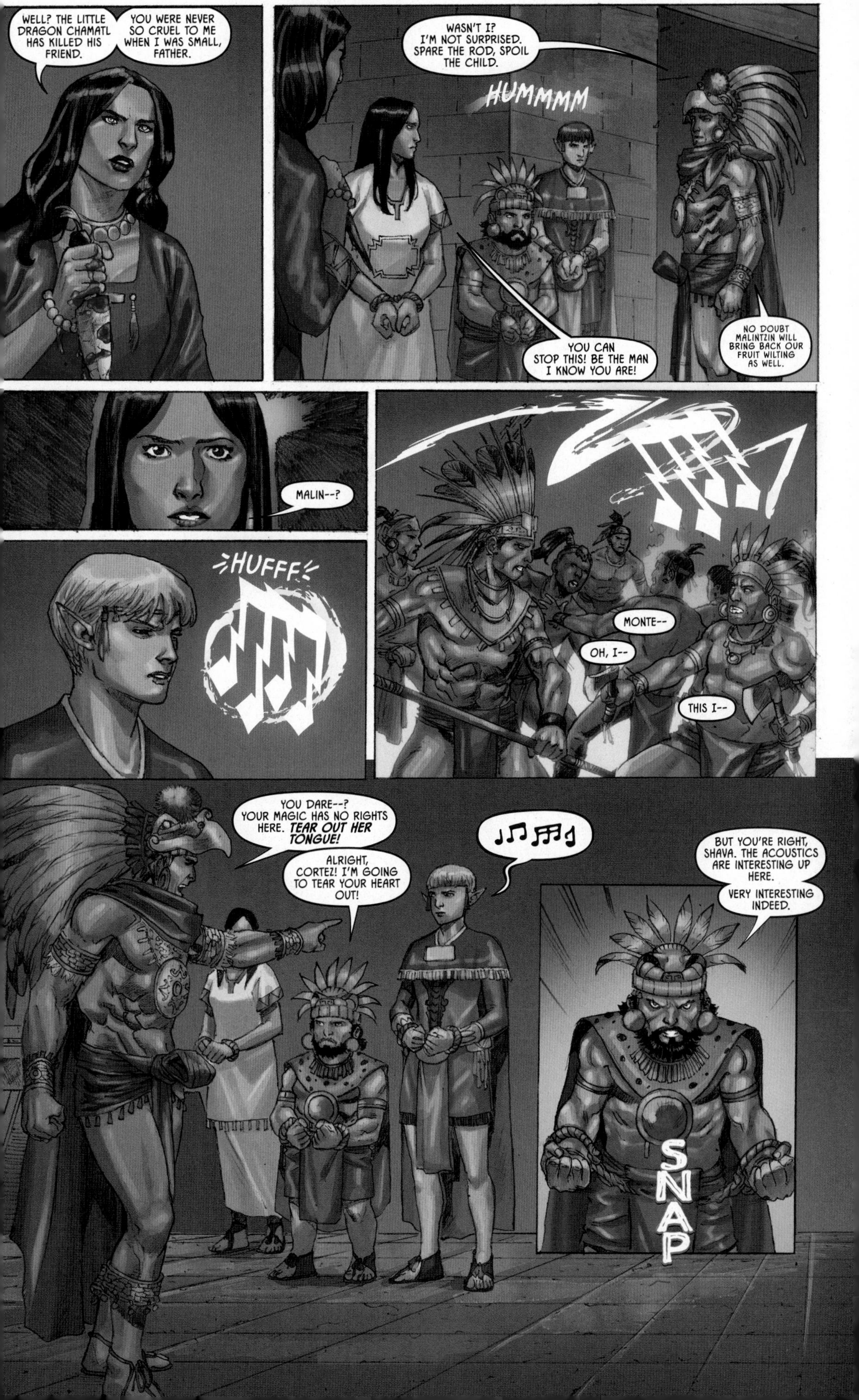
WELL? THE LITTLE DRAGON CHAMATL HAS KILLED HIS FRIEND.
YOU WERE NEVER SO CRUEL TO ME WHEN I WAS SMALL, FATHER.
WASN'T I? I'M NOT SURPRISED. SPARE THE ROD, SPOIL THE CHILD.
HUMMMM
YOU CAN STOP THIS! BE THE MAN I KNOW YOU ARE!
NO DOUBT MALINTZIN WILL BRING BACK OUR FRUIT WILTING AS WELL.
MALIN--?
HUFFF
MONTE--
OH, I--
THIS I--
YOU DARE--? YOUR MAGIC HAS NO RIGHTS HERE. ***TEAR OUT HER TONGUE!***
ALRIGHT, CORTEZ! I'M GOING TO TEAR YOUR HEART OUT!
BUT YOU'RE RIGHT, SHAVA. THE ACOUSTICS ARE INTERESTING UP HERE.
VERY INTERESTING INDEED.
SNAP

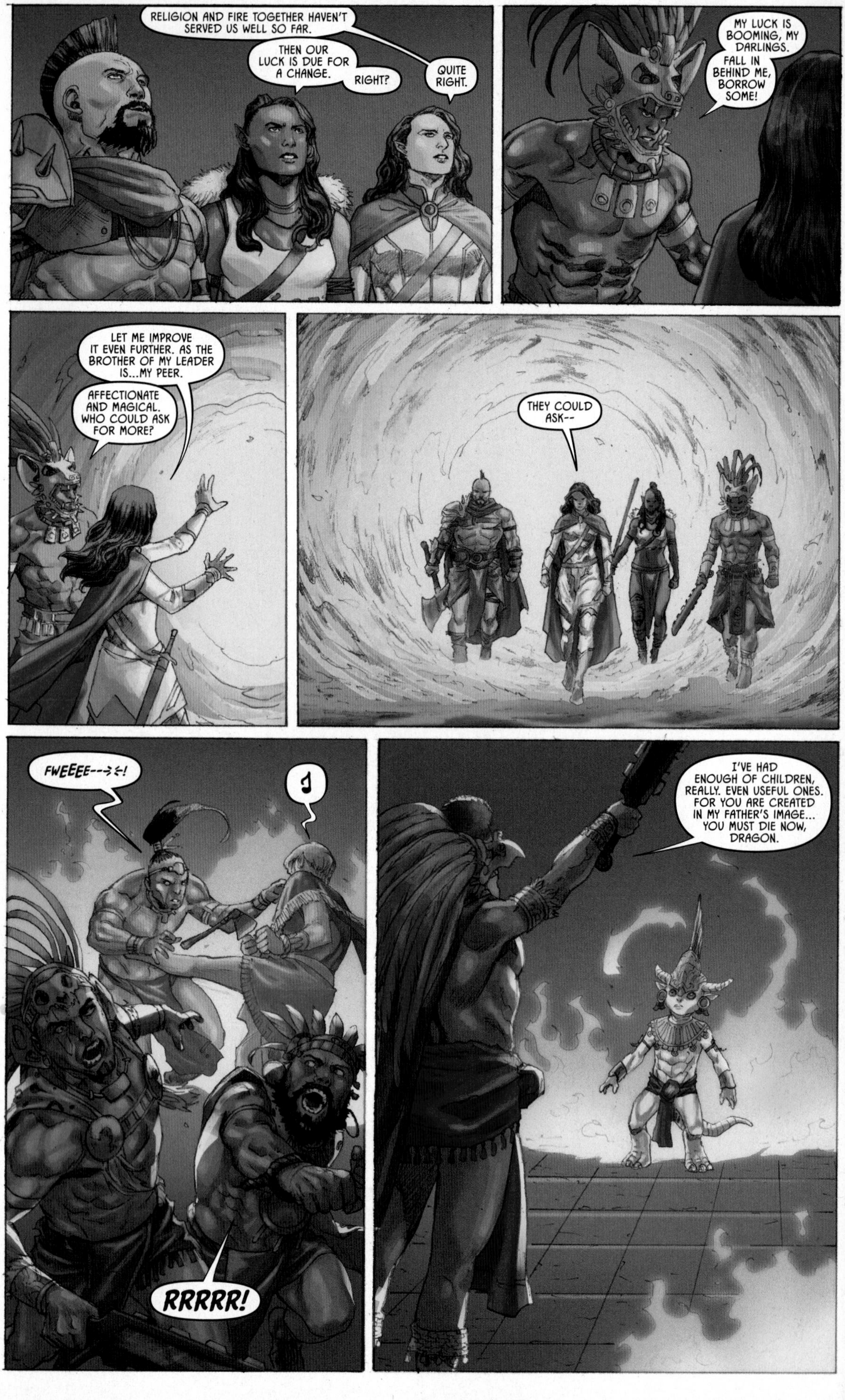
RELIGION AND FIRE TOGETHER HAVEN'T SERVED US WELL SO FAR.
THEN OUR LUCK IS DUE FOR A CHANGE.
RIGHT?
QUITE RIGHT.
MY LUCK IS BOOMING, MY DARLINGS.
FALL IN BEHIND ME, BORROW SOME!
LET ME IMPROVE IT EVEN FURTHER. AS THE BROTHER OF MY LEADER IS...MY PEER.
AFFECTIONATE AND MAGICAL. WHO COULD ASK FOR MORE?
THEY COULD ASK--
FWEEEE--
RRRRR!
I'VE HAD ENOUGH OF CHILDREN, REALLY. EVEN USEFUL ONES. FOR YOU ARE CREATED IN MY FATHER'S IMAGE... YOU MUST DIE NOW, DRAGON.

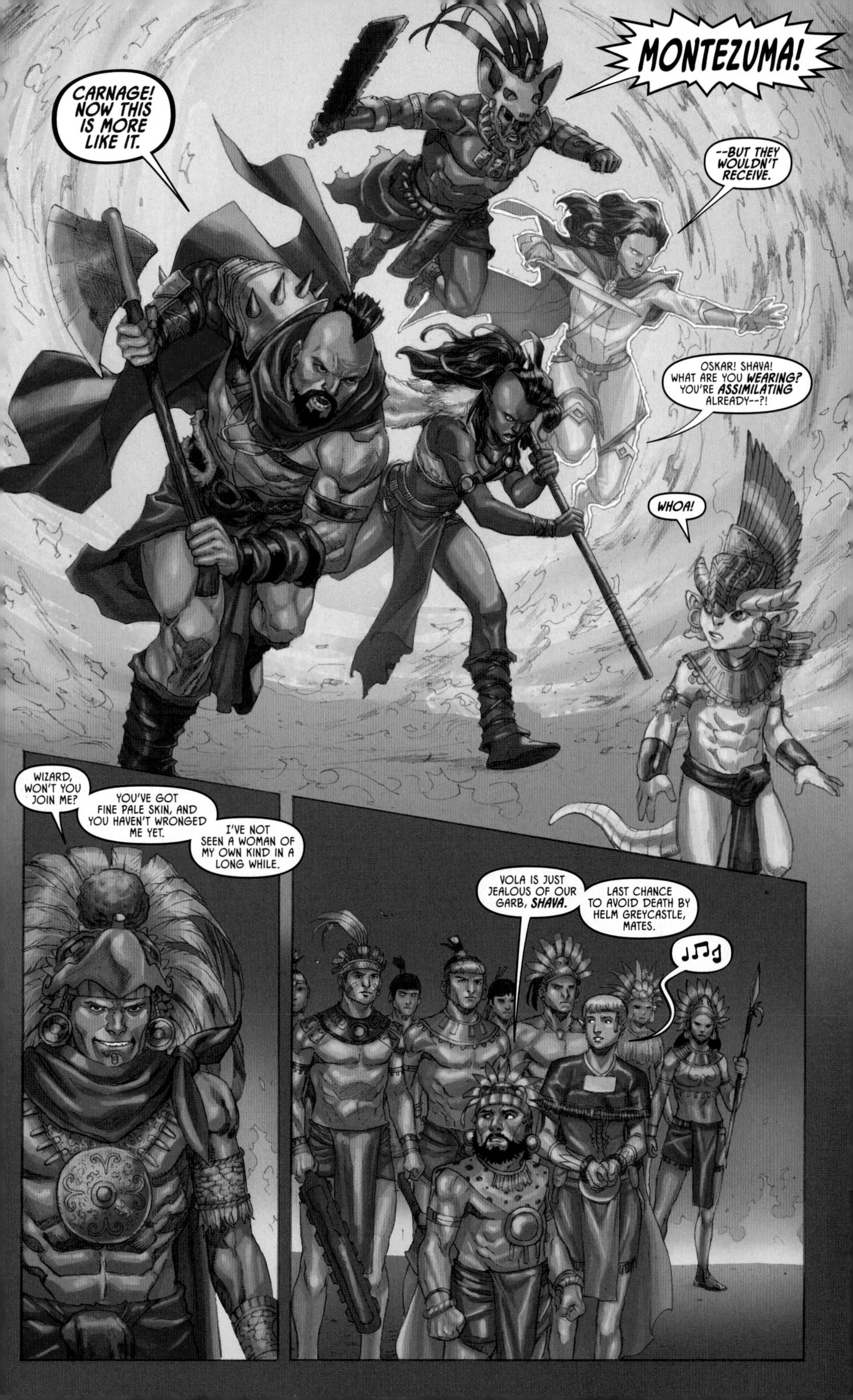
MONTEZUMA!
CARNAGE! NOW THIS IS MORE LIKE IT.
--BUT THEY WOULDN'T RECEIVE.
OSKAR! SHAVA! WHAT ARE YOU WEARING? YOU'RE ASSIMILATING ALREADY--?!
WHOA!
WIZARD, WON'T YOU JOIN ME?
YOU'VE GOT FINE PALE SKIN, AND YOU HAVEN'T WRONGED ME YET.
I'VE NOT SEEN A WOMAN OF MY OWN KIND IN A LONG WHILE.
VOLA IS JUST JEALOUS OF OUR GARB, SHAVA.
LAST CHANCE TO AVOID DEATH BY HELM GREYCASTLE, MATES.
♪♫♩

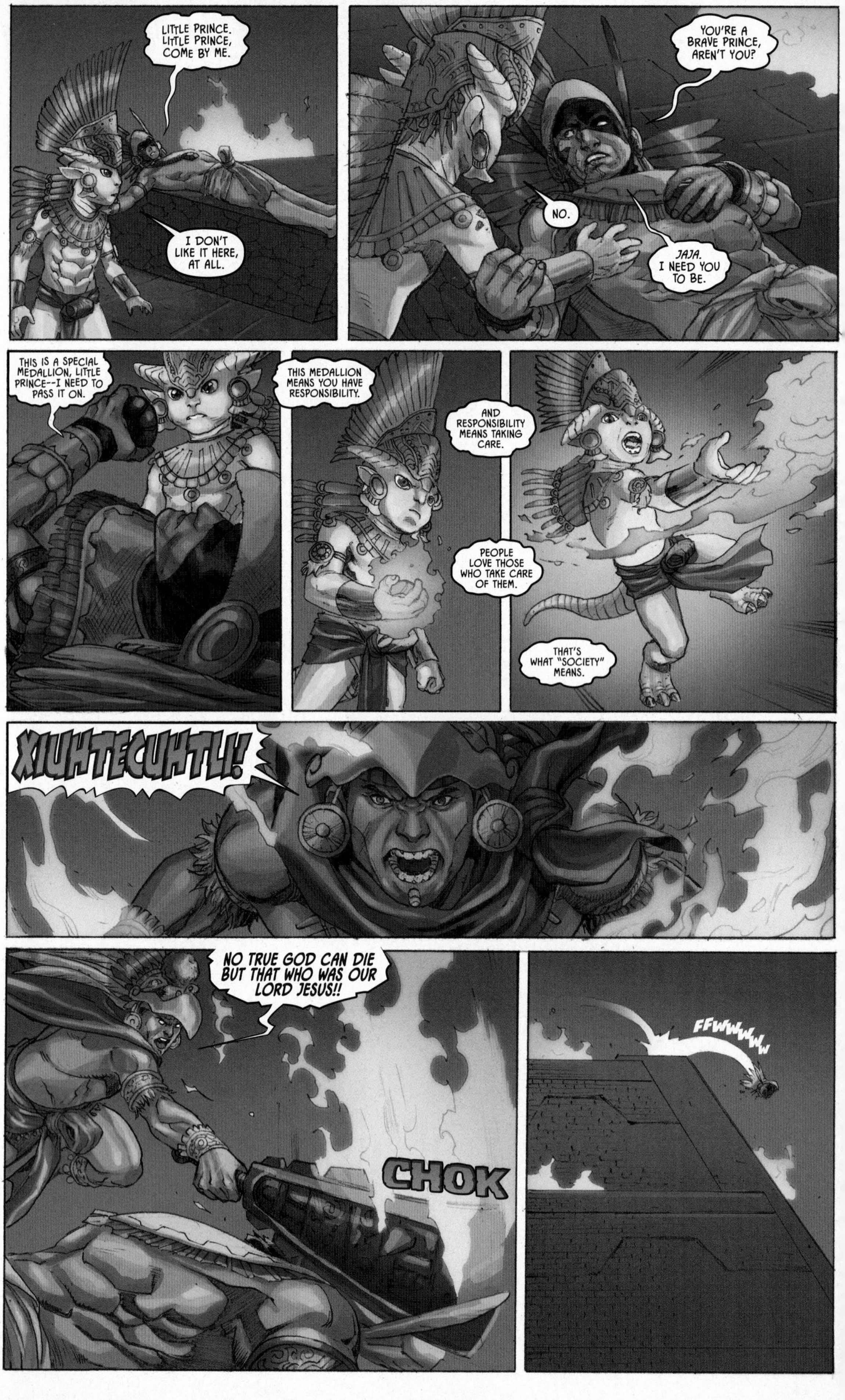
LITTLE PRINCE. LITTLE PRINCE, COME BY ME.
I DON'T LIKE IT HERE, AT ALL.
YOU'RE A BRAVE PRINCE, AREN'T YOU?
NO.
JAJA. I NEED YOU TO BE.
THIS IS A SPECIAL MEDALLION, LITTLE PRINCE--I NEED TO PASS IT ON.
THIS MEDALLION MEANS YOU HAVE RESPONSIBILITY.
AND RESPONSIBILITY MEANS TAKING CARE.
PEOPLE LOVE THOSE WHO TAKE CARE OF THEM.
THAT'S WHAT "SOCIETY" MEANS.
XIUHTECUHTLI!
NO TRUE GOD CAN DIE BUT THAT WHO WAS OUR LORD JESUS!!
CHOK
FFWWWWW

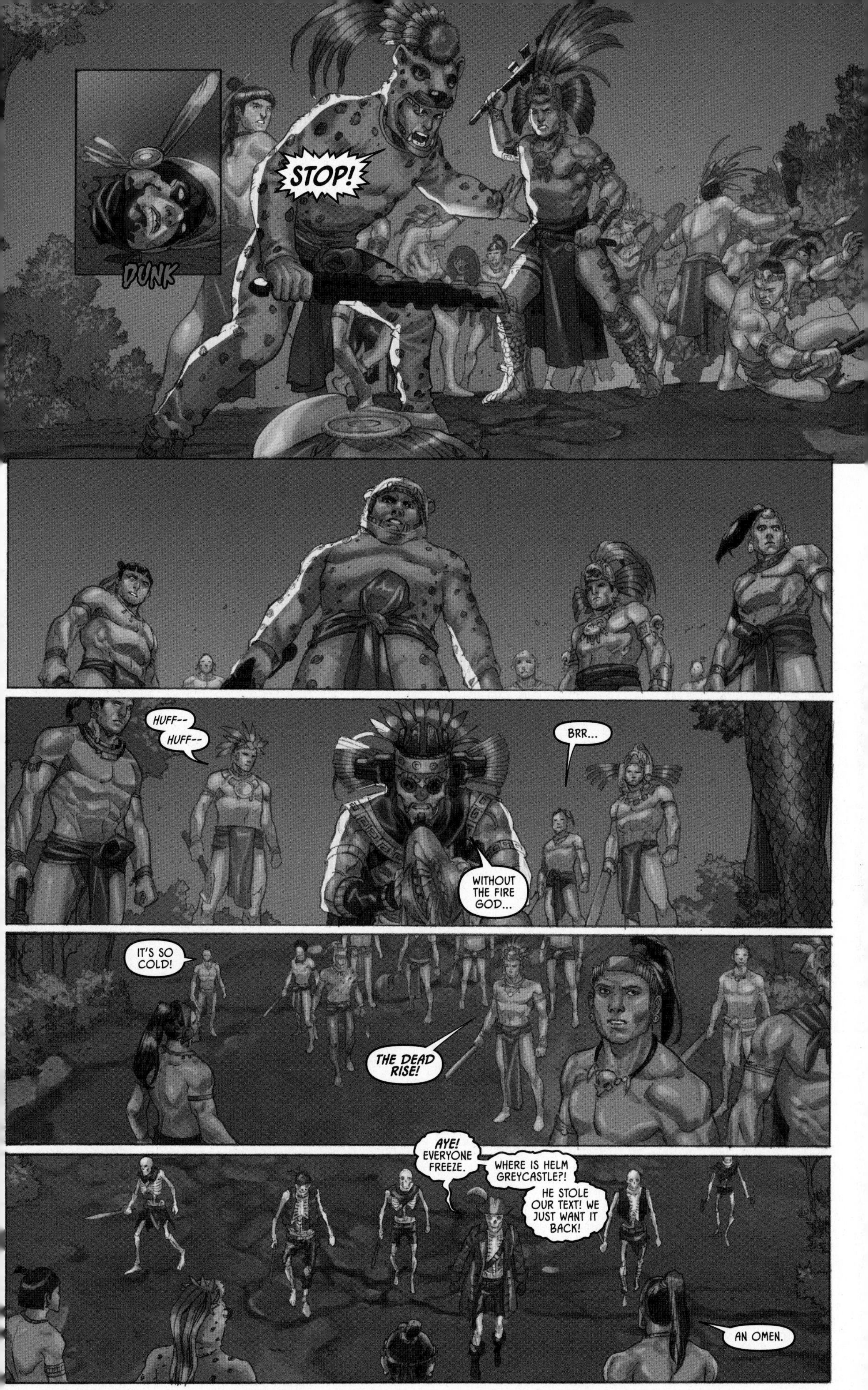
STOP!
DUNK
HUFF--
HUFF--
BRR...
WITHOUT THE FIRE GOD...
IT'S SO COLD!
THE DEAD RISE!
AYE! EVERYONE FREEZE.
WHERE IS HELM GREYCASTLE?!
HE STOLE OUR TEXT! WE JUST WANT IT BACK!
AN OMEN.

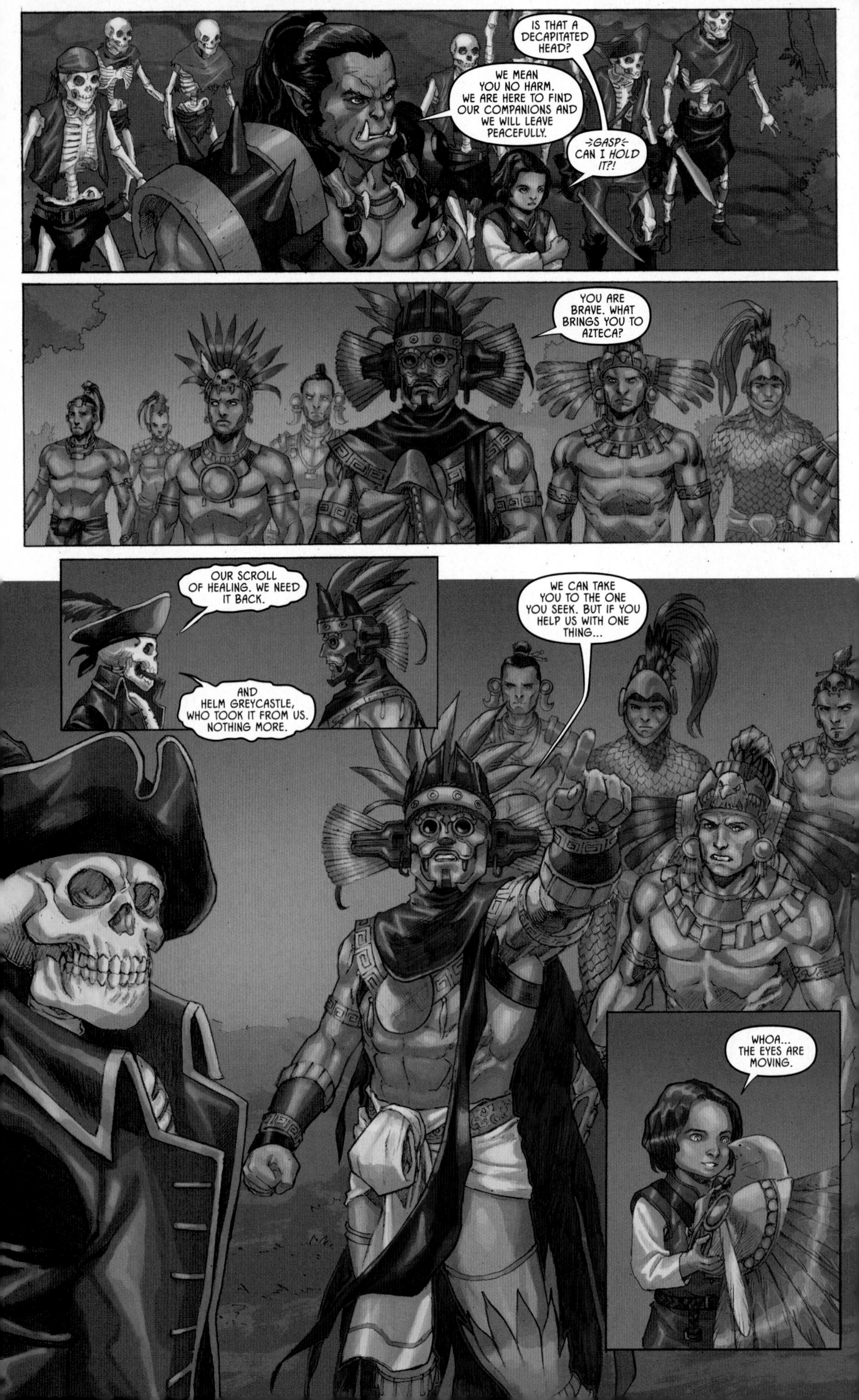
WE MEAN YOU NO HARM. WE ARE HERE TO FIND OUR COMPANIONS AND WE WILL LEAVE PEACEFULLY.
IS THAT A DECAPITATED HEAD?
⇒GASP⇐ CAN I HOLD IT?!
YOU ARE BRAVE. WHAT BRINGS YOU TO AZTECA?
OUR SCROLL OF HEALING. WE NEED IT BACK.
AND HELM GREYCASTLE, WHO TOOK IT FROM US. NOTHING MORE.
WE CAN TAKE YOU TO THE ONE YOU SEEK. BUT IF YOU HELP US WITH ONE THING...
WHOA... THE EYES ARE MOVING.

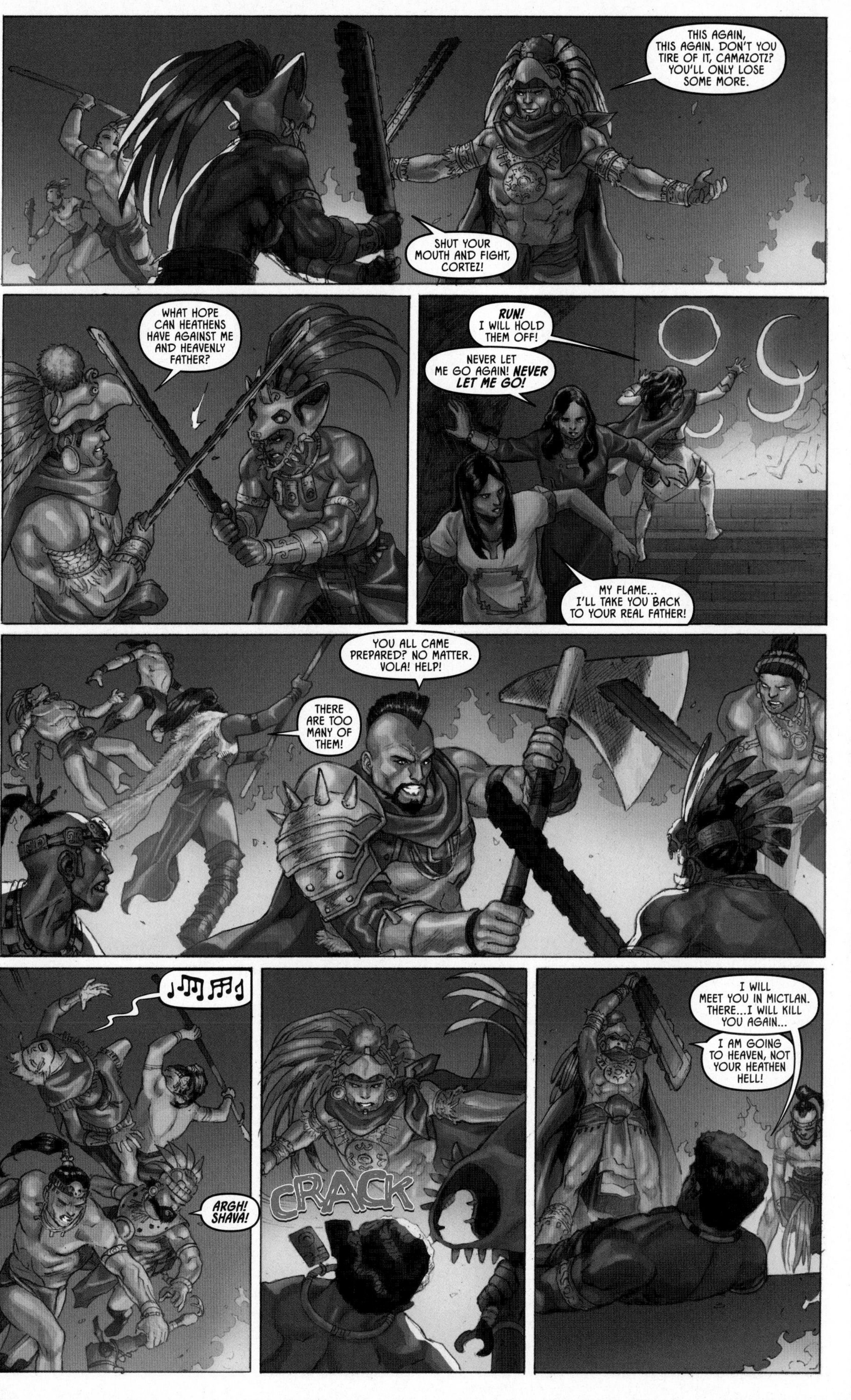
THIS AGAIN, THIS AGAIN. DON'T YOU TIRE OF IT, CAMAZOTZ? YOU'LL ONLY LOSE SOME MORE.
SHUT YOUR MOUTH AND FIGHT, CORTEZ!
WHAT HOPE CAN HEATHENS HAVE AGAINST ME AND HEAVENLY FATHER?
RUN! I WILL HOLD THEM OFF!
NEVER LET ME GO AGAIN! NEVER LET ME GO!
MY FLAME... I'LL TAKE YOU BACK TO YOUR REAL FATHER!
YOU ALL CAME PREPARED? NO MATTER. VOLA! HELP!
THERE ARE TOO MANY OF THEM!
ARGH! SHAVA!
CRACK
I WILL MEET YOU IN MICTLAN. THERE...I WILL KILL YOU AGAIN...
I AM GOING TO HEAVEN, NOT YOUR HEATHEN HELL!

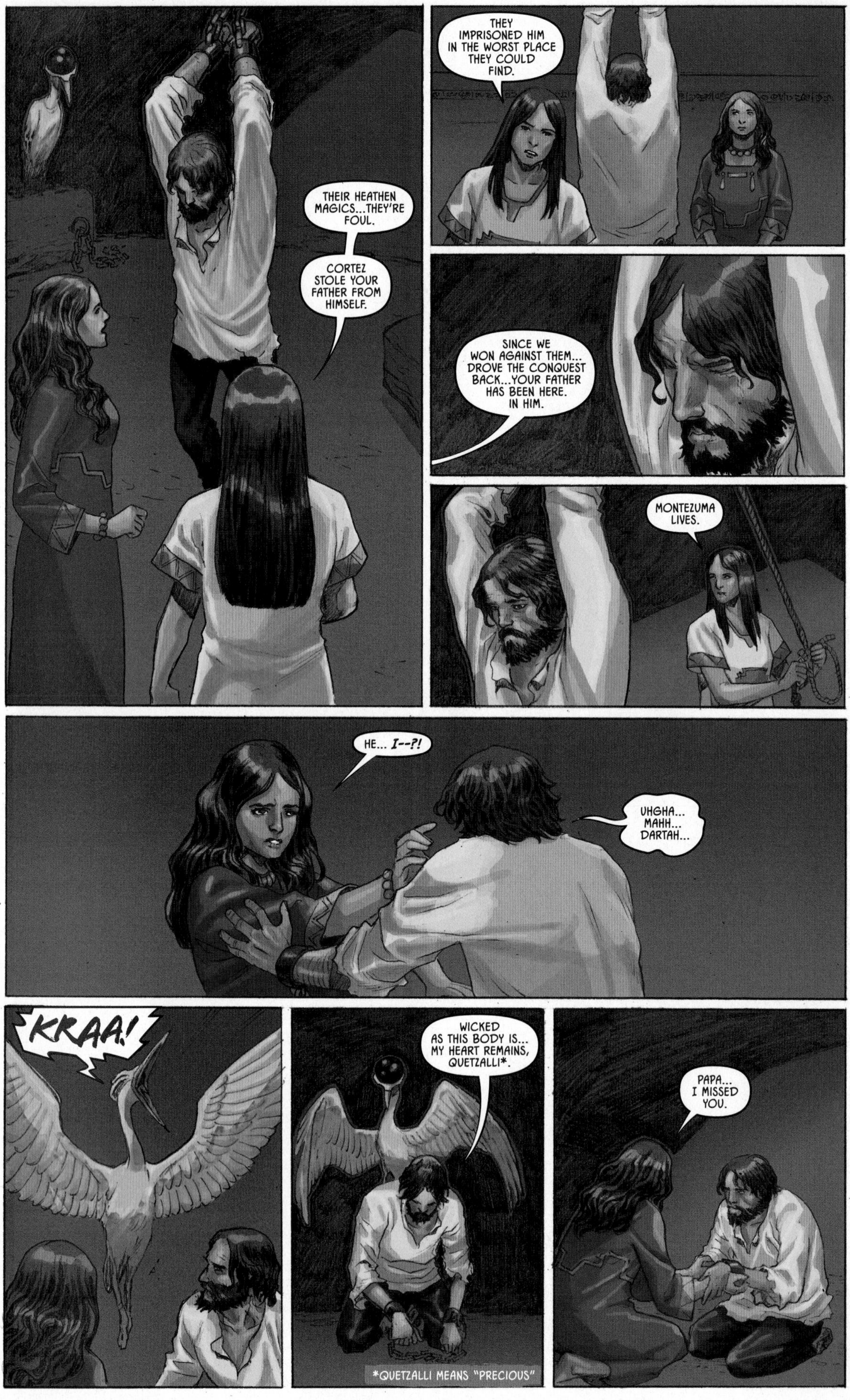
THEIR HEATHEN MAGICS...THEY'RE FOUL.
CORTEZ STOLE YOUR FATHER FROM HIMSELF.
THEY IMPRISONED HIM IN THE WORST PLACE THEY COULD FIND.
SINCE WE WON AGAINST THEM... DROVE THE CONQUEST BACK...YOUR FATHER HAS BEEN HERE. IN HIM.
MONTEZUMA LIVES.
HE... I--?!
UHGHA... MAHH... DARTAH...
KRAA!
WICKED AS THIS BODY IS... MY HEART REMAINS, QUETZALLI*.
*QUETZALLI MEANS "PRECIOUS"
PAPA... I MISSED YOU.

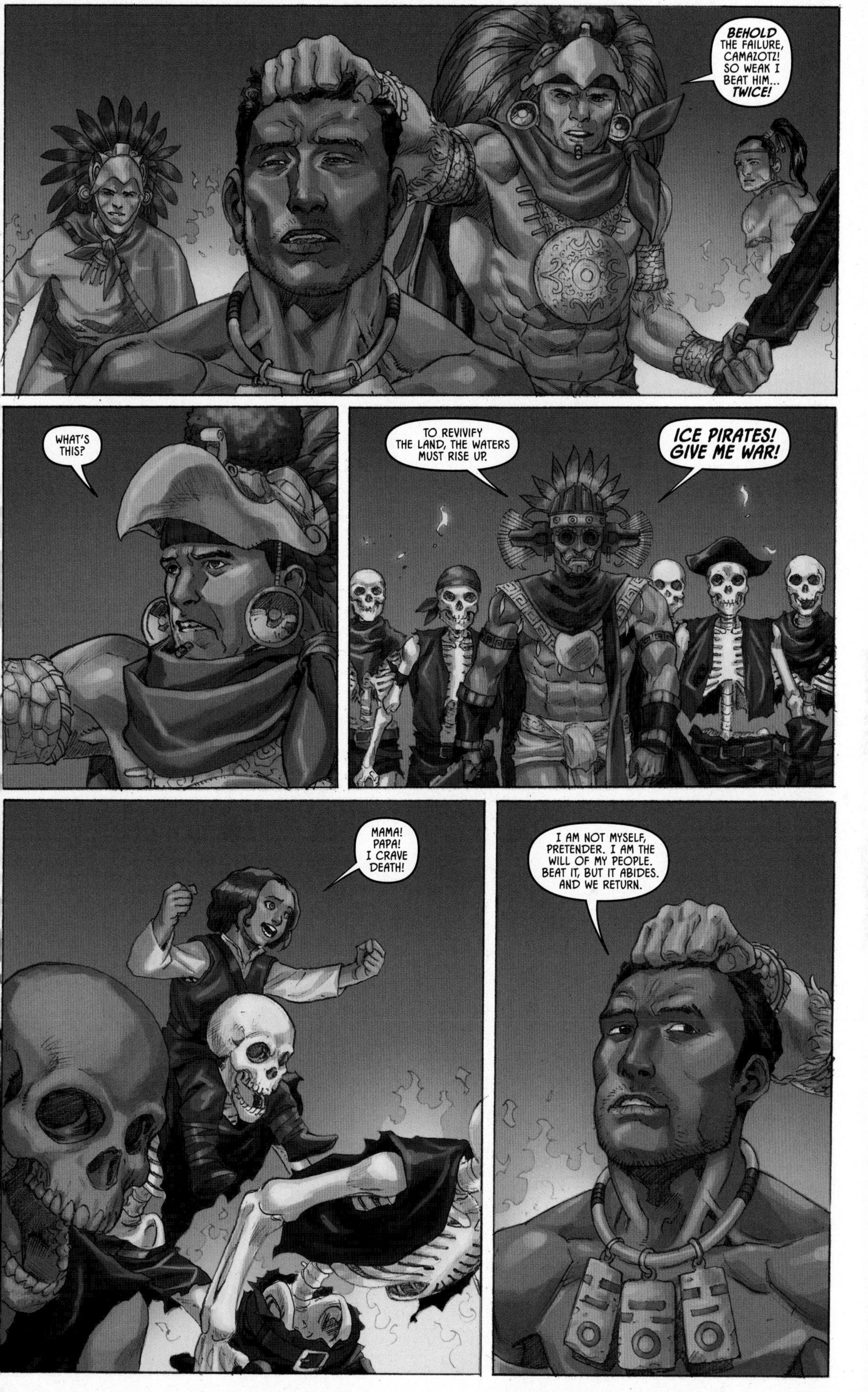
BEHOLD THE FAILURE, CAMAZOTZ! SO WEAK I BEAT HIM... TWICE!
WHAT'S THIS?
TO REVIVIFY THE LAND, THE WATERS MUST RISE UP.
ICE PIRATES! GIVE ME WAR!
MAMA! PAPA! I CRAVE DEATH!
I AM NOT MYSELF, PRETENDER. I AM THE WILL OF MY PEOPLE. BEAT IT, BUT IT ABIDES. AND WE RETURN.

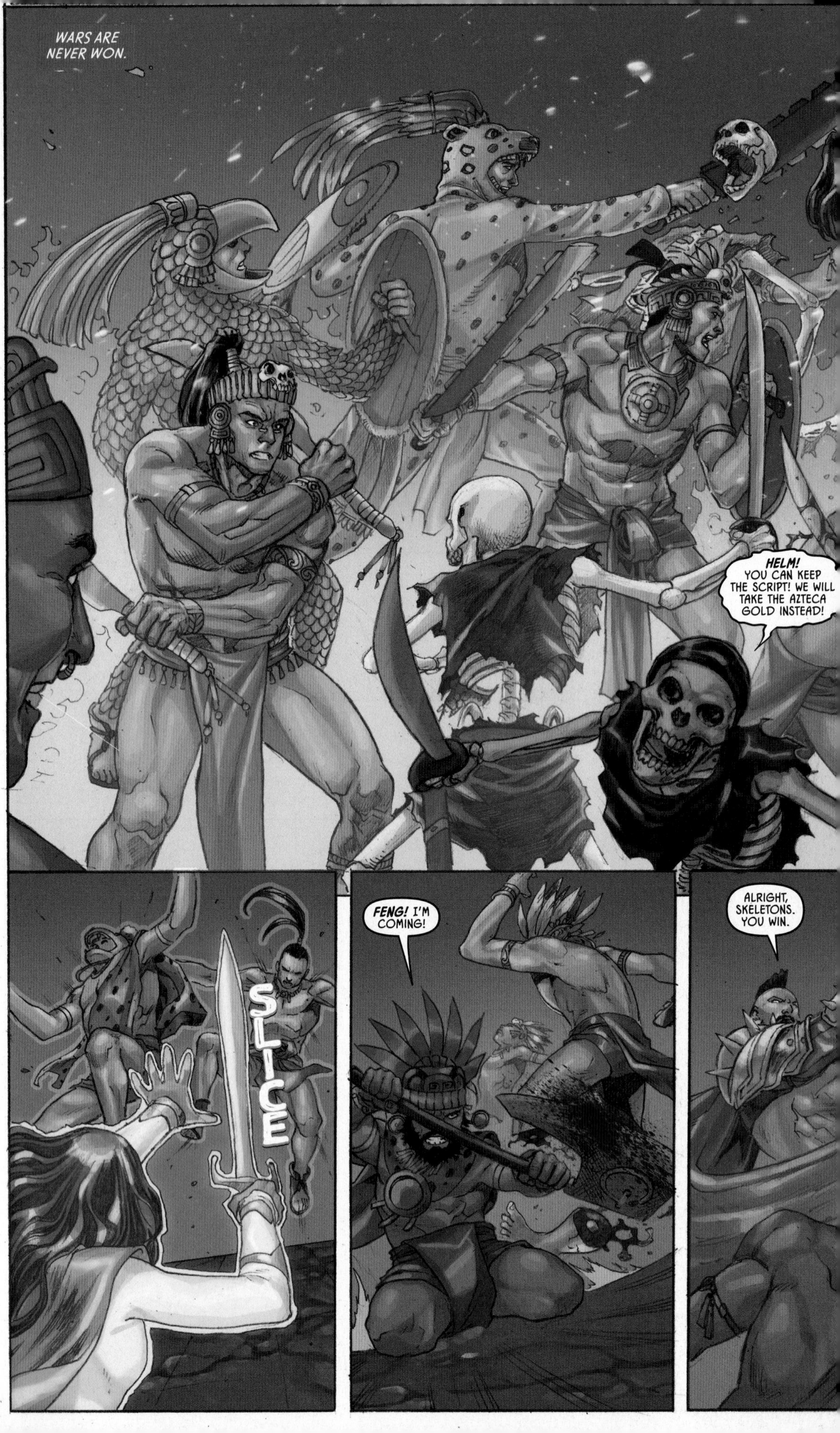
WARS ARE NEVER WON.
HELM! YOU CAN KEEP THE SCRIPT! WE WILL TAKE THE AZTECA GOLD INSTEAD!
SLICE
FENG! I'M COMING!
ALRIGHT, SKELETONS. YOU WIN.

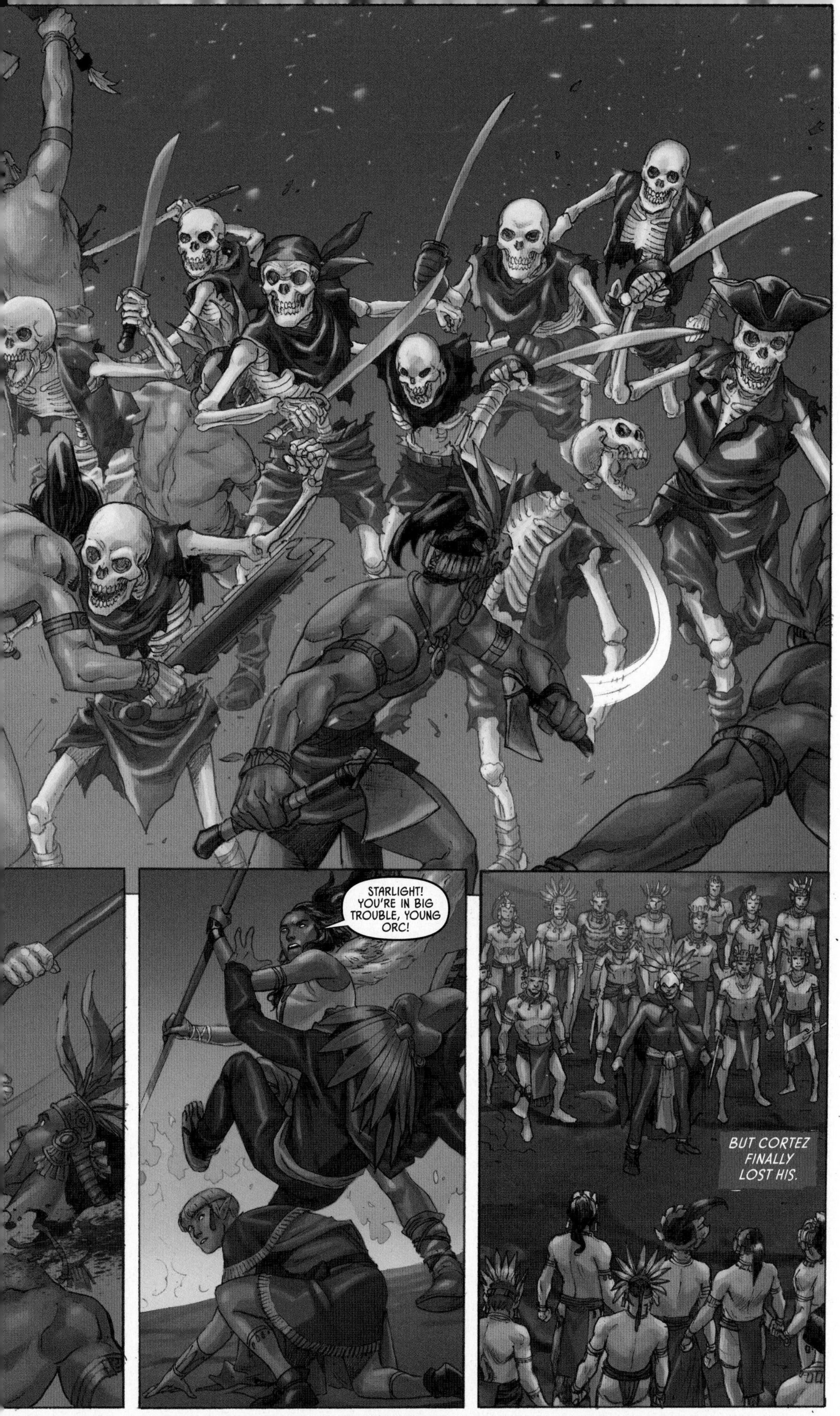
STARLIGHT! YOU'RE IN BIG TROUBLE, YOUNG ORC!
BUT CORTEZ FINALLY LOST HIS.

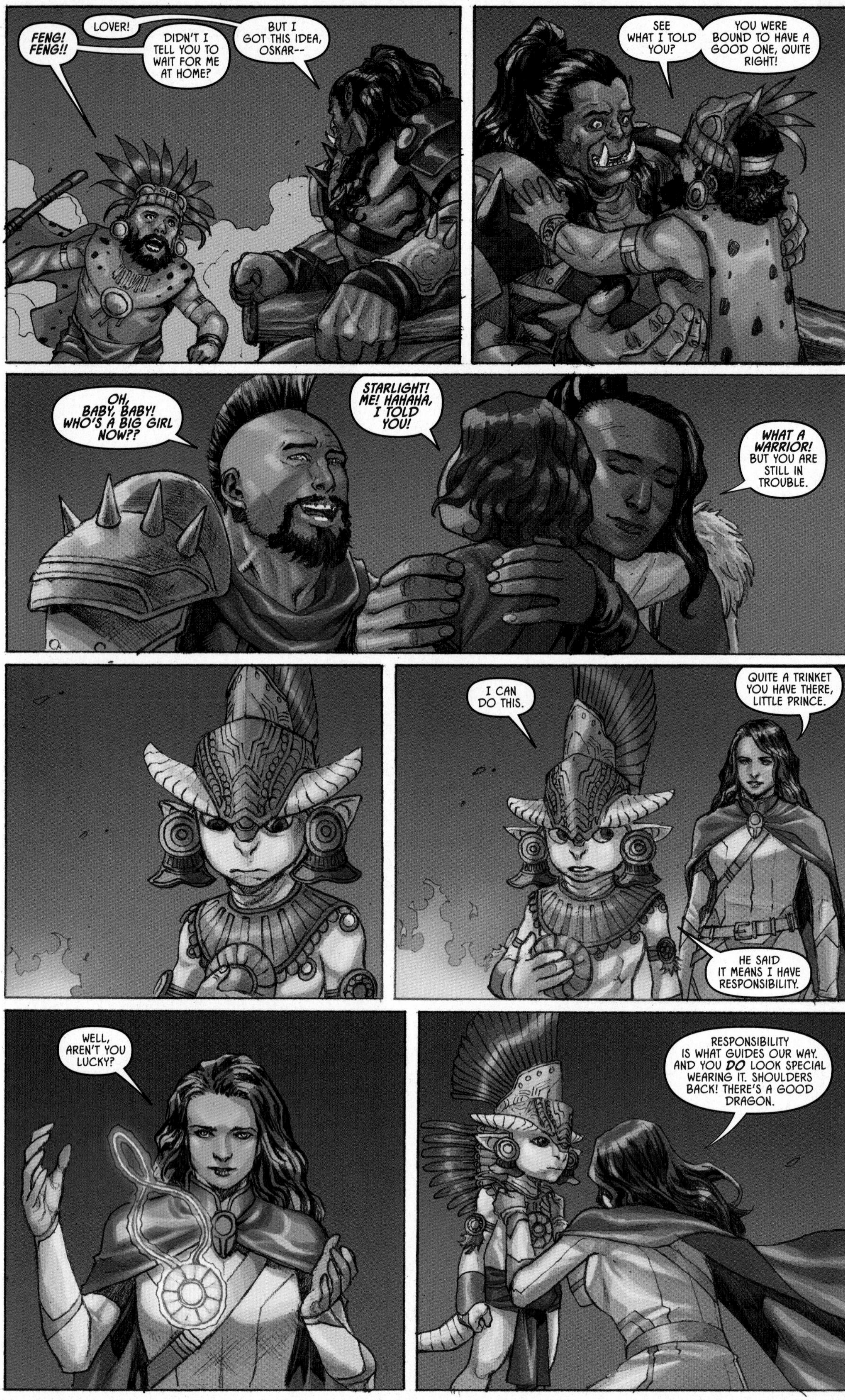
FENG! FENG!!
LOVER!
DIDN'T I TELL YOU TO WAIT FOR ME AT HOME?
BUT I GOT THIS IDEA, OSKAR--
SEE WHAT I TOLD YOU?
YOU WERE BOUND TO HAVE A GOOD ONE, QUITE RIGHT!
OH, BABY, BABY! WHO'S A BIG GIRL NOW??
STARLIGHT! ME! HAHAHA, I TOLD YOU!
WHAT A WARRIOR! BUT YOU ARE STILL IN TROUBLE.
I CAN DO THIS.
QUITE A TRINKET YOU HAVE THERE, LITTLE PRINCE.
HE SAID IT MEANS I HAVE RESPONSIBILITY.
WELL, AREN'T YOU LUCKY?
RESPONSIBILITY IS WHAT GUIDES OUR WAY. AND YOU DO LOOK SPECIAL WEARING IT. SHOULDERS BACK! THERE'S A GOOD DRAGON.

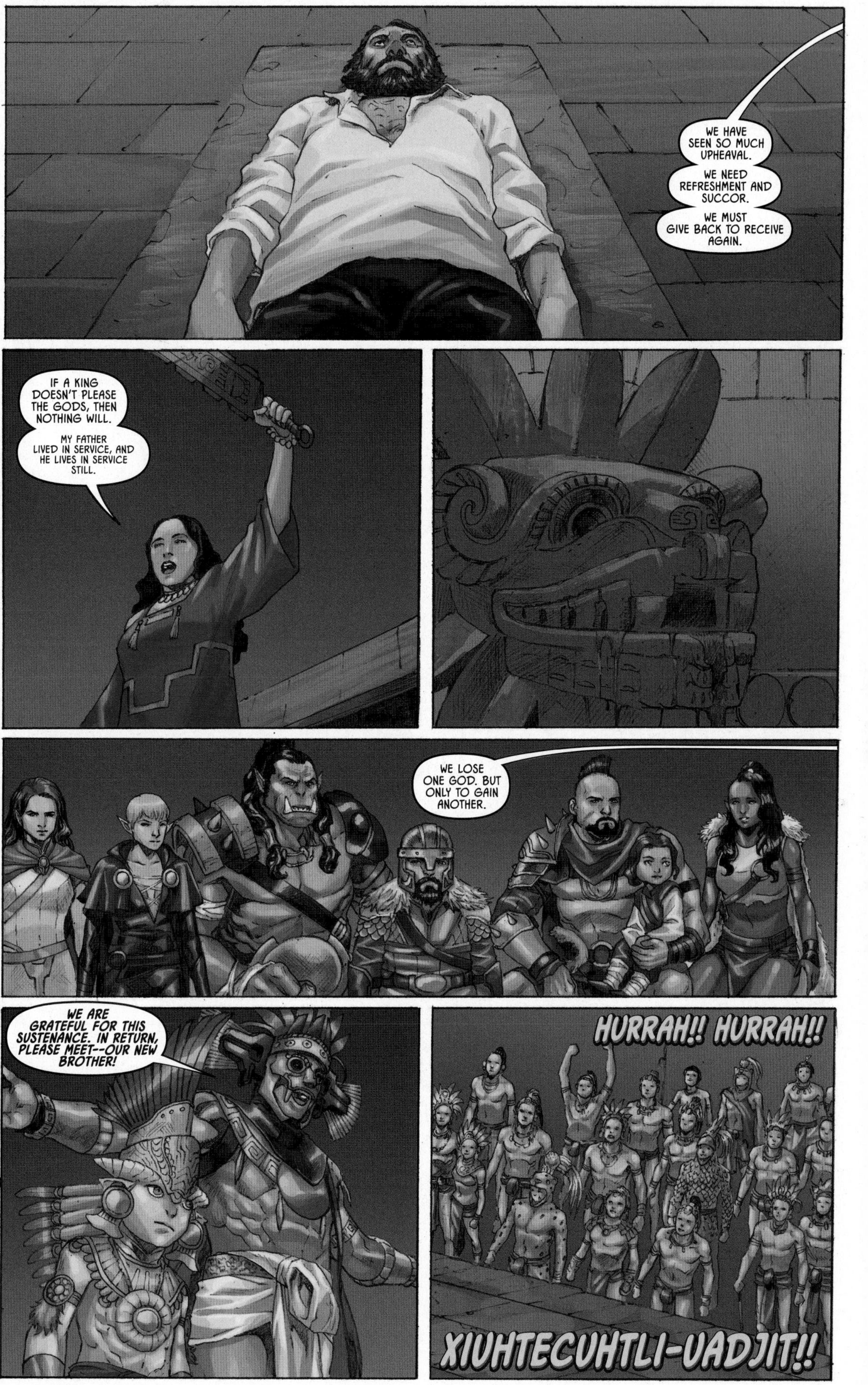
WE HAVE SEEN SO MUCH UPHEAVAL.
WE NEED REFRESHMENT AND SUCCOR.
WE MUST GIVE BACK TO RECEIVE AGAIN.
IF A KING DOESN'T PLEASE THE GODS, THEN NOTHING WILL.
MY FATHER LIVED IN SERVICE, AND HE LIVES IN SERVICE STILL.
WE LOSE ONE GOD. BUT ONLY TO GAIN ANOTHER.
WE ARE GRATEFUL FOR THIS SUSTENANCE. IN RETURN, PLEASE MEET--OUR NEW BROTHER!
HURRAH!! HURRAH!!
XIUHTECUHTLI-UADJIT!!

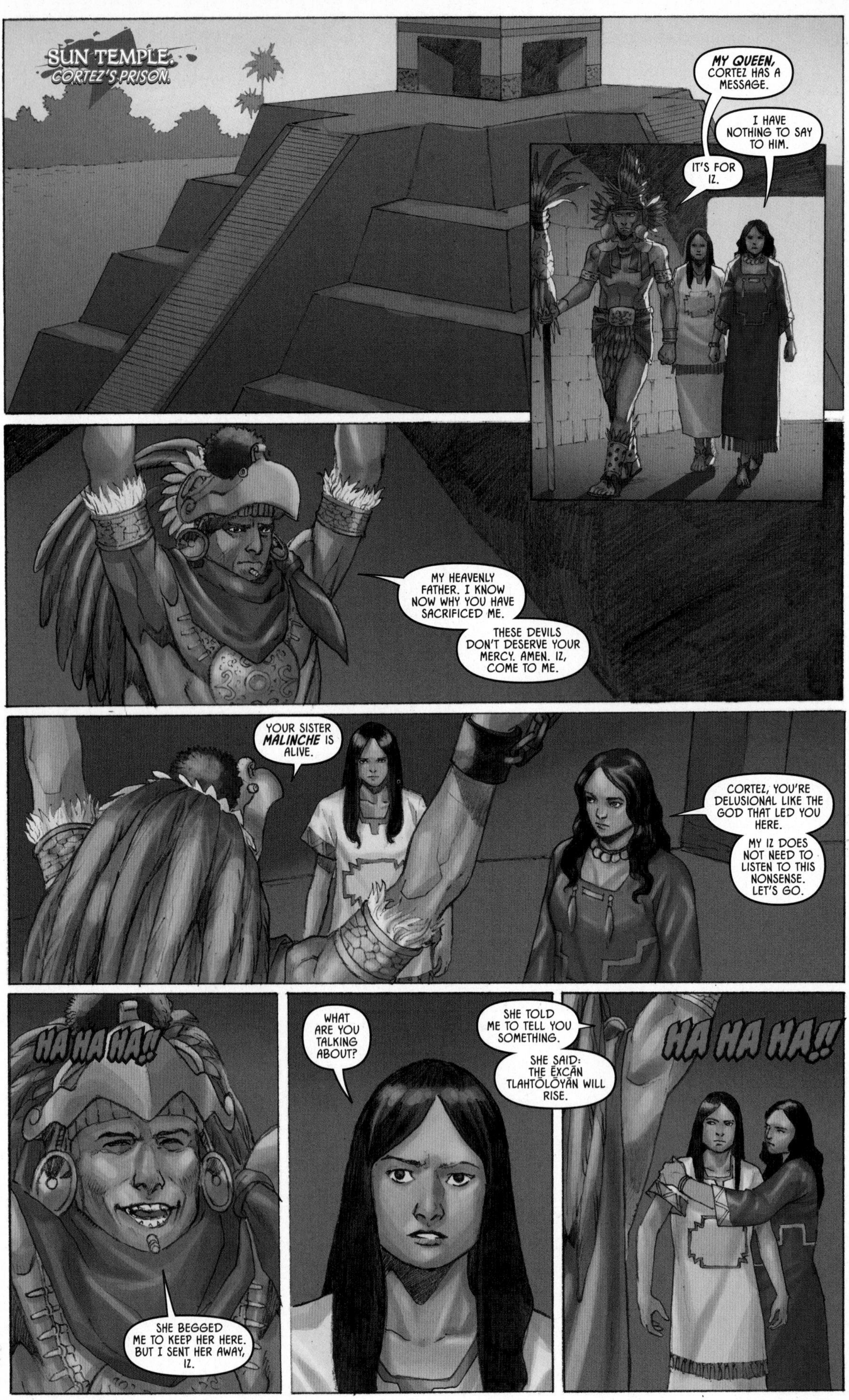
SUN TEMPLE.
CORTEZ'S PRISON.
MY QUEEN, CORTEZ HAS A MESSAGE.
I HAVE NOTHING TO SAY TO HIM.
IT'S FOR IZ.
MY HEAVENLY FATHER. I KNOW NOW WHY YOU HAVE SACRIFICED ME.
THESE DEVILS DON'T DESERVE YOUR MERCY. AMEN. IZ, COME TO ME.
YOUR SISTER *MALINCHE* IS ALIVE.
CORTEZ, YOU'RE DELUSIONAL LIKE THE GOD THAT LED YOU HERE.
MY IZ DOES NOT NEED TO LISTEN TO THIS NONSENSE. LET'S GO.
HA HA HA!!
SHE BEGGED ME TO KEEP HER HERE. BUT I SENT HER AWAY, IZ.
WHAT ARE YOU TALKING ABOUT?
SHE TOLD ME TO TELL YOU SOMETHING.
SHE SAID: THE ĒXCĀN TLAHTŌLŌYĀN WILL RISE.
HA HA HA!!

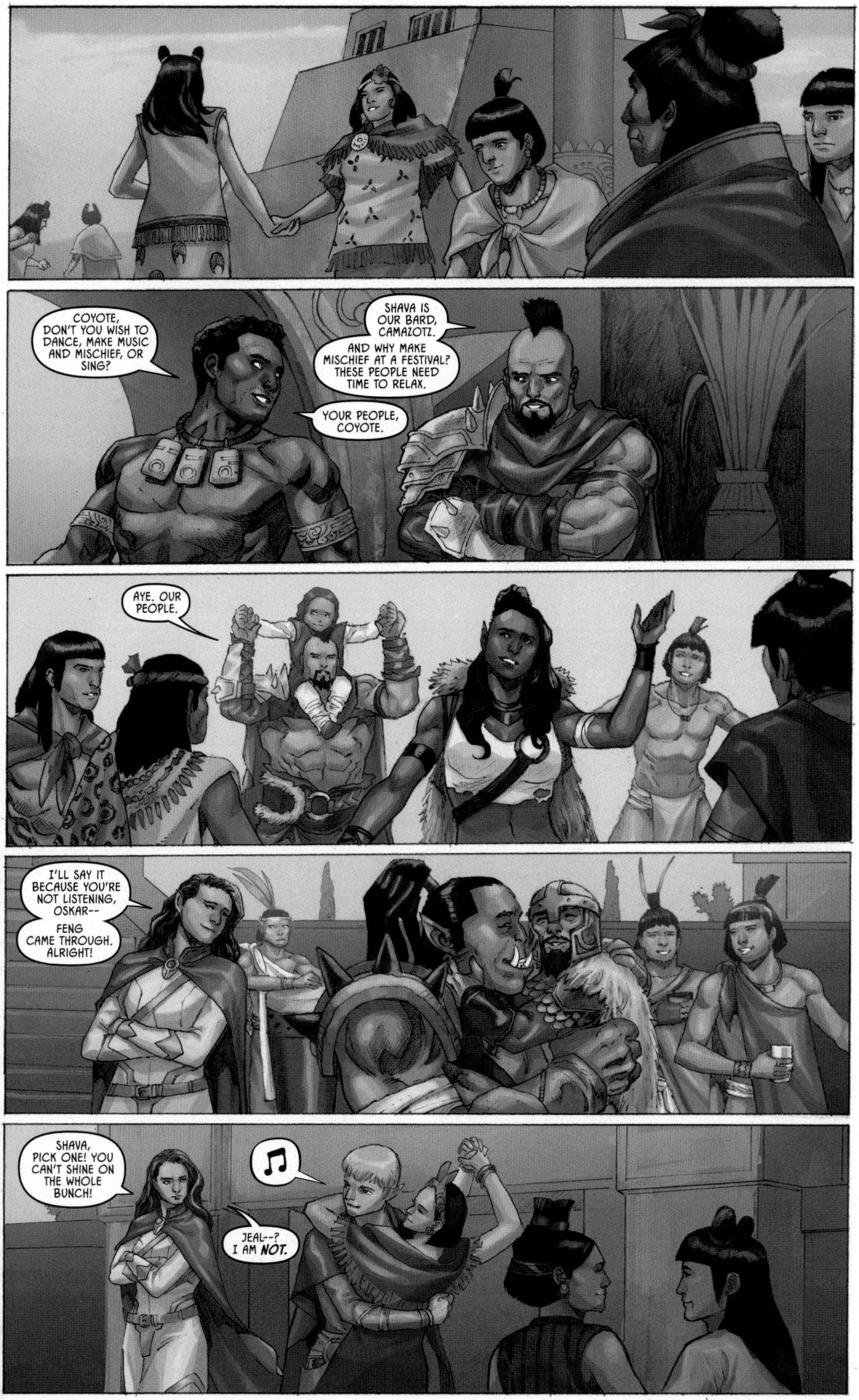
COYOTE, DON'T YOU WISH TO DANCE, MAKE MUSIC AND MISCHIEF, OR SING?
SHAVA IS OUR BARD, CAMAZOTZ.
AND WHY MAKE MISCHIEF AT A FESTIVAL? THESE PEOPLE NEED TIME TO RELAX.
YOUR PEOPLE, COYOTE.
AYE. OUR PEOPLE.
I'LL SAY IT BECAUSE YOU'RE NOT LISTENING, OSKAR--
FENG CAME THROUGH. ALRIGHT!
SHAVA, PICK ONE! YOU CAN'T SHINE ON THE WHOLE BUNCH!
♫
JEAL--? I AM NOT.

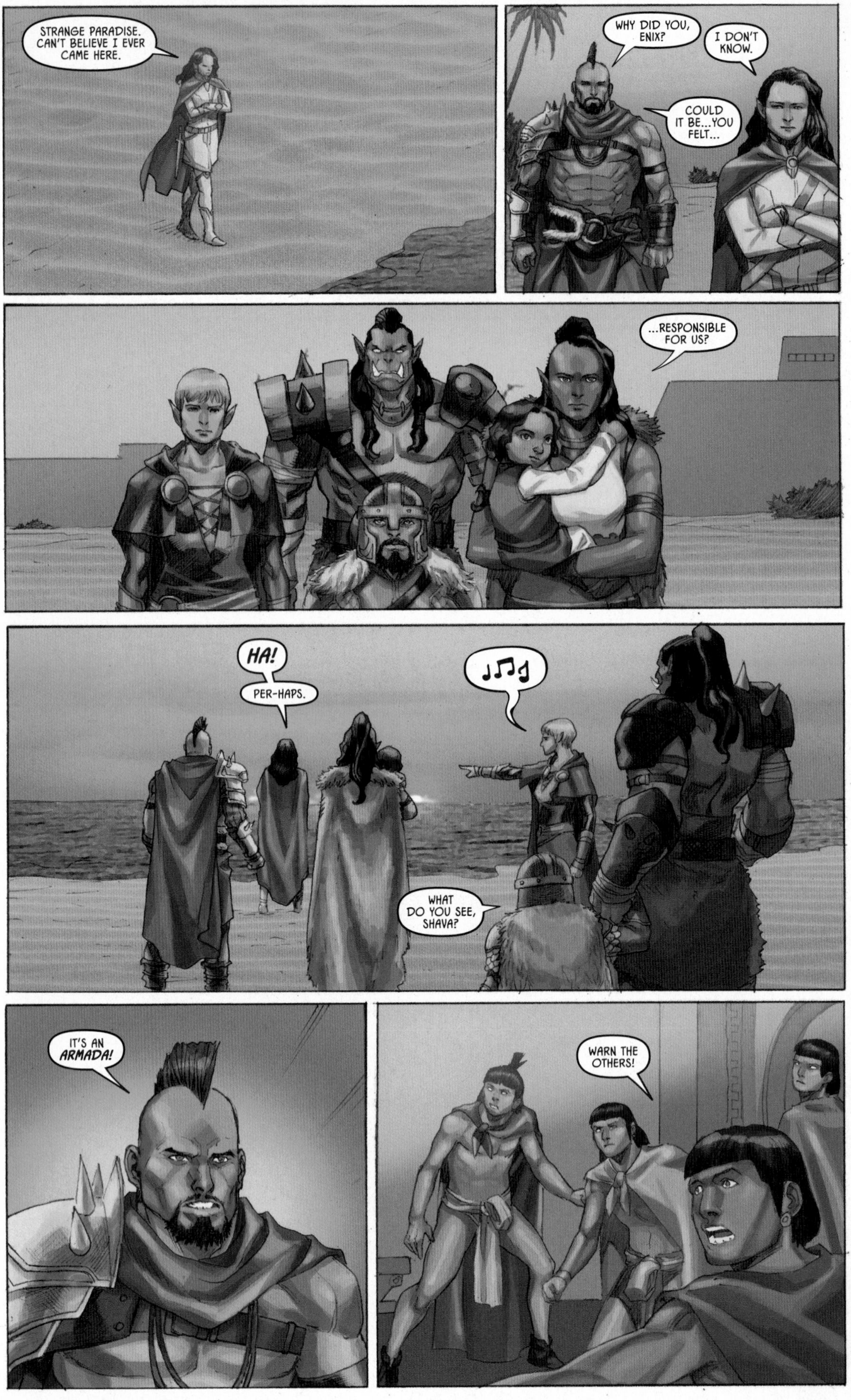
STRANGE PARADISE. CAN'T BELIEVE I EVER CAME HERE.
WHY DID YOU, ENIX?
I DON'T KNOW.
COULD IT BE...YOU FELT...
...RESPONSIBLE FOR US?
HA!
PER-HAPS.
♩♫♩
WHAT DO YOU SEE, SHAVA?
IT'S AN ARMADA!
WARN THE OTHERS!

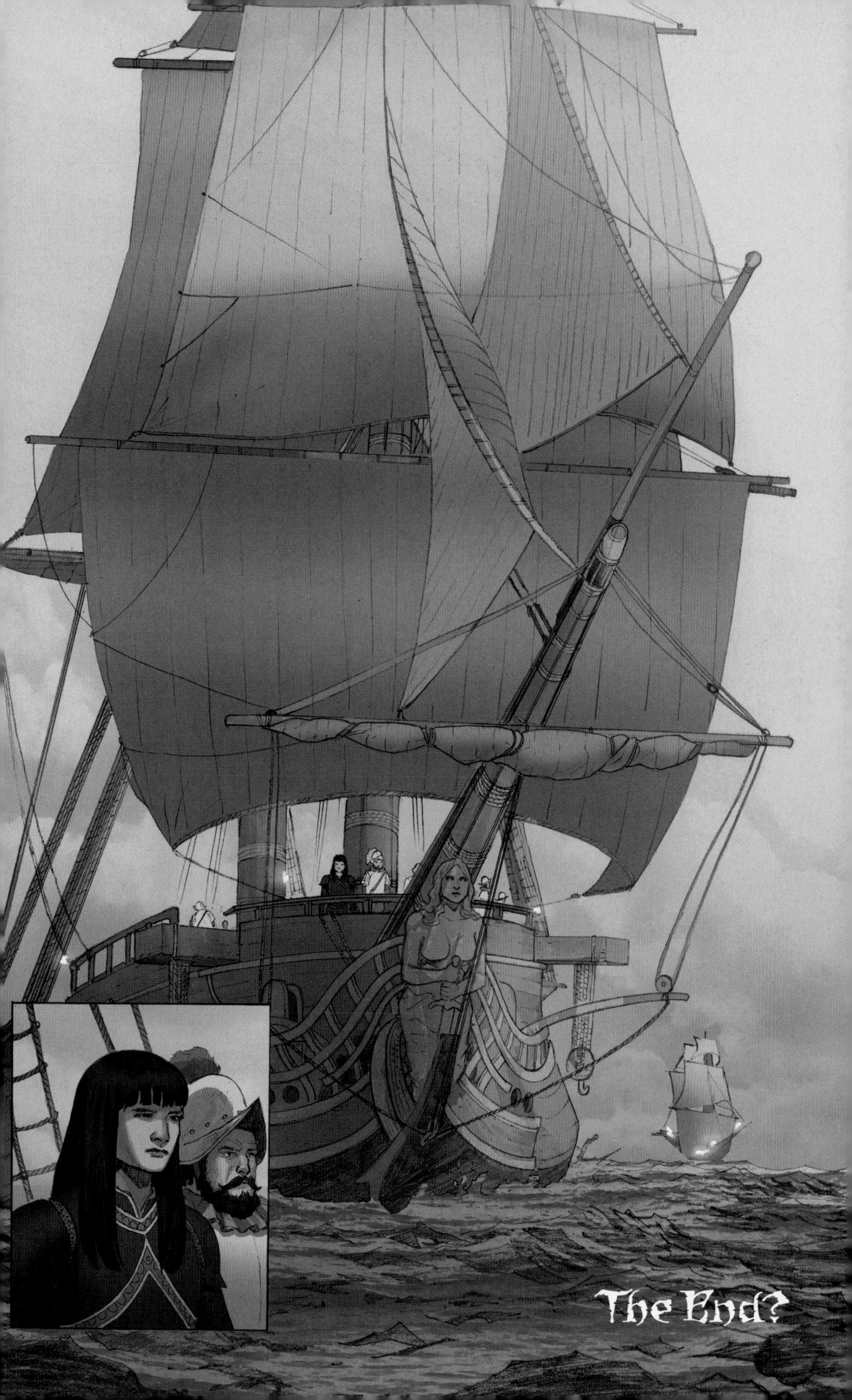
The End?

SACRED ARMOR

game by **TRISTAN J. TARWATER**   art & editor **JEN VAUGHN**

In a village on the outskirts of the Aztec Empire, a dire omen manifests to a group of adventurers charged with obtaining a piece of mythic armor. The future will be full of blood and smoke, but if these adventurers find the Ichcahuipilli of Divination, their town may stand a chance of surviving the fallout of the wars between the Mexica and the mysterious Castillians.

The heat of red blood, the glimmer of black mirrors, the crackle of white electricity: all of this lies in the path of your party in the world of Helm Greycastle!

An adventure for 3–5 players from 4th – 6th level, Sacred Armor invites them to go on a quest to find a fabled piece of armor that will help them face a prophesied threat. Compatible with 5E, adventurers will travel through steaming forests, chilling cave systems, and the mythology of the world of Helm Greycastle to find their desperately needed prize.

In addition to this text, gaming groups will also need:

- SR5D, which will have instructions on how to make characters and run the game. This is available online!
- Dice or dice rolling software.
- The maps included in this adventure.
- Tokens or miniatures to represent characters if using a physical map.

It's a good idea for GMs to read through the adventure to get the narrative down before the gaming session. If you've already got some play under your belt, you already know reading ahead as the GM helps to keep things running smoothly. If you don't, it will give you all the preparation you need!

A Bit About the Setting

Sacred Armor is set in the world of Helm Greycastle, a reimagining of the Mexica/Aztec world. This empire radiated out from the Mexico Valley and included the amazing Tenochtitlan, a jewel of engineering and power, as well as satellite city states, towns, and villages. It incorporated many cultures that were sustained through agriculture, fueled via tribute and war, and steeped in their beliefs of the gods and the order of the world. The technology, environment, and magic make it different from many fantasy RPG settings, but it is equally hazardous, awe-inspiring, and deadly.

Players will have the chance to play Mesoamerican-inspired characters who are more comfortable with obsidian blades than steel and with atole than oat porridge. The world of Helm Greycastle and the gaming adventure you are about to play are not meant to be precisely historically accurate, nor are they meant to be your standard European inspired fantasy setting but with pyramids instead of temples. It is a world inspired and informed by aspects of the Mexica and other Mesoamerican cultures around the time of contact with the Spanish. It is an adventure told within the framework and limitations of 5E game mechanics. And it is an awesome time brought to you by the imaginations of the creators of this amazing comic and what the players and GM bring to the table.

The campaign consists of two arcs: the first arc, where the players are introduced to the world, have social interactions, and receive their quest; and the second arc, where they must fight to show they are worthy to receive the Black Mirror Ichcahuipilli. While hitting all of the spots along the narrative will give your group a few hours of fun, feel free to adapt the adventure to your playstyle, using the info about the location and the comic to build on and modify your campaign.

About the Adventure

When rumors and omens spread fear through the Aztec Empire at a fevered pace, an ominous omen offers a chance of survival to a group of adventurers: an enchanted piece of armor that will protect its wearer from the magic of their enemies. Adventurers will face the dangers of the forest and fantastic adversaries as they follow the call of prophecy.

Before the game: Spend 10–30 minutes figuring out how the players fit into the world and if/ how they know each other. In addition to their player classes, they may have jobs in their town or community; possibilities include farmer, noble, soldier, hunter, teacher, merchant/spy, sex worker, artisan, doctor, and shaman. They may have relatives and families in town, and feelings about the Mexica Empire, the Castillians, or any of the characters, or events in Helm Greycastle.

The Town of Cuappatollitlan

The adventurers begin in Cuappatollitlan, a town on the southeastern border of the empire. It consists of about 60 families who are mostly farmers but also artisans who make pottery and jewelry, weave textiles, paint fabrics, and more. Their homes are made of adobe and have a separate building used for sweat baths. The town has a central plaza with a busy market where people trade their goods for things made in other parts of the empire and other nations. A small pyramid that serves as a temple to the gods rises above the market square.

Fields spread around the outskirts of the town, buffeted by forests and then hills. People grow corn, squashes, chili peppers, beans, and cotton; terraces are built into hillsides to expand farmland and prevent erosion. People keep turkeys and dogs as protein sources and hunt for deer, rabbits, and other animals in the forest. They drink at home, saving public intoxication for holidays where it is appropriate to overindulge in alcohol.

FOR GM TO READ: The golden light of the morning sun begins to illuminate the fog of the small town nestled between the forest and long, thin marsh that eventually gives way to a small river. Waterbirds poke through the mud and reeds for food while bugs hum in the grass. The sounds of the village float on the air: the barking of dogs, warbling of turkeys, and flapping of ducks flying down from their roosts in the trees. Children laugh as their parents call for them while neighbors greet each other on the way to their fields and shops. The air is perfumed with the smell of morning fires and corn, though the first meal of the day isn't for several hours. People carry water back from the river in clay jars. An old woman is selling atole in the village market, and as she sings about her wares, the sound of corn being ground on her metate adds a cheery note.

For GM to know: *The following information details things the townsfolk are all talking about as the players go about their morning routines and get a feel for the setting. The purveyors of the message mentioned here are suggestions! Important information should not be missed just because the players didn't interact with the correct person—they will just get it from a different source. As the GM, make sure your players get the info they need.*

- **A few women carrying water** talk among themselves about rumors they have heard about Emperor Montezuma calling an end to the Flower Wars. While this development led to momentary peace, people are saying towns and villages are taking the opportunity to shore up their forces, attacking each other and taking hostages to sacrifice before they make their moves on the capitol. So far the town hasn't been attacked, but one woman says a nearby village was just raided; the many young people taken by soldiers will either be forced to march to Tenochtitlan or sacrificed to ensure victory.
- **Two old women drinking from gourds** and watching children talk of an influx of jaguars in the area. They wonder what this could mean, as jaguars are jungle animals. No one has been attacked, but large paw prints have been spotted in the fields around the village and some people have reported missing dogs.
- Under the careful watch of **an older man with a cane, two teenage boys with carved sticks** loudly reenact a sword fight between an Aztec soldier and a Castilian soldier, the former berating the latter by calling them a coward and a heathen. This reenactment is inspired by the fact that the Castillians have apparently fled the capitol, getting on their boats and going back over the ocean to wherever they came from.
- **For some reason, merchants are being arrested** and sent to the capitol. Some are saying the Emperor is imprisoning them.The Emperor is also encouraging the use of the strange language the foreigners speak.
- **The Emperor is also encouraging** the use of the strange language spoken by foreigners.
- **A local merchant has** a strange, curved metal object on his blanket next to some clay pots and bows. He says he traded it for a bag of cocoa beans. These objects were seen on the feet of some of the large deer the Castillians rode, which are apparently called "horses." A few people say they can be eaten like other animals, and some were captured after they escaped. While they're dangerous and capable of killing people, their legs are very vulnerable; Castillians have been seen killing horses that suffer from broken legs. It's unclear what the objects on their feet are for, but they are clearly important.

What were Flower Wars?

The Mexica regularly engaged in predesignated battles with rival nations. These battles served political and cultural purposes, helping the Mexicas assert their military prowess as well as ensure a supply of captives for sacrifices as well as dampen the fighting ability of enemies. Because these conflicts have only occurred for roughly the past 70 years, there may be elders who remember the famine that prompted the Flower Wars or the time before this martial campaign of propaganda was a thing.

Colorful Fortunes

NPCs in this interaction
Merchant: Ichtaca
Soldier 1: Yaotl
Soldier 2: Chimalli

A merchant named Ichtaca who arrived before dawn is setting up his wares: thick, green bricks of spirulina; heady spices; and dozens of types of dried chilis that make your eyes water when you bring them to your nose. The two Mexica soldiers flanking his table stare grimly ahead, each armed with a beaded shield and a macuahuitl.

If the PCs try to strike up a conversation, the soldiers are close-lipped, but if pressed they express concern over recent changes in the capitol. A Persuasion check (DC 15) results in the player saying something that wins the soldiers over. An Insight check (DC 15) results in the player seeing that the soldiers and merchants are from the capital, their manner of speech and the merchant's clothes more common among more urban citizens of the empire. The soldiers and Ichtaca have been on the road for a few weeks and while they are tired of travelling, they are not eager to get back. The rumors of some of the changes the Emperor has been making concern the soldiers, though they do not say they disagree with him outright. The merchant is dismissive of their worries, even when the local raids are mentioned. When the soldiers mention that many merchants are being summoned back to the capitol in order to report to the Emperor, Ichtaca becomes flustered. He feels confident that he will be allowed to continue his business uninterrupted, with the two soldiers at his disposal.

The PCs should not feel inclined to fight the armed soldiers, as they are mostly there to protect the merchant, doing nothing to provoke anyone. An Intelligence Check (DC 10) tells players they are decorated soldiers who have fought in battles and killed enemies before. An Insight Check (DC 15) reveals the soldiers are torn; if they are summoned back to the capital, they are not sure what they will do if the Emperor orders them to do something they think is against their way of life.

The merchant is looking to hire some people in the village and the party fits the bill. He has heard a rumor that some peculiar jungle parrots have made their way to an area about a day's walk away: If the adventurers can procure the parrots, they will be compensated in the form of cocoa beans and cotton, and he will put in a good word for them with his boss if they want to do this kind of work in the future. (The merchant is trying to get promoted within his guild and procuring these parrots will definitely impress his superior given their bright feathers.) He provides the adventurers with a hastily drawn map and a bag of high-quality cornmeal mixed with spices to make atole, basically providing their provisions for the trip. He will pay 50 cocoa beans for each parrot they find, but if they find a rare Quetzal bird, he will pay 100 coca beans, or 1 piece of fine cotton.

Parroting

The first activity is a simple traipse through the rainforest as the adventurers try to find parrots to take back to the merchant. The party can use this day-long walk to talk over the information they heard in the village.

FOR GM TO READ: The sounds of civilization melt away as you walk down the path into the forest. A pair of hunters carrying rabbits passes you, and they say hello as they head back to the town.

You approach the location on the map that the merchant has given you. A flash of red out of the corner of your eye blazes as the cry of the macaw echoes through the air. The sound of the birds in this part of the forest is strange. Bright colors occasionally flash through the leaves.

For GM to know: *Through a combination of Nature, Animal Handling checks and/or attack roles, the adventures can find and capture several parrots. Please refer to the table on the next page to determine what they catch. The birds are not in their natural habitat and so are easy to spot in the sparser foliage of the forest. They player can try to catch each bird individually with standard attack rolls, or attempt to trap the birds with a net, or other type of trap. The birds are cinsidered Tiny creatures.*

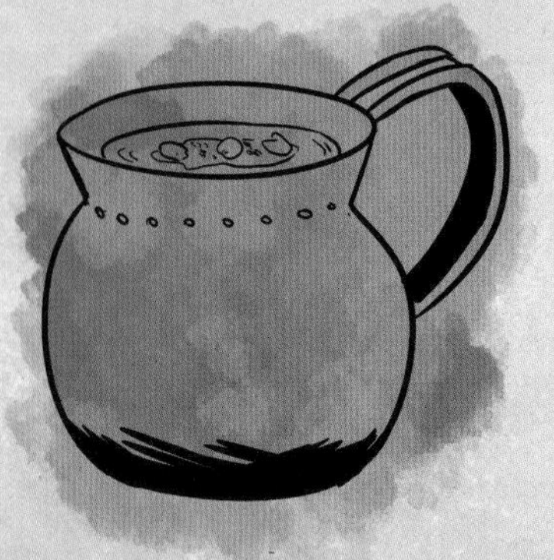

TYPE OF BIRD	AC	PERCENTAGE (roll a d100)
Squirrel Cuckoo	11	00-40%
Scarlet Macaw	13	41-55%
Hyacinth Macaw	14	56-70%
Military Macaw	13	71-90%
Quetzal Bird	16	91-100%

Omen

FOR GM TO READ: Sounds ripple through the forest—crackling wood, whipping winds, and the screams of birds. A weird, deep warbling emits from the bush as something large crashes through the greenery. The light in the forest drops as if a cloud has crossed the face of the sun, and suddenly the air stills, sticky humidity enveloping you as the forest goes completely silent.

A beast of strange proportions leaps out from the forest like a peculiar deer, robust and brown, screaming strangely. Its hooves flash in the scant light as it rears up on its back legs. Hot red blood streams from wounds on its body, which is covered in both odd ropes and metal plates that clank when it moves, filling the air with a metallic smell.

A giant eagle with blue-tinged feathers sits atop the beast's head, talons dug into its skull. The bird's wings are spread wide, and it tears at the flesh on the strange beast's face and neck with its sharp beak. The beast's slender legs—kicking in vain—finally buckle as it crashes to the ground.

The mysterious bird doesn't open its mouth, but as it looks at the adventurers, they hear a voice in their heads which says:

> ***Death worse than this approaches from the east. In the Cave of Cold Lightning, the Black Mirror Ichcahuipilli is the key to protecting you from your enemies.***

The bird then beats its large wings as if to fly off, but it simply disappears before your eyes as the beast it harried lies dead on the ground, blood pooling around its head.

For GM to Know: *A Nature check (DC 15) confirms that this is a horse, one of the strange creatures the Castilians brought with them from over the water.*

The ropes and plates it wears are a well-used leather saddle, a bridle, and light armor. In addition to the wounds it sustained on its face, it also has broken arrows sticking out of the flesh on its back haunches. They are made of obsidian, which is typical of Aztec arrowheads. The saddle is stained red and brown with blood.

In the saddle bag are the following objects:

- **A map of Tenochtitlan** and the surrounding area, written in Nahuatl and Spanish
- **A rosary of wooden beads** (An Intelligence (Nature) check of 15 reveals they are made of boxwood, but not from any type that grows in the area)
- **A handkerchief** embroidered with roses
- **Some dried meat and hard bread**, both very salty
- **A diary** written in Spanish*

By casting Comprehend Languages or with a Wisdom check of 17, the book is revealed to be the log of a conquistador that talks about the area, the land, and their impression of the Aztecs, which is a bit black and white. They are convinced the Aztecs worship demons yet cannot help but admit they are a very clean, orderly people with beautiful cities and farms, pleasing in their features and polite in their manners. How such a beautiful place could be fueled by so much violence and blood defies all logic. There are also passages about gold and the shock with which Aztecs respond to its use, as they value the substance for its beauty but don't use it for money.

Despite the saddle and bridle, the horse's rider is nowhere to be found. Players can make an Investigation or Perception check to track the origins of the horse. DC 15 reveals the tracks came from the north and started abruptly. DC 20 reveals the tracks came from the direction of the capitol and that the hoof marks are deep; it looks as if the beast was dropped from a considerable height. There is no trace of any humanoids in the forest, but as the players approach the place that seems to be the origin of the tracks, the forest is quieter, the sounds of birds and insects dampened.

The walk back to the village is uneventful, and when they arrive, it is as busy as any other day. The merchant is delighted to see the parrots the party has procured for him, and he pays them handsomely in cocoa beans.

If the adventurers do not know where to go to have the omen read, they can roll an Intelligence (Arcana or Religion DC 10) to realize they should go to the temple and see the high priestess.

The Reading of the Signs

NPCs in this interaction
High Priestess: Teoxihuitl

For GM to Know: *The steps up to the temple, while not steep, are many. The high priestess stands atop them on the temple platform and wears a green skirt and xicolli.*

She listens to the story of the travelers, her eyes glinting with excitement as they speak of the Ichcahuipilli of Mirrors, and asks them to come into the temple. Copal incense is burning on the pyre and two priests are kneeling before the altar, their hands covered in blood. They do not notice the priestess or the adventurers as they walk by.

FOR GM TO READ: The priestess pulls out a piece of paper and begins to paint a map. Deep in the forest several days from the town is a very cold lake, its water black as obsidian. It used to be a mirror of the sky, and those who knew how could read the future in its reflection. An island sprung up from the water when the great warrior Tlacalal asked the god of the earth to hide the armor "until a great change is needed in the land again." The island "broke" the mirror of the lake, and the warrior descended into the earth to hide the armor.

The adventurers must travel south beyond the lands of the Aztecs and into the cloud forest to reach this place. The priestess invites them to sleep in the temple while she intercedes on their behalf to be sure this is the right path.

The party can sleep for the night and get ready to leave the next day with the aid of the priestess and any NPCs they befriend. For the journey, the priestess gives them the following:

The players may level their characters, having accepted the intercession of the priestess.

- **Two potions** of Cure Moderate Wounds per player
- **Enough food for the trip** (cornmeal, dried chilis, etc)

Entering the World of Legend

FOR GM TO READ: The familiar landscape gives way to thickening trees and lush greenery. Birds call to each other in the sun-dappled understory as insects swarm and skitter over the leaf-littered ground. The light that reaches the very bottom of the rainforest is scattered at best—splotches of yellow light that manage to creep between spaces in the canopy. Clouds hug the ground, giving way to clearings, only to rise up again from the ground. The occasional snap of twigs overhead is followed by the scampering of a monkey or the flight of a colorful parrot. Insects of all sizes, from tiny yet dangerous ants to large and gorgeous butterflies hum and move about. The air is thick with humidity and heat as well as the smells of warm greenery and decaying plant matter.

It is a two- to three-day trek from the town to the location the priestess has directed you to. The map indicates there are three stone monoliths along the way; each bears a symbol—a glyph of a mirror with an axe above it—that will indicate which way the adventurers should go. If they put the symbol to their back and head away from it, they will hit the next landmark.

For GM to Know: Each monolith is surrounded by stone ruins covered in overgrown plants, and a Nature check (DC 15) reveals they have been abandoned for more than five generations. The walls that still stand are carved with images of people and animals. Parts of the artwork seem to have been destroyed, the stone chipped away. Trees and vines grow over what were once cultivated fields. Orchards grow in abundance by the ruins, bearing fruit for those who pass by.

As the adventurers travel between monoliths, the remnants of roads occasionally show themselves, and stone markers spanning the waterways indicate bridges once existed. But they see no one along the way.

Energy Crackles Over the Broken Bowl of Divination

FOR GM TO READ: Ahead is a clearing filled by what appears to be fog. Silence engulfs everything until the only sounds are water lapping at a nearby shore and your own heartbeat. A blue light shines in the fog, growing in intensity as the adventurers draw near but remaining distorted by the thick fog. As the party steps out of the forest, a wild wind picks up, whistling through the trees and scattering the fog like an invisible hand pulling back a blanket. A lake so still it resembles a piece of polished obsidian stretches before you, the air above it now humming with energy. Mangrove trees surround the water, and any animals within their branches or among their arching roots are still and silent. At the center of the lake is an intriguing blue light emanating from a cave on a small island.

A splash sounds somewhere from over the lake, followed by a crackle and a zap. The smell of ozone permeates the air. Yet the surface of the water is still, and though it's crystal clear, the dark, rich earth of its bottom makes it appear black as night. Occasionally something partially buried in the lake bottom catches the light, the glint of something fleeting, gone as soon as it is perceived.

For GM to Know: No stones lie between the shore and the small island. While the island is not in the center of the lake, it is, at the very closest, 100 ft. from the shore. There is no boat along the entire bank of the lake, nor any sign of human life. There are animal tracks in the mud. A DC 15 Nature check reveals the tracks to be those of deer and jaguars.

Within the pool are either multiple regularly-sized electric eels or a giant electric eel. Please refer to the chart below to determine the encounter. Electric eels obtain a majority of their oxygen from the air and surface every 10–15 minutes to breathe. In addition, they have been known to leap out of the water to attack predators with their electric charge.

Electric Eel
Medium-sized beast, unaligned

STR	DEX	CON	INT	WIS	CHA
10	11 (+0)	10 (+0)	3 (-4)	13 (+1)	3 (-4)

AC:
12 (natural armor)

Hit Points:
30

Speed:
0 ft., swim 30 ft.

Damage Immunity: lightning
Skills: Perception +4

Senses: passive Perception 15
Languages: ---

Challenge: 1 (200 XP)

Electric Senses: An electric eel has advantage on Wisdom (perception) checks on live creatures in the same body of water it is in.
Shocking Tactics: An electric eel will try to stun its opponent before attacking with its Bite.

ACTIONS
Shock: The electric eel lets out an electric charge when it perceives a threat. Creatures within a 20-ft radius of the electric eel take 1d10 + 4 lightning damage and must make a Constitution check (DC 12) or be stunned. Once per round, on the player's initiative, the player may make another saving throw; if they succeed, they are no longer stunned.

Bite: Melee Weapon Attack + 4 to hit, reach 5 ft one creature. 1d8 + 2 crushing damage as the electric eel tries to suction chunks of its victims into its wide mouth.

Giant Electric Eel

Large sized beast, unaligned

	STR	DEX	CON	INT	WIS	CHA
	14	9	14	5	15	5

AC:
15 (natural armor)

Hit Points:
40

Speed:
0 ft., swim 40 ft.

Damage Immunity: lightning
Skills: Perception +5

Senses: passive Perception 15
Languages: ---

Challenge: 3 (700 XP)

Electric Senses: The giant electric eel has advantage on Wisdom (Perception) checks against any living creature in the same body of water.

Shocking Tactics: A giant electric eel will try to stun its opponent before attacking with its Bite.

ACTIONS

Shock: The electric eel lets out an electric charge when it perceives a threat. Creatures within a 30-ft radius of the electric eel take 2d8+ 6 lightning damage and must make a Constitution check (DC 15) or be stunned. Once per round, on the player's initiative, the player may make another saving throw; if it succeeds, they are no longer stunned.

Electric Bubble: Ranged Weapon +4 to hit, 1d6 + 2 lightning damage Stunned, save takes half and is not stunned. This attack can be done in the water or above water.

Bite: +5 to hit, reach one creature 2d6 + 2 crushing damage as it tries to suck up its victims with its large, wide mouth.

Please refer to the table to determine the encounter for the party. Eels may take turns using Shock, giving other Eels the opportunity to use their Bite attack. To streamline gameplay, if on their initiative multiple Eels use Shock, have players roll one save vs. all the Eels rolls.

LEVEL	ENEMY CREATURES
Level 4	4 Electric Eels or 1 Giant Electric Eel and 1 Electric Eel
Level 5	5 Electric Eels or 1 Giant Electric Eel and 3 Electric Eels
Level 6	7 Electric Eels or 2 Giant Electric Eels and 2 Electric Eels

(Table assumes party size of four players; may be adjusted for smaller or larger parties)

With the electric eels vanquished, the players are free to investigate the glints of light at the bottom of the lake. They turn out to be obsidian arrowheads and spear tips, some shattered. There are also many small jade and gold beads and a single pair of coral earrings.

Into the Cave

FOR GM TO READ: The interior of the cave glimmers, its walls completely encrusted with crystals; it's like stepping into a geode. The glow you saw was merely the light scattering across the facets of the millions of surfaces. The colors range from completely transparent to inky black and every shade of grey in between. The crystals range from short nubs to large clusters of points; regardless of size, they are very sharp to the touch. Even the floor is covered in the crystalline structures, their uneven surface felt through the soles of your footwear.

In the center of the cave is a hole in the ground that leads to a spiral staircase, which descends below the surface of the lake. Sound bounces off the rough surfaces of the walls and floor strangely, and the winding staircase is wide enough to accommodate people descending single file at first. It then widens so that two medium-sized individuals can stand side by side.

The air is cold and damp, with the occasional drip of condensation on the glimmering walls. The staircase leads to an empty chamber, devoid of light.

For the GM to Know: *If the players have a light, they notice something laying across the bottommost step of the staircase: a skeleton. A hole in the back of the skull gives the likely cause of death, but there are no spear or arrow points among the remains. Upon a successful Investigation DC check of 16, it looks like the body wore armor made from bones, a collection of straight, white bones as long as a human finger, scattered among the ribcage. In addition, the hole in the skull is rimmed black, as if the edges of the bone burned. A lone black beetle scuttles out from among the bones, disturbed by the movement of the remains. A few beads made of jade and coral are scattered around the body, the remnants of an ornate collar worn by the deceased warrior.*

Setting: A cavern with walls 20 ft. high and 100 ft. in diameter. The spiral staircase the PCs came down is in the center of the room. There are four stone pillars, each of which are 30 ft. from the staircase. The terrain is slightly sloped and standing water covers about half of the cavern floor, which is littered with bones that are scattered among the jagged facets of the crystals. Lying in wait in the standing water are the Axolotl Warriors, camouflaged against the water and stone texture of the floor (Perception DC 20 to see them).

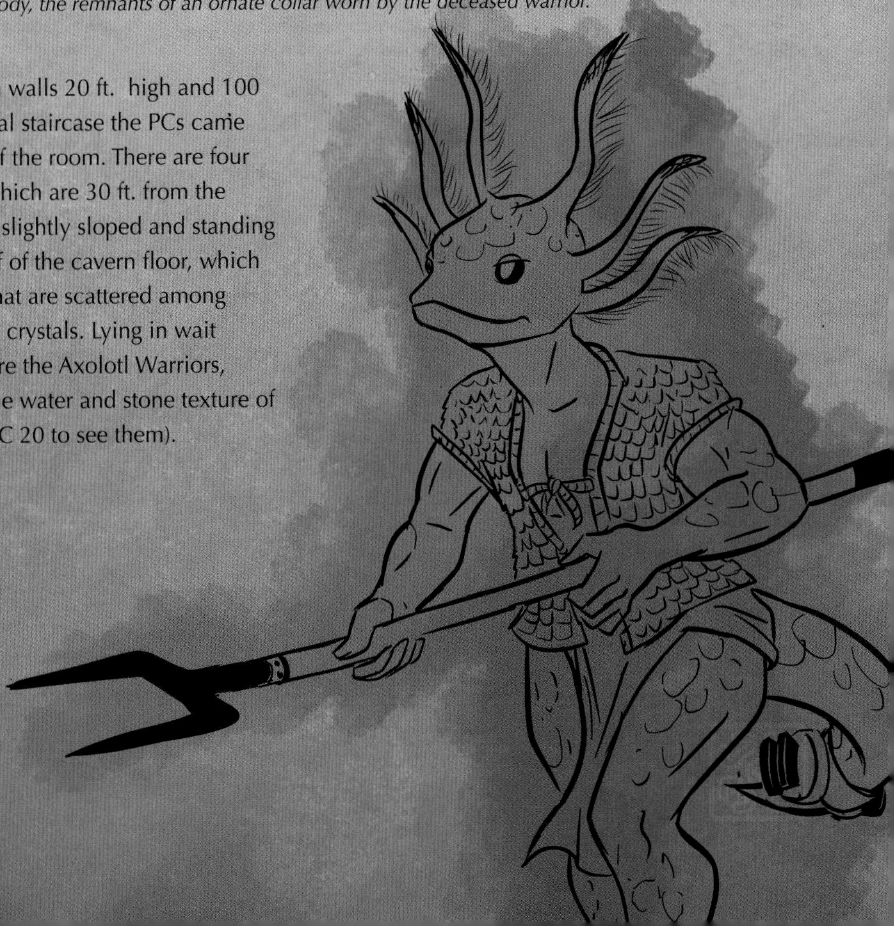

As soon as any warm-blooded creature gets within 50 ft. of any Axolotl Warrior, it wakes up from its slumber. The dark beings begin to glow as a crackling sound bounces off the walls. As they stand erect, sparks ripple through their feathery gills. Their blank expressions are discordant with the fighting stance they take as they point their shining spears at the intruders.

Axolotl Warriors
Medium humanoid

STR	DEX	CON	INT	WIS	CHA
15	10	14	9	13	5

AC:
15 (natural armor)

Hit Points:
30

Speed:
30 ft., swim 30 ft.

Skills: Perception +5, Stealth +5
Senses: Passive Perception 15, Blindsight

Languages: ---
Challenge: 2 (450 XP)

Misplaced Warmth: The Axolotl Warrior can sense a warm-blooded creature within a 50-foot radius.

ACTIONS
Spear: +5 to hit, 1d6 + 2 piercing

Lightning Fast: The Axolotl Warrior makes two melee attacks with their spear.

Shocking Success: On a successful hit, the Axolotl Warrior may try to stun the character by sending anelectric shock through the spear as a Free Action. The player must make a Constitution Save (DC 13). On a failure the player takes 1d6 + 4 lightning damage and is Stunned. On a successful save, the player takes half damage and isn't Stunned. The player can reroll the save at the start of their turn.

Surprising Lunge: If the Axolotl Warrior is within 5 ft. of an enemy, it can use its Move to Feint, rolling against the player's Wisdom (Perception DC: 10) roll. On a success, the Axolotl lunges at the target and delivers a Bite (+2 to hit) for 1d6 crushing damage and 1d4 lightning damage. The target must save against the lightning damage (DC 13) or be Stunned. Save takes half damage and isn't stunned.

Throughout the fight the Axolotl Warriors scream at the players in their monotone, hissing voices Only the worthy shall leave with what they desire. Your strength or your blood shall bloom in this sacred place. We will show your hearts to the gods.

Refer to the following table to see how many Axolotl Warriors to include in the encounter.

LEVEL	ENEMY CREATURES
Level 4	4 Axolotl Warriors
Level 5	5 Axolotl Warriors
Level 6	6 Axolotl Warriors

FOR GM TO READ: Once the Axolotl Warriors have been defeated, the smell of copal fills the cave. Of the four pillars, only the one at the north end of the cave is carved to look like a being. Its face is the fierce visage of a jaguar, its mouth open in a soundless snarl full of sharp teeth, and it "wears" an ichcahuipilli. At the base of the statue, an inscription reads:

Blood brings about the future. Sacrifice summons tomorrow.

As the inscription is read, the teeth of the statue gleam.

For the GM to Know: *The Black Mirror Ichcahuipilli is summoned when the adventurers offer their own blood to the statue, placing any amount in its mouth. A Religion or Arcana check (DC 12) has players recall the importance of blood sacrifice to the deities and recognizes the teeth of the statue as looking similar to the tools priests and nobles use to perform bloodletting rituals on themselves. The Ichcahuipilli pattern on the statue becomes the Black Mirror Ichcahuipilli, which the adventurers can remove.*

Black Mirror Ichcahuipilli

Mundane ichcahuipilli are dipped into salt water, and the salt crystallizes within the layers of cotton as the water evaporates, hardening the armor and making it impervious to arrows. The Ichcahuipilli of Divination, however, has been dipped in waters used for divination, and its magical properties have imbued the protective garment with the following properties:

The Black Mirror Ichcahuipilli

Armor (padded) legendary, requires attunement

The Ichicahuipilli is a tight-fitting garment worn on the torso. It is secured with ties at the front that are made of thick, stark-white quilted fabric stuffed with cotton fiber. It has short sleeves and extends past the waist. From afar the Ichcahuipilli appears white, but up close is a scintillating black, having absorbed the magical energy of the waters of divination.

The Black Mirror Ichcahuipilli is a legendary item, created by Tezcatlipoca for the warrior Tlacalel. It does not deflect arrows but rather catches them, and it is efficient against macuahuitl. The stats for the Ichcahuipilli are as follows:

Light armor
13+ Dex modifier
Weight: 9 lbs.

Damage Resistance: +5 piercing and slashing weapons
All attacks against the wearer are done at disadvantage. All attack rolls the wearer makes are at advantage.

Divined Duel
Once per day at the beginning of an encounter, the wearer may choose one enemy. The wearer gets an additional action they may use on the enemy's initiative, as if the enemy's initiative triggers an action. After the enemy's action, the player may take their action and choose to have it happen before or after the enemy's action. If the enemy falls out of initiative, the effect ends and the wearer cannot use the ability again until a new encounter starts.

Other Rewards
Each Axolotl Warrior has a spear; each spear is plated in a thin layer of gold.
Among the scattered bones, the adventurers also find: a bag of 20 arrowheads, three obsidian bladed hand axes, the remnants of two bags of moldy corn, one pair of jade earrings, a collar of turquoise beads, a gold labret ring in the shape of a serpent, and a necklace of jade with gold skull beads.

The Road Back

FOR GM TO READ: When exiting the cave, the weather is clear and breezy; the crystal-clear water sparkles under the light of the sky, and if there are any electric eels in the lake, they are not visible.

The journey back home is uneventful. Occasionally the feeling of eyes upon the travellers draws attention to the green foliage of the forest. The yellow eyes of a jaguar peer out from the darkness, watching but never threatening, and while it occasionally slips away, by evening its presence is heavily felt.

Culmination

Soon the smell of extinguished fires hangs in the air, acidic and thick. The town has been attacked, the roofs of several buildings burned and the plaza deserted except for a few people picking through the scattered and destroyed goods.

The merchant, Ichtaca, is among them. His guards are gone. If asked, he says the town was asleep when all of a sudden there was a howling sound and a commotion. When people looked outside, there were lights all around that were made of something other than fire. The attackers were an army of soldiers from Chalco. They went into people's homes and captured young men and women, tying them up and attacking anyone who got in their way. The priestess tried to stop them, but they called her a traitor and threw her down the temple stairs. She is alive but barely. To keep the townspeople from following them as they marched away, they set fire to the buildings. Ichtaca has no idea where his two guards are; they may be dead or captured. People fear their newfound enemies are marching to Tenochtitlan and will sacrifice those they captured to ensure victory in the capitol. Among those taken are people the adventurers knew.

The stakes are even higher, the enemies greater in number than before. This, unfortunately, is just the beginning.

ATTENTION GMS!: Scan this QR code to download images and maps to enhance your virtual session!

Special thanks to Gabriela Downie, Matthew Emmons, Chris Sanchez, Cheyenne Hohnam, and Fabian Lelay.

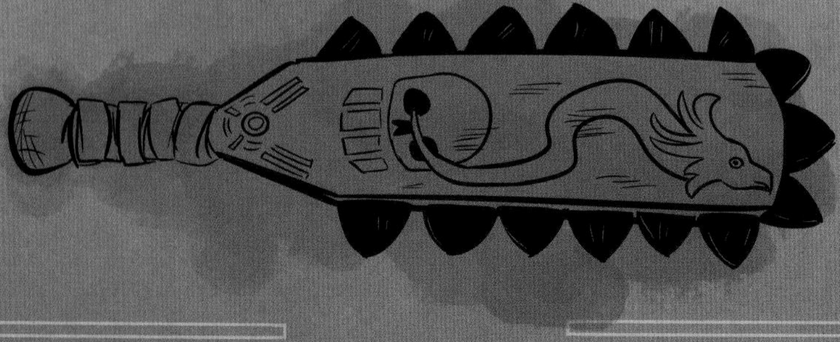

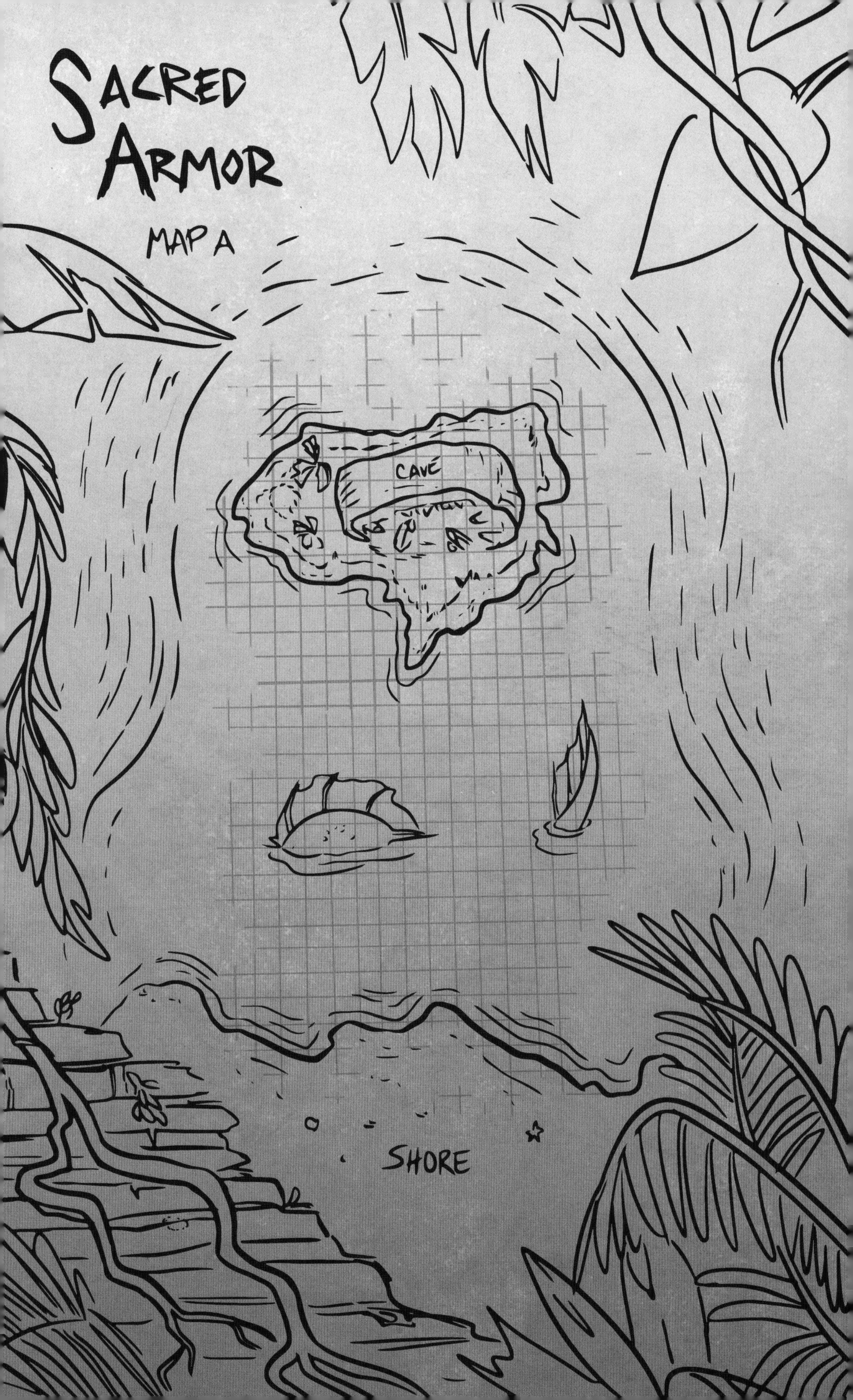
SACRED ARMOR
MAP A
CAVE
SHORE

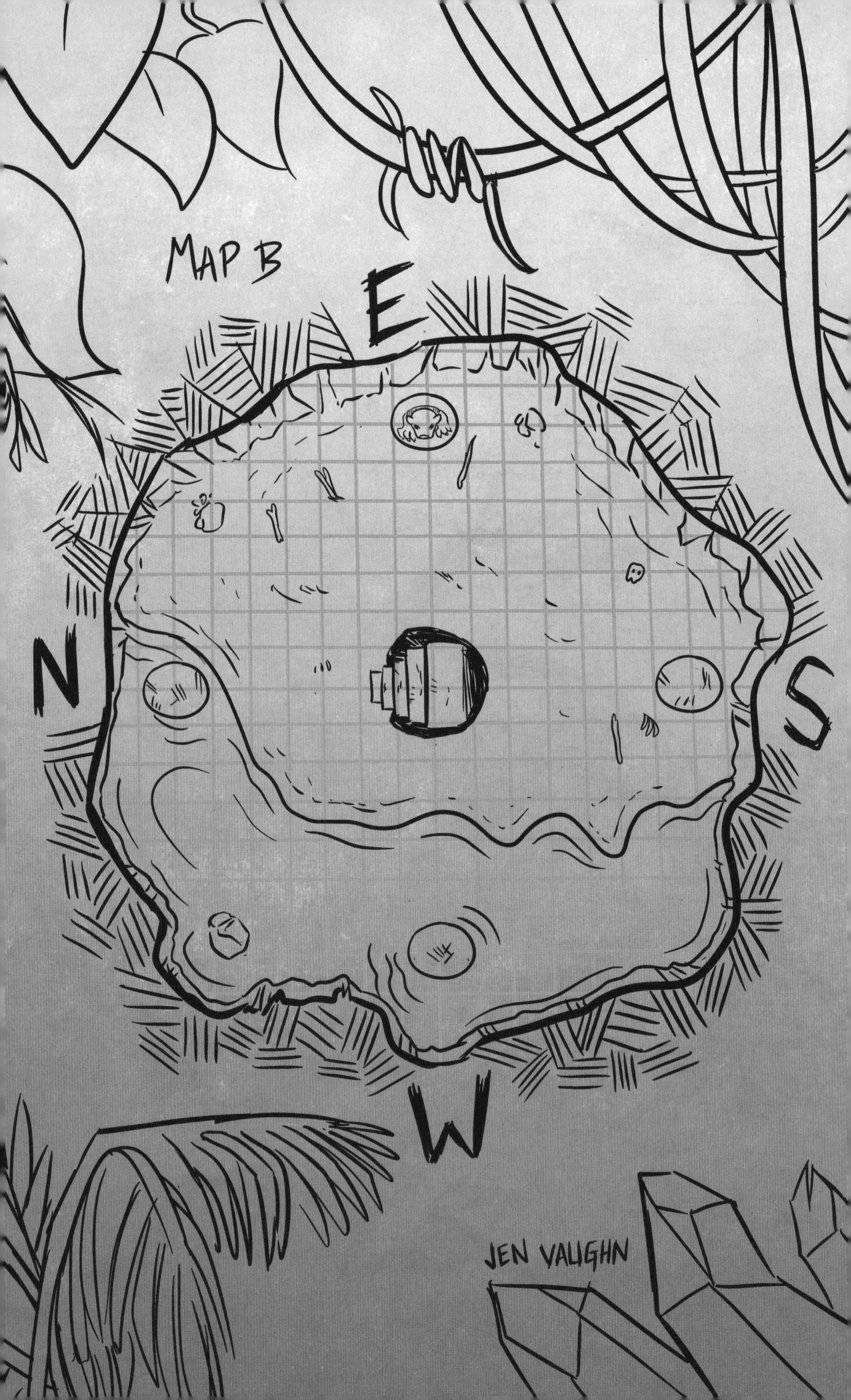
MAP B
E
N
S
W
JEN VAUGHN

THE BLOOD BETWEEN WORLDS

game by **TRISTAN J. TARWATER**   art by **JEN VAUGHN**

A town torn apart by war. Death, fearsome and liberating. The fate of the world written in blood. These are the adversities you will face in the one shot adventure, The Blood Between Worlds!

This 5E adventure set in the world of Helm Greycastle will take a band of player characters from a town on the outskirts of the Mexica empire to the scene of a violent struggle. In order to get there in time, the players will have to travel through the spirit world and face spirits and gods who reside there. When the players look in the mirror, what will they see?

The Blood Between Worlds

The Blood Between Worlds is an adventure for 3-5 players from 5th-7th level and meant to be a sequel to "Sacred Armor," featured in Helm Greycastle #1. In the previous adventure, the adventurers traveled into the jungle to retrieve the Black Mirror Ichcahuipilli from a sacred hiding place. The stats for the Black Mirror Ichcahuipilli are in Helm Greycastle #1 but are also supplied in this adventure.

The world of Sacred Armor and The Blood Between Worlds is the same as that of Helm Greycastle: a fantasy version of the Mexica/Aztec Empire around the time of their first contact with Hernán Cortez. Magic is real, homes are made of adobe bricks and Nahuatl is the common tongue. This adventure cannot possibly include all the worldbuilding of the comic or aspects of the 16th century Mexica civilization, so while you can play the adventure as is, we encourage you to read Helm Greycastle and read up on the history of the Mexica, as well as the other cultures which flourished in what is now Mexico.

FOR GM TO KNOW: *As always, it's a good idea to read through the adventure before running it. That way you can get an idea of how the game will flow and what will happen. Some parts of the adventure are marked "**For the GM to Read,**" which indicates the GM can read these sections out loud to the players. Others are marked "**For the GM to Know**" which gives information about the section and things the GM can take into account when running the game. The adventure is a one shot but can also be a template for or dropped into a longer adventure.*

In addition to this text, gaming groups will also need:

- SR5D, which will have instructions on how to make characters and run the game. This is available online!
- Dice or dice rolling software.
- The maps included in this adventure.
- Tokens or miniatures to represent characters if using a physical map.

If you haven't played Sacred Armor but still want to play The Blood Between Worlds, please note the following differences in playing!

IF PLAYING AS A SEQUEL:

- Have the players level before playing.

- The High Priestess and the Merchant would be familiar with the players and their previous quest.

- In the previous quest they went hunting for brightly colored parrots for the Merchant and heard him and his two guards discuss the unrest at the capital and the strange changes that the emperor was making, such as citizens having to learn Castilian and a hold on sacrifices. If the merchant sees them, he directs them to the High Priestess.

- The High Priestess would remember the strange omen which the players witnessed and their quest into the jungle for the Black Mirror Ichcahuipilli. The piece of armor is important for the defeat of an approaching enemy the omen warned about.

IF PLAYING AS AN ENTRY POINT:

- The adventurers come across the town, smoke still rising from the burnt buildings. Most of the warriors have been killed or taken away. The attack happened in the middle of the night two nights ago, everyone off guard.

- Not knowing anyone, the townspeople are distracted with trying to get their lives back in order; if asked, almost everyone knows someone who had been kidnapped. Eventually someone notices the players as being from outside of the town and tells them the High Priestess has told the people someone was coming to help them.

The Town, Buried in Ashes

FOR GM TO READ: The town of Cuappatollitlan lies in ruin. Smoke still rises from the ashes of several homes, and smears of blood on the dusty ground and splashed against the walls have darkened to a rusty red. Occasionally the reality of what has happened hits one of the citizens and they cry out, breaking the rhythm of quiet murmuring and the whimpers of the wounded and the despairing.

The town is full of a strange energy: people are mourning, some still in shock from the attack, sitting in front of their homes and staring into space. Others are busy, carrying water, salvaging what is left of their fields, or making bricks. Life pushes on and there are stomachs to fill, wounds to tend to and tomorrows to plan for.

FOR GM TO KNOW: *If they stop to ask any of the people what has happened, they are told that an army from Chalco invaded their town several days ago, in order to capture sacrifices. The army is on the march to the capital, where they intend to confront Emperor Montezuma and restore the order of the world as it was before the Castilians came. Almost everyone has lost someone and is in mourning and trying to rebuild, yet they apologize to the travellers for not being able to offer them their hospitality. The adventurers see the following as they enter the town:*

- Some of the sick have been taken to the market square to be tended to, priests and healers walking among the many injured. Most of the injuries are wounds from falling as people fled or were attacked with clubs but more than a handful of people are bleeding from wounds made from obsidian blades, either sliced with an atlatl or punctured from an arrow.
- Family members tear cotton into bandages to tend to people's wounds, while some weave on looms trying to keep up with demand. The dead are being wrapped in cotton, to be placed in their final resting places, under the homes of their relatives.
- The sound of woodwork is a strange note on the otherwise somber day. Wood crafters are making effigies of the dead, working hard to make sure the dead are supplied with the proper materials for their funerals.
- People are trying to repair the damage to their homes, walking with bundles of reeds to repair roofs. In the field, some people are hunched over the earth, making adobe bricks for repairs. Others are looking over smashed crops, trying to salvage what they can. One or two people just sit in their field, head in hands, crying.
- Two children are walking around, awkwardly carrying buckets of water on a shoulder pole. They are asking if people need water, offering sips from a ladle made from a gourd. They see the adventurers and ask if they want water.
- An old woman is stirring a pot of atole, offering the spiced, thick beverage to anyone who asks and brings a cup to partake of the nutritious drink. Even still, the aroma of spices cannot mask the stench of death and decay from those who have perished.

IF THE PLAYERS PLAYED SACRED ARMOR:

The people the players talk to recognize them; they definitely recognize the armor, if the adventurers have it out. News of their quest spread through the town shortly after they left, and so many look upon the players hopefully, urging them to go see the High Priestess so she can know they were successful.

IF THE PLAYERS DID NOT PLAY SACRED ARMOR:

The people nervously regard them, not sure who their alliances lie with. As soon as the players express any interest in helping, they are directed to the High Priestess, who said aid was coming to the town in some form.

FOR GM TO READ: The temple is easy to find, the largest building in the town. A tall pyramid built of huge stone blocks, many steps lead to the top. People sit in the lower steps of the pyramid, some of them dazed, others trying to get some space from the morbid frenzy of their homes. At the top of the pyramid in the temple building, an old woman, the [bold] High Priestess [end bold], lies on a mat. Her right arm and leg are tied with splints, cotton bandages wound around her head. A [bold]Junior Priestess[end bold] sits on the ground beside her, crying. Two priests are off to the side, mixing and grinding medicine in bowls made of stone.

The Junior Priestess hears your approach and looks up, frightened. When told the adventurers are there to see the High Priestess, the Junior Priestess gently taps her on the shoulder, awakening her.

The High Priestess tells the Junior Priestess to help her sit up. She smiles at the adventurers, though she winces right after, pain shooting across her face.

FOR GM TO KNOW:

IF THE PLAYERS HAVE PLAYED SACRED ARMOR:

The High Priestess asks if the players were successful in their endeavor.
"Praise the gods", she says. "You have been supplied for battle. Do you know where your path now leads?"

IF THE PLAYERS HAVE NOT PLAY SACRED ARMOR:

The High Priestess says "The gods have answered my prayers, quiet as my words have been, and sent us those who could set things right. If you have come to our aid, we will supply you with tools to defeat our enemies."

One of the priests says the players should surely get the captives back from the army of Chalco. Another suggests the players go after Montezuma himself, as his recent reforms are the cause of all of their troubles.

The High Priestess says given what has happened, perhaps the gods should be consulted. The High Priestess offers to have someone divine the future for them. If the adventurers agree, she tells the Junior Priestess to help the adventurers.

Sign of the Spirits

FOR GM TO READ: The Junior Priestess opens a wooden chest and pulls out a metal bowl used for divination and a small leather pouch. She sets the bowl on the ground and fills it with water from a nearby pitcher. She then removes her jade earrings and places them in the bowl of water, before reaching into the leather bag. In her hand is a handful of dried corn kernels of many colors. She counts them carefully before she holds them over the bowl, praying words to the gods, asking for their guidance as to what the adventurers should do. She drops the kernels into the water.

A hot, dry wind blows through the temple. A mote of fire sparks on the stone floor before tracing the outline of a circle. The flames leap up and then lower, a pool of something dark, thick and red rising out of the ground. When you look right at it, you can make out something on the other side: trees, grass, birds. Another world.

The Junior Priestess gasps, the other priests falling to their knees.

The Junior Priestess looks into the bowl and says, "There is someone the order of the world hinges on. If you find her, you can bring about the end to the chaos of today. But it is far, so the gods have offered you a shortcut. If you travel through the spirit world, you can get there quickly."

The Head Priestess says, "Before you go, please take these items with you to help you on your way."

FOR GM TO KNOW:

IF THE PLAYERS HAVE NOT PLAYED SACRED ARMOR:

The High Priestess whispers something to the young priestess who read their fortune. She goes into the inner temple and comes back with a box made of extremely dark, polished wood. She opens it and offers the Black Mirror Ichcahuipilli.

The priestess also includes the items from the section below.

The Black Mirror Ichcahuipilli

Armor (padded) legendary, requires attunement

The Ichicahuipilli is a tight-fitting garment worn on the torso. It is secured with ties at the front that are made of thick, stark-white quilted fabric stuffed with cotton fiber. It has short sleeves and extends past the waist. From afar the Ichcahuipilli appears white, but up close is a scintillating black, having absorbed the magical energy of the waters of divination.

The Black Mirror Ichcahuipilli is a legendary item, created by Tezcatlipoca for the warrior Tlacalel. It does not deflect arrows but rather catches them, and it is efficient against macuahuitl. The stats for the Ichcahuipilli are as follows:

Light armor	***Damage Resistance:*** +5 piercing and slashing weapons
13+ Dex modifier	All attacks against the wearer are done at disadvantage. All attack rolls
Weight: 9 lbs.	the wearer makes are at advantage.

Divined Duel

Once per day at the beginning of an encounter, the wearer may choose one enemy. The wearer gets an additional action they may use on the enemy's initiative, as if the enemy's initiative triggers an action. After the enemy's action, the player may take their action and choose to have it happen before or after the enemy's action. If the enemy falls out of initiative, the effect ends and the wearer cannot use the ability again until a new encounter starts.

The priestess offers each of the players:

Weapons: the priestess offers each player one Mesoamerican weapon similar to a weapon they have proficiency with. Each weapon is a +2. Refer to the chart below for approximations.

- **Macuahuitl:** any slashing weapon; a club edged with shards of razor sharp obsidian, can be used one or two handed
- **Tlahuitolli:** Long or shortbow; comes with 20 arrows with points of obsidian or flint
- **Cuaualolli:** Any bludgeoning weapon; a mace made of hardwood topped with a copper ball
- **Tepoztopilli:** Spear with an obsidian spearpoint
- **Itztopilli:** axe or handaxe with a blade made of copper; one end of the blade is sharp while the other is blunt.
- **Tematlatl:** Sling made of maguey cactus fibers; comes with 50 clay balls flecked with obsidian shards
- **Topilli:** a quarterstaff ornately carved, a copper ball at either end.
- **Tlacochtli:** throwing knives or darts made of obsidian.
- Other: If a player requires something there is not an approximation for (for example, a crossbow) there is simply a +2 version of it decorated with turquoise and copper.

The priestess also gives each player:

- A piece of greenstone to keep on their person for each person (Arcana or Religion Check DC 15: In their culture, greenstones are given to the dead, in order to pay their way to the Underworld).
- 2 potions of Cure Moderate Wounds.

Enter the Blood Between Worlds

FOR GM TO KNOW: *This section is a simple traipse through a spirit world where the players encounter a deity. The goal of the section is to get them to the final battle but have the characters learn more about what is happening in the world of Helm Greycastle and the Mexica world in*

The players are NOT dead. The deities are aware of their presence. They also have their jobs to do and their prayers to fill and their sacrifices to receive. It is not that their relationship with their worshippers is transactional. It is that they understand the balance of the universe, the flux which rushes to fill what is empty, the energy which must be put in things to grow, the room things make for things when they die. Movement, orderly and chaotic, occurs throughout the universe. Life is meant to end. Even the deities do not escape death and destruction. All things on the earth, under it and over it move. But the deities are never foolish enough to think their actions will not have consequences.

FOR GM TO READ: As you slip through the portal, you can feel the thick, viscous feeling of blood roll over your skin, as if you were traveling within a vein. The world goes red around you and then a bright light shines in the distance, drawing rapidly closer. You fall to the ground, the feeling of blood clinging to you but you are completely dry and unharmed.

The sun shines in the sky, higher than it normally shines in the world but bigger; it looks like a ball of fire, flames circling the golden orb.

A warm, damp wind blows, the scent of iron and copal on the air. The wind ripples the grass, which in some patches is a green so vibrant it looks like it is carved from precious jade. In other stretches the grass is so dry and brown, it rattles in the breeze.

The earth beneath your feet is soft and in the brief moments that the wind stops blowing, it is completely still... the earth seems to move beneath you, as if it is quietly slumbering and breathing softly.

Flower blooms peek their colorful faces out among the grass, tufts of bright purple amaranth, dazzlingly orange marigolds and pink dahlias. Hummingbirds flit among them, the flap of their wings droning, their bright colors scintillating. Colorful butterflies hover languidly, their wings like colored glass.

Trees dot the landscape, some blasted as if struck by lighting, not a leaf, bug or bird among their withered branches. Some trees are an explosion of green leaves, their branches dripping with fruit so ripe, their sweetness almost masks the smell of rotting fruit underneath. The roots of the trees look like skeletons piled at the bottom, clinging to the tree with boney hands.

In the distance, a medium sized Xoloitzcuintli (or Xolo dog) jumps in the air, snapping at the butterflies. The dog sees them and its ears perk up before it ducks into the grass. The dog pokes its head up and keeps sneaking towards the group.

FOR GM TO KNOW: *The players can make a Wisdom (DC 15) or Animal Handling Check or Nature: This dog is not a threat. A Religion or Arcana Check (DC 15) reveals the Xolo dog is associated with Xolotl, the god of fire, lightning and deformities, as well as being a psychopomp. It is Xolotl who guides and protects the Sun as it travels through the Underworld.*

If anyone calls to the dog, the dog jumps up and runs through the grass towards them. When it emerges from the grass, it is carrying a large bone (Nature Check DC 10: it is part of a human pelvis). The dog drops the bone at the feet of whoever called it and runs away a few feet before running back, trying to entice the players to throw it. The dog is all black with a few scruffy hairs on its muzzle and a birthmark on its back in the shape of the wind jewel. (Religion or Arcana Check 15: this is a symbol associated with Xolotl and Quetzalcoatl).

If the players throw the bone, the bone will change course and always head west. It will go for a few meters in the direction thrown before changing direction and heading west. The dog chases the bone and picks it up and waits for someone to take the bone from him and throw it again.

If someone tries to speak to the dog, the dog's thoughts are "You throw," and "I show." It is not a normal dog; it actually drops the bone when asked. If offered food it refuses the food. It only eats dog meat and human meat. It only drinks blood. At one point while travelling, the dog runs off and laps at a pool of something that does in fact turn out to be blood. However, the dog is non-threatening and doesn't bite or growl at the players. Occasionally the dog will look up at the sun and bark at it. The dog chases the bone and holds on to it, waiting for the players to catch up before dropping the bone so they can throw it again.

FOR GM TO READ: The sun speeds through the sky, the light quickly dropping into sunset. The sun approaches the horizon. With one final throw, the hipbone flies...into the hand of a man. The man looks at the party. He wears a breastplate much like the shape on the dog's back. Where his eyes should be are empty sockets, yet his gaze is penetrating. His feet are backwards and his skin is black like that of the dog.

The man regards you all, the dog going to sit at his feet obediently.

"I must guide the sun along its journey through the Underworld," he says. "But I will open a way back to your world. It is not yet your time to descend through the Nine Worlds. Though if you return here bravely, you may be transformed into one of these he says." He holds out his hand and a hummingbird alights on it.

"You cannot go until you feed my servant," Xolotl says, the god pointing to the Xolo dog. The dog yips and paws at the air, whimpering.

FOR GM TO KNOW: *The players can roll a check (Religion or Arcana, DC 10) to remember the greenstones that the High Priestess gave them. If they hold them out to the dog, the dog gulps them down.*

FOR GM TO READ: When the dog eats them all it stops moving and the symbol of the Wind Jewel on its back begins to glow. The dog's legs grow long and it stretches, warping its form until it becomes a large, obsidian mirror held in a stone casing carved with the story of the making of the first humans of the 5th Sun.

Xolotl says, "You must each stand before the mirror and see the possibility that lies within you. If you will accept it, you may go through. This world is full of so much: Pain. Suffering. Joy. Companionship. Our hearts and our minds and our actions matter. Even the deities do not escape the effect of other beings and the consequences of our actions. Know this and be mindful of your thoughts, your feelings and what you create with your hands.

FOR GM TO KNOW: *Each player must stand before the mirror. Roll a d4 and consult the following table to see what each player sees.*

ROLL:
1. What or who they most fear
2. What or who they most love
3. What or who they most desire
4. The location of someone or something the player is looking for.

Let the player describe what or who shows up in the mirror; ask them questions to expand the scene vividly and their character's reaction upon seeing it. Everyone can see the image, but only the player can hear any dialog which may be happening (for example, if their greatest fear is their god rejecting them, they alone will hear the rebuke of their deity) in the scene. After seeing it play out, the player must then step through the mirror into pitch black. They do not automatically pass on to the next encounter!

The next player rolls on the table and has their scene., etc.

Although not every player is physically present to witness each other's scene, they still somehow know what everyone saw once they emerge from the portal. Once everyone has entered the portal, they are all within a dark space. All they can hear is something breathing, something that is not them. After three breaths, they all fall out onto the beach.

Red Writing on the Sands of Time

FOR GM TO READ: As you fall onto cold, white sand, the roaring sound of the ocean crashes against your senses. Stepping out of the darkness of the portal, it takes a while for your eyes to adjust before you realize it is night, a sliver of a moon in the sky. The air smells of salt...and blood. A massive boat is on the beach, too far up on the sand to have simply been pulled up through human effort. Its hull is cracked open like an egg, massive splinters of wood litter the sandy shore. Men scream and beg for what sounds like mercy before their cries turn to gurgles and then fade into the sound of the ocean and battle.

On the deck of the wrecked ship, a young woman is being pushed by a Mexica soldier. The young woman looks like the other people of this area, her jet black hair pulled into a strange hairstyle. She wears a huipilli, but her skirt is large and full and she wears a cloak of heavy dyed fabric over her shoulders. A Mexica soldier in impressive armor on the beach shouts up to the boat and the young woman is picked up and thrown down to the beach. She screams, the soldier on the beach catching her. He lets her stand on her own two feet, but points his macuahuitl at her, saying something, before pointing with a jerk of his chin off into the distance. Her dark eyes glimmer with tears, but she wipes her eyes with a handkerchief and turns to go where directed.

The crackle of arcane energy lights up the forest as men fall to the ground, their clothes singed and their flesh burned. Out from the forest steps a priest, an obsidian knife in hand, lips still moving with prayers to the deities for power.

FOR GM TO KNOW: *Have players roll initiative.*

In the chaos of the beach, the players are seen as threats by the other soldiers on the beach. On their way to the woman they are assaulted by various soldiers whose stats are as follows:

Soldiers in the Fray

Medium Humanoid

STR	DEX	CON	INT	WIS	CHA
10	10	10	10	10	10

AC: 12

Hit Points: 1

Attack: +4 to hit, 1d6+2 slashing damage

Important Note: *Effectively, one hit will take any of the soldiers out, replicating a frenzied rush through the battlefield. The soldiers can be either Castilians or Mexica in the GMs description as it is all out violence on the beach, all parties involved. If any player asks "is there a random soldier close enough for me to attack," as they move through the battlefield, the answer should be "yes."*

There is no set number of Soldiers in the Fray; roll initiative for the Soldiers as a whole and on their initiative, any/all of the players may be attacked as it makes sense.

The Chosen Warrior is situated by the boat; the Priest of Chaloc is located closer to the forest, giving the players two areas to focus on.

The Creation of Paths Through Warfare

FOR GM TO READ: The Chosen Warrior pushes the woman to the ground, pointing his macuahuitl at her before proclaiming:

"More blood to rewrite the story of the world."

He screams, raising his macuahuitl in the air, facing the adventurers.

FOR GM TO KNOW: *The stats for the Chosen Warrior are as follows.*

Chosen Warrior	STR	DEX	CON	INT	WIS	CHA
Medium Humanoid	15(+2)	14(+2)	14(+2)	2(+1)	13(+1)	13(+1)

AC:	Hit Points:	Speed:
16 (padded armor and shield)	148	35 ft.

Skills: Perception +5, Stealth +4
Languages: Common

Senses: Passive Perception 14
Challenge: 7

ACTIONS

Macuahuitl: +7 to hit, 1d10 + 4 piercing
Multi Attack: *The Chosen Warrior gets two melee attacks per round.*
Reflexes of the Gods: *Once per encounter, the Chosen Warrior can cast the spell Slow at-will. The save DC for this spell is 14. The Chosen Warrior cannot use this again until they have had a Short Rest.*
Saved to be Sacrificed: *When an attack from the Chosen Warrior would drop a creature to 0 hit points or below, he can choose to knock the creature unconscious instead. The creature does not need to make a Death Saving throw but they fall to the ground and are Stunned for three rounds. The effect can only be removed before the three rounds lapse via magic which can undo effects. Restoring hit points does not remove the effect. If the effect is removed via magic, the targeted creature must immediately make a Death Saving throw.*

During the fight, the Chosen Warrior may talk to whoever is fighting with him, urging them to fight bravely so when he subdues them, they will make a better sacrifice. Their efforts in battle will not be in vain

High Priest of Chalco
Medium Humanoid

STR	DEX	CON	INT	WIS	CHA
13	14	15	13	16	16

AC:
14

Hit Points:
78

Speed:
30 ft.

Skills: Perception +6, Stealth +4
Senses: Passive Perception +7

Language: Common

ACTIONS

Tecpatl (obsidian dagger): +6 to hit, 1d4+5 slashing damage.
Quauhollli (mace): +6 to hit, 1d8 + 5 bludgeoning damage.

SPELLCASTING

The High Priest of Chalco is a 5th level spell caster; his spells have a save DC of 14 and a Spell Attack Modifier of +6. The High Priest has the following spell slots open, as well as the spell "Blood Fog" listed below.

Cantrips known:

Spell Slots	Spell Slots
1st: 3	**0:** Light, Sacred Flame, Spare the Dying, Thaumaturgy
2nd: 3	**1st:** Inflict Wounds, Cure Wounds Command, Healing Word
3rd: 3	**2nd:** Spiritual Weapon, Augury, Aid
4th: 1	**3rd:** Spiritual Guardian, Blood Fog
	4th: Guardian of Faith

BLOOD FOG *3rd level enchantment*

Casting Time: One Action
Range/Area: 60 feet/Target
Components: V,S,M (copal incense mixed with the blood of the caster)

Duration: One Round
School: Enchantment
Attack/Save: Wisdom
Damage: Psychic

A targeted creature sees a fog of blood rise up around them. The target must make a Wisdom Saving throw or take 4d10 psychic damage and is Frightened, as the thick, red fog envelopes them, their heart pounding so loudly, it is all they hear. On a successful save, the targeted creature takes half damage and is not Frightened. When cast at a higher spell slot, the caster can target one additional creature.

FOR GM TO KNOW: *If the High Priest is killed, with his dying breath he says, "You fools. You do not know the world you are creating with your bloody hands."*

Conclusion if the players lose

The Chosen Warrior stands over each adventurer, tying them up securely before yanking them to your feet. He pushes them into line behind the woman, ordering them to follow the other captives being taken into the forest besides the beach.

"You fought well but victory lies ahead for us," he says.

The woman turns back to look at you. Despite being in the same situation as you, she looks upon you with pity, or perhaps guilt.

"Keep moving, Doña Marina," growls the Chosen Warrior, prodding her in her back with his macuahuitl. "You will be sacrificed last, the key to our victory over Tenochtitlan." The soldiers hurry you along as you walk through the night towards the death your enemies have for you.

Conclusion if Successful

FOR GM TO READ: The warrior defeated, his body lies on the ground, red blood seeping out onto the white sand. With his last words, he prays to the deities.

"We tried to stop them...to preserve this path…."

The woman stands up, brushing her clothes clean. A small cut on her forehead is bleeding and she is trembling but other than that, she seems unharmed.

She says hello in Nahuatl and Castilian, trying to see which you understand. She curtsies deeply, before introducing herself.

"Thank you for saving me. I am Doña Marina. I've come from over the ocean to try and make things right."

FOR GM TO KNOW: *Doña Marina tells the party that there are captives in the woods, people who were going to be taken to Tenochtitlan to be sacrificed. Some of the captives have already run onto the beach, using the blades of the dead warriors to cut their bonds. Doña Marina tells the party that there were provisions on the ship, and that they can give the provisions to the captives for their journeys back to their homes. Among the captives are people from the town of Cuappatollitlan. They thank the players and tell them they will throw a feast for them when the town has recovered their losses and will pray for them every day. Most of the captives are young adults and teenagers.*

If asked how the ship got onto the beach, Doña Marina tells them they were sailing to Tenochtitlan when suddenly the ship began to glow, a wild wind blasting over the ship, throwing two men overboard. The next thing they knew, the ship had crashed onto the beach, as if god had picked it up and dropped it there like a toy. The beach was covered in soldiers...she then goes quiet.

If any of the Castilian soldiers survived, they fled into the night. Doña Marina asks the players to escort her to Tenochtitlan, as she must speak with Montezuma. She says there were horses on the ship that are probably close by; they can ride those to Tenochtitlan (Nature Check DC 15 to know what a horse is, as horses are not endemic to the area). She says she can pay them as well.

ATTENTION GMS!: Scan this QR code to download images and maps to enhance your virtual session!

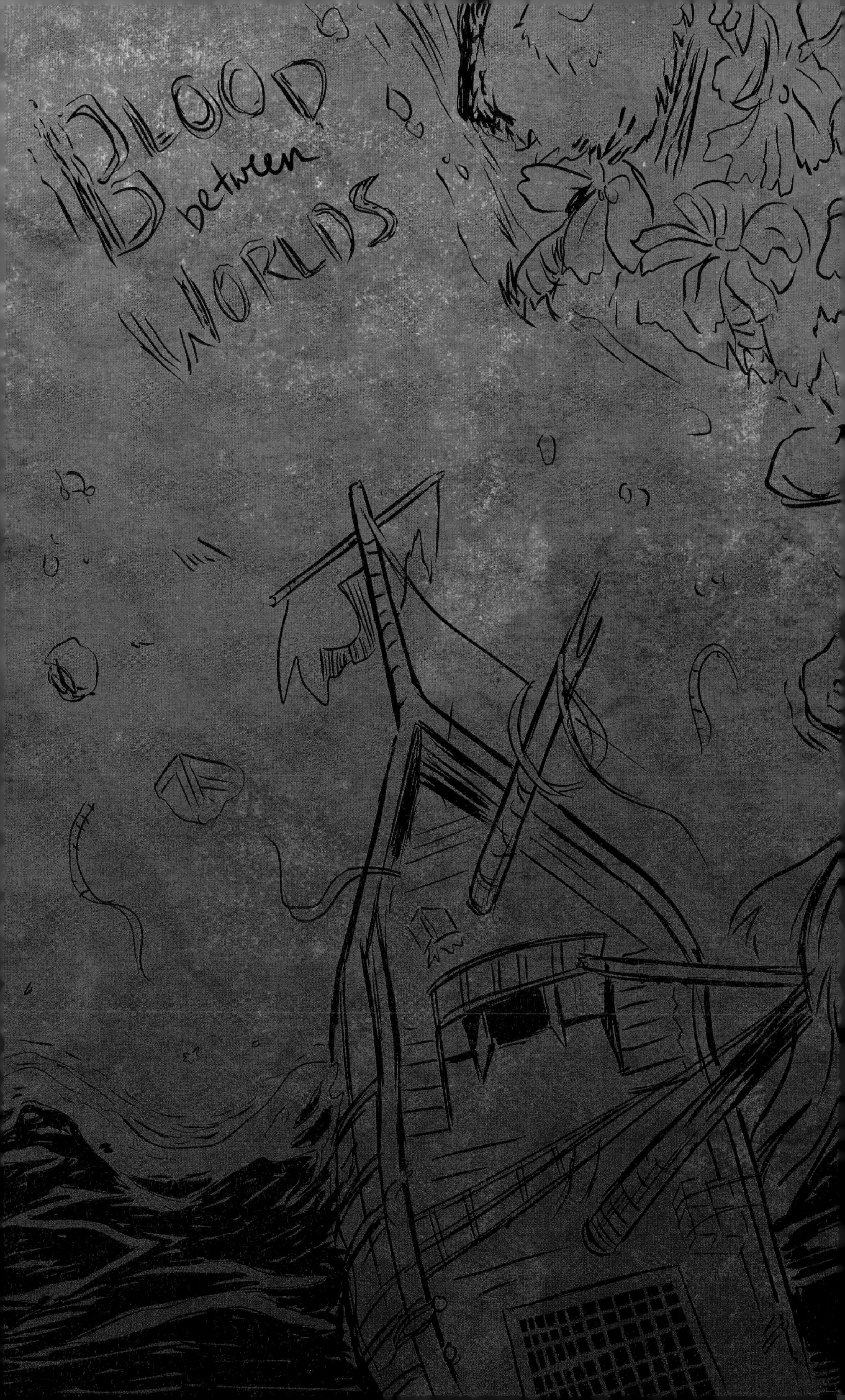
BLOOD
between
WORLDS

THE BELLY OF THE BEAST

game by **GEOFFREY GOLDEN**   art by **JEN VAUGHN**

Adventurers will explore the deadly Templo Tlaltecuhtli with Helm Greycastle himself! Helm heard a rumor that Uadjit was being held captive there, but the rest of Helm's crew believe it's a trap. A suicide mission. Helm, drunk, promises the adventurers any treasure they find together. He just wants the dragon prince.

Inside they find pits of venomous snakes to kill, invaluable treasure, and walls of screaming skulls – former conquistadors in endless pain. All throughout the temple, adventurers hear a beating, a rhythmic pulse, and walls show traces of pink slime. At the center of the pyramid, the temple awakens and condemns the adventurers to death. To protect the temple from the invading Spaniards, Montezuma III used his magic to bring Templo Tlaltecuhtli to life. The temple, aching from hunger pains, ate the trespassers who wished to destroy it. Rather than give the pyramid peace, Montezuma keeps it alive and feeds his own people to this magical beast.

Suddenly, the adventurers are in a race against time as sticky pink slime spews from the walls. If they don't find their way out in a hurry, Templo Tlaltecuhtli will trap them inside and eventually digest them!

Adventure Hook

Explore a Living Temple… and Fight to Escape – Traps and treasures await the adventurers inside Templo Tlaltecuhtli. The paths they choose will alter their journey, but they mustn't deliberate too long, because time is of the essence. Inside, they will battle snakes and skeletons, solve deadly traps, and avoid being devoured by the temple itself. They might even choose to come to Templo Tlaltecuhtli's aid.

Adventure Background

Belly of the Beast is designed for 3-5 players at levels 1-3. To play, the GM will need this text, a SR5D, and dice. Optionally, the enclosed map (see the **Templo Map** section in back) can be used with tokens to represent the players and monsters, either virtually or in-person.

The adventurers find themselves lost in a lush, green forest in the nighttide. They're far from the Aztec village they left an hour ago, where they met a powerful half-orc cleric named Vola. She offered a 1000 gold reward to the adventurers to watch over her husband and father of her child, Helm, who went on what she believes is a suicide mission to a cursed temple. Vola notes that Helm always acts recklessly when he drinks. She didn't know much about Templo Tlaltecuhtli (pronounced "Tlal-teh-koo-tlee"), only that the local villagers have called it a legendary deathtrap.

It's the dead of night, but glowing moonlight peeks through the tree branches, lighting a dirt path. Whimpering quetzal birds cut through the silence with their chirps. Up ahead, they see glimmers of torchlight and hear the churlish laughter of a desperate warrior...

Set-Up: This adventure takes place in 16th century AD Mexica in the world of Helm Greycastle. If your players are already adventuring here (say, from issue 1), that's terrific! If not, how they originally arrived in this Aztec world – magic portal, time travel – is up to the DM.

Outside the Templo

The trees give way to a grass clearing. The moon is high in the sky and now perfectly visible. In front of them is a sight to behold: Templo Tlaltecuhtli, a tall pyramid surrounded by lit torches. A stone staircase leads up to a semi-circle entrance at the very top. Rectangular pillars protrude from the roof. With an Arcana check of DC 10, an adventurer will note how it mimics the ones on the head of the Aztec Earth goddess Tlaltecuhtli, for whom the temple is named.

The stone temple is decorated in a knife and spear tip pattern. An Investigation check of DC 15 will reveal tiny cracks forming in the stone around the armaments. These weapons aren't merely decoration. They're actual weapons. These armaments are being pushed out of the temple walls. (They're being excreted, unable to be properly digested by the living temple.)

Entering the Temple: There are no visible entrances to the temple. The adventurers need to climb the stairs and enter through a trap door at the very top. (See **M1 - Spike Pit**.)

At the base of the stairs sits **Helm**, a muscular, mohawked Human barbarian. (See the **Stat Blocks** section for more on Helm.) He's shirtless with spiked metal armor covering just one arm. In the other is a waterskin filled with ale, which Helm is currently abusing. He's humming a little tune to entertain himself. When the adventurers approach, Helm laughs and flashes them a welcoming grin.

> **"Let me guess. My lovely Vola sent you? I don't need a babysitter. What I need are a few brave adventurers with guts, who love treasure. If that's not you, then beat it back to the village."**
> **– Helm**

Helm's Drinking: Helm is a strong, steely-eyed warrior with a weakness for drink. Drinking makes him more reckless and sociable, but not buffoonish. If adventurers confront Helm directly about his drinking, Helm will brush them off. Possible excuses: it's his "pain medicine;" drinking adds excitement to any adventure; they wouldn't like him when he's not drinking. A Persuasion check of DC 12 or higher will lead Helm to consider an adventurer's advice or concern, and not immediately shut them down. At DC 17 or higher, he won't drink again in the temple.

Helm explains his situation. He's on a quest to find Uadjit, the last dragon prince, kidnapped by this land's ruling sorcerer, Montezuma III. One villager claims Uadjit is being held in Templo Tlaltecuhtli, but Vero and his companions refuse to accompany him into the pyramid. Everyone in the village says the same thing: no one who enters leaves. If Uadjit was taken to this temple, there's no way he's still alive. Helm split from the group to see this "so-called cursed temple" for himself.

He makes the adventurers a deal: accompany Helm to the altar room inside, where he believes Uadjit is being held. In exchange, the adventurers can keep all the treasure they find. If they say yes, the quest begins. If they refuse, Helm curses to the air and triumphantly, drunkenly stumbles up the staircase. The DM should encourage the adventurers to join Helm, reminding them they already promised Vola they would watch over him.

The staircase is smooth textured, made of polished red rocks. The edges of the staircase zig-zag in and out, and with an Arcana check of DC 10, they'll realize the staircase is patterned after the blood that flows from Tlaltecuhtli's mouth in statues. The Aztec goddess is worshipped with human sacrifices.

Inside the Temple: The temple was magically brought to life with an insatiable appetite for human flesh. Throughout the temple are pipes. At midnight, the pipes spew deadly digestive acid into every room though little holes in the walls. The gooey pink slime traps humans inside, then breaks down their flesh and bones, to be irrigated through small grates in the floors. To notice the holes and grates, adventurers must pass a Perception check of DC 10. At DC 15, they'll notice the walls are tinted by the pink, flaky residue of the slime.

There are torches throughout the temple, lighting up every corner, but even with the fire, it all feels strangely... warm inside. Like bodily warmth. The adventurers can hear a faint, pulsing beating in the distance. It's the sound of slime running through the pipes, which gets louder as they get closer to the altar room, beneath which are the central pipes.

M1 – Spike Pit

When the adventurers reach the flat landing at the top of the pyramid, they find no entrance, only artwork. A thin horizontal line cuts across most of the platform, with flat stones surrounding the line, resembling a mouth and teeth. **This is a pit trap!** It's a 15 foot tall drop with rock spikes at the bottom! Helm is in the very center of the platform, so unless someone warns him in time or pulls him away, he'll likely fall into the pit.

Give a Moment: Every room in the Templo has hidden dangers, but also mechanisms for its former worshippers to avoid those dangers. So before traps go off, allow a minute or two for adventurers to explore their surroundings.

✳ PIT TRAP

Trigger: Anyone who steps on the flatstone teeth could fall in.

Effect: Adventurers who trigger the trap must make a DC 15 Dexterity saving throw. On a save, the adventurer could grab the edge of the pit. Or grip the steps built into the side of the pit, designed to climb down safely. On a failed save, the adventurer hits sharp spikes carved from volcanic rock below to take 5 (1d6+2) piercing damage.

Countermeasures: A successful Wisdom check of D10 or higher will reveal that a few of the flagstones are protruding suspiciously, and may have a purpose beyond mere art.

Whether Helm takes damage or not, he'll note that he was careless and needs to sharpen up. Then he'll absentmindedly take another drink.

The spikes are only in the very center of the torchlit room. There's a stone walkway encircling the spikes, which leads to a downward staircase. Inside the room, there's a painting on the wall depicting Tlaltecuhtli squatting before bowing Aztecs. The crocodile skinned goddess has fistfuls of humans in her claws, blood dripping from her mouth. However, her face has been scratched out with a large "X." The paint is also faint and worn, like it's being washed away. The moon is depicted high in the sky, just like tonight.

They'll notice something else, too: disgusting bits of rotting flesh and tiny, smooth shards of bone. They look like the leftovers a voracious predator would leave behind (but it's actually the parts of humans the Templo hasn't fully digested).

Helm approaches the long stone staircase. He blinks slowly, then jokes that stairs are the drunk man's greatest enemy. The staircase leads them around a curved corner, into a new room.

M2 – Fire Serpents

The circular room prominently features six stone statues of Xiuhcoatl, the Aztec fire serpent. These scaly serpent sculptures have spiral patterns on their heads. They're about 8 feet long, twisting and bending around the floor into "S" like curves. None of them have tail tips. Instead, the Xiuhcoatls seem to meld into the floor. Also on the floor, the adventurers will step past long, thin, rotting strips of snake hide.

Every Xiuhcoatl has an open mouth, bearing sharp fangs, and ruby eyes shining in the torchlight. The adventurers have entered **a snake trap!**

 ## SNAKE TRAP

Trigger: When any adventurer looks into the sparkling ruby eyes of any snake statue.

Effect: A heavy metal blockade drops behind them. The other door is a stone slab across the room that won't budge. Out of the Xiuhcoatl mouths slither **10 Poisonous Snakes**, filling the room with venomous monsters! The statues rattle back and forth when the snakes exit them

Countermeasures: An experienced magic user may intuit that the energy emanating from the rubies is foreboding with a Wisdom check of DC 25 or higher. However, if they've already looked directly at the rubies to do this, the point is moot! They could look at the rubies indirectly, out of the corner of their eyes, to avoid the trap.

How to Escape: The statues are moveable, and not as heavy as they look. At DC 7, an adventurer may notice that the shapes of the snakes appear to mirror one another, because they fit together. The adventurers can do the following to lift the stone slab and escape:

- Destroy at least 7 Poisonous Snakes. Helm will start slaughtering them without hesitation.
- Rotate the six Xiuhcoatls so they lock together, forming three interlocking pairs. When they do this, a circular pillar will rise from the floor, revealing a gold tunic! It's not designed for combat, and will slow an adventurer down.

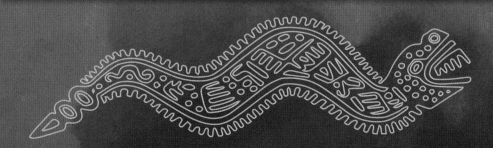

Ceremonial Ēhuatl

Armor (medium), very rare

This gold plated tunic with a jewel encrusted jaguar insignia gives the wearer +1 to AC and +3 to Intimidation rolls. However, the wearer or holder is encumbered. Their speed drops by 10 feet and is heavily encumbered.

Helm screams off any snakes that remain when the stone door opens. They'll slither back into the Xiuhcoatl statue mouths. When the door opens, it reveals another downward stone staircase. Helm wonders aloud how many more stairs there'll be as he takes a swig! The pulsing grows louder as the adventurers descend into the belly of the beast.

M3 – The Altar

Who is the Templo? – The adventurers are about to meet Templo Tlaltecuhtli herself. Built by the Aztecs to worship the goddess Tlaltecuhtli, the Templo itself was brought to life by Montezuma III to devour the conquistadors who invaded her, intent on destroying her. Now she must eat anyone who enters to satiate her appetite. She doesn't want to, but she has to. She has no formal name.

Help the Templo – The Templo doesn't fully understand how her body works mechanically, but she senses that if her insides were smaller, she wouldn't have to eat as many humans, and perhaps could subsist on snakes and rats. This is a clue for the adventurers to destroy the Jaguar room, like a bypass surgery.

The final staircase is much shorter, leading to a larger and more spacious room than the previous ones. It's a grand stone hall with intricately carved patterns on the walls and pillars: planets, suns, skulls, snakes, and jaguar heads. There are bone and flesh bits stuck in various crevices throughout the room, and the smell is putrid. In the center of the room is what looks like a destroyed, partial pillar, but a successful Perception check of DC 6 will reveal it's hollow inside the "pillar," and the beating noise is emanating from this structure. Soon, they'll know it's a well about to overflow with pink slime. The pulsing is the thick slime moving through the temple's intricate pipe system.

Ahead of them is a raised platform. A 20 foot tall stone statue of the goddess Tlaltecuhtli looms over them, smiling with her claws raised to the sky, but its face has once again been destroyed. Her nose was shot off with gunfire, and her earrings were chiseled off. Before her is a raised tablet with a patterned brown and beige blanket covering what looks to be a body. Helm worries that's the dragon prince and runs to the altar. He rips off the cover to reveal the decaying skeleton of a Spanish conquistador in a burned, chewed through metal skirt, covered in pink slime. The torches glow brighter and a powerful female voice echoes throughout.

"As long as I live, I shall hunger for flesh. I ache for it. All who enter shall be devoured. I welcome your questions, and then, your last words."
– Templo Tlaltecuhtli

The adventurers may ask the Templo a few questions before Helm drunkenly dares the sacred building to do its worst. If Helm isn't drunk, the Templo's stomach growls and it begins...

Digestion

The well in the altar room erupts with pink slime! The floor quickly fills with the deadly viscous liquid. All players roll for initiative and take turns, like in combat. Here's a chart for the digestive slime's effects over time. Remember to keep track of how many full rounds have taken place.

ROUND	SLIME HEIGHT	EFFECTS
3	1 Foot	Difficult Terrain. Move at half speed.
6	2 Feet	Burning. Take 1d4 acid damage every turn.
12	3 Feet	Intense Burning. Take 2d6 acid damage every turn.
18	4 Feet	Exhaustion. DC 15 Athletics check required to move 5 feet.
25	6 Feet	Drowning. (See SR5D p. 183).

Strong waves of slime are splashing through the doorway they entered from, so the adventurers would be wise to move forward. Past the altar are three doorways.

M4 - Jaguar Room

If the adventurers take the left door, they'll soon enter the cramped Jaguar Room. The walls are painted with a mural of angry jungle cats devouring villagers. It's filled with treasure, both Aztec and Spanish, but it's also quickly filling with slime. The highlights include 500 gold, 50 platinum, 20 lbs of cacao beans, a silver war mask, ten metal helmets, five silver plated swords, 10 lbs of brightly colored feathers, a mother of pearl bottle stopper set, and bags of jade and turquoise.

Against the walls are five tightly sealed kegs of gunpowder. If the adventurers manage to destroy the room – hopefully without destroying themselves – it will fill with dirt and become unenterable. Now the slime will only fill as high as 2 feet, since the temple won't need to eat as much flesh, and will begin draining. Use the slime height chart (see **Digestion**) in reverse to determine the speed at which the slime drains.

M5 - Steam Room

If the adventurers take the central door, they'll walk up a dark 12 foot flight of stairs. They'll enter a small stone room with a dome ceiling. There's a single torchlight on the wall in front of them, beneath which is a stone mask of Tlaltecuhtli, untouched. In the center of the room is a two-tiered stone platform. The bottom layer is for resting with carved grooves designed for sitting. The top layer has a cavity containing a pile of volcanic rocks called tezontles. In the corner is a wooden bucket filled with water.

If the adventurers need to heal, they'll take the torch off the wall, light the volcanic rocks, then throw the water on the hot stones to create steam. The steam revives all players, healing them for 12 (3d8) hit points and cures poison condition. The eyes of Tlaltecuhtli glow a soothing white while the fire burns.

M6 - Walls of Skulls

If the adventurers take the right door, they'll find themselves in a dank and dirty cavern, with its own flooding pool of pink slime. However, the slime is the least of their worries. The cave walls are lined with tzompantli (pronounced "som-pantli") skull racks. The 200 skulls shriek and shout in endless pain! These are the decapitated skulls of the conquistadors who tried to destroy the temple. Most just scream, but one or two shout "mátame!" ("Kill me!")

Out of the slime pool, **6 Conquistador Skeletons** emerge, decked out in scraps of metal armor, covered in burn marks. They block the pathway through the cavern to freedom. They're unaffected by the pink slime. The adventurers may choose to fight them head on. With an Investigation check of DC 8, they'll notice the same burn marks on 20 of the skulls on the rack. That's because they were from the same battalion that was burned to death. For every burned skull the adventurers find and destroy, it will distract a Conquistador Skeleton for a round of combat as they go to check on a fallen comrade.

SKULL

AC:	Hit Points:
15	3 (1d6)

After laying waste to the skeletons, their path is clear: a long tunnel, illuminated by the light of enchanted crystals, leads the adventurers to a well-hidden secret door, covered in dirt and grass several feet behind the temple.

Conclusion

Dawn is breaking. The deep purple sky will soon be overtaken by the hot orange sun cresting the horizon. Helm thanks the adventurers for their help, then makes his way back to the forest path. You accompany him to the village, back to Vola and his crew. What a night.

Special Ending – Drinking

If the adventurers convince Helm to stop drinking in the temple, a realization dawns on him. The temple struggled with uncontrollable impulses, destroying and ruining the lives of local villagers. Maybe his drinking would do the same to his friends someday.

Helm takes his waterskin, unscrews the cap, and starts to tip it over… but then cringes, stops himself, and takes another swig of liquor. He laughs. Some monsters aren't easily slain.

Special Ending – Jaguar Room

If the adventurers destroyed the Jaguar Room, the ground will shake before they leave the area. It feels like a light earthquake. Out of small holes in the temple walls, treasures left behind in the Jaguar Room will spew out of the dirt (gold, swords, bags of feathers), along with an additional 2000 gp.

Among the treasure, one item glistens in the new sun, commanding their attention: a shining gold fire serpent necklace. Along the curves of the snake reads the word "Tlazocamati." An Arcana check of DC 7 will reveal the word means "Thank You" in Nahuatl.

Rewards/XP

When the adventurers return to the village with Helm, Vola gives them 1,000 gp total. Everyone in the party earns 250 XP to thank them for their service.

Helm Greycastle

Medium humanoid (human), lawful good

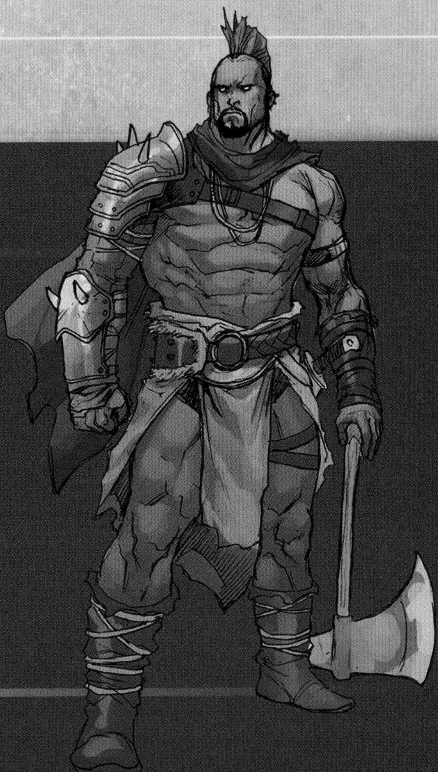

STR	DEX	CON	INT	WIS	CHA
17(+3)	14(+2)	15(+2)	11(+0)	14(+2)	9(-1)

AC: 14 (leather, scale mail, shield)

Hit Points: 59 (6d12)

Speed: 40 ft.

Skills:
Perception +5, Animal Handling +5, Survival +5, Athletics +3

Saving Throws: Strength +6, Constitution +5
Languages: Common, Halfling
Challenge: 4 (1,100 XP)

Reckless Attack: When Helm makes his first attack on his turn, he can decide to attack recklessly, giving him advantage on melee weapon attack rolls using STR during this turn, but attack rolls against him have advantage until his next turn.

Extra Attack: Helm can attack twice, instead of once, whenever he takes the Attack action on his turn.

Intoxicated: When Helm takes a drink, he gets advantage on Strength and Charisma ability checks, and disadvantage on all other checks. If Helm doesn't drink through a full combat encounter, he "sobers up" and is no longer Intoxicated. Intoxicated is a free action.

ACTIONS

Great Axe: *Melee Weapon Attack*: +6 to hit, reach 5 ft, one target. Hit: 9 (1d12 + 3) slashing damage.

Javelin: *Melee or Ranged Weapon Attack*: +6 to hit, reach 5 ft. or range 20/60 ft., one target. Hit: 6 (1d6 + 3) piercing damage.

Rage: Helm gains advantage on STR checks and saving throws (not attacks), +2 melee damage with STR weapons, resistance to bludgeoning, piercing, slashing damage. His rage ends early if he is knocked unconscious or if his turn ends and he hasn't attacked a hostile creature since his last turn or taken damage since then. He can also end his rage as a bonus action.

DESCRIPTION

Helm is a proud, charismatic, and forthright barbarian warrior. His purple mohawk, barrel chest, greataxe, and single sleeve of metal armor strikes fear into Helm's enemies. Though he's a fierce warrior, Helm bristles against authority, always believing himself to be the leader of any team. He struggles with a range of addictions: alcohol, smoking, and magic mushrooms. When someone's in trouble, Helm doesn't hesitate to act – and slash!

Ideal: "It's my destiny to save the dragon prince. Stand in my way and your destiny is a swift death!"

Bond: "Stand behind me. I'll protect you."

Flaw: "Drinking helps the pain. Not the scars of battle, but the scars of the past."

Poisonous Snake

Tiny beast, unaligned

STR	DEX	CON	INT	WIS	CHA
2(-4)	16(+3)	11(+0)	1(-5)	10(+0)	3(-4)

AC:
13

Hit Points:
2 (1d4)

Speed:
30 ft., Swim 30 Ft.

Senses: Blindsight 10ft., Passive Perception 10
Challenge: 1/8 (25 XP)

ACTIONS

Bite: Melee Weapon Attack: +5 to hit, reach 5 ft., one target. Hit: (1d6) piercing damage plus (2d4) poison damage. The target must make a DC 10 Constitution saving throw, taking the poison damage on a failed save, or half as much damage on a successful one.

Conquistador Skeleton

Medium undead, lawful evil

STR	DEX	CON	INT	WIS	CHA
10(0)	14(+2)	15(+2)	6(-2)	8(-1)	5(-3)

AC:
13 (Armor Scraps)

Hit Points:
13 (2d8 + 4)

Speed:
30 ft.

Damage Vulnerabilities: Bludgeoning
Damage Immunities: Poison
Condition Immunities: Exhaustion, Poisoned

Senses: Darkvision 60 ft., Passive Perception 9
Language: Understands Spanish
Challenge: 1/4 (50 XP)

ACTIONS

Thirst for Combat: After a successful attack, Conquistador Skeletons make two melee attacks the following turn.
Shortsword: Melee Weapon Attack: +4 to hit, reach 5 ft., one target. Hit: 5 (1d6 + 2) piercing damage.

ATTENTION GMS!: Scan this QR code to download images and maps to enhance your virtual session!

Special thanks to game testers Gabriela, Jazzlyn, Matt, and Chris!

Story Flow Chart

Here's a TLDR overview for Belly of the Beast

VILLAGE
Vola asks adventurers to protect Helm for 1000 gp. He went to a dangerous temple.

FOREST PATH
Where the adventure begins.

OUTSIDE TEMPLE
They reach the Templo Tlaltecuhtli. Helm is drunk on the front steps. He needs to find the Dragon Prince. The adventurers agree to accompany him.

TOP OF TEMPLE
Take the main stairs up. This is the only way inside. It's a trap door with spikes at the bottom, triggered by stepping on stones. There is a ladder to get down safely.

SPIKE ROOM
The paintings on the wall show the goddess Tlaltecuhtli, who required human sacrifice, with her face scratched off. There's a beating pulse sound. A staircase leads downward.

SNAKE ROOM
There are 8 snake statues. Out of them comes 10 Poisonous Snakes! Defeat 7 in combat -or- shift the statues together like puzzle pieces to scare the snakes and reveal a gold tunic.

ALTAR ROOM
Helm runs to the altar and lifts the blanket to reveal... a corpse. The temple is alive! She tells the adventurers to devour their flesh by filling up with deadly acid. The adventurers have limited time to escape.

JAGUAR ROOM
The room is full of treasure, gunpowder, and rising acid. Light the gunpowder to destroy the room to lessen the temple's appetite. The acid won't rise past 2 feet and will drain.

STEAM ROOM
Light the volcanic rocks in the center of the room and pour the bucket of water on them to create steam. The magical steam heals the adventurers for 12 HP.

CAVERN
A wall of skulls scream at the adventurers, as 6 Conquistador Skeletons rise from an acid pool! Adventurers can destroy skulls to distract the skeletons or fight them head on.

OUTSIDE
Helm thanks the adventurers, who accompany him back to the village.

IF HELM STOPS DRINKING
He seriously considers sobriety, though he knows it'll be tougher than any monster he's fought.

IF THEY DESTROY THE JAGUAR ROOM
Treasures will spew out of the holes in the temple walls, including 2000 gold.

VILLAGE
Once Helm is returned, Vola gives them their reward and the adventurers each gain 250 XP.

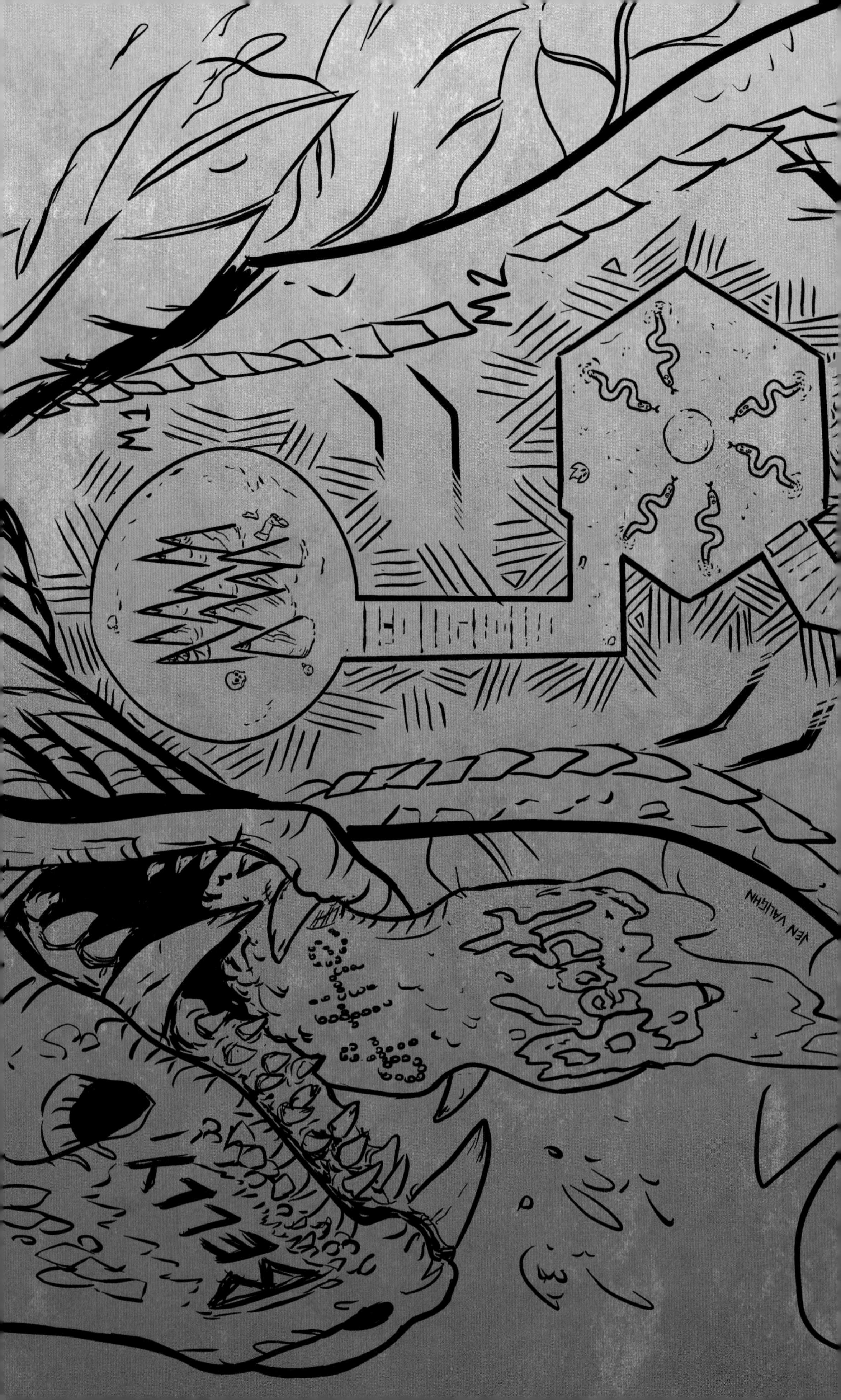
JEN VAUGHN

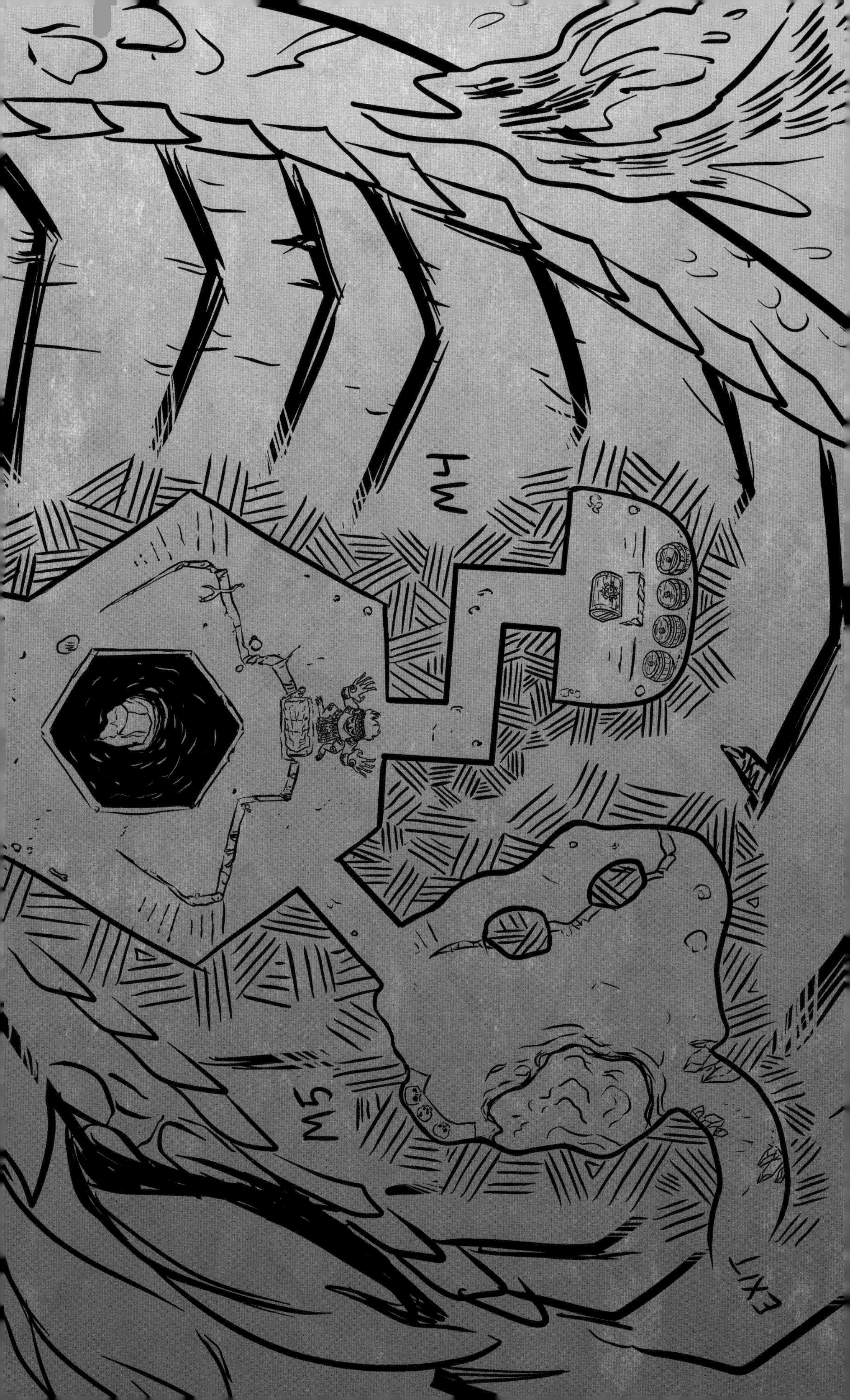
EXIT
M5
M4

COVER GALLERY

COVER 1A

RAHMAT M. HANDOKO
& BRYAN VALENZA

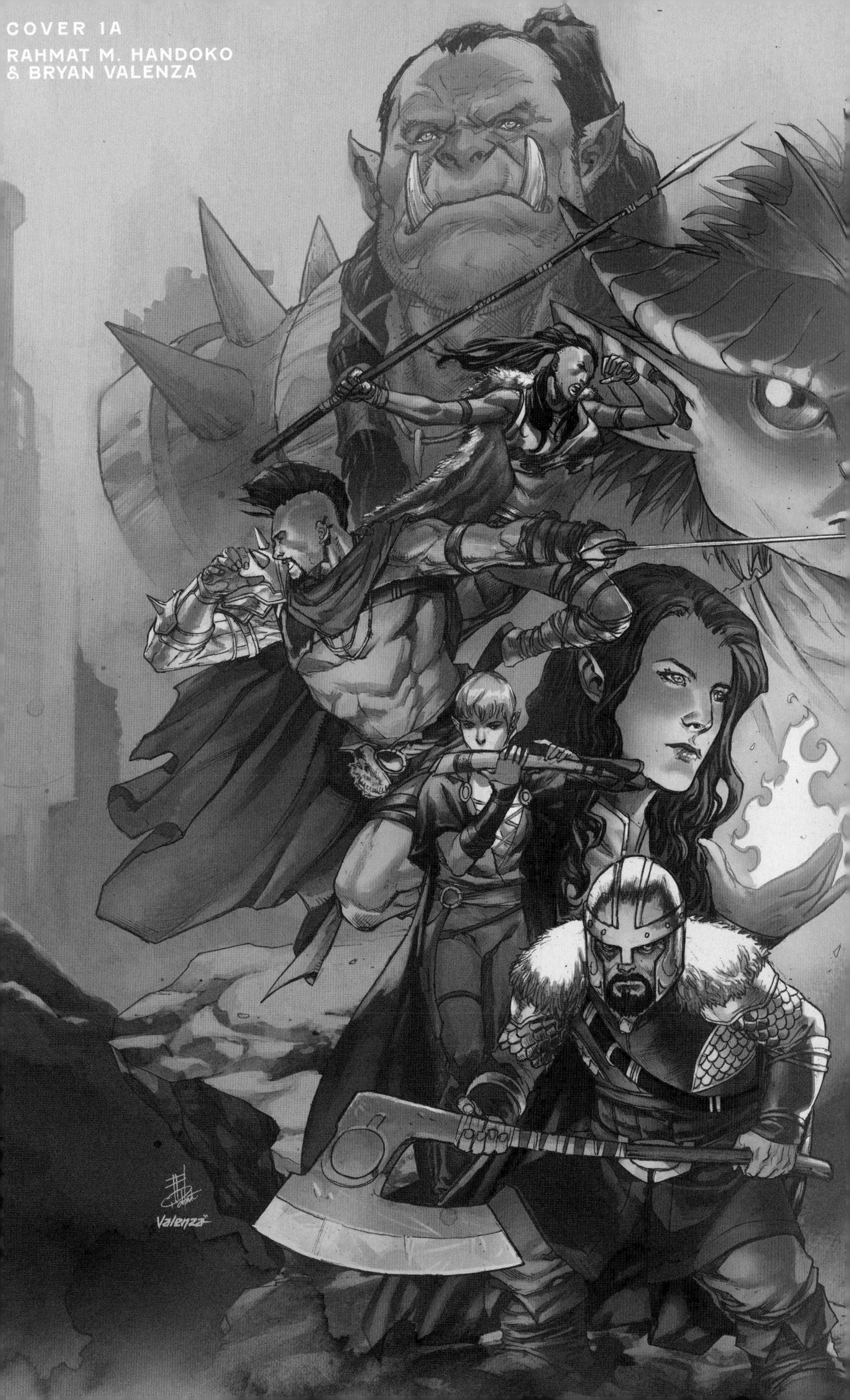
Valenza

COVER 1B

DAVID LAPHAM
& BRYAN VALENZA

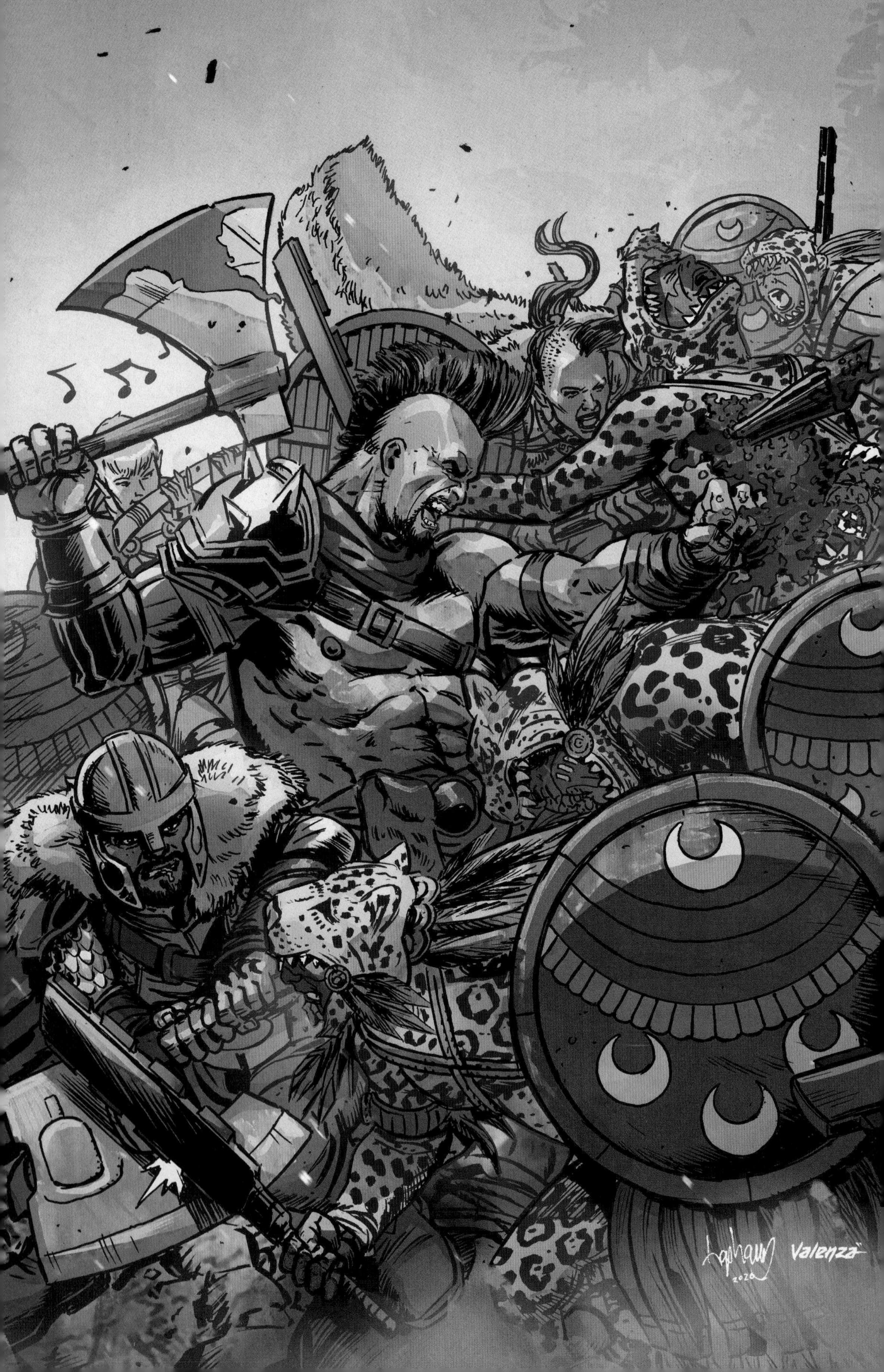
Valenza

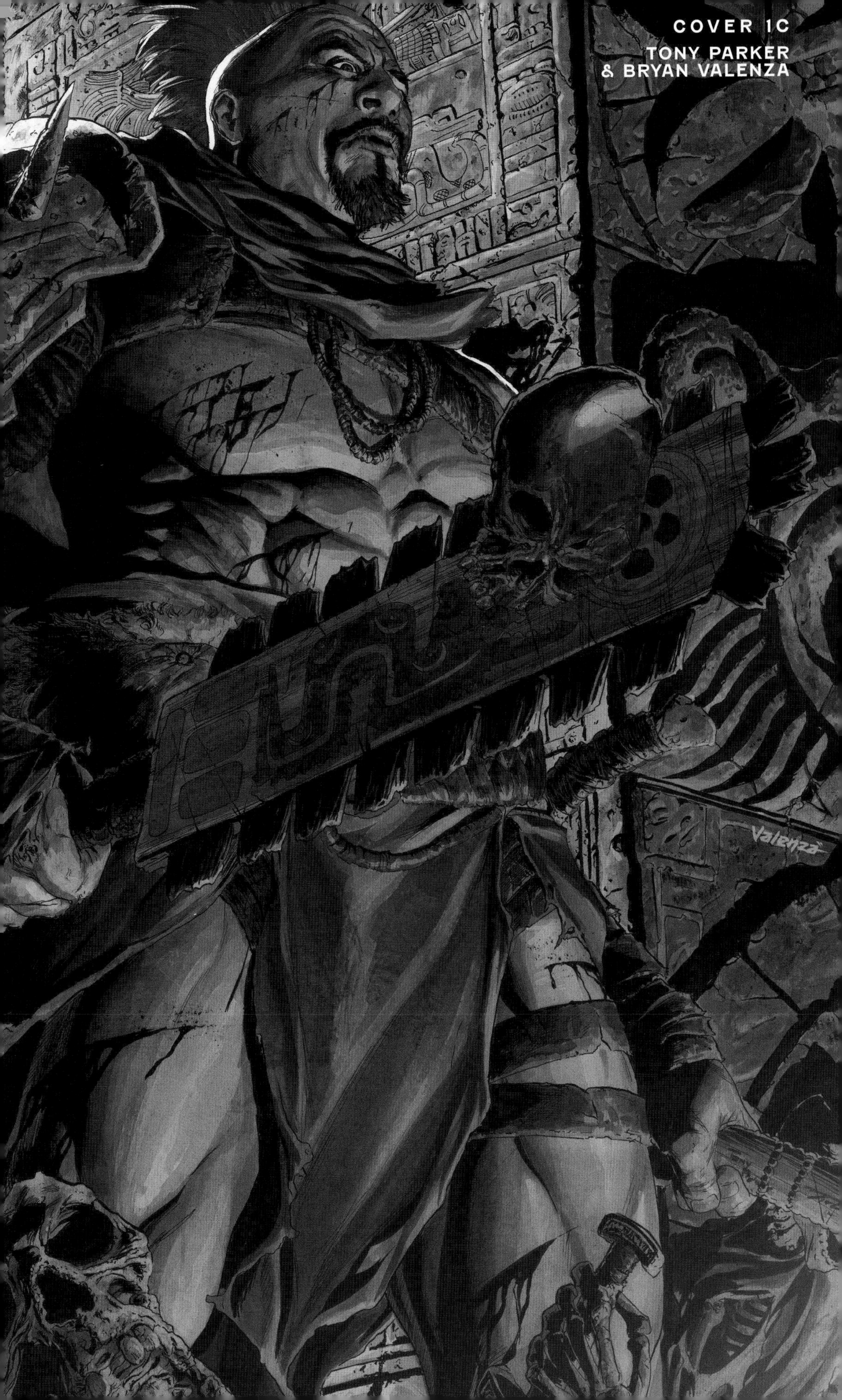
Valenza

COVER 1C
TONY PARKER
& BRYAN VALENZA

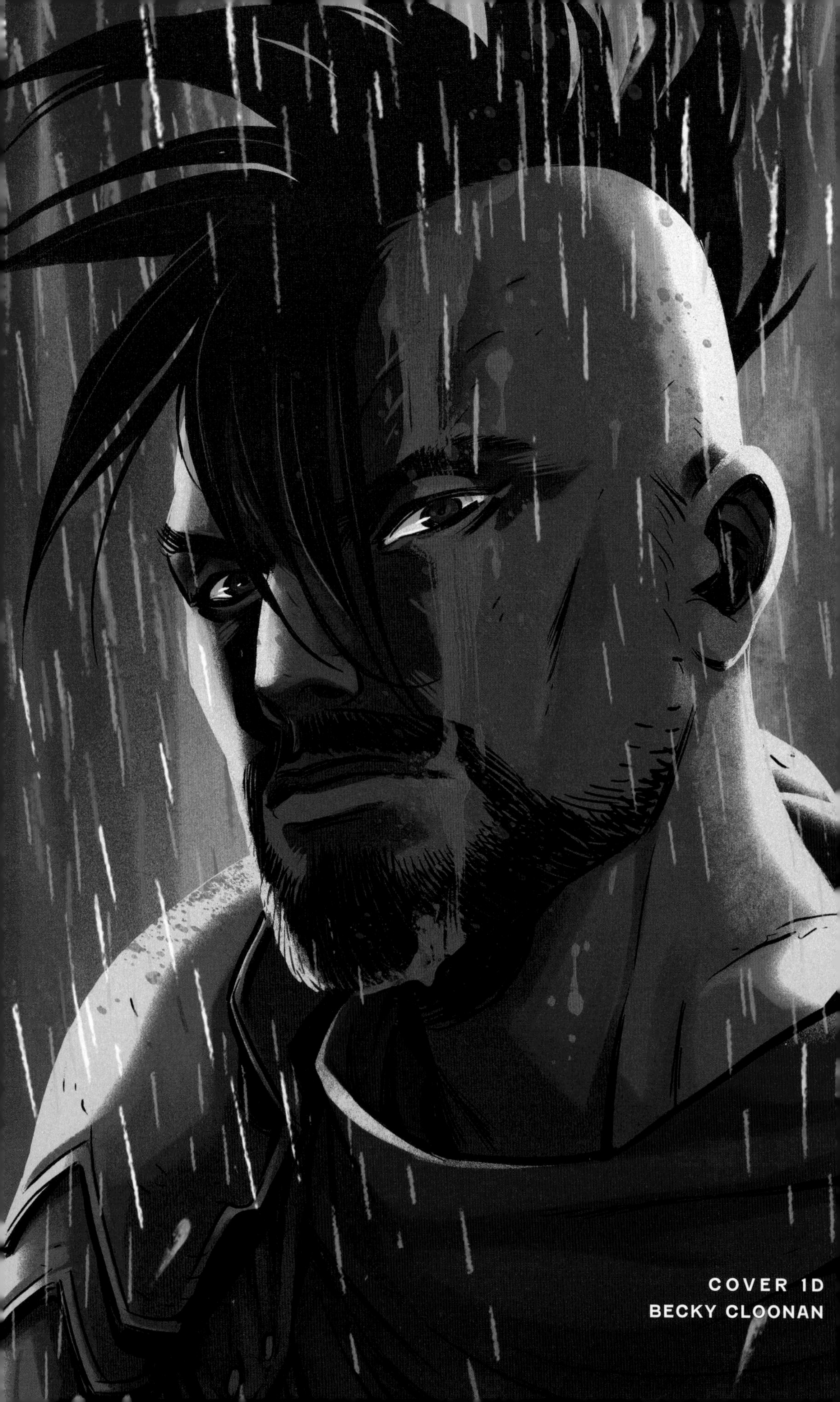

COVER 1D
BECKY CLOONAN

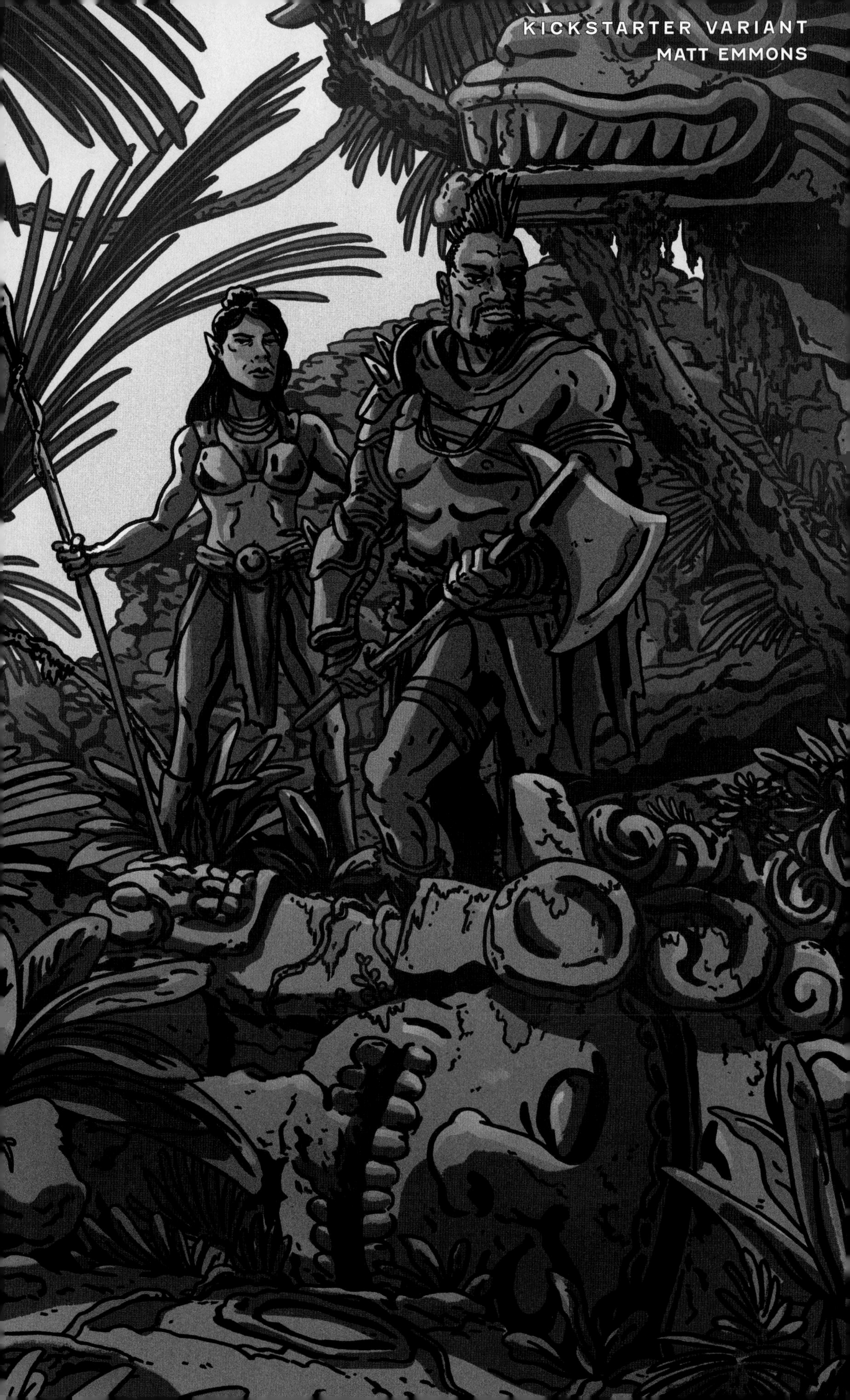
KICKSTARTER VARIANT
MATT EMMONS

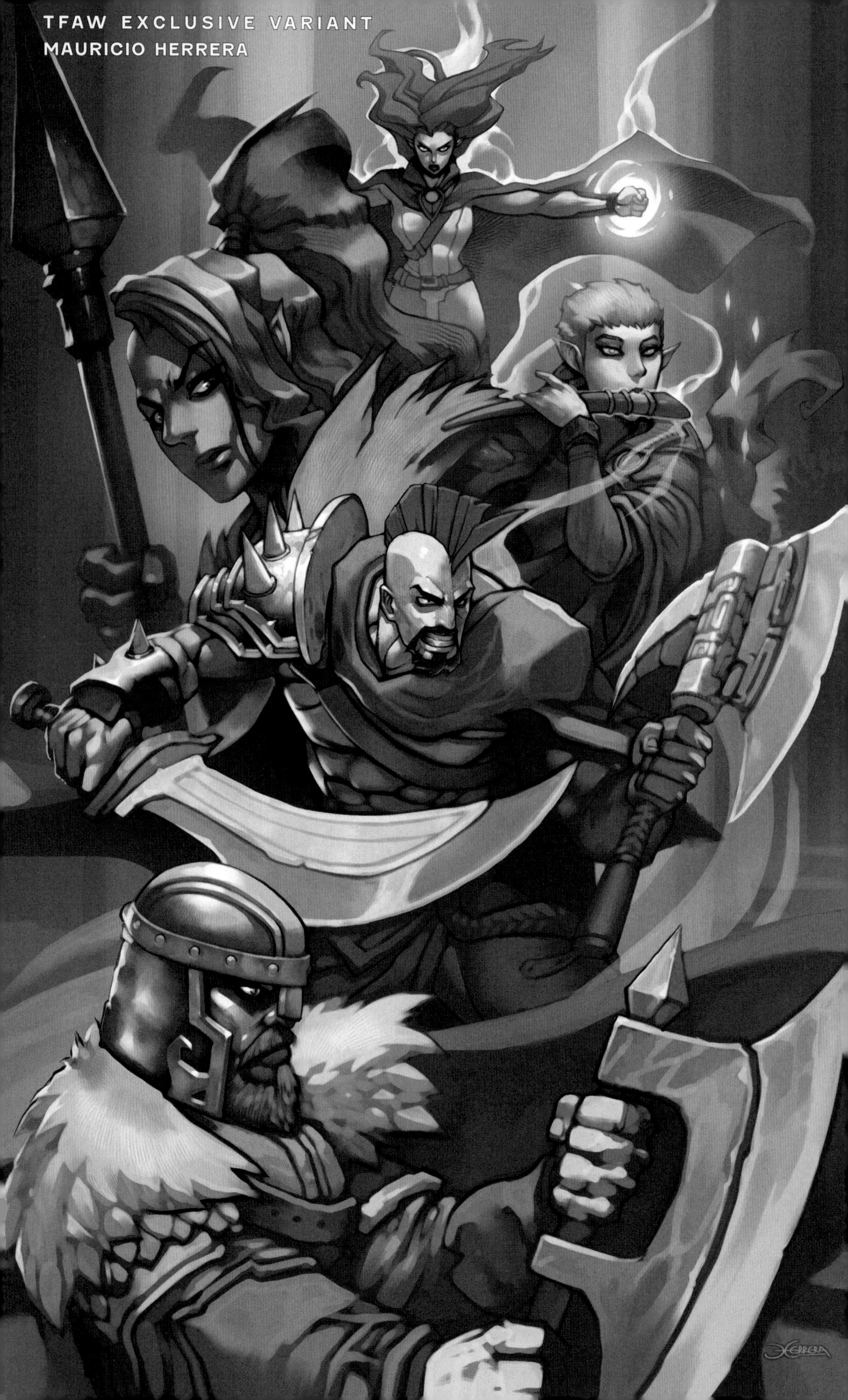

TFAW EXCLUSIVE VARIANT
MAURICIO HERRERA

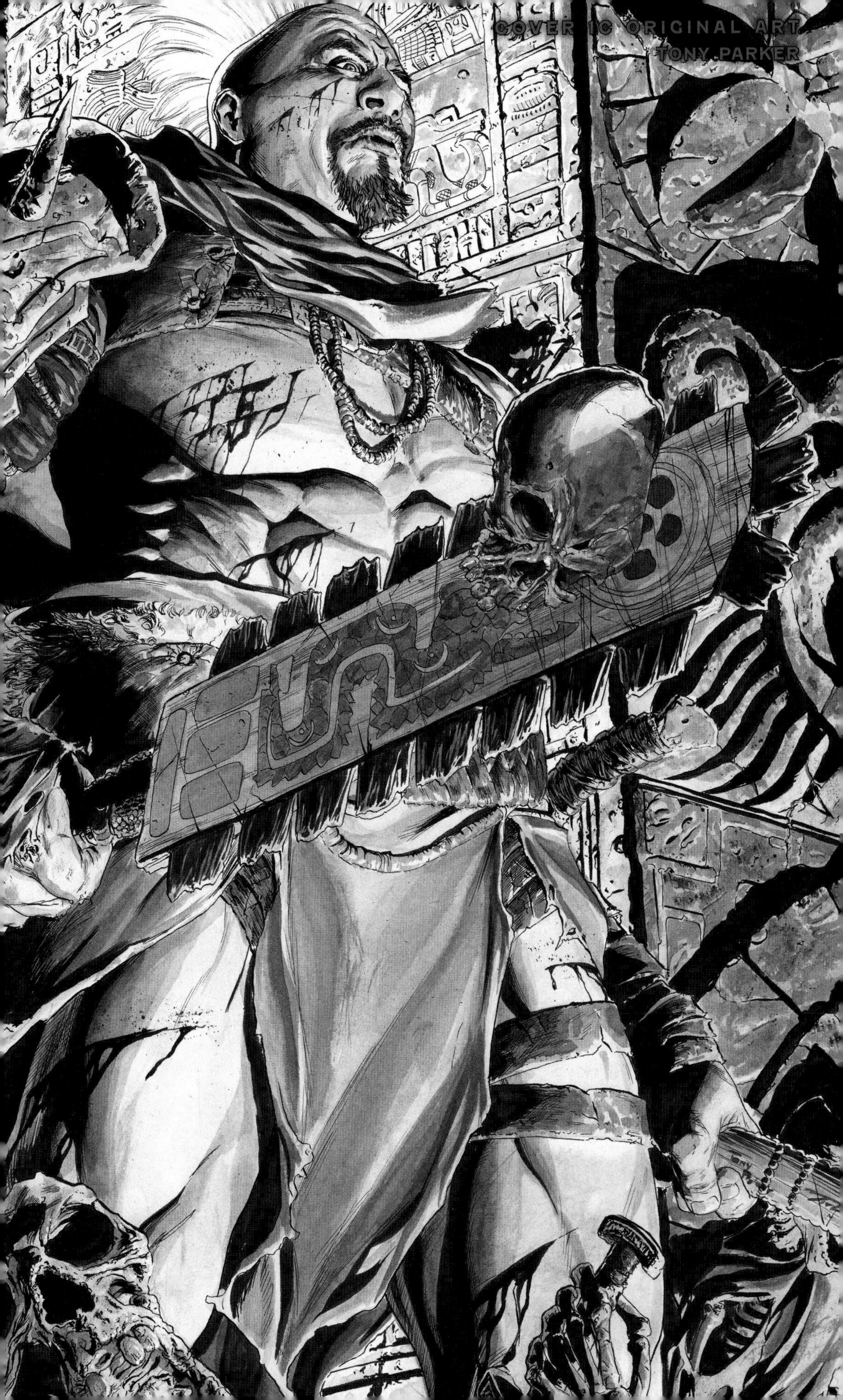
COVER 1C ORIGINAL ART
TONY PARKER

COVER 2A
DALE DEFOREST

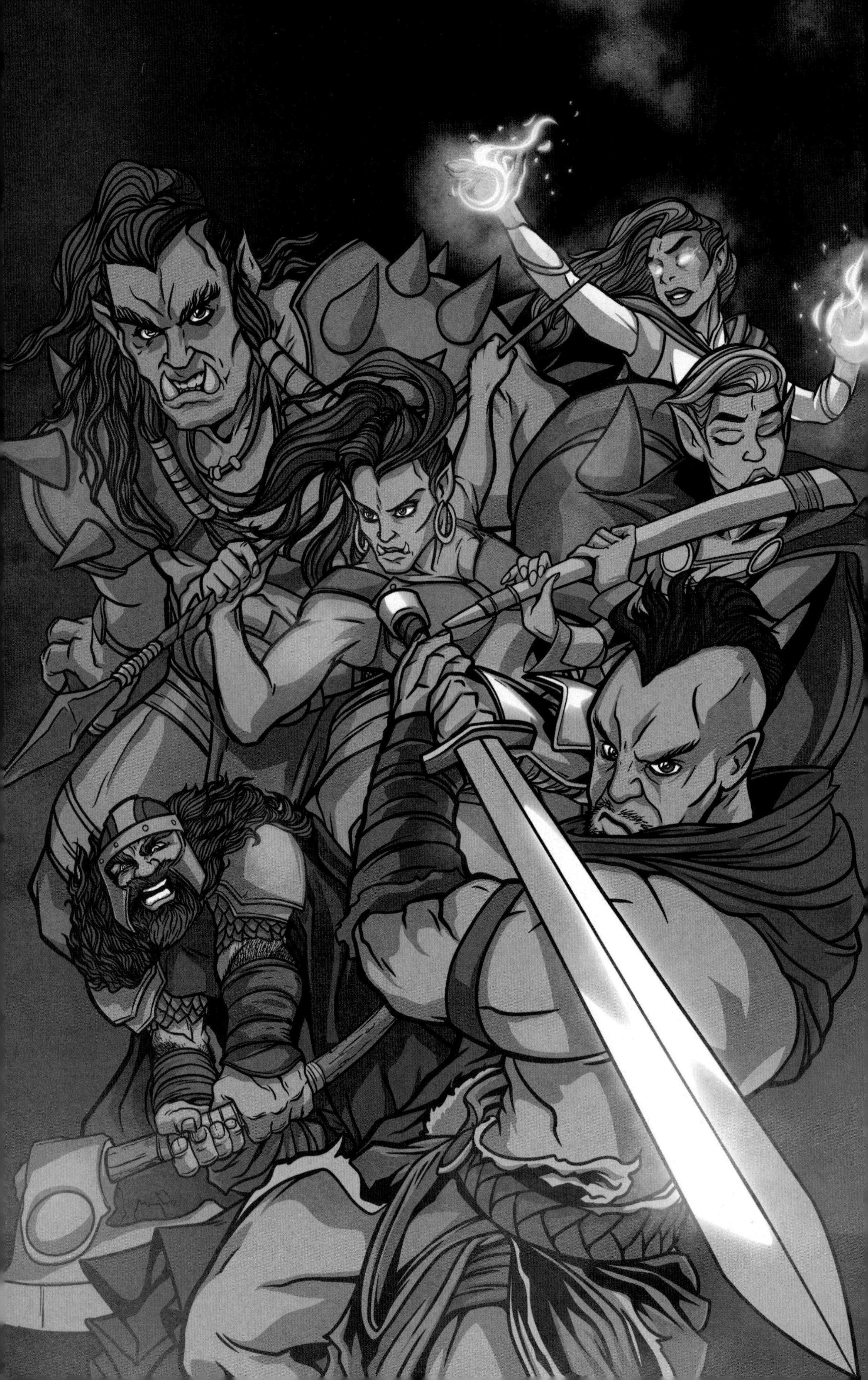

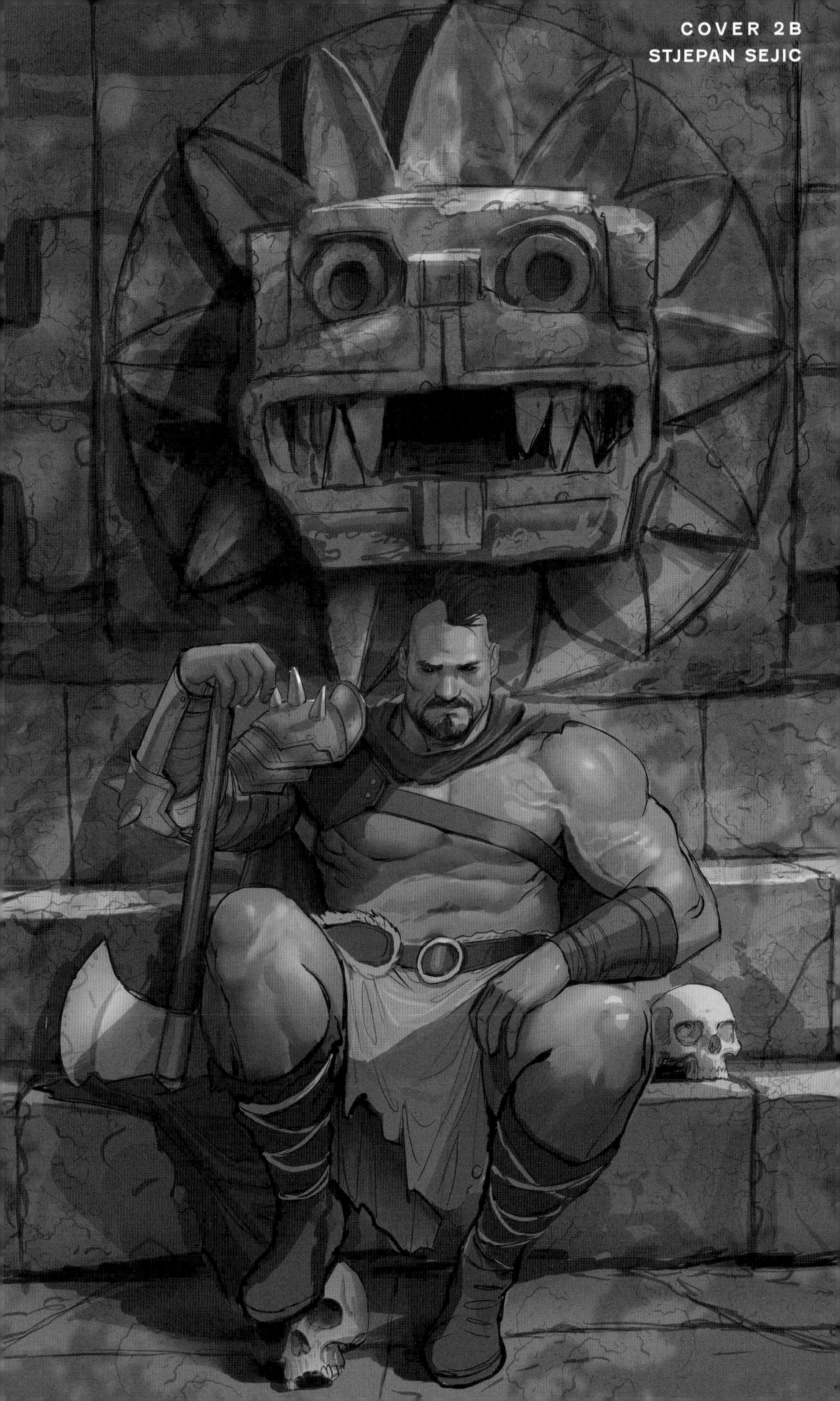

COVER 2B
STJEPAN SEJIC

COVER 3A
CHLOE M. GIROUX

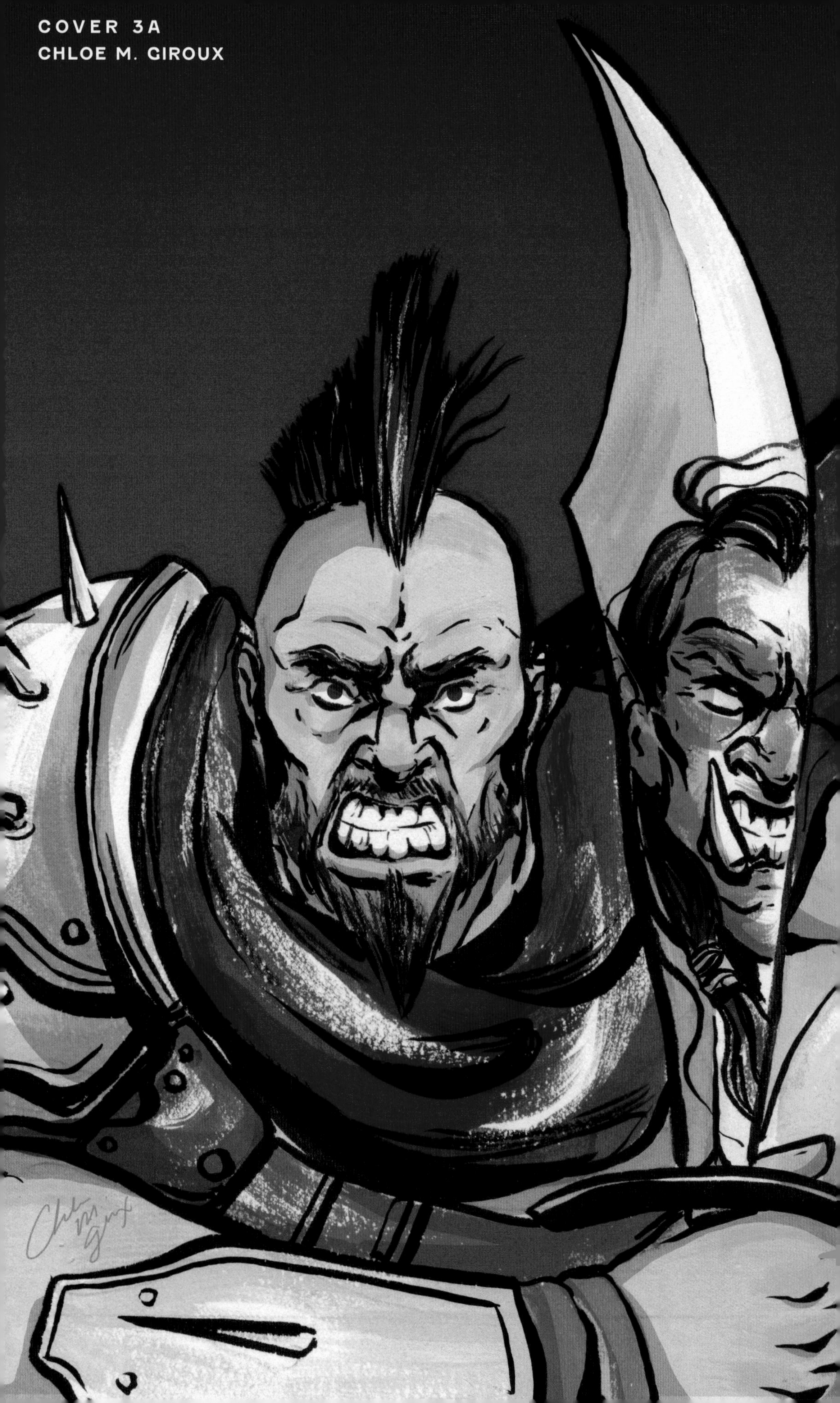

COVER 3B
GABRIELA DOWNIE

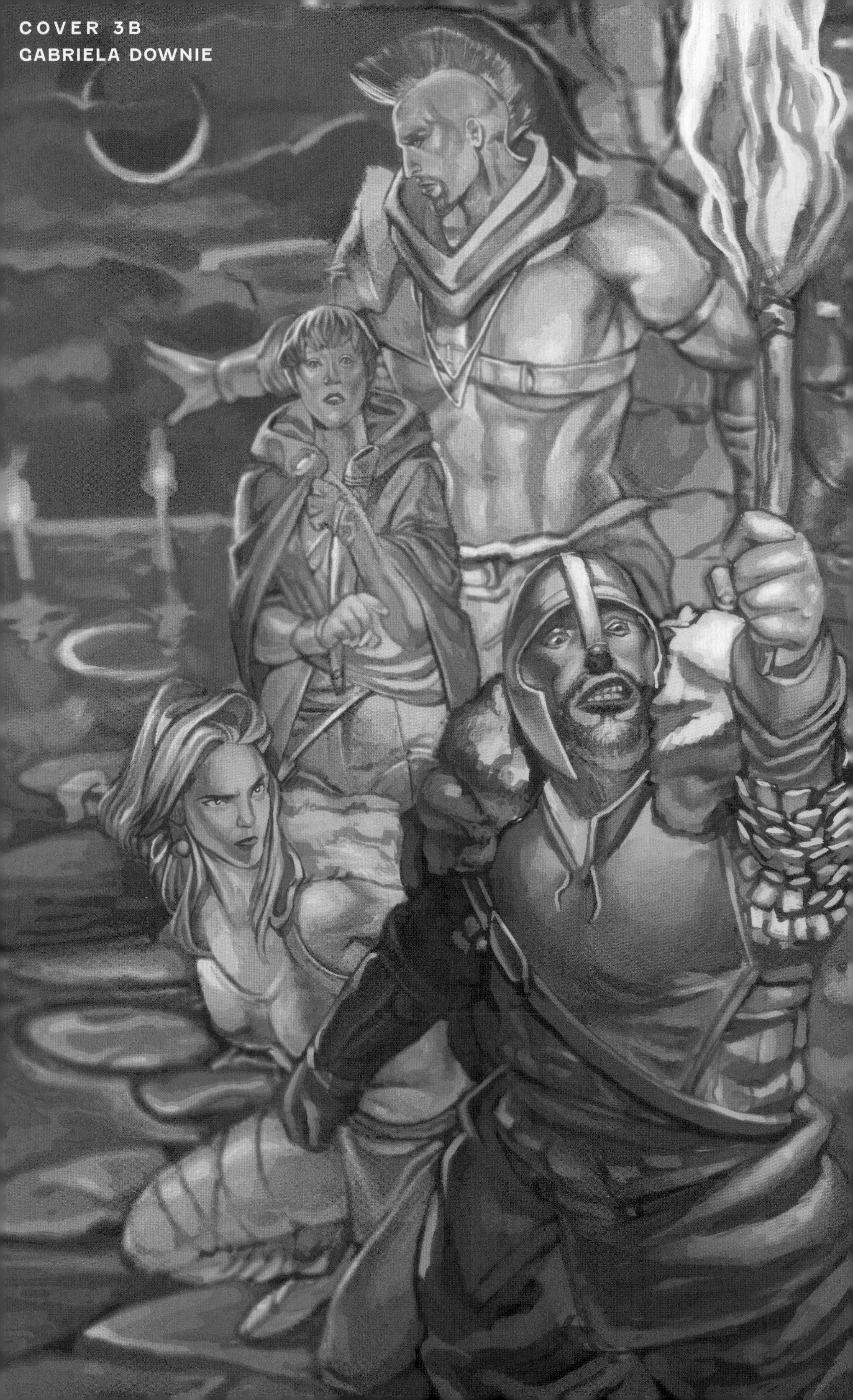

COVER 4A
BJORN BARENDS

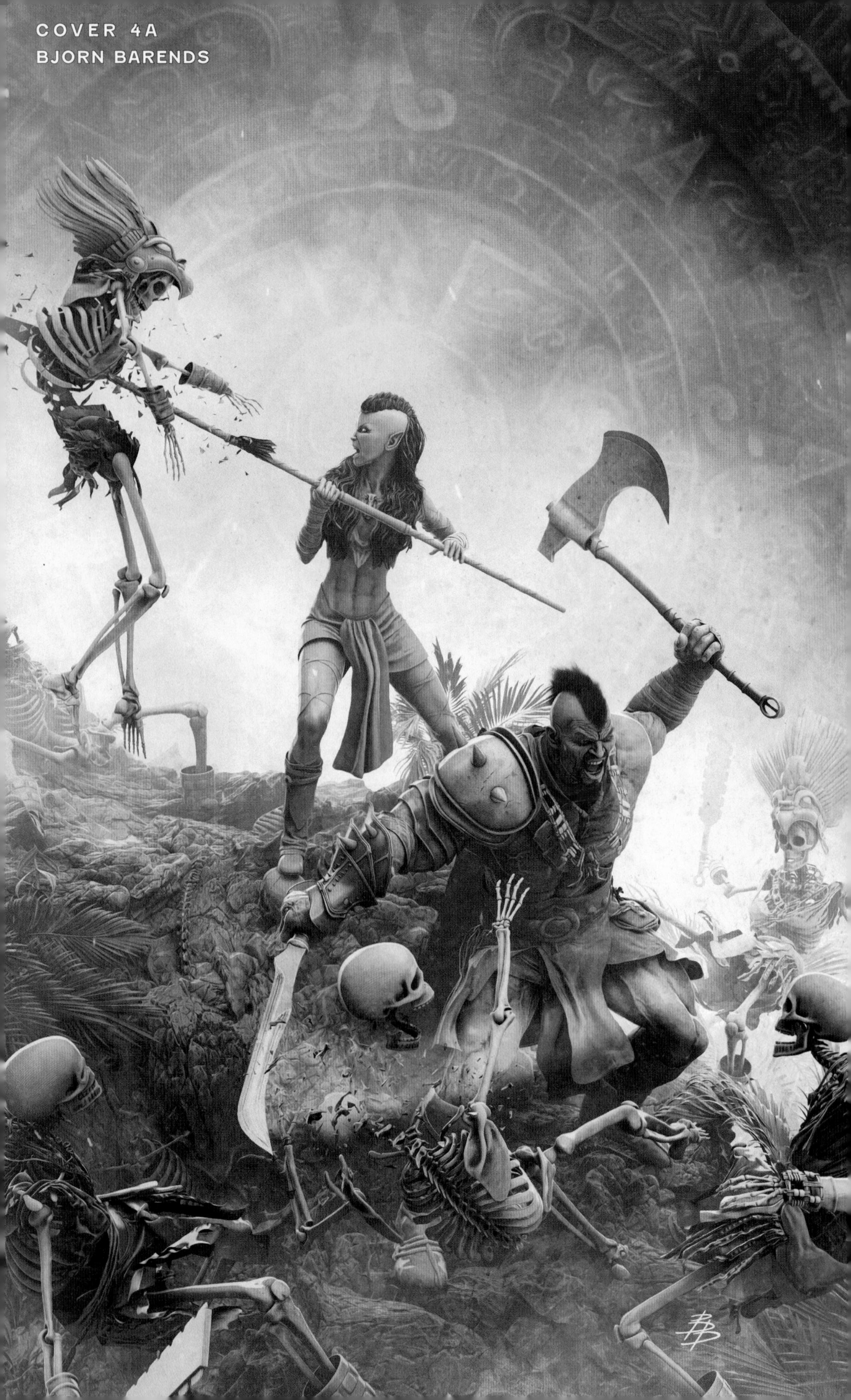

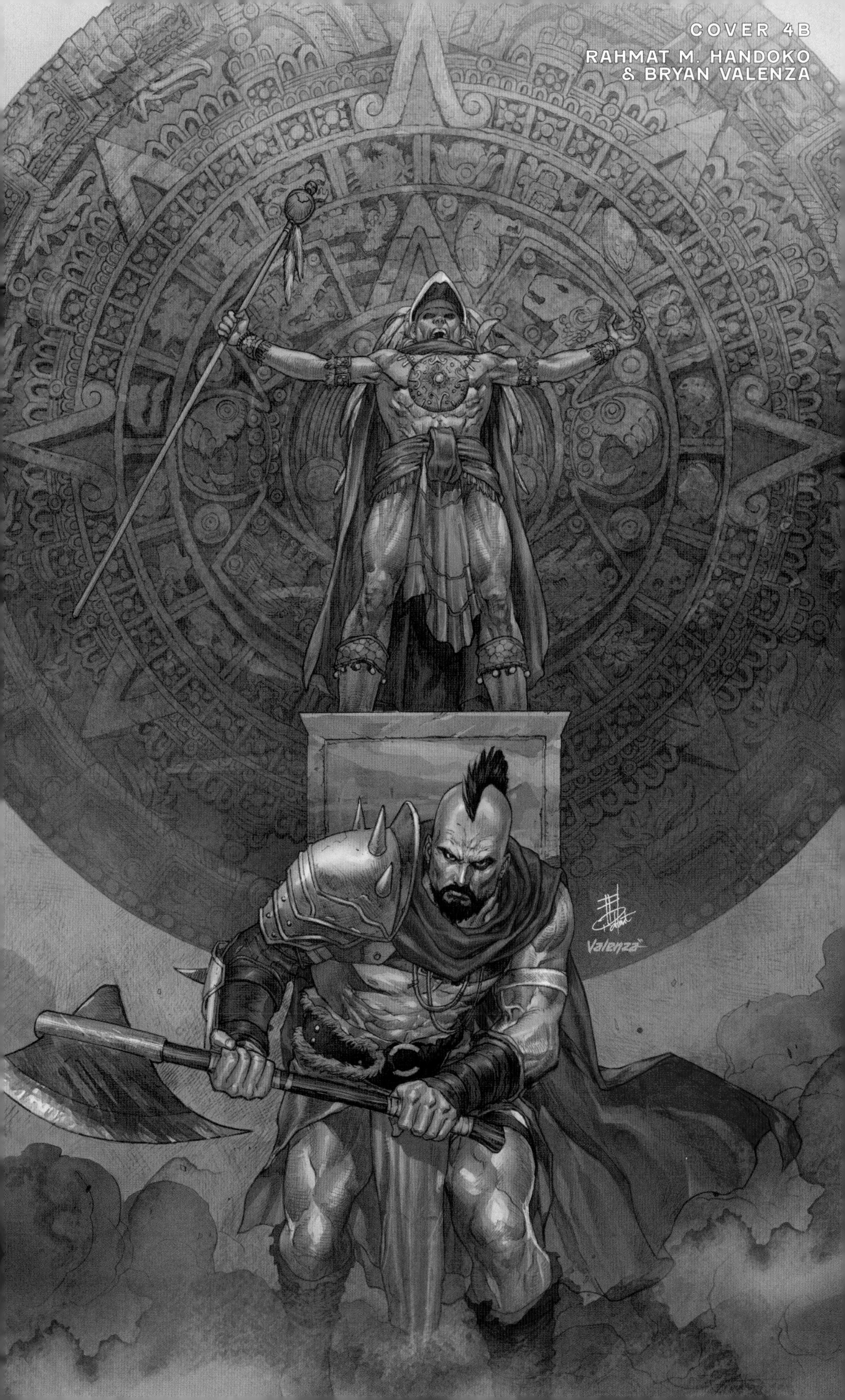
Valenza
COVER 4B
RAHMAT M. HANDOKO
& BRYAN VALENZA

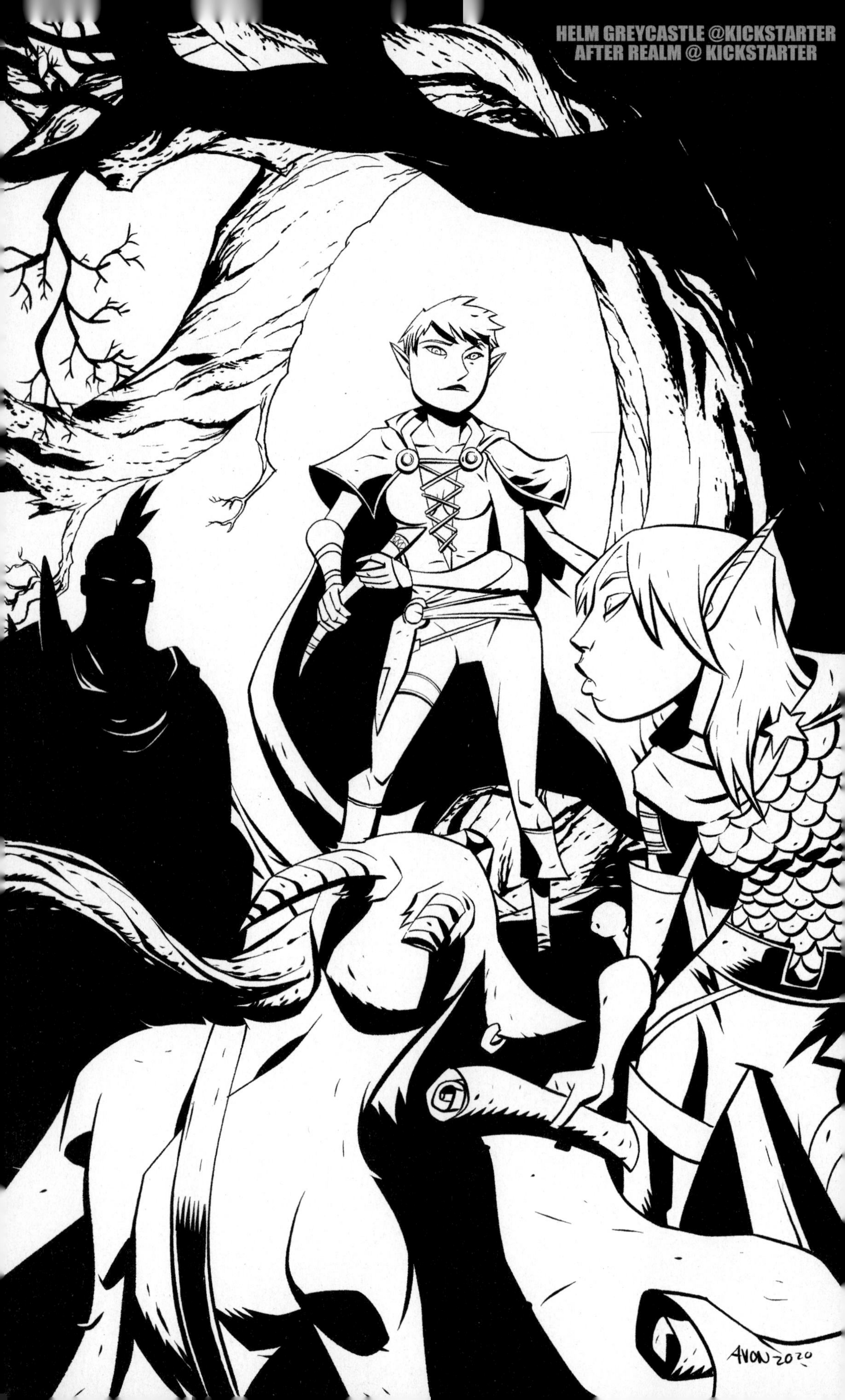
AVON 2020

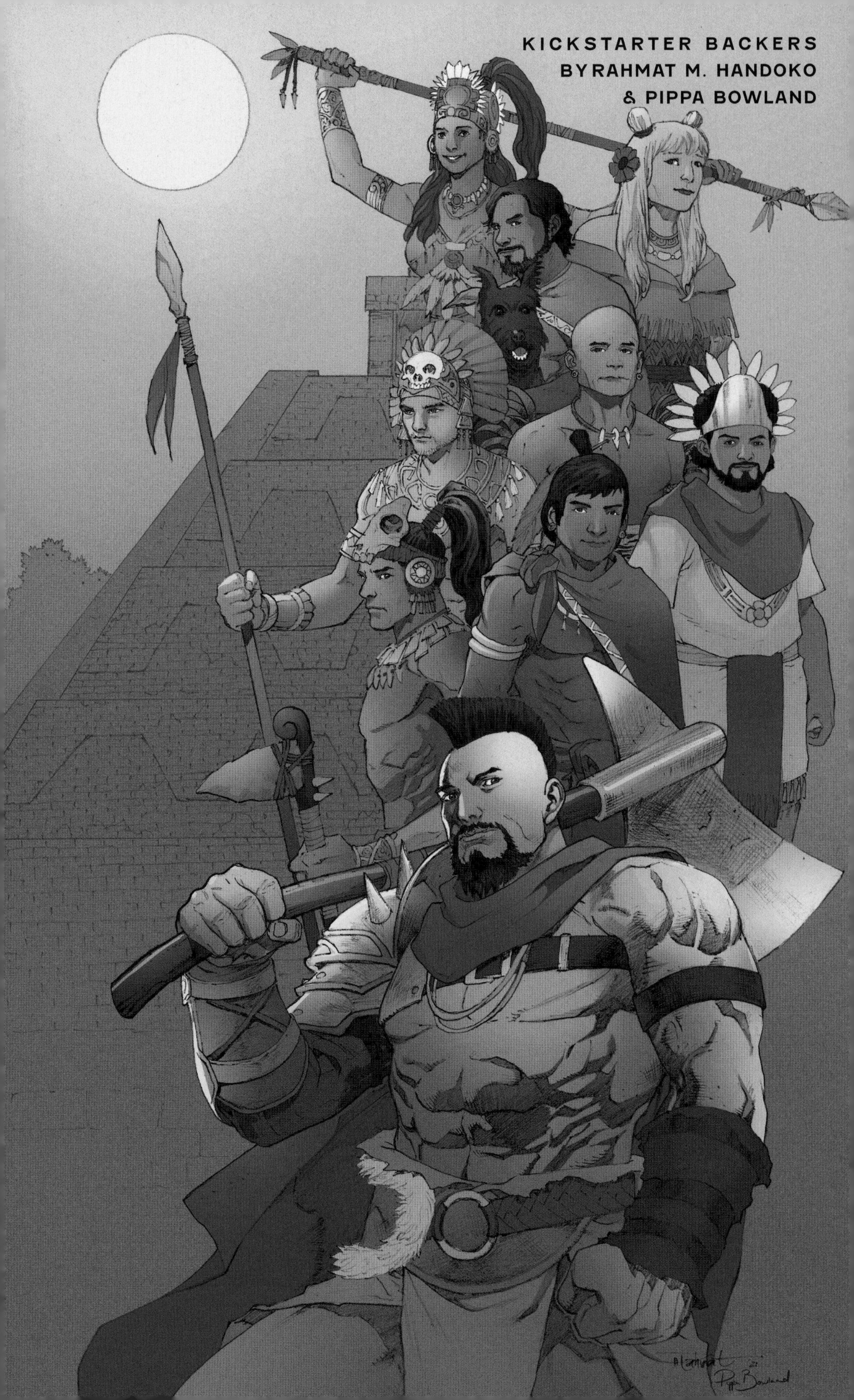

KICKSTARTER BACKERS
BY RAHMAT M. HANDOKO
& PIPPA BOWLAND

THANK YOU TO OUR KICKSTARTER BACKERS!

Omar Yehia Spahi
Tyler Button
Deborah Barajas
Andy Liegl
Arturo Salazar
Fred Higgins
Andrew Spieldenner
Samuel Ortiz
Laura Jones
Michael Conrad
Lucas A. Ferrara
Bridget Silvestri
Alex Garcia
Mario R Flores
Lauren Adkisson
Jeff Lemire
Janelle Asselin
Bethany Sell
Dan Wood
Diego Lucero Lopez
Tom Donnelly
Ron Green
Chip Mosher
Elsa Abs
Ted Lange
Patrick Bächli
Joe Crawford
DAVID CRISPINO
Ronell Whitaker
Robert Wilson IV
Mel V
Bobby Hernandez
Daniel Petersen
Katy Rex
Luke Martinez
David Mariotte
Jacob Cox
Jason Gonzalez
Francisco Ferrer
David Mendez
Julia Potter
rory monserat
Yvette Arteaga
Kate Rothgaber
allen bethel
Becky Cloonan
Joe Barrette
Joe King
Sam Smith
Jeff Simpkins
Adrian Martinez II
Kayleigh Giorgio
Jeff Torres
Rico Taveras
Amedeo Turturro
Jason M Lavochkin
Tony
Tymothy Peter Diaz
Mike Saxon
John H. Bookwalter Jr.
Stacey Adams
Chris Doray
Roberto Marquez
Chris Tollafield
David Clarke
Sean Wynn
Erik T Johnson
Donald Stewart
Johnathan Tessmer
Holly Aitchison
Christine Davis-Corona
Katrina Reid
Denis Leining
CHUNK Kelly
Brett Davis
Scott Buoncristiano
Jarred Lujan
Hope Nicholson
Andrew Snow
Vincent Zalkind
Jesus Diaz
Geoffrey Golden
Eric Spiker
Bob Quinn
Jen Vaughn
David A. Tauster
Steenz
Anthony Dash
Jean-Pierre Vidrine
Matt Roberts
Rant Howard
Lori Matsumoto
Pat O'Malley
Ben Abernathy

Curtis
Rogelio Buenrostro
Jess Taylor
Gregory Eide
Alberto Gonzalez Jr
William Boehmer
Margaret
Jordan Lee
Roddy Williams
Alexa Dickman
Matthew Lazorwitz
Liana Kangas
David Fitzsimmons
Myron Fox
Tristan Mathews
John Jutoy
David Watkins
Fredie Mejia
Alexander Eklund
Chelsea Barghout
Aviva Artzy
JACKSON W LANZING
Kent Heidelman
Kent Reinbold
Harley Jebens
Dylan Paris
Jennings Mergenthal
Alvaro Montoro
Michelle Parros
Mary Gaitan
Joel A. S. Butler
Kyle Matthews
Marty Valencia
Jaclyn Iskra
Rebecca Bryson
Jim Chadwick
Hernán Guarderas
Jillian Adams
Ramsey Sibaja
Jason Verdugo
Patrick Lugo
Aaron Yee
Dan Berry
Jon Duckworth
Peter Lennox
Jon Schlaffman
Eduardo Martinez
Thomas Mackiewicz
Jorge Garza
Anthony Pereda
Ramon Olivo
Scott Phelps
Vincent Kukua
Shawn Kirkham
Luis Carrasco
Genna Ford
Jose Pimienta
Robert Belgrave
Jenn Corella
andrew belanger
Josh Smith
Jazzlyn Huerta
Terry Blas Green
Owen Ryan
Gerardo Gutierrez
Matthew Rosenberg
Phillip Bergquist
Brian Guerrero
Kirk Spencer
Chuck Roman
Armando Ramirez
5 Meats Comics
Michael St. George Matatics
Gabriela Romero
Andrew Gonzalez
Ellen Hummel
Catfish Baruni
Kristen K Simon
Gilbert Rodriguez
christian vilaire
Jonathon Lawless
Joey Esposito
Kate Newton
David Quiles
Rodney Anderson
Sebastian Kadlecik
Nadia Uhl
Ed Brisson
Dennis T Culver
David A. Rodriguez
Gregory M Lickteig
Phillip Hanlon
Isobela Georgiades
Vincent Deloso

Joe M. Sonntag
Roland Edwards Jr
Justin C de Baca
Omar Escobar
Joel Elad
John Hull
Alex Swindle
Andrew Connor
Daria Aksenova
Edward Allen III
Kevin Alexander Bides
Gregory Lincoln
CINDY WOMACK
Eric Palicki
Zack Quaintance
Brittany Matter
Jonathan A Auerbach
Eugene Alejandro Santiago
Nick Eliopulos
Matt Nixon
Wade P Kapanke
WILLIAM ANDERSON
Rick Quinn
Kat Englin
tobey zehr
Eva Jarkiewicz
Michael Pang
CHRISTOPHER WALKER
Jeremy Holt
Salah Hassanpour
DEAN MORTON
Marcus A Jimenez
SHAUN GILROY
Rodney Dollah
Stonie Williams
Luis Enrique Leal-Munoz
Ernie Estrella
Brian Wickman
Ariel Baska
William J Dennis
Shawn Demumbrum
Jonathan Diener
Julio Anta
Alex Segura
Michael DeLong
Kate Meyers
Morgan Hampton
Mike Macropoulos
Scott Koblish
Albert Ching
paul meyer
ROSS E RICHIE
Braeden Jones
Kristy Quinn
S. Stevenson
Ivan A Salazar
Michael Cassella
Geoffrey D. Wessel
Terence Dollard
Efflam Mercier
Jack Baur
Josh Blaylock
Christian Carnus
Scott Schmidt
Mark Roslan
Anthony Barajas
Brian Thomer
Ben Prenevost
Alinna Stinnett
George Carmona
Matt Smith
David Kinsel
Shaun Peterson
Jiba Anderson
Jason Davis
Scott Maynard
Ryan Smith
Stephanie Phillips
Chris Hernandez
Tom LaGatta
Logan Naugle
Phillipe Bojorquez
Mr Alexander J Waldren
Zack Kaplan
Phillip Kirby
Alexandra Robinson-Burns
Barbara Perez Marquez
Asher Powell
D.J. Kirkbride
Felipe Cagno
Jeremy Mohler
9th Level Games
Travis Rivas
Moni Barrette

Bryan A Conner
Jim Hanna
Jacob Breckenridge
Dan Kroon
Joseph Chong
Drew Fitzgerald
Carson Anderson
Jennie Cochran-Chinn
Andrea Rosales
Peter M Schmeer
Norm Harper
Grace Gordon
Jason Hammons
Brandon Lee Nelms
Hector Rodriguez
Matthew McBee
Andrew W Grisham
Phillip Hester
Daniel Kleen
Todd Avery
Michael Bryant
Patrick LaBruzzo
Erin Collins
Daniel Templin
John Greiner
Steven Charles Brown
Derek Barsness
Eben Burgoon
Amy Kleman
Wendoline Infante
Chris Foster
Ashley Washington
Ronald Zabala
Thomas M. DeVaughan
Luke Gartner-Brereton
Cairn Riney
Charlie Stickney
Scary Stuff Podcast
Rich Boyle
Chris Call
Steven Prince
Chris Ayyoub
Peter Engebos
Brenton Lengel
Kiel Phegley
Michael Tanner
Frank Zanca
John J Riley
Jeffrey Tokman
Zach Anderson
Michael Pokorny
F. James Martin
Eric T. Sorlien
Jeffrey Lee
Jonathan Bowen
Erik Rinard
Jamal D Narcisse
ro lamb
Franky J DeJesus
Matt Wolfe
Travis Lovellette
Kelly Evans
Andrew Nisbet
Michael C. Fedoris
Simon Birks
Shaun Manning
Donald Claxon
Leisha-Marie Riddel
Bruce Bevens
Andy
Andrew Kaplan
Ibrahim Moustafa
Don Cardenas
Joseph Cooper
Danny Djeljosevic
Craig A. Taillefer
Adam Ferris
Ellen Power
Elizabeth Brei
david brothers
Izzi
Günter roithmeier
David Crocker
David Marquez
Christof Bogacs
Aubrey Sitterson
Brian Weibeler
Corgi Boss
Mike Rooth
Oeming
Cristina Lazala
Joe Ranoia
wolf
Bernardo Briceño

Alex Paknadel
Ryan K Lindsay
Todd Matthy
Adam Bauser
Sequart Research & Literacy Organization
Ashardalon89
Andrew Maxwell
Curse of Sebs
Paul Baumeister
Chris
Ray Chou
Andrew Mauney
Komavary
Hula Mcula
Robbie Smith
Stephane PHILIPPO
NangijalaIF
William Carranza
K
George O'Connor
Nightwing
Matt Harding Productions
Veronica Tyus
BHP Comics
Joe Illidge
Matthew Sibley
Stephanie Cooke
Ryan Ruppe
Jann Jones
Nola Pfau
PM
Samir Sayed
Mike Rapin
Bartimaeus
Marco Cunalata
Matthias Ackerl
Richard Parker
Declan Shalvey
Gary Moloney 42
JP Jordan
Jake Shyer
G.I.
Ian
Marco Moll
Jonathan Whiteley
Justin Greenwood
Jennie Gruber
James
Ben C
Trevor D. Perry
T.J. Wiley
Chloe Ramos
Chuck Robinson
George Peterson
Lars Peter netchaef
Matthew Demelio
Craig Hackl
Hassan Otsmane-Elhaou
dgwohl
Shaun Kronenfeld
Stephen Morris
Frazer Brown
Jon Morris
Douglas Broome
Anthony
Matthew Gray
Jonathan Thompson
Giovanni P. Timpano
Jon Moisan
Tim Mcburnie
Ben Krieger
J. L. Johnson Jr.
Shea Austin
Jacob Edgar
Jakub Šebesta
Andy "Shaggy" Korty
Switch
Sarah Gordon
Chris Mole
Nic ter Horst
Sylvia Moon
Alberto Rayo
Tharathip Opaskornkul
Robin
Jody Houser
Brandon Eaker
Tim Malone II
Jon Trainer
Charles D. Moisant
Timothy G Smith
Gene Verley
Nafmi Sanichar-van Her-wijnen

DeepFoxJude
Daniel Huntley
Daniel D. Calvo
Kohilan Mohanarajan
Christopher Kranz
Joe Davidson
Jim Demonakos
Jacob Haller
Jared 'pirate' Foley
Joe
Mathew Wahrman
Kendrick Hernandez
Rex Co.
Catherine
Tim Stroup
Shelly Bond
Heather
Kathryn Calamia
Luca Beltrami
Niko O.
Eric Müller
tvest
Gavin Greene
Ronald
Dan
Chris Tomlinson
David F. Walker
Shaun Sunday
Gaëtan Voyer-Perrault
Brant Fowler
Nalin Taylor
Adimo37
Charlie Harris
Einar Petersen
Craig McKenney
Elmi
Hannah Rose May
Martin John
Vince Hernandez
Christine
Rebecca Bateson
Nadine Roselle
Jack Holder
JOJO
Ernest Romero
Fran Delgado
Randall Nichols
The Creative Fund by BackerKit
Allen & Donna Breckenridge
Oscar Alfredo Pérez Cordoba
Meaghann Tomahawk Clark
Jessicah Cheyenne Hohman

Praise for Helm Greycastle

"By following the traditions of high fantasy, HELM GREYCASTLE serves to push boundaries with its Latin American setting and perspective...the series that feels more real and original than some kind of forced corporate attempt at diversity. The result here is joyous and immersive world-building with recognizable yet relatable characters."

– Hannah Rose, CBR

"HELM GREYCASTLE is a great template for a way to decenter whiteness while telling a highly imaginative, compelling story that feels much more reflective of the genre's readers."

– John Schaidler, Multiversity Comics

"...if you're looking for a new perspective on the standard western high fantasy setting, then HELM GREYCASTLE may be worth checking out."

– Michael Thao, Geek'd Out

"Henry's passion for inclusion of Mesoamerica in pop culture is palpable in the pages of this book. From the beautiful art, the lovingly researched setting, and the fun and very human characters. The twist of including the Mexica as part of the main plot, with interesting and multifaceted characters, was a breath of fresh air."

– Sofia E. Alexander, EP & Creator of Onyx Equinox

"HELM GREYCASTLE is a wonderful adventure told through lively writing and beautiful art. Henry Barajas is bringing much needed diversity and inclusion to comics and the fantasy genre."

– Sydney Phillips

"A roaring, well-characterized fantasy story elevated by the deft inclusion of Mesoamerican myth and culture; it also includes a whole playable module in the back, making it a must-buy for RPG fans."

– Alex de Campi (DRACULA, MOTHERF*CKER)

"What HELM GREYCASTLE does for high fantasy action-adventure stories is what polyhedral dice did for the advent of tabletop gaming. Both changed the game. Don't sleep on what will assuredly be your new favorite comic book series."

– Jeremy Holt (MADE IN KOREA)

"From the beautiful art and vibrant colours to the exuberant characters and story; everything pops off the page and breathes new life into the adventure genre. If you're part of the ever-growing fanbase of Dungeons & Dragons and TTRPGs, HELM GREYCASTLE is for you."

– Stephanie Cooke (Oh My Gods!)

"HELM GREYCASTLE is a fantastic, immersive debut - and speaks to me creatively and personally. An epic Latinx fantasy that revels in the elements of the genre but also manages to feel relevant and of-the-moment, Barajas, Valenza, and Handoko lay the foundation for what will hopefully be a long, winding run."

– Alex Segura (Star Wars Poe Dameron: Free Fall, The Black Ghost, Miami Midnight)

"HELM GREYCASTLE is both classic, and endlessly surprising - serving up the fantasy calories we all crave but with provocative new twists in every scene. Step into a world you only think you know, and eyes up for Jaguar Knights. Kids that hunger for some good old fashioned killing, and a world of Middle American Myth as you've never seen before."

– Steve Orlando (COMMANDERS IN CRISIS)

Henry Barajas is a Latinx author from Tucson, AZ. He is best known for his graphic memoir about his great-grandfather Ramon Jaurigue titled *La Voz De M.A.Y.O. Tata Rambo*. He has contributed to anthologies that benefit mass shooting Route 91 victims and The Southern Poverty Law Center such as *Where We Live* and *The Good Fight*.

Bryan Valenza has been a comic book colorist since 2012. In 2017 he founded the coloring studio BEYOND Colorlab, based in Jakarta, Indonesia. He currently occupies his time coloring various projects, including *Witchblade, Golgotha, Skies of Fire, InSEXts,* and *Mighty Morphin Power Rangers*.

Claire Napier is a freelance editor and cartoonist. She was a features editor at Women Write About Comics for six years, and Editor-In-Chief 2017-2018. She still writes for WWAC, as well as at ComicsMNT and Shelfdust. Among others, Claire edits Hari Connor's award-winning *Finding Home,* the activist memoir *La Voz De M.A.Y.O.: Tata Rambo*, and is currently editing the story comics magazine *BUN & TEA*. She can be found at @illusclaire and will be delighted to work with you.

Rahmat Handoko has worked on various illustrations and comic projects during his career as a professional illustrator. Some of his famous works are DC Universe Online Illustrations Cards, *G.I. Joe* cards, and *Iron Man* for Marvel Comics. Currently, the artist behind *Helm Greycastle* from Top Cow Productions.

Gabriela Downie was born and raised in Los Angeles—the daughter of Central American Refugees—and is at the helm of diversity and inclusion in the entertainment industry. Downie is self-taught and inspired to keep paving the way for more Latinx artists. Follow her at @gabrieladownieincomics on Instagram.

FLESHING OUT HELM

By Claire Napier

When I came on board for this project, it was already well away—Henry and Bryan had established their worlds, their characters, their plot, the majority of the events of the books. Half the first issue had already been lettered! That means, as an editor, there wasn't a great deal for me to immediately do, beyond wrangle the scripted dialogue into its best form and in that the form that best complemented the drawn and coloured pages. Indeed, by the second issue my role had rolled over into co-writer, which to be specific in this case meant that I laid down dialogue options and some additional detail over Henry's plotting and panel descriptions, made suggestions back and forth with him after he'd added his own preferred lines, and adjusted that team dialogue again once the pages were drawn and the space for the lettering defined, inarguable, in two dimensions. Essentially, my part in things was very much of the old school "Marvel method," making the illustrated plot sing as well as it could through character speech and captioning, which I enjoyed enormously. It's just fun.

So, creatively and consultationally, all of my focus went into identifying the appropriate "voice" for each of the billion characters within this story. There are a lot of them, a notable lot of them over at least three factions, which is daring and agreeable; it means there's a favourite available for everyone (who's yours?) and a lot of different moods and perspectives to consider, which is inspiring and engaging for those inclined towards roleplay and game thinking.

Henry had character bios in his pitch packet, which I had access to, and with those and the first script, plus the plotted events and the indications on motivation and perspective that those implied, I set about triangulating the vibe for each character. This is a very good job to have. Let me offer some examples!

Oskar was fairly easy: Peter Jackson's Gimli founded the passionate dwarf template for the twenty-first century, and as Henry's resources made it clear that Oskar was both devotedly romantic and gay that was enough of a disruption to make his dialogue come fairly easily. What would Gimli say, if he were a more central character, queer and not subject to homophobia? Add a little Brian Blessed for beard-guy flair, and—easy. An indignant, tender, rich-voiced lover of life who enjoys making his opinions on events known, perhaps obliquely through use of a conversant—usually Shava, as her communication through musical notes meant that the space taken by her responses need not be large, leaving Oskar a bit of yardage for his verbosity. They're also both gay, and therefore provide each other immediate backup in a way that is hopefully soothing in a world (ours) that DOES contain homophobia and queer isolation. Shava, for her part, gets to be piquant without becoming arch or distant like Enxina, as Oskar's exposition-through-response puts a different tone to any disagreement or suspicion implicit in her position. Oskar's passion is a good foil for her ambiguousness, I hope—she gains some irony through his presence as an explicitly passionate interpreter.

Enxina's archness grew out of her matter-of-fact statements and orders in the draft script for issue one, as well as her obvious power as a sorcerer. Sorcery suggests study; she has knowledge and intelligence, which nobody else in her party especially prioritises. She outranks everyone almost innately, and to soften that you either have to really soften it, the Final Fantasy-style pleasant girl healer type, make her apologetic (irritating), or lampshade it by making her standoffish and challenging. Obviously I chose the latter! Rahmat's choices in her design on the page gave her quite a flat affect on top of her competence, what's often known as a "resting bitch face," so—why not make her a resting bitch? Nothing Enxina does is cruel or dominating, she's essentially an honest and helpful person, so allowing her to be judgemental and outspoken makes her an "unlikable character" while everything she actually does is for the greater good (and therefore "likable"). It's fun to mix these oppositional aspects together in various ways—creativity often benefits from juxtaposition and emotional paradox.

A character of this strength (whose statements are forceful) is useful to have amongst a large cast, because they provide opportunity for other characters to be impacted and to make statements in direct opposition to Enxina's. Dona Isobela, for example, is a gentle girl on the whole, she has an air of quietness and an attitude of retiring elegance, but she's also a princess, and a princess might have enough entitlement to deference to force even a gentle person toward a cowing interjection when someone is sufficiently rude in front of her—as Dona does, outright stating that Enxina is judgemental after Enxina disrespects the cultural values of her hosts. A brasher character than Dona could say more, could really scold or criticise Enxina, but for Dona Isobela a simple statement is enough. Enxina is judgemental, which is both evidently true and itself an implicit judgement on whoever it's used to describe! A very subtle way of shutting down a rude acquaintance. Hopefully this gives some indication of how distressing it must have been for Dona to see her father become the mess that Cortez made of him.

Helm Greycastle #1

Written By Henry Barajas

Page One
Four Panels

1. Helm Greycastle stabs an ice pirate with his long sword. He is fighting with his crew outside of the STORM CASTLE. It's like Alaska but always daytime and you can't see the sun.

   sfx smash!

   a. **HELM**: I think they're getting tired!
   ICE PIRATE: Kill the colonizer!
   CAPTION: HELM GREYCASTLE
   SUB-CAPTION: FEARLESS LEADER

2. Shava Nailo plays her flute (made of elephant bone) causing the ice pirates to crack before they can strike her.

   SFX MUSICAL NOTES

   SFX CRACK!
   CAPTION: SHAVA NAILO
   SUB-CAPTION: ELVEN SIREN

3. Long shot on Oskar Frostbeard running out of STORM CASTLE with a scroll. He's beaten and bloody, but he's happy that he has what they came for. Ice Pirates are trying to catch up but he's too fast for a short, stout dwarf.

   b. **OSKAR**: I've stolen their sanctified text! RETREAT!
   CAPTION: OSKAR FROSTBEARD
   SUB-CAPTION: PASSIONATE DWARF

4. Over the shoulder shot from the ice pirates. They're almost see-through. They surround Vola. Blood drips from her mouth as she readies her warhammer to strike her foes.

   c. **Vola**: I can hear him, but I can't see him!
   CAPTION: VOLA
   SUB-CAPTION: LOVER. MOTHER. FIGHTER
   d. SKELETON: Why are you stealing from us?!

PAGE TWO
Four panels

1. Oskar slides past her right as she smashes the ground.

   a. **VOLA**: When did you learn how to fly, Frostbeard?

   b. **OSKAR**: More are coming!

2. The group starts to run the other way because the water below them is swallowing everything.

   c. **Helm**: You can. But we are **leaving**, Vola!

3. Shava frantically drawing the teleportation circle on the floor while the others are fighting the frost pirates and the ground is collapsing.

   d. Vola: Scribble faster!

4. Shava blows amber dust while whistles a musical.

   e. **Shava**: Musical note

Page Three
Splash page

1. The whole crew standing in the Teleportation Circle appears at a church in Thar. There are some elves caught by surprise. Helm has a frost pirate by the throat. Oskar pulling his axe from the chest of a pirate and excited to see Enxina Holimion. Shava in the middle. Vola mid-swing down. Enxina Holimion is relieved to see them back.

   A. Caption: PALO MESA.

   B. **Oskar**: Enxina! We retrieved it!

   C. **Shava**: Musical note

   D. **Enxina**: Who are your new friends? They seem to be melting.

   CAPTION: ENXINA HOLIMION
   SUB-CAPTION: GENERALLY UNIMPRESSED

PAGE FOUR
Six Panels

1. Helm looks relieved. Vola looking down at the melting pirate, smiling.

   a. **Helm**: Feng better appreciate this. My nose nearly froze off.

   b. **Vola**: It looks like our drizzling foes have final words.

   SFX: HSSS

2. The Ice Pirates are trying to keep themselves together. One raises her short sword.

   C. Ice Pirate: HELM GREYCASTLE, you wiley dog. You and your mates will pay!

3. Helm and Vola laugh.

   D. Helm: I've never drunk my foe before. I'll fetch me my flagon!

4. Oskar walks with Enxina. Oskar looks hopeful. Wizard examines the scroll they stole. Oskar on right of the panel, Wizard on left.

   E. Oskar: Are we too late?

   F. Enxina: Time is relative, Oskar son of Frostbeard.

   Can we have a speech bubble for the scroll, indicating that it contains the symbol Enxina speaks in the next panel?

5. Enxina Holimion delays time for everyone but Oskar and himself. The background goes grey while they retain their color. Oskar is amazed.

   G. Enxina Holimion: *Musical Note*

6. The sick orc, Feng, is in bed frozen in time.

   H. Enxina Holimion: We will have to do our best with what little of it we have left.

PAGE Five
Six Panels

1. Oskar stands near the sick Orc while Enxina Holimion reads the scroll.

   a. **Oskar**: He feels dead.

   b. **Enxina Holimion**: The poison still has him out cold.

   CAPTION: FENG
   SUB-CAPTION: BAD IDEAS BOY

2. Enxina Holimion's eyes glow.

   C. Enxina: Hopefully, he will return to us...now.

   D. Feng: Huh?!

3. Time resumes. The color starts to fade back. Feng is shocked, the orc starts to cough.

4. Feng looks relieved. Oskar holds his hand.

   E. Feng: I knew you would you save me--

   F. Oskar: Rest, my heart.

5. Enxina Holimion casts a spell over a clay cup to grow a plant that will slow down the poison that's killing feng.
   G. Feng: I can't move--

   H. Enxina Holimion: This will help slow the effects.

6. Enxina Holimion's spell shows a sprout that's frozen.

   I.   **Oskar**: Who did this to you, Feng?

PAGE SIX

Six Panels

1. Close up on Feng. Angry.

   a. Feng: I don't know...

2. Flashback. Feng is leading a wagon through a forest in the night. They are transporting an albino dragonborn princess, Uadjit.

   b. **Feng**: (Caption) ...I was employed to secretly guide Uadjit, the last dragon prince, to ...safe harbor.

3. Fire balls launch at Feng and wagon.

   c. **Feng**: (Caption) We didn't see them coming.

4. The wagon erupts in flames.

5. Feng is attacked from behind via fireblast.

   d. **Feng**: GRAH!

   e. **Feng**: (Caption) They looked like... giant cat people. I know it sounds ridiculous.

6. Uadjit screams for feng.

   f. **Uadjit**: FENG!

Caption: I can still hear Uadjit screaming my name...

PAGE SEVEN

Six Panels

1. The rest of the crew gathers around Feng.

   a. **Feng**: ...How long have I been out?

   b. **Enxina Holimion**: We found you during the eclipse.

   c. **Shava**: *Musical note*

2. Feng fears for Uadjit.

   d. **FENG:** I know you have gone to great lengths to revive *me*, but Uadjit needs--

3. Close up on Oskar. Determined.

   e. **Oskar:** We will rescue Uadjit.

   f. **Helm:** You're on your own, Frostbeard.

4. Helm is not interested and tries to storm off.

   g. HELM: I'm not chasing death **again** for this **traitor**.

5. Feng disappointed in himself.

   h. **Feng**: I know you'll never trust me after leaving you for dead at the Saguaro of Sacrifice... And this threat **is** far too great. It's **best** you hide--

6. Helm, angry, loses his temper. Shava, worried, holds him back. Vola ready to fight.

   i. **Helm:** Hide?! Where were **you** when **we** slayed the King of Demons?!

   j. **Enxina Holimion**: Helm, enough!

PAGE EIGHT

Six Panels

1. Enxina Holimion faces Helm. Helm is upset. Enxina Holimion is stoic.

   a. **Helm:** I have a daughter to protect! This is a goose chase--

   b. **Enxina Holimion:** We **all** protect her. Where are you going to take her? You're banned from your homeland. Vola has been disowned. We're all wanted for **murder**.

2. Helm defeated.

   c. Helm: We are all without a home. And I promise we **will** find a permanent place. But--

3. Close up on Uadjit scared in a dark place.

   d. **Enxina Holimion:** Somewhere a scared child, possibly the same age as your Starlight, is in danger.

4. Aztec warriors carry the cage that's covered with a blanket. They're in a tomb that's full of old Aztec relics.

   e. **Enxina Holimion:** Their death is near. We have no idea what threat we will face.
   f. WARRIOR: We found this demon. Their escort got away.

5. One of the warriors swipes the blanket off to reveal the albino dragonborn.

   g. AZTEC MAN: We must bring them to Montezuma III!

6. Uadjit is scared. Shielding their eyes from the light.

   h. **Enxina Holimion:** But we are their only hope. Do you rise or hide, Helm?

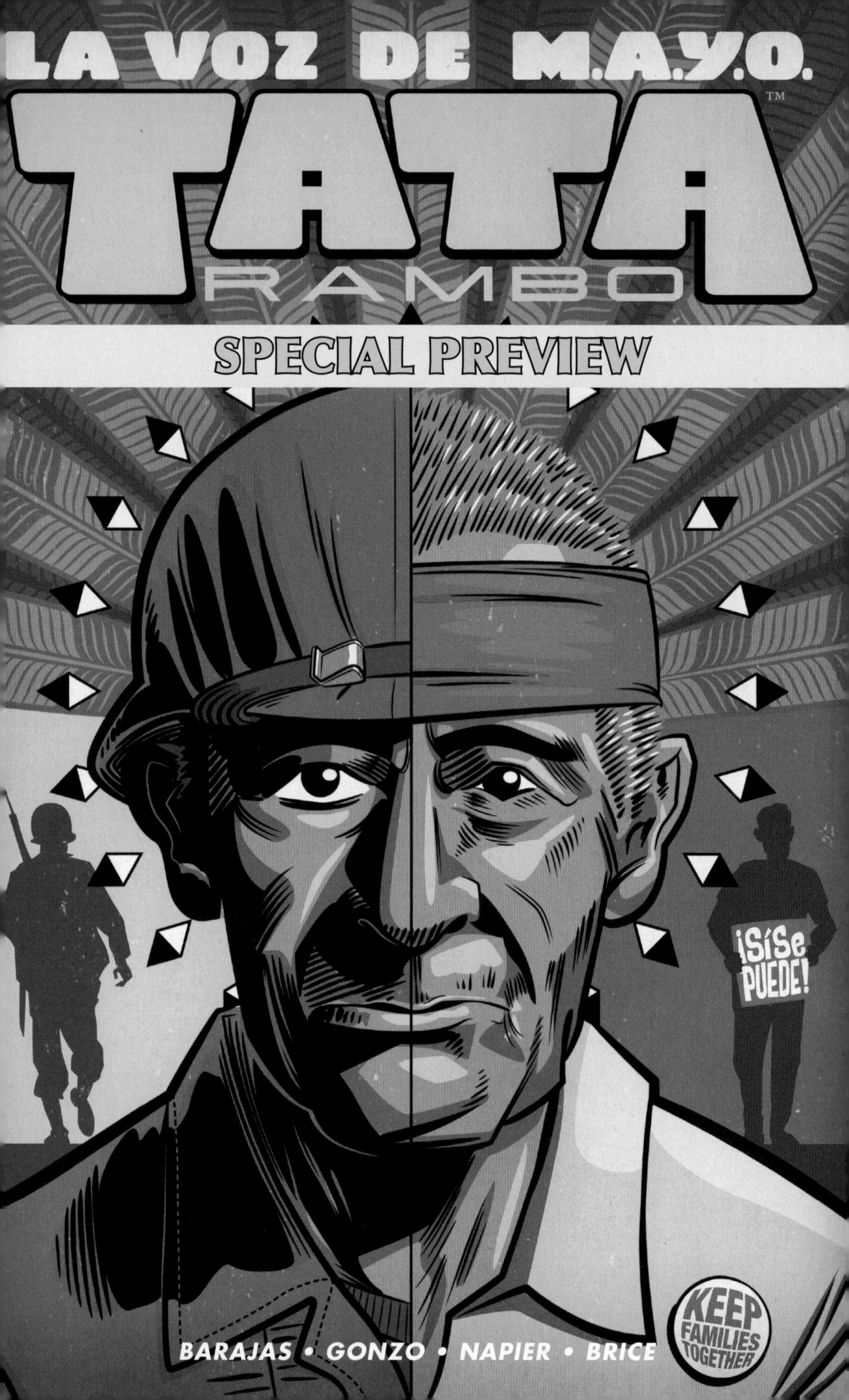
LA VOZ DE M.A.Y.O.
TATA
RAMBO
™
SPECIAL PREVIEW
¡Sí Se
PUEDE!
KEEP
FAMILIES
TOGETHER
BARAJAS • GONZO • NAPIER • BRICE

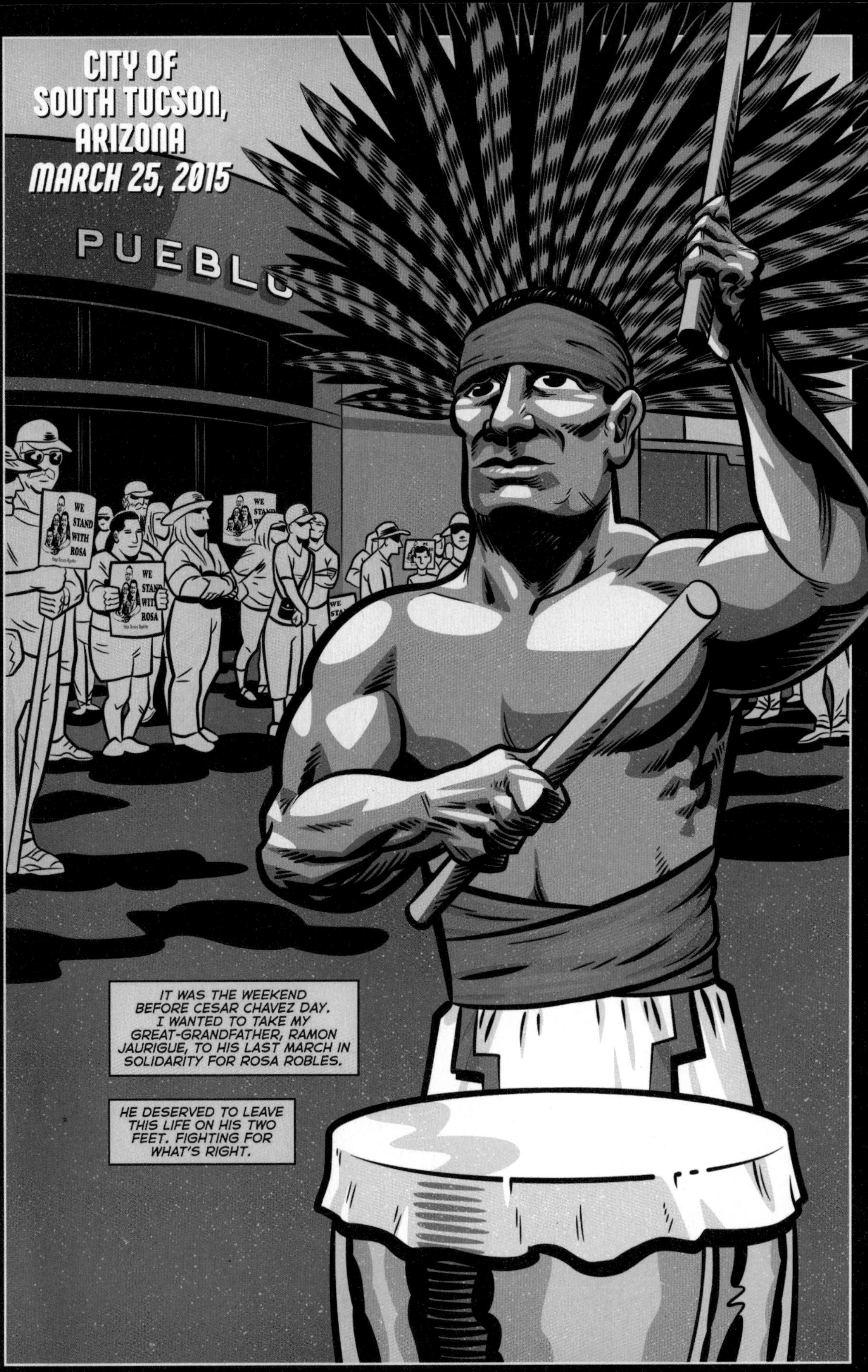
CITY OF SOUTH TUCSON, ARIZONA
MARCH 25, 2015
PUEBLO
WE STAND WITH ROSA
WE STAND WITH ROSA
IT WAS THE WEEKEND BEFORE CESAR CHAVEZ DAY. I WANTED TO TAKE MY GREAT-GRANDFATHER, RAMON JAURIGUE, TO HIS LAST MARCH IN SOLIDARITY FOR ROSA ROBLES.
HE DESERVED TO LEAVE THIS LIFE ON HIS TWO FEET. FIGHTING FOR WHAT'S RIGHT.

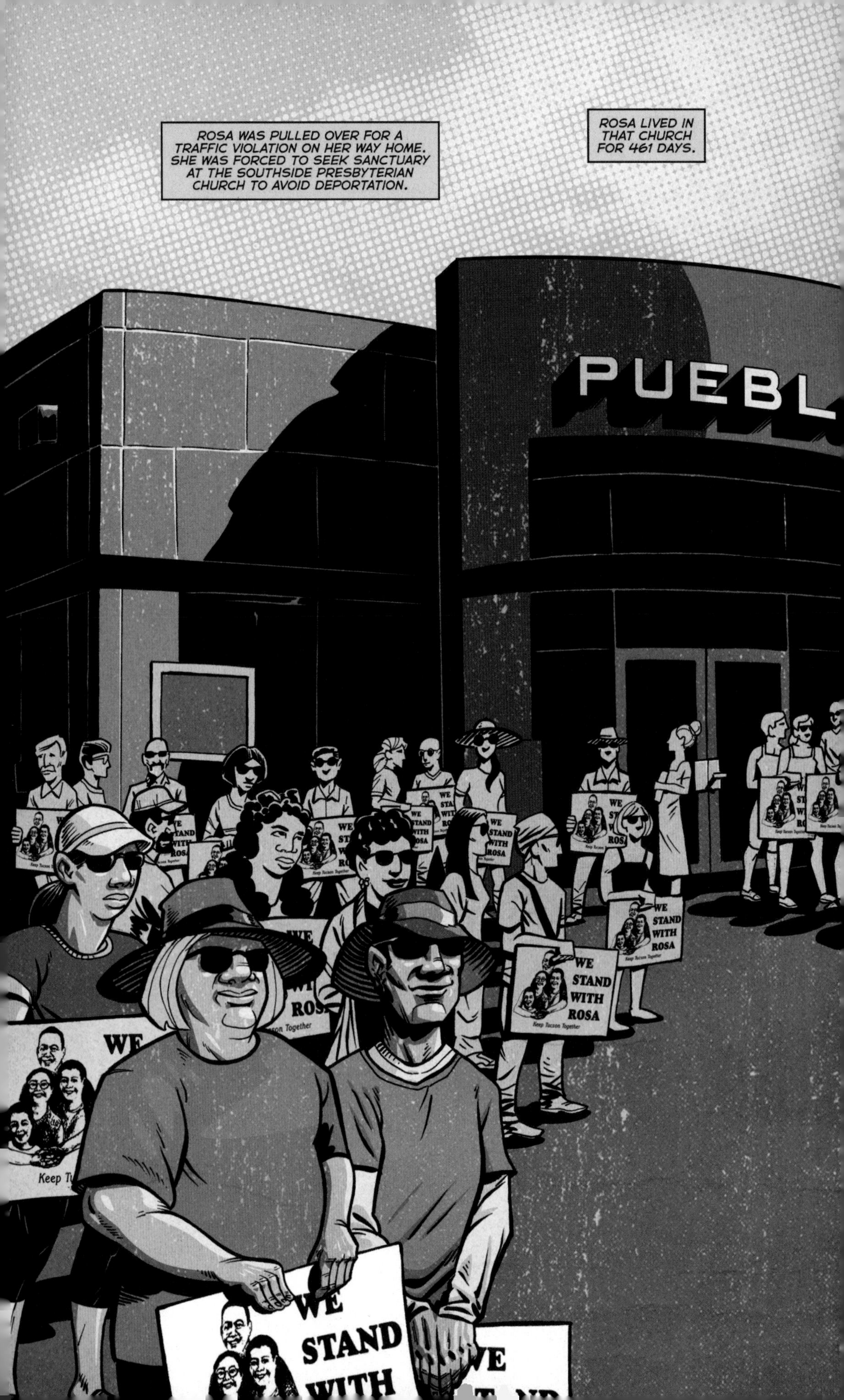
ROSA WAS PULLED OVER FOR A TRAFFIC VIOLATION ON HER WAY HOME. SHE WAS FORCED TO SEEK SANCTUARY AT THE SOUTHSIDE PRESBYTERIAN CHURCH TO AVOID DEPORTATION.
ROSA LIVED IN THAT CHURCH FOR 461 DAYS.
PUEBL
WE STAND WITH ROSA
Keep Tucson Together

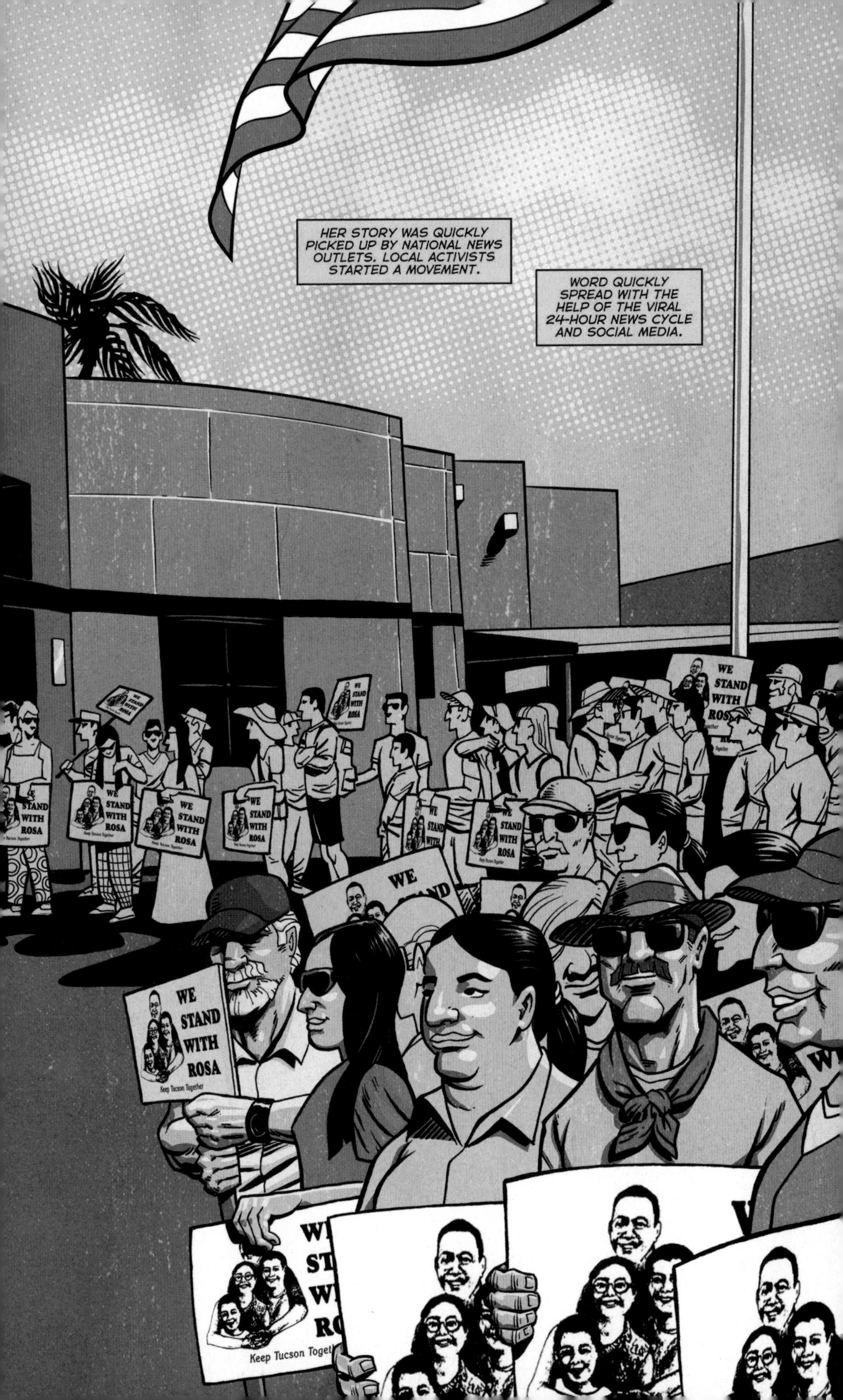
HER STORY WAS QUICKLY PICKED UP BY NATIONAL NEWS OUTLETS. LOCAL ACTIVISTS STARTED A MOVEMENT.
WORD QUICKLY SPREAD WITH THE HELP OF THE VIRAL 24-HOUR NEWS CYCLE AND SOCIAL MEDIA.
WE STAND WITH ROSA
Keep Tucson Together

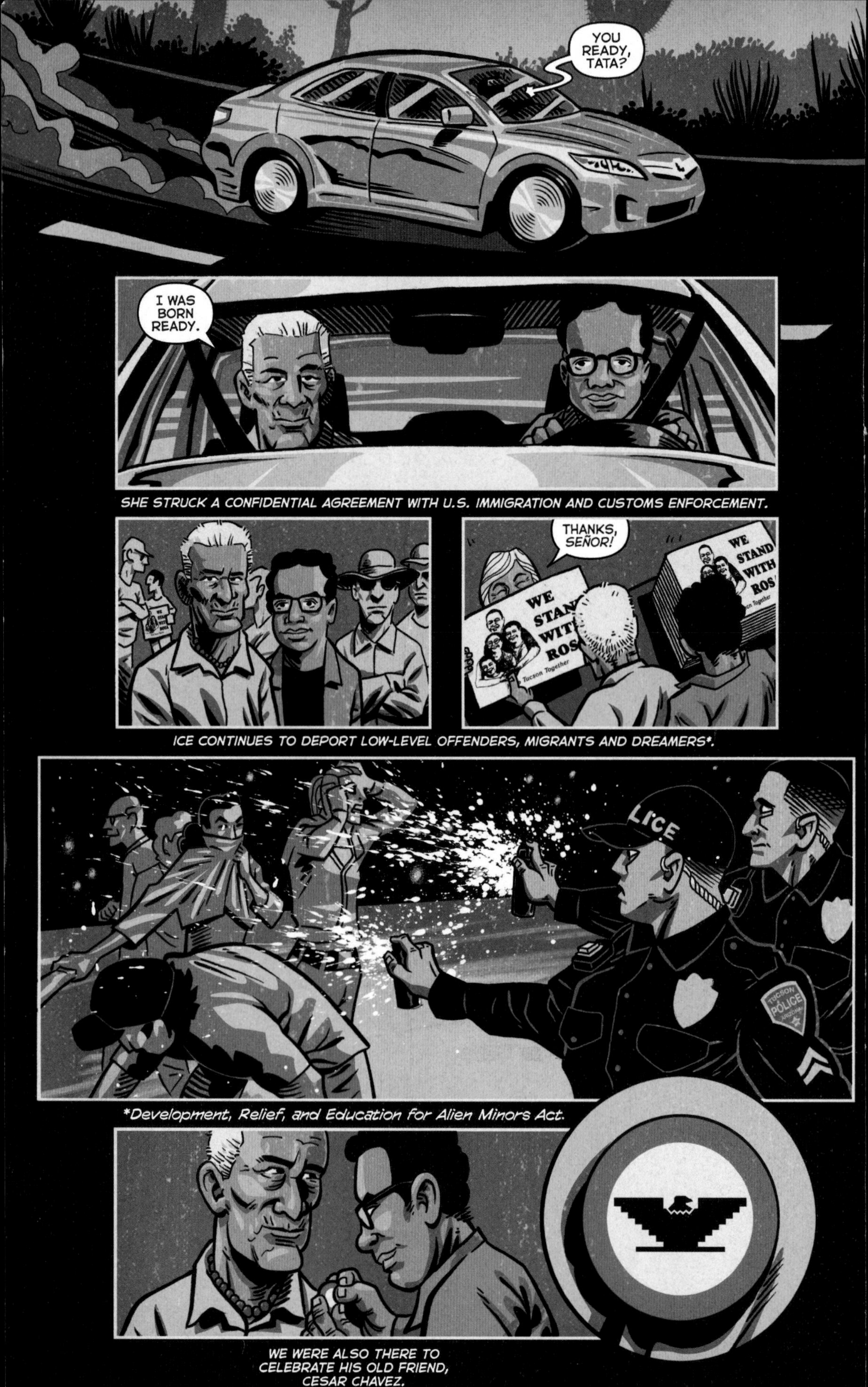
YOU READY, TATA?
I WAS BORN READY.
SHE STRUCK A CONFIDENTIAL AGREEMENT WITH U.S. IMMIGRATION AND CUSTOMS ENFORCEMENT.
THANKS, SEÑOR!
WE STAND WITH ROS
Tucson Together
ICE CONTINUES TO DEPORT LOW-LEVEL OFFENDERS, MIGRANTS AND DREAMERS*.
ICE
POLICE
*Development, Relief, and Education for Alien Minors Act.
WE WERE ALSO THERE TO CELEBRATE HIS OLD FRIEND, CESAR CHAVEZ.

RAMON DIED ON OCTOBER 11, 2017.

IN THE 70S, RAMON HELPED THE PASCUA YAQUI TRIBE INSTALL SIDEWALKS, ROADS, ELECTRICITY, PLUMBING AND BRING JOBS TO THEIR COMMUNITY. HE CO-FOUNDED M.A.Y.O. AND THEY HELPED THE TRIBE KEEP THEIR LAND FROM BEING TAKEN BY THE CITY OF TUCSON TO MAKE WAY FOR INTERSTATE 10.

I SPENT A WHOLE MONTH INTERVIEWING RAMON AND SURVIVORS THAT WERE ACTUALLY THERE.

I SPENT YEARS RESEARCHING TO TELL TRUE FOLKLORE. NONE OF THIS WAS DOCUMENTED PROPERLY.

RAMON DIDN'T WANT ANY RECOGNITION FOR WHAT HE HAD DONE. RAMON DID A LOT BUT DIDN'T WANT THE SPOTLIGHT.

THIS IS A STORY ABOUT WHAT I CAN PROVE AND I THINK MIGHT HAVE HAPPENED.

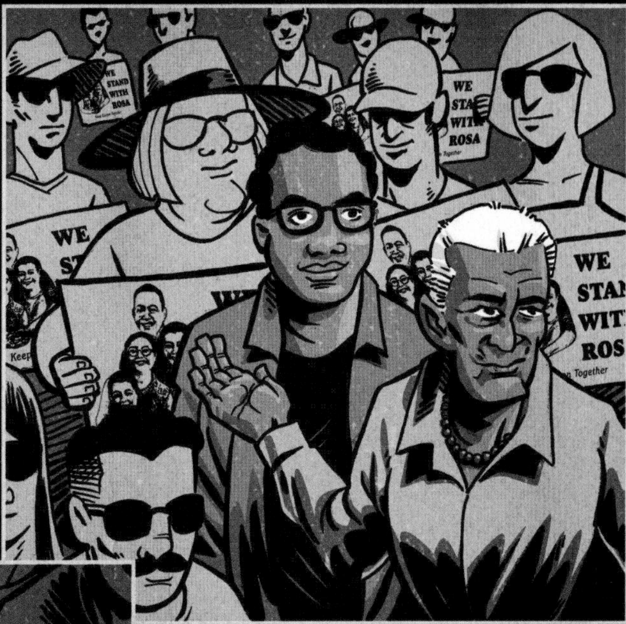
WE STAND WITH ROSA
WE STAND WITH ROSA

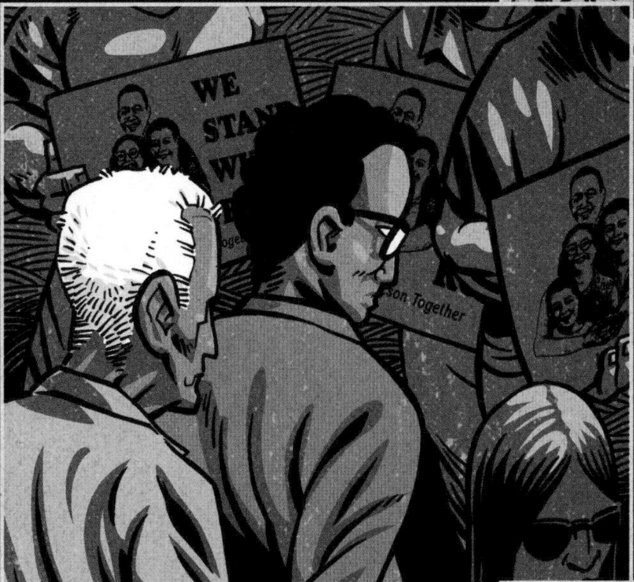

MY FAMILY USED TO TELL ME THAT HE WAS A GOOD MAN, AND HE HELPED A LOT OF PEOPLE-- BUT NEVER WENT INTO DETAIL ABOUT HIS ACTUAL ACCOMPLISHMENTS.

THE REPORTER IN ME COULDN'T LET THAT HAPPEN WHILE HE WAS STILL ON THIS EARTH.

SADLY, HE DIDN'T LIVE LONG ENOUGH TO READ THIS. I REALLY WANTED TO GIVE HIM A COPY SO HE COULD FINALLY SEE HIS WORK RECOGNIZED. BUT HE NEVER WANTED THAT. BUT AT THE END OF THE DAY, I HAD TO DO THIS FOR MYSELF.

I WANT TO BE ABLE TO HAND DOWN WHAT YOU'RE READING SO MY FAMILY WILL KNOW WHAT TO SAY WHEN SOMEONE IS CURIOUS ABOUT THE ORPHAN, WORLD WAR II VETERAN AND POLITICAL ACTIVIST.

MOST PEOPLE DON'T GET TO GROW UP WITH THEIR GREAT-GRANDPARENTS. I'M LUCKY TO HAVE THESE MEMORIES, INTERVIEWS, AND HIS RECORDS TO TELL THIS IMPORTANT STORY THE YAQUI TRIBE HAS EITHER CHOSEN TO OMIT OR DIDN'T HAVE THE MEANS TO DOCUMENT.

IT'S HARD TO PUBLISH THIS BECAUSE I FEEL LIKE I'M SAYING GOODBYE TO RAMON, AND I'LL NEVER BE READY FOR THAT.

THIS IS FOR THE PEOPLE OF OLD PASCUA. I HOPE THEY EMBRACE THIS AND SHARE IT WITH THEIR PEOPLE. IT'S AN IMPORTANT SLICE OF NOT ONLY THEIR HISTORY BUT FOR TUCSON AND OTHER NATIVE PEOPLE. AT THE END OF THE DAY, I HAD TO DO THIS BUT FOR MYSELF.

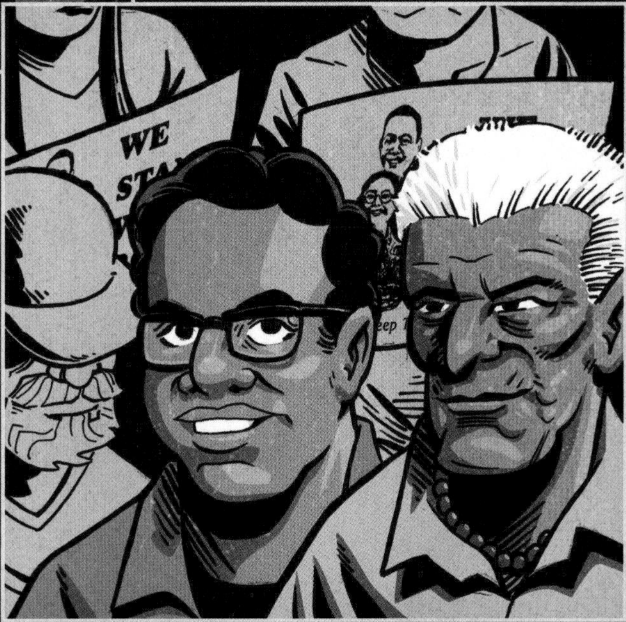

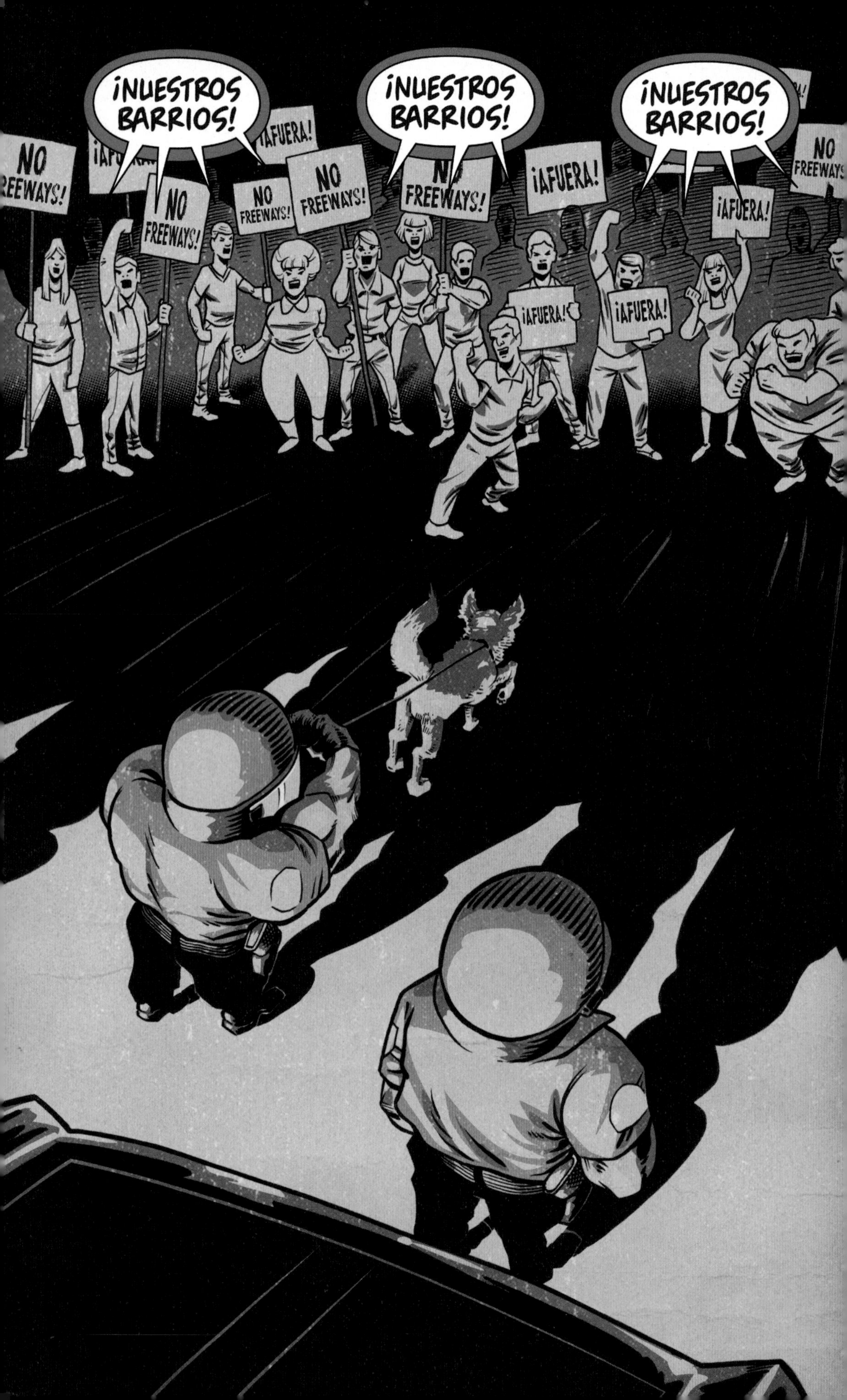
¡NUESTROS BARRIOS!
¡NUESTROS BARRIOS!
¡NUESTROS BARRIOS!
NO FREEWAYS!
¡AFUERA!
NO FREEWAYS!
¡AFUERA!
NO FREEWAYS!
NO FREEWAYS!
NO FREEWAYS!
¡AFUERA!
¡AFUERA!
NO FREEWAYS
¡AFUERA!
¡AFUERA!

The Top Cow essentials checklist:

A Man Among Ye, Volume 1
(ISBN: 978-1-5343-1691-1)

Aphrodite IX: Rebirth, Volume 1
(ISBN: 978-1-60706-828-0)

Blood Stain, Volume 1
(ISBN: 978-1-63215-544-3)

Bonehead, Volume 1
(ISBN: 978-1-5343-0664-6)

Cyber Force: Awakening, Volume 1
(ISBN: 978-1-5343-0980-7)

The Clock, Volume 1
(ISBN: 978-1-5343-1611-9)

The Darkness: Origins, Volume 1
(ISBN: 978-1-60706-097-0)

Death Vigil, Volume 1
(ISBN: 978-1-63215-278-7)

Dissonance, Volume 1
(ISBN: 978-1-5343-0742-1)

Eclipse, Volume 1
(ISBN: 978-1-5343-0038-5)

The Freeze, OGN
(ISBN: 978-1-5343-1211-1)

God Complex, Volume 1
(ISBN: 978-1-5343-0657-8)

Infinite Dark, Volume 1
(ISBN: 978-1-5343-1056-8)

La Voz De M.A.Y.O.:
Tata Rambo, Volume 1
(ISBN: 978-1-5343-1363-7)

Paradox Girl, Volume 1
(ISBN: 978-1-5343-1220-3)

Port of Earth, Volume 1
(ISBN: 978-1-5343-0646-2)

Postal, Volume 1
(ISBN: 978-1-63215-342-5)

Punderworld, Volume 1
(ISBN: 978-1-5343-2072-7)

Stairway Anthology
(ISBN: 978-1-5343-1702-4)

Sugar, Volume 1
(ISBN: 978-1-5343-1641-7)

Sunstone, Volume 1
(ISBN: 978-1-63215-212-1)

Swing, Volume 1
(ISBN: 978-1-5343-0516-8)

Symmetry, Volume 1
(ISBN: 978-1-63215-699-0)

The Tithe, Volume 1
(ISBN: 978-1-63215-324-1)

Think Tank, Volume 1
(ISBN: 978-1-60706-660-6)

Vindication, OGN
(ISBN: 978-1-5343-1237-1)

Warframe, Volume 1
(ISBN: 978-1-5343-0512-0)

Witchblade 2017, Volume 1
(ISBN: 978-1-5343-0685-1)

For more ISBN and ordering information on our latest collections go to:
www.topcow.com
Ask your retailer about our catalogue of collected editions, digests, and hard covers
or check the listings at: Barnes and Noble, Amazon.com, and other fine retailers.

To find your nearest comic shop go to:
www.comicshoplocator.com